D1219779

Young Woman of 1914

ARNOLD ZWEIG

☼

THE CASE OF SERGEANT GRISCHA

ARNOLD ZWEIG

☼

Young Woman of 1914

TRANSLATED FROM GERMAN BY ERIC SUTTON
PUBLISHED BY THE VIKING PRESS NEW YORK
1932

Printed in U. S. A.
Distributed in Canada by the Macmillan Company of Canada, Ltd.

For Marie Zweig

Contents

BOOK ONE

BERTIN

Chapter 1

BERTIN PACKS

Schmielinsky, the postman, on his evening round, stood sorting his mail with practised fingers in the doorway of No. 6 Brixenerstrasse. One registered letter for the artist at the top of the house, two field post letters for the lady on the third floor, one of them ominously official; a picture postcard for that friendly cook at the Zimmermanns' flat, and, among various unremarkable missives, for the student on the ground floor right, the order to join up. Schmielinsky contemplated it with silent loathing. He was a reservist, and one day just such a scrap of paper would blow up for him too—how soon, who could tell? Had not Parliament, and many, many citizens, both great and small, poured forth their savings in subscriptions for the second war loan? Nine thousand and eighty million marks—nine billion marks! So they all meant the War to go on. It was hopeless.

The student here seemed to have changed his lodgings twice. "Fine for him," muttered Schmielinsky; "he'll have to be up good and early tomorrow morning." The young man was in, opened the door himself, heard the postman say: "Fall in for the polonaise," took the officially folded paper, seemed to grow a shade paler, said politely: "Thank you very much," and shut the door.

Such letters are quickly torn open with trembling fingers, in the scanty light of the ceiling lamp. Panic seized him as he read: "8.00 a.m." And he could not ring up Lenore. Then he reminded himself that Paula Weber would tell her. Eight o'clock, Army Service Corps Reserve battalion, stationed at Küstrin. Well, it might have been worse.

Werner Bertin, when the call of destiny came upon him, was

twenty-six years old, of middle height, pale, with red lips and dark brown eyes. Behind him lay a penurious youth; he had gradually gained confidence in his abilities, and had developed them by eager and laborious effort; he had studied law, philosophy, modern languages, and after his first bar examination he went further, and began to write short stories, a novel, and dramas. He fancied he saw himself as he really was, and viewed his own character with a trained and critical eye; in reality he knew but scanty fragments of himself. He now began to pace round his sitting-room with his hands behind his back. The calling-up order lying on the writing-table seemed to exercise a sort of suction; it whirled up into itself all his former life, just as the smoke-laden air of a room pours into a ventilator. So he was to be a soldier without combatant training, and thus without hope of advancement as long as the War should last. What had been the use of his school tests, his military exemption examination, and his diploma? And to what end had he spent seven years at various universities? It was all delusion, wasted life, now sucked up by the ventilator. To the military authorities he was merely a recruit, not quite fit for active service; the fact that he was a writer only served to make him ridiculous. And yet—he became conscious of a throbbing at his heart. These same authorities were insignificant in themselves; but behind them stood home and usage, all the forces of the soul, all the good spirits of the Fatherland. Rough hands, indeed, had seized him, brutal and bloody was the task to which they would put him—no matter. War was in the world, and war prevailed. A man must now be equal to all claims, with nerves more sensitive, emotions keener, and spirit more alert. Now Germany was calling, and he must be prompt to answer.

He sat at the table, which was half covered by a cloth, meditatively cutting up his food, bit by bit—bread, ham, and a little cheese; and, as usual, his thoughts served as seasoning to his meal. The genius of life and indeed of humanity cared nothing for individual existences; over the most gifted of them it passed unheedingly. It recked only of the expansion of species, the onflowing surge of forms and types in which it found embodiment.

Mutual adaptation rather than war best served its ends; but sometimes, after long labours with such instruments of peace, units called nations, turgid with their strength, dash upon each other, and grasp at what shall make them greater. He, Werner Bertin, had been born unawares into such a time, a fate which no one could have foreseen. He might be one of the many who, gifted or no, would be flung into the rubbish heap as dung for the future. His pride did not suffer him to stand aside or creep into obscurity. Still, it was better, if less glorious, to be a soldier in the Army Service Corps, and survive, than to fight and fall with the field artillery. He had in fact been assigned to the latter unit in the previous August.

With such thoughts in his mind he ended his meal. His muscles, tense and eager, began to quiver within him. Privations had no terrors for him. He had never been a man for ease, and physically he would certainly hold out. His weak points were his heart, his throat, and his eyes. From very early days he had had to earn extra money by giving lessons, he had lived on about seventy marks a month during his first student years, and subsequently on small scholarships until his stories brought him added earnings which meant better clothes and brief holidays. This period came to an end today. A card to Frau Laubschrey giving formal notice that he was leaving his lodgings could be posted early tomorrow morning, together with a note to Paula Weber, which he hurriedly sat down and wrote. He asked her to ring up Lenore in the morning, tell her he had been suddenly called up, and help her to clear up his effects; and also to take a yellow-covered packet from his writing-table, and give it to her on May 17th. There were really now only four things left for him to do: pack his trunk, dispose of his manuscripts, undress, and go to sleep.

The room was papered and decorated in a faded brown, and it looked out on to the yard: in front of Bertin the dark expanse of a wall towered up into the sky, that seemed poised above it, pale and unreal, like a fanlight through which the spring had begun to shimmer. All day long a fine rain had washed the flagstones of the yard, and in their shining surfaces was mirrored the electric glitter of lit houses. Bertin sighed and drew the curtains. He recalled the morning when, with Lenore to help him, he had taken this lodging, three hundred marks having suddenly dropped on to his table from the third thousand of his novel, *Love at Last Sight*. How eagerly they had walked into the agent's office that morning, arm in arm, happy as a young married pair looking for their first home. Frau Laubschrey—for that and no other was the lady's name—showed them all her vacant rooms, diverting them the while with the most refined of monologues. They had solemnly surveyed every room with a great air of decorum, while they grimaced and giggled and nudged each other behind Frau Laubschrey's broad upholstered back, and generally behaved disgracefully. Frau Laubschrey was a trifle magniloquent over the merits of her domain. She called attention to the painted tiles of the bathroom, which were set in a series of three, depicting respectively a flatfish, a water lily, and a sailing ship, and she called them *majolica* or *faïence:* she pointed proudly to the leather cover of a very angular sofa, to which, she said, two gentlemen in "smokings" would give the true club atmosphere. With her high-laced bosom, and the fresh skin of her face, crowned by the piled mass of faded brown hair, on which a hat was perilously perched, she made an oddly enlivening figure. Over the brown-papered room she burst into the following eulogium: "A real *dolce far niente* for a refined gentleman, secluded but sociable," and with these words she opened the door of a neighbouring double-bedded room. How could one resist so picturesque a personage? They decided, and they did not regret the choice. Six happy months of work and secret love confirmed it.

The young man opened all the drawers of the writing-table and took out letters, university papers, magazines, large folio pages of written manuscript, notes, picture postcards, every kind of rubbish that accumulates in several months. He looked it over, tore up a great deal, and made a parcel of the rest. A cigar helped him through this operation, although he had to keep putting it down on the ash tray. He was in the right course; he had already put off from the familiar shore, and he was rowing with cheerful composure towards a new one. Now for his aged trunk, packed and unpacked when so many terms had begun and ended. He dragged it by one of the leather handles into the full light and threw back the lid; there it lay, a hollow vessel, brown outside, striped red and white within, ready to receive the possessions of a traveller. (What might be needed for a longish journey on foot, he thought he would take with him in a rucksack; and he accordingly arranged in due order all that lay before him.) With the deftness of one now practised in such modest removals, he spread a layer of books at the bottom: dictionaries, English, French, and Latin, in grey slip-covers, a selection of Goethe's correspondence, handbooks of law, two volumes on the history of philosophy, some modern poetry, and the Hebrew-German bible. The gaps were stuffed with the yellow-red volumes of the Reclam library, mostly Russian stories and plays, twenty pfennigs a volume. Violin and piano music, novels by contemporary authors, three well-thumbed little volumes of Friedrich Nietzsche, two of Stendhal's great romances, and three volumes of Gottfried Keller's short stories; all these, with a mass of miscellaneous literature, magazines and even newspapers, were bundled into the trunk, taken out, examined once again, and hurriedly crammed down. How long would it be before all these loved companions again saw the light? He sat for a moment meditative on his chair, with a silk strip of pictured Chinese stories in his hand. He did not delude himself. The War would last six months more; statesmen could hardly call upon their nations for a new winter campaign after the awful experiences of the one lately ended. By Christmas there would be an armistice, and in January—the new year—negotiations for peace. And then a month, or six weeks, before the troops could get back to civil life again. For ten months at least he must be parted from the contents of that trunk, those stiff collars, shirts, and neckties, the Japanese woodcuts, and the little Satsuma vase. The suits lay neatly folded on the books and the music; on top of them the manuscripts—short stories, twelve or fourteen, some still unpublished, but most of them with copies of the various papers in which they had appeared; articles likewise, and his two dramas. Thoughtfully he balanced in his hands the thick bound MS. volume, of English handmade paper, in which he had written his first-born. *A Man Called Hilsner* was its title, and it dealt in short staccato scenes with a strange trial that had taken place in Austrian Bohemia, some half century before, of an otherwise obscure individual for the mysterious murder of a child. Bertin's idea had been to show how the grasp of fate had snatched the man into a light that rendered him transparent. He dropped it into the trunk, where it lay much as it reposed in the cupboard of the Censorship; the publisher even hesitated to print it. Only three or four typescript copies were in circulation. Bertin found himself wondering if anything would come of it: and he picked up what came next to hand to go on with his packing. A bronze inkpot was cunningly wrapped in woollen stockings, a black stone pen-tray was stowed into the arm of a jacket; then, with a heavy heart, he laid away the volume of old yellowed Venetian paper that contained his second play. The last year, spent upon this work and with Lenore, had made up for all the hardships of his youth. It was as though a husk had burst; the words poured forth as they had never done before. She had made him young through happiness, through the utter bestowal of herself. . . . Dearest heart. . . .

A watch ticked on the table; the room swam in a haze of cigar smoke. The cubed object constructed of compressed cane, barely a yard long, and half a yard broad and high, now seemed like a hollow stone in which a man's past was embedded. Tomorrow he could press down the arched lid, sit on it, and snap the locks. Only a flat portfolio remained to be crammed down on the top; from it Bertin took a manuscript, twelve poems for Lenore, as a surprise and a last present for the second anniversary of their first meeting, which was dearer to them and more significant than their birthdays. The yellow envelope in which he was to send it lay ready to hand; kindly Paula Weber would see to this. She would also look after his violin, as Lenore could at most receive and conceal poste restante letters. Now for final instructions: clapping his hands to his forehead, he took a plain sheet of paper, sat down, and wrote:

"Testamentary Disposition." (The phrase "Last Will and Testament" seemed too pompous.) "Although, on being called up for the Army Service Corps, it may seem inappropriate to conjure up the shadow of death, I appoint as follows. My manuscripts, and such of my books as she shall choose, belong to Fräulein Lenore Wahl, Potsdam, Parkring II. I ask her to deal with my printed and unprinted works as she shall see fit, without destroying them. Any proceeds from them shall belong to her. This legacy involves her in no obligation. She is indeed completely free, and I only hope that she may find someone worthy of her, in case I do not survive. From the day on which we met she has brought me nothing but happiness, encouragement, and help. I offer her my thanks; I feel my whole being centred upon her; whether I live or die, seems to me, here and now, almost indifferent. No. 6 Brixenerstrasse, Berlin, April 20, 1915, in complete possession of my faculties, and great gratitude and peace of mind. Werner Bertin."

On reading this over, he thought the tone of it a little too sentimental; he frowned for a moment, but he would not allow himself to cut anything out or rewrite it. It was time to stop being ashamed of one's feelings or their expression.

He put the paper in a special envelope, wrote on it "Testamentary Disposition," forgot to add, "Not to be opened until my death," as he sat dreaming of his friend, addressed it "Frl. Paula Weber, to be called for," and looked at the time; eleven o'clock already. He opened the sitting-room windows, undressed in the next room, stretched himself comfortably in bed, lay awake for a while in anticipation of the active life that would now seize and shake him, and dozed off with the intention of waking up punctually at six o'clock next morning. And so he slept, his finely moulded forehead, edged by arched brows over the closed lids, outlined against the pillow into which his left cheek was sunk. His parted lips gave him an expression of childlike self-abandonment.

Nothing betrayed the unknown chambers of his being, which might now perhaps spring open and bring forth strange matters. Impenetrable lay that sleeping face in the dark atmosphere of the room. Above him towered a pile of hollow rooms, habitations of men, right up to the attics, the domain of bats and full of dusty chests, worn-out furniture, children's toys, and threadbare flags. But beneath, beneath even the cellar, ran drains and sewers, the mighty veins of that vast entity, Berlin.

A fine rain sprinkled the glimmering roofs of the great city, wreaths of cloud-like mist moved over the houses, sank into the abysses of the streets, and enveloped the lamps in a pale globe-like radiance. They whirled over the whole North German plain, they swept in from the West, and even reached the entrenchments in the East. No voice spoke in them, they brought no sound of grief nor lamentation. And yet beneath the earth, or on the naked ground, already lay armies of dead Germans: two hundred thousand in the West alone, two hundred thousand in the East. Of wounded there were near a million, apart from the missing, who lay mouldering in the marshes, or ate their hearts away in prison. For their sake there was agony, and tears, and bitterness, in countless closed rooms; but never for other eyes to see.

Chapter 2

ON THE TRUNK

Two young women in light spring dresses and small straw hats, stood in a lodging sitting-room and looked curiously about them. Frau Laubschrey, a careful landlady, had already had the curtains taken down. The light glared crudely on the dark brown wallpaper of the sitting-room; and had a bedroom ever displayed so shamelessly the grey flowered ticking of its mattresses and bolsters? Into this plundered lodging the two friends had come, to do what remains to be done after the removal of a tenant so unusual as not to be able to take his trunk with him.

In three rooms had Lenore Wahl been happy in the course of her life; in her earliest nursery at Potsdam; in the attic high up above the tree-tops by the forest at Polling, near Munich; and in this one. Between the first and the second came childhood and youth, almost twenty years, full of growing unrest; between the second and the third yawned but one abyss—the War.

In the meantime Paula Weber had been inspecting all the rooms with a rather superior air. "Well—I really think this time Werner might have risked the Wahl family's disfavour and rung you up." She had fled from Altweiler in Alsace, after many conflicts with her parents' obstinacy, to study the violin, and now she was the favourite pupil of a famous old artist.

"My dear, he wasn't thinking of himself; he wanted to save me from the wrath of my household gods—that was all. And just as well."

Paula Weber shook her head, frowned, and glanced abruptly at the writing-table.

"There's something missing in this room besides the curtains," said Lenore meanwhile, and sat down on the trunk, which disclosed all its scars and stains in the gay light of morning. Her bright gaze darted about the room. "And yet I can't see what it is. There's the old engraving, here's the writing-table, the bookcase, and the sofa. What is it that's gone except the lodger and the curtains?"

Paula Weber meditated; Lenore could not know. Bertin had written to her about a large yellow envelope, which she was to take from the writing-table unobserved. But she could see nothing of the kind; Frau Laubschrey had clearly taken charge of it.

"We must find out, Lenore."

Lenore nodded, caressing the trunk with her fingers. "Dear old trunk, more faithful than your master. All that time in Munich, that lovely spring and summer at Polling, you stood in the corner, you nice old thing, so neatly covered up; how often have I sat on you. And now it's to you I'm saying good-bye, you that are still here, full of the fragrance of this last winter of ours. If only you could speak! You used to stand in the bedroom. You have seen me with very few clothes on; not to say—with nothing on at all. It's nice to sit on you and stroke your shabby sides." But she concealed what she really felt and said: "We must take this young man down a little, Paula. What a conceited creature it is, to be sure."

"So they all are. Proud of their intellects and yet so childish!"

"Childish! I believe they're only going on with the War to impress us; and they talk about the spirit of the universe and the great times to come."

Paula drew her chair up to the writing-table and pulled at the locked drawers. "That's perhaps where our mistake begins, Lenore. We mustn't let them too long out of our hands; they change in two days. André hadn't been six weeks with the labour battalion, in East Prussia—in those days they sometimes put the Ersatz Reserve men on to trench digging—and he came back with such manners—you can't think! I blushed in the dark to hear the expressions he had learned; and he suddenly began to pretend he was master! He didn't flirt with me any more, he ordered me about, as if I was on duty in bed. Oh," and she burst into a ripple of laughter, "what eyes he made when he had to spend the night on the sofa in the sitting-room, poor fellow, until he had learnt how a man should approach a lady to whom he isn't married. No, a soldier's life isn't good for the lords of creation."

They both laughed; and then Paula Weber became serious again. They had come here with an object. First, where was the violin? They found it behind the green curtains of the bookcase. And as they were looking for it, Lenore at last realized that the rug in front of the sofa was missing. She had felt the need of it when Bertin moved in, and had bought a cheap one at a store, a German imitation of a Persian pattern. Could Frau Miele, who looked after the building for Frau Laubschrey, have taken it away that morning by mistake?

"It's wartime, Lenore," observed Paula Weber, sagely; "the men on active service also take what they need. They call it requisitioning; a strange word makes it seem all right. As Werner couldn't have turned up at the district headquarters with a roll of carpet under his arm, I suppose women have started requisitioning."

Lenore listened in astonishment. Had the spirit of the War spoiled simple people, too? Her mother who was deep in relief work for the soldiers' women dependants, had certainly told her how they often had not money enough to buy the children a modest bowl of milk every morning, or to pay the rent. But to take a carpet away like this—surely that was going a little far, even in wartime. "We'll ask Frau Laubschrey," she said.

A key turned in the lock outside; and Frau Laubschrey bustled into the dismantled room and peered about her. "Well, here we are, Fräuleinchen," she said. "I hope you haven't been crying too long, it isn't good-bye for ever. You want to take the trunk away, if I understood you rightly on the telephone?"

Lenore said, "Yes." Something dangerous lurked in this astute landlady's eyes and amiable voice. And indeed, before five minutes had passed, she made the completest scene that the two startled and amused young women had ever witnessed. Not merely did she deny that she had ever seen a rug—there had been none in the room when she let it; she refused to allow the trunk to be taken away until the April gas, telephone, and electric light had been paid for. Who would guarantee these payments? How could one trust anyone in these times? Nothing doing. The trunk would stay until the meters had been read.

Lenore Wahl would have been glad to hold her ears against this raucous outburst, and looked at the landlady as though she had been a familiar old horse which had suddenly begun to misbehave. Paula Weber let her shriek herself to a finish; she then pointed out that the landlady had no sort of right to detain the trunk, as any policeman from the street would make quite clear; and he would also be remarkably inquisitive about the vanished rug. (Heavens, thought Lenore, Police! What if the Commissary of Police rang up the Wahl family, or called upon them about a missing rug at No. 6 Brixenerstrasse.) But she told the woman that there was some sense in her anxiety over Herr Bertin's few debts, and to that end she would pay something on account of what would be due for April, estimated in accordance with the larger amount that had been paid in March.

So saying, she dropped a piece of money, large and silvery, with a clink on to the writing-table, and promised that at the beginning of May either she or Fräulein Wahl would not fail to appear in Frau Laubschrey's drawing-room and settle what remained, on production of the receipts.

" . . . And now let us forget about the rug," added Lenore. "You're quite right, there never was one there."

Frau Laubschrey laughed. These were two young women after her own heart. Generous enough over trifles, they knew how to carry the main point. They were well able to look after themselves; indeed one had to be, to survive in this manless world where a pretty face alone was no longer enough. "Schlossarek will be glad to carry the trunk down for a small tip," she said calmly; "there's no sense in troubling poor Miele. Her husband has been called up, and it isn't easy for a woman with three children to keep going these days. The War is a bad time for the little ones, Fräuleinchen—well, perhaps it will end soon."

Paula Weber, taking advantage of the restoration of peace, eagerly agreed; then she asked Lenore to get two luggage labels from the stationer's at the corner, and fill them up, as Bertin had forgotten to do so. It would be simplest to send for the things later. Lenore obediently hurried out.

She did not like to think any ill over Frau Laubschrey; the woman had impressed herself upon her in much too strange a way. On December 1st last, about five o'clock in the afternoon, she had rung at Bertin's door to collect the rent. She had just come from a funeral feast; an elderly miser had left a cheerful widow behind him, and Frau Laubschrey had had rather more than a nip of strong waters. The two friends were just then finally revising two articles for a weekly magazine, in which Werner Bertin had tried to do justice to the reasons that had led Japan and Turkey to declare war. Frau Laubschrey had burst somewhat inharmoniously upon this peaceful occupation; she took a chair, fell into ecstatic admiration of these works, and chattered away affectedly; then she became natural, took her fifty marks and gave a receipt, and suddenly insisted on laying the cards for the Fräulein. She happened to have them with her. Oh, she had quite a reputation for telling fortunes.

Lenore came from a faithless age, and a faithless school. For that reason the woman made a certain impression on her as she sat under the lamp with a faintly glazed look in her eyes, her hat with its absurd feather fantastically shadowed beside her on the table. She produced a pack of cards and asked her to choose nine for herself and nine for him, and lay them in rows, face upwards. Frau Laubschrey seemed to grow smaller and older; muttered words and exclamations burst from her lips. (In point of fact Dame Laubschrey was very wide awake. It was obvious that the pair would marry, and also that the man would be called up. The girl would naturally have all the trouble over the marriage, since war had never yet prevented a wedding. Here Frau Laubschrey spoke out of a deeper knowledge then she knew; the indestructibility of life, that by the agency of woman preserves itself against the male madness of destruction.) Before her lay an array of brightly coloured slips of cardboard, covered with age-old designs; in words that bore the impress of established formulæ, Frau Laubschrey prophesied: "I see danger, for you and for him; here lies much money, and here lies marriage. The Queen of Hearts will carry through the marriage by herself." (Lenore grew pale, and thought: "All by myself! But I'm not strong enough." Which was just what the Sybil intended.) "But it won't happen at once; there are difficulties—near relations, father and mother. . . ." ("Right," thought Lenore; as Frau Laubschrey said to herself in the broadest Berlin dialect—"The young lady's people don't exactly fall on the young gentleman's neck. . . . ") And then, so as to give the little fool something to chew: "It will take to the very day, exactly as long as the time you have known each other; the time card lies between the ten of hearts and the ten of spades. But you'll bring it off, Fräulein, and I congratulate you." She took Lenore's hand from the table, shook it, seemed to wake up, and went.

Of course the whole thing was absurd. Was she, Lenore Wahl, to bring off a marriage against the opposition of the world? And yet, Macbeth could have felt no more deeply grateful to his witches than Lenore Wahl to the prophetess Laubschrey. And now was a rug to spoil it all? . . .

Scarcely had the door closed behind her when Paula Weber began to draw on her gloves: "I've deliberately put off the most important point until now, Frau Laubschrey. Our friend Bertin left a large yellow envelope on his writing-table, directed to me, which contained a birthday surprise for Fräulein Wahl. I should hate to think it had been destroyed. Manuscript, Frau Laubschrey, poems, such as lovers send each other. I've no doubt you've taken charge of it, to prevent it falling into wrong hands, and I'm very grateful to you." There was no avoiding the steady gaze of her dark eyes.

"So he left something important as that lying about in the

room? Just like a man." And with this she produced the key of the writing-table and handed Paula Weber the missing envelope. "Ah, if young love might never perish," she quoted soulfully. As she had now definitely secured the rug, she would not mind abandoning any other plunder.

Paula Weber slipped Bertin's papers between the sheets of music in her portfolio, and snapped the lock, just as Lenore, flushed with haste, came in again.

A quarter of an hour later she gazed in affectionate farewell at the medievally weathered façade of the house at No. 6 Brixenerstrasse, with its crouching stucco dragon over the doorway; on the left, St. George transfixed it with his lance, while on the right, St. Michael brandished his sword, both in full armour, and compounded of the same sort of stucco as the writhing dragon.

Chapter 3

PATERNAL POWERS

But for one incident, the two girls would have had the opportunity of doing this service for their friend six months before —and who knows whether Lenore would not thus have been spared many things. The fact that it did not so happen was due less to Herr Hugo Wahl than to the character and concerns of the man with whom he had an appointment.

Albert Schieffenzahn, Colonel, attached for the time being to the General Staff in Berlin, paced heavily up and down the red and grey carpet. At every step he carefully shifted his considerable weight from one foot to the other, with a sort of rolling swaying gait; and the gaunt room quivered faintly at his tread.

It was the end of October, '14; after a brilliant beginning, the war had come to a depressing deadlock. As he strode up and down the room, the Colonel ground his fine strong teeth; and if he looked short-legged, his outthrust body and square jaw gave him the force of a dangerous fighter. He had no need to worry about the East; there the right people were already at work; and he, Albert Schieffenzahn, knew that his place with them was secure. But yonder, across the Rhine, where the All-Powerful were raging! A man must be on the spot to see the facts as they stood—the pitiable ruin of what had once been a plan. For a week past he had been slaving in Berlin to do what he could to relieve the desperate case of the artillery, which, wisely enough, was only allowed defensive fire in cases of extreme emergency. Indeed, the ammunition had to be guarded by sentries. Every night someone from the Staff of the Fourth Army hung on to the telephone shouting for shrapnel, field-gun ammunition, and explosive. They were flinging volunteer battalions, thousands of future officers, against English positions without artillery preparation; trained soldiers with machine-guns were posted behind railway embankments in Flemish cities. But even his gift of organization, his power of pumping energy into lethargic personages, could not make good the follies of many years; and this Herr Wahl from Potsdam, whom Geheimrat von Bahr had urgently telegraphed to him to receive at once, could not open his eyes any wider. There would be no atmospheric nitrogen before March or May. Until then the war must be a sort of table tennis, or they must treat for peace—in the last resort by the surrender of Lorraine and the evacuation of Belgium. Such a peace was to be had. But would that be victory? It would spell defeat. Excuses? No, by heaven! Schieffenzahn had seen things far too much from within, he was far too prone to fling himself, with the ruthless sincerity of the artist, upon the object that confronted him to content himself with the cheap pretext of the English blockade. If, after barely eleven weeks, the German armies saw their victories slipping from their grasp for want of explosive, gun-cotton, and nitroglycerine, the causes of this were certainly not to be sought in London, but in Berlin.

The man in the black-collared tunic of the artillery officer and the crimson-striped breeches of the General Staff, pacing up and down on that four-cornered space, twisted a cigar in the fingers of his right hand and puffed at it from time to time. Confound these blunderers and wiseacres and sycophants. They had let loose a war and taken no account of modern artillery technique. For they knew that it must come to war sooner at later. Six years before, they had given in to Austrian persistency, and in secret agreements between the Chiefs of the two General Staffs, they had made all proper alterations in the provisions of the Triple Alliance. Thus, behind the backs of parliaments and even governments was created a spearhead against Russia, in case that Empire saw fit to oppose certain schemes devised by the elegant denizens of the Ballplatz against the Serbs. Had they taken this into account or not? And why had he, Schieffenzahn, then captain on the Great General Staff, had been attached to the Japanese in 1905 to write reports for Berlin? To what end had he trailed about Manchuria in the icy wind, covered with mud from head to foot; why had he scrawled pages of notes with frozen fingers by the light of one candle in his tent, and taken so much pains to delude the suspicions of the insinuating yellow gentlemen, in trying to calculate, from the ammunition expended by the Japanese, what would be needed for the artillery battle of the future? And the arrogance with which they had praised his work! And now they lay howling in their beds, drank themselves stupid, or, in the All-Highest places, fell into a fury that was succeeded by a dull despondent determination to avoid any definite decision. It was small comfort to him that the French, the English, and the Russians themselves were in like case. They, too, stood disgraced before their peoples from the highest to the lowest.

Albert Schieffenzahn buttoned up his tunic, placed his hand on his hip, and still padding up and down the silent room, with its thick walls and closed double windows, looked the Medusa in the eyes. The defeat on the Marne—that was where it had begun. A battle fought on a front of three hundred and fifty kilometres between the Vosges and Paris must inevitably be lost by generals who fought with one eye on an All-Highest personage far behind in peaceful Luxemburg, and deferred to the plain ignorance that there prevailed, when their duty was to go and see for themselves and take the measure of the facts. This was the chief and fundamental error; it lay in the system, and had ruined all the so-called Kaiser manœuvres; and even though certain generals were made to pay the penalty for advancing too far in the heat of victory, or leaving a gap between the Brandenburgers and the Saxons, and though, between four walls, such humbug might pass current, he, Albert Schieffenzahn, was not to be so deluded. True, there had been a certain amount of whispering and gossip among the higher officers; the Army Command had sent a Colonel to the fighting line with full powers to make what decisions he thought fit; and he, ill from the responsibility and a pessimist by nature, had broken off the battle just when events were taking a favourable turn. Well, the truth would be known in years to come; it was no use trying to dig it out now.

In that hour of pallid morning light, when the wind and rain howled round the corners of the isolated house, Colonel Schieffenzahn grasped the indefeasible outlines of what was to come. If the present crisis could be surmounted, it was still possible to conquer. True, the War would then last for years, more than could be counted on the buttons of a tunic. The question of food supplies might become difficult, many raw materials would run short, and the nation itself might lose its nerve; but a few stout hearts would preserve the will to victory, and all might be well! It was therefore essential to forestall any possible disorders: everyone not doing indispensable work in field or mine or factory, must be sent to the War as soon as possible, or at least put into an army tunic and subjected to military law. Properly considered, the non-combatant services were an important section of the army. In the beleaguered fortress that was Germany there must be no vacillations of mood; a man who was not in the firing line was, in any event, a very fortunate person. Thus would he shut the mouths of all those gentlemen for whom a war lasted a little too long, the trades unionists, the unskilled workmen, and the so-called intellectuals from the liberal professions. He would bundle them all into uniform and train them gradually for the battles to come. And women—he would raise home armies of women and post them where they could take the place of men; on the railways, in the postal service, in every factory, and behind every sort of desk and counter. No State in the world offered so many conditions for such a Spartan regime; no other State could imitate it; Germany could not be beaten. Victory was not a gift, but he who grasped at it thus defiantly must win. Let democratic babblers beyond the frontiers drivel about the free co-operation of an instructed people: the best thing in the world was an Order—so a poet had said, and by the Flag of Prussia he was right, and deserved a *schnapps* for saying so. There should be no lack of Orders.

Not the future, therefore, but the munitions crisis of today and tomorrow would break Germany, unless a miracle happened.

By bitter inter-departmental conflicts a little ammunition might be extracted from the Navy, and explosive could be imported across the Baltic from the Swedes, the only neutrals who were well disposed. Perhaps, too, Italy would produce some of the nitrates that she imported from South America for agricultural purposes, if that traitorous little ally were promised a bit of the Trentino, payable at the conclusion of peace. But these were vague prospects. And von Bahr's telegram seemed to suggest that a banker might be able to help.

A bare minute before the appointed time, Colonel Schieffenzahn, leaning against the window and immersed in these painful meditations, saw Herr Hugo Wahl get out of his great car. He was punctual, at all events, this gentleman from Potsdam—a Jewish gentleman, as the glimpse of profile, the black moustache, and heavy shoulders at once betrayed. Colonel Schieffenzahn laughed shortly. He was very welcome! In a war with England he would gladly have entered into an alliance with the devil, since neither Junkers nor Ministers seemed to realize the necessities of war in the matter of raw material, grain, and oil: how much more with one who merely wanted recognition as a citizen at last.

Herr Hugo Wahl sat down opposite the Colonel with his overcoat thrown back, still a little out of breath. Among his clients there were officers of every rank, many of them much higher than a colonel. But here, in these rooms, encompassed by the spirit of military infallibility, he had a sensation almost of awe. He began by observing deferentially that he assumed Herr von Bahr had informed the Colonel of the object of his visit. Anyone who wanted to import so much as a rabbit from occupied Belgium, had to get a permit from the competent military authorities. But this consignment of guano, genuine Chile saltpetre, was most urgently needed for agricultural use in Brandenburg.

Albert Schieffenzahn's eyes involuntarily began to glare like those of a hunting owl; and there were few men who could have gone on talking under that gaze. Herr Hugo Wahl stopped short. Had he done something wrong? Did the Colonel object to interference by third parties?

But with a courteous gesture, his eyes again half-hidden by dropped lids, Schieffenzahn bowed slightly, and said: "Where are you going to get the guano without stealing it, sir?"

Herr Wahl then explained that the man in charge of his agricultural credits business, one Leo Brümmer, now lance-corporal in the Landwehr, in the course of his duties as sentry in the Antwerp docks, had observed a train of forty, and possibly fifty, trucks of guano, of first-rate quality, probably just unloaded.

"Ah, that consignment," said Schieffenzahn, and nodded with an air of complete composure. "No, my dear sir, that is long since disposed of. The new Commander-in-Chief couldn't let you have it; we have to think of international law—the Americans are so damnably inquisitive—and everything we discover has to be applied to the needs of the country first."

"Ah," said Herr Wahl regretfully, "Belgian soil is so much better anyhow than our Brandenburg sand, they wouldn't want more than half of it."

Albert Schieffenzahn laughed like a boy. "True enough. But you must get on to the right Department in Brussels; it's no good coming to us—we can't help you. The telegrams to and from Brussels already fill a good-sized cupboard, and we've only been occupying the country three months."

"But," Herr Wahl put in, "couldn't we suggest to these Belgians that they should draw up a statement of their essential needs and make it fit in with our own? I know many of our important industrialists in the West would be glad, under favourable conditions, to be spared a great deal of tiresome competition and enter into some such scheme."

"Later on, perhaps, my dear sir, later on; at present they're extremely hard to deal with, and wouldn't hear of such a thing." And, in ecstasy at this glorious news, he added: "But the man who spotted the stuff seems to be a bright sort of fellow. The local administration in Belgium will want as many like him as they can get. We'll have him promoted sergeant, and seconded for service with the Base-Command in Belgium." And he made a note of the name, unit, and company of the Landwehrsmann, Leo

Brümmer. Now he must get rid of this thick-lipped herald of good news, as quickly as might be, or he would then and there die of joy behind his writing-table. Fifty trucks of Chile saltpetre! —five months' supplies for the artillery. Surely, if the words could ever be used, God was on the side of the Germans.

Herr Wahl, on the other hand, had no notion of taking his leave. He had already forgotten his disappointment. Why not? It was worth the journey to get acquainted with Colonel Schieffenzahn. And if Brümmer got a position in Belgium, something could be made out of that, sooner or later. A banker had enough on his hands already. After two troublesome months of stagnation, some sort of war industry would have to be organized, which, with fewer men available, would call for all heads and hands. But as he was sitting here calmly smoking and talking to one whose scribbled memoranda controlled men's destinies, couldn't he mention the fellow Bertin and dispose of him by getting him called up? Such an objectionable young man, who had made good use of his opportunities in Munich to turn the head of his daughter, Lenore, and last Sunday at his, Herr Wahl's, own coffee table, had expressed views about the Emperor, the Siegesallee, the repertoire of the Hoftheater, and the objects of the war, that were not becoming from anyone at such a time. What was entertaining enough in the July number of *Simplizissimus,* had, by October, become irritating and offensive. Discipline and military training would be most beneficial to this dubious literary gentleman.

But before he could open his mouth and pass, by way of observations on those who decried German treatment of Belgium, to the subject of the unfortunate Bertin, Albert Schieffenzahn got up. In courteous and even cordial tones, he thanked Herr Wahl for the pleasure of the interview, and excused himself on the plea that he was urgently needed at an important conference at the Reichstag. "I hope," he said mysteriously, "to be called away from here very shortly in connexion with certain events that may take place in the East. Otherwise I should count upon the pleasure of working with such leaders of industry as yourself. Perhaps

I shall be able to do more for you one day—we've plenty of time before us. Try to remember my absurd name; I have already taken careful mental note of yours, Herr Wahl. In any event, I am always at your service." And with the pleasant laugh of an important personage who is setting himself to secure a man's goodwill, he shook Herr Wahl by the hand, accompanied him to the door, and through it into the corridor, set his visitor on his way, clicked his heels like a cadet, leapt back into his room, shut the door, sat down at his writing-table and hammered on it with both fists like a Negro on the verge of hysteria, and finally burst into tears—tears of happiness, tears of wild deliverance; the war would go on; and, of course, Germany would win. A telegram to Antwerp, urgent and secret, within three hours, requisitioned a freight train on such and such a quay in the docks. Now the new nitrate works could take their time.

On the way back Herr Hugo Wahl, with impassive countenance, meditated, to the accompaniment of the pleasant rocking motion of the car, on what he had gained and lost during the last few hours. He had made the acquaintance of an able and important personage, a most outstanding plus. On the other hand this fellow Bertin was not disposed of, an undeniable minus—but of how trifling a kind! It would be all right if his wife and he kept an eye on the girl and impressed upon the innocent creature whom she ought, and ought not, to know. He would speak to Mathilde at once about it. And suddenly, as the car sped onwards and his thoughts dwelt upon the harmless student Bertin, Herr Wahl's face contracted into a wry expression of disgust. These were noisy ruffians that poisoned the life of every patriotically minded Israelite—by their corroding criticism, their ever-open mouths, and their lack of instinct for social order. The corpulent Herr Wahl hated no man; he believed in peace and quiet. But this fortune-hunter, it was true, he honoured with an aversion that admitted of no compromise.

In holding these views, Herr Wahl was no different from other fathers, who think their children are easily led, and paint black pictures of the characters of their unwelcome friends. What Werner Bertin really thought and would have said, if a fat banker had not provoked him into contradiction, he was expounding that very day, in the company of a few friends and one stranger, in the house of the author and art expert, Dr. Theodor Lederer, whom he admired as heartily as he condemned most of his fellows.

On that afternoon around the circular old-fashioned table, on which two book-lined walls looked down, the three generations sat. A Dutch merchant, Dr. van Rijlte, who had come to Berlin on business, represented the oldest, and was regarded with envy by his juniors and the younger generation, for behind his back the wide world opened out: waterways to Sumatra, Borneo, Java, and the Fortunate Isles. He was moving about the country, trying to get into touch with liberally minded Germans, because he and many other Dutchmen would have gladly used the time of the great munitions crisis to pave the way to a speedy peace; but this was known only to Hermann Lorcher, the author, who was leaning against the stove warming his bony hands, his pince-nez poised askew before his expressive eyes. The ladies, knitting vigorously at grey mittens, mufflers, or socks, agreed with their hostess, who maintained that we were a great nation, which must expand, and incorporate Belgium and Antwerp in the German Reich. A cynical voice from the stove interjected that in so doing we should annex the most thickly populated industrial State on earth; but they did not heed it. Dr. Berchtl, formerly a lecturer at Munich University, his arched brows resting on his folded hands, and a glitter in his set eyes, expressed the hope that the Church would use her good offices to reconcile the Belgians to their German kindred of the Rhineland; it was known that Pope Pius X had blessed the arms of Apostolic Austria. Dr. Albert Loth, barrister and Rhinelander, then fell into disfavour with his hostess (Mela Hartig-Lederer, a famous pianist of a rather violent temperament), because he dismissed these fantastic dreams, and described a veiled annexation as being as discreditable as it was impossible; he even ventured to say that he had always disavowed war as organized force, and saw no reason to abandon a view which the facts had merely served to confirm. No one agreed with him. The host, stroking his beard with ivory fingers, looked deprecatingly across at his wife, whose knitting needles clicked out sparks of wrath. Obstinate little Frau Dr. Berchtl, from the corner of the curved sofa, inveighed against certain intellectuals among the Western Powers, Belgians, Irish, French and Swiss, who, owing their reputation and no small amount of money to German theatres and publishers, had now with equal folly and discredit to themselves, turned their backs on us. Every fair-minded person knew that Germany and Austria had only started the war because they could do no otherwise.

Dr. van Rijlte, ruddy and white-haired, nodded meditatively. As he crumbled the little cakes on his plate, and nibbled at the fragments, he led the conversation away from this hopeless theme. These people knew only of German victories; the state of siege prevented their having any knowledge of the reality: they lived in a haze of false security which must one day fatefully collapse. "Nasty little country—Belgium," he said with a twinkle. "Too many nuns and priests, and nothing but rain. Everyone curses it who hasn't got business there." He looked round that circle of fine, keen faces, with Frau Mela's Tyrolese peasant's head in the centre, and asked quietly what was thought of the destruction of Rheims cathedral. Here was a gathering of artists and authors, philosophers and pretty young women. He had found it commonly held in Germany that this unique masterpiece was not worth the bones of a single Pomeranian Grenadier, to use a phrase of Bismarck's, and if such buildings as the Cloth Hall at Ypres were wrecked by gun-fire, those who had posted the artillery observers on the towers were solely responsible.

But this, he went on with a smile, was not a matter for elderly gentlemen. The younger generation must speak and contradict him—those who would be soldiers if the war went on long enough.

Werner Bertin undertook to reply. He was a prospective

artilleryman, and a writer of plays; and if it was not arrogant to speak before so many much more qualified persons, he would do his best.

Some of the company looked at him encouragingly. No one suspected how eagerly Lenore Wahl awaited what her friend would say. Now he was to defend before the world an act that had stricken them both so deeply.

In his embarrassment he fell into the lilting cadence and the broad vowels of his Silesian home, and he blushed as he began. The destruction of such a masterpiece was not a matter that could be cleared up by argument, it was much more in the nature of a tragic event, fit theme for a great drama, if indeed so recent an occurrence could be thus utilized. It would have been a crime had the French omitted to post observers on this stone mountain and it would have been an equal crime had the Germans allowed themselves to be prevented by the irreplaceable artistic value of the building, from firing on it. Necessity had entangled both sides in a tragic knot, and only the eye of destiny, that saw and saw through them both, could decide on which of them would fall the glory of that destruction and the light of inner justification.

"Well said," replied van Rijlte; "incidentally, the French deny that there were any such observers. Now, my young friend, you who place such matters beyond argument, would you fire on Strassburg cathedral, if it came to the point?"

And Bertin replied, still with a faint Silesian accent: "I would fire on Strassburg cathedral if an evil fate should make it necessary; though my heart would bleed to do so, and I daresay one would suffer for it all one's life. . . . "

"Then you would not refuse?" asked Frau Dr. Lorcher, gentle and grey-haired, from the other corner of the sofa.

And Bertin: "No, I would accept my burden."

Then a short silence fell, while all of them, absorbed in their own thoughts, looked at the young man and pondered on his words. Van Rijlte thought Germany's case was hopeless; Frau Mela was confident of victory; Hermann Lorcher thought: Poor fool; and Lenore Wahl thought: Dear lad.

Chapter 4

IN KÜSTRIN

A ponderous travelling trunk was trundled along the platform on a porter's truck, and then shot up in a lift to the luggage shed. There it waited for a while until a lengthy freight train rumbled into the station during the night. In a closed car, not for the moment needed for the transport of forty-eight men or six horses, it lay firmly wedged between barrels of herrings consigned from Stettin to Bielitz in Austrian Silesia, and dispatched via Kreuzburg, as the shorter connexion via Beuthen-Kattowitz was congested by the transport of coal, troops, war material, and pit-props for the industrial area. Flat cases with handles from the Spandau factories were loaded into the Kreuzburg car—practice ammunition for the machine-gun company of the infantry battalion stationed at Kreuzburg; wicker containers from Berlin containing glass globes of acid, also for Austria; and, finally, miscellaneous crates of all sizes, made of white, cheap wood, with Rhineland goods for Breslau. Breslau was a large city of many needs, and a vast market was opening up towards the East—Poland, and the occupied area generally. The superintendent of the freight station at Kreuzburg did not fail to notice the brown trunk in its sequestered corner, consigned to Herr Berthold Bertin. The porter who had put it on the car had wrapped it in a bit of sacking to protect it against the briny reek of the herring barrels; Pawlitzky, the forwarding agent, took delivery of it, together with the invoice, and carted it off with various other packages to the shop of Herr Berthold Bertin, cabinet-maker.

In her smock of washing velvet, figured in a gay design of browns and greens and yellows, and with slippers on her feet,

Frau Bertin, small and silent, accompanied the trunk, still faintly odorous of herring, on its passage through the shop and the house. Her heart throbbed with agitation. There it was—all that was now left to her of her boy. Fräulein Wahl had written most kindly, really very nicely indeed for someone she did not know, and sent the key; and as business was quieter than it had ever been—there were few customers in these days for a bachelor suite in oak, or a lacquered bedroom suite—she could devote long and loving hours to unpacking and disposing of the contents. The windows of the living-room looked out on to the courtyard, surrounded on three sides by low buildings, all belonging to Herr Bertin's business. To the right and left they were overshadowed by the high walls of the neighbouring houses, which her Werner so detested. He had such odd habits, such strange sensibilities and outbursts of emotion. He was very original, and not like other young men. She could not help being angry with him sometimes; but there—he was in love, and she loved him all the more. Alas, it would be a long time before he took his degree, now that he was stuck in the Army Service Corps in Küstrin, where Old Fritz and his poor friend Katte had got into such trouble when Fritz was still Crown Prince. The war would certainly last into the summer; he had already lost so many terms that one more would not greatly matter. He was always away—he had been away for years now—and she missed him terribly; and yet after the first three or four days of a holiday there was certain to be a quarrel—because he would not share a room with his brother, or write a poem for the cabinet-makers' summer celebrations, or call on Herr Justizrat Czempiner. He much preferred to wander in the fields and the woods, to spend hours lying on a narrow plank across a stream, watching the antics of a nasty little brown water-rat, and then be late for dinner so that the soup had to be warmed up again—that was her Werner. There she was, thinking these unkind thoughts about her boy, and see how neatly he had packed his trunk. With loving care she took out one thing after another, shook out the clothes, smoothed the shirts, brushed the felt hat and tried to pat it into shape, set out the ornaments, unwrapped the bronze inkstand from the stockings, and polished the black marble bowl that this young Fräulein Wahl had sent him for his writing-table on his birthday. Yes, the boy had always been unlike the others. His constant headaches, his catarrhs, his sensitive throat, his heart so prone to palpitations—how on earth would he get on as a soldier? His father and brothers laughed—the conceited lad would need to be put through it pretty thoroughly before he looked like a soldier. Indeed, who would ever have thought that she would see her boy in uniform? She must not say anything against the War, the Russians had begun it; would the filthy Cossacks ever get into Kreuzburg? She had never seen one, thank heaven; but she had read about them in the paper. So long as the enemy did not want peace, we must go on hammering them, and war was very good for business. What torments they had gone through between 1894, when Werner had the measles and then scarlet fever immediately after, and 1908, when he went to Munich. What a time it had taken them to reach a point when they knew that they would not have to tremble at the prospect of pay-day at the beginning of the month, or borrow the money from a credit society, because it was so difficult to get in what they were owed. But now that Fritz had persuaded his father to start manufacturing cases for munitions of all sorts and kinds, they looked like doing very well indeed. The yard was stacked with piles of crates, flat for infantry cartridges, long and narrow for hand-grenades—these lined with zinc; large and square for the artillery, to hold sacks of gunpowder or mysterious substances of which they did not know the use.

She laid the suits first over the backs of the chairs and then arranged them on the coat-hangers; they must all go to the little local tailor Cohnreich, who would put them in order—at any rate he could clean and press them, and put new bindings round the inside of the trouser legs. The shoes must be put on trees, and the dirty clothes could be taken downstairs at once in the basket. Werner would be sure to write soon for stockings or underclothes.

The manuscripts had better stay where they were in the drawer of the trunk; the music could go into the bookcase to begin with, it could be taken out later, dusted, and then properly arranged. She knew how much he valued those manuscripts; her Werner invented all manner of stories in his head and then put them down on paper. Who could have predicted it, when she brought him into the world so many years ago one happy noontide? Such a little laughing child, and now a writer of books and plays that the Censor did not like. He had never been able to adapt himself to other people. He would find life difficult in a stupid place like Küstrin.

Seated on a yellow-backed cane chair beside the emptied trunk, surrounded by a litter of shirts, suits, shoes, and a pile of dirty linen, Frau Lina Bertin pressed her handkerchief to her eyes with thin faded fingers, because she was so sorry for her unhappy son, who had been dragged from the life that was his, and flung into the Army Service Corps.

But the mother-heart was wrong. The son needed no sympathy; indeed, he was very well content. When, eight or ten days after he had been called up, he read in his second letter from Kreuzburg that all his things had arrived safely and had been unpacked—("I wish it wasn't so long before you come to fetch them away again")—he was really almost surprised. Was the day of his packing up no further away than this? He ate other food, began the day in different fashion, divided it as he had never done before, filled it with strange movements, brandished his arms and his legs, stretched his back, hollowed his stomach, responded to stimuli that had lain buried for half a dozen years, and found himself doing physical exercises, marching and running races. He heard new voices without and within, and an odd but heartening confusion of orders that came from other men and from his own inner self. It was strange that his handwriting had not altered; it remained just the same, like his mother's.

He was arrayed in a uniform that made him look like a convict;

the clumsily cut grey tunic was far too tight across the shoulders and much too loose lower down. Red squares, indicating his unit, adorned his collar, and intensified the pallor of his face, while his cropped hair made his ears stand out abruptly from his head. A cap, a grey and shapeless object like a potato-pancake, was pulled down to his eyebrows in the prescribed manner. It effaced his forehead and the outline of his head, and made him look as imbecile as the trained soldier, in his proper pride, expected the recruit should be made to look. But that was no more than a joke. The Fatherland called for greater sacrifices than that. What especially pleased him was the prospect of leaving the garrison town in a few days, and being transferred in a smaller unit to some neighbouring village, "to get settled down," as Sergeant Boost observed with a wink. Until then, the raw recruits were billeted in a large dance hall on the outskirts of the town, where they slept on straw for their first night as soldiers, and tasted their first coffee from a field kitchen. The day was filled with walking, saluting, marching, running, exercise, and drill, which latter they soon picked up, and indeed they were now forming fours with precision. There was also instruction on the hierarchy of N.C.O.s and officers, their badges, their authority, and the all confusing varieties of salute. They had taken the oath on the Articles of War—to Bertin's regret, without the slightest ceremonial; a long list of harsh injunctions was read out, the refrain of which ran—"A repetition of the offence will be punished with death": a somewhat less impressive ceremony than a head cook announcing the menus for the week. But he, Werner Bertin, entered into all this with the utmost cheerfulness. He enjoyed the sensation of being a part of a gigantic entity, with joint responsibility for a firmly welded group, of which the members were fused into a unity; the soldier's *esprit de corps*. He, a man who had lived by his mind, was no longer alone, and this was the first source of happiness. As soon as one had learned to grasp intuitively what was expected and how an order should be carried out, one felt a sensation of freedom, of a new collective freedom, such as a man had never dreamed of hitherto. It was glorious not to have to think any more, or at least, not to the exclusion of every other activity; to put the overdriven intellect out of commission, arouse an infinitude of new brain-cells and nerve-currents, and with them revitalize the whole body. He was now among soldiers, as he had hoped to be in his boyhood, when the infantry battalion marched through Kreuzburg with its band playing. The splendid marches of the days of the Great Frederick, the Hohenfriedberger and the Torgauer, were now his music; and they stirred sleeping ardours in his soul. In the days of peace, a man had to be on his guard against militarism, defend the intellect against the onslaught of force, and stand firm against the abominations of the sabre-rattlers. But now intellect and force were at one, the war had fused them, the might of the armies served the spirit that was Germany, and the emotions of a soldier-lad were worth as much as the heart's blood and high endeavour of a great writer.

All this passed through the head of Werner Bertin, private in the Army Service Corps, in Büderling's Dance Hall, during the midday interval, while he, surrounded by a crowd of his fellow-soldiers, sat down to write a letter home, a warmer and more affectionate letter than he had written for a long while. He wondered whether Lenore would understand all this? Needless to ask: a Prussian girl, brought up in Potsdam, and a woman who loved him. He was delighted to hear that she had got into touch with his mother, who had now asked him whether she should send a letter of thanks, or merely send a postcard acknowledging the safe arrival of the trunk. He must speak to Lenore about it. Perhaps she would be able to come and see him next Sunday like any other soldier's girl, and sit beside him here in Büderling's garden, with a glass of raspberry-juice before her, arm in arm with a soldier. If he wrote her a card now, she could arrange to get away from home, and it wouldn't take her long to get there and back in a D-train. She would surely invent some excuse. Oh, for a sight of those great grey eyes and that girlish mouth. Later on she would come and see him in his village. If he only knew where it would be. What it was to be loved! Never in all the years of his youth would he have dared to believe that he would win such a girl for his own.

It was strange to sit here in the straw and ruminate, amid the snores of the noonday sleepers and the wafts of hot spring air that came through the windows. It was good to be alive and to be a soldier, and to sit writing letters and postcards stamped "Field Post."

Chapter 5

EARLY CHERRIES

Lenore hurried down the steps with an air of smiling satisfaction —the reflection of good news. Dr. Lederer had just telephoned that an important theatrical producer, an Austrian like himself, wanted to read Werner's piece, *A Man Called Hilsner,* that exciting drama which the Censor did not like. Had she got a copy? It might be very important, he had added. And it must be quickly forthcoming—tomorrow morning, if possible. ("You have to be on the spot with theatrical people, or they will have forgotten you by next day.") Oh, she understood. If Werner's play was acted, all their troubles would be over; the parents could be easily brought round. Was there a spell in Frau Laubschrey's cards after all? How glorious if she could manage it all by herself!

At the moment Lenore was wearing a white kitchen apron; she was keeping Frau Mahnke company. The house lay in a noonday stillness, almost void of people. Father and grandfather at business, David at the gymnasium, mother on her rounds of inquiry for the War Wives Relief Association. Poor mother! She lived in a pleasant house, esteemed by all who knew her; her charities now held an important place on the official list. But her social isolation, her want of human contacts and of neighbours, had always depressed her, and the smartest visitors from Berlin had brought her no comfort. Lenore could never understand how much it mattered to her mother if Frau Ducherow did not come to tea, or if Frau Sanitätsrat Paulke did not invite her to her Ladies' Circle; but now she understood. She needed the warmth and movement and regard without which it was hard to thrive in any environment. And Mother was certainly thriving now. Red cheeks, good humour, and sound sleep at nights brought her happiness, simply because she was allowed to help.

The kitchen, which was in the basement, glittered with white tiles, brass fitments, and an array of porcelain, pewter, and copper. Frau Mahnke, cook to the Wahl household, was busy at the great wooden table bottling early cherries, which she had bought for good money from a Werder cherry-grower, against the still distant winter. For this purpose the stalks had to be picked off the large pink and yellow berries, and Lenore, well aware of the excellent impression that would be produced on the more important members of the family by such housewifely activity, got a great deal of amusement out of it. She was often away from home, always with an excellent excuse, and no one asked her questions; however, from time to time she liked to emphasize her position as daughter of the house. But her true life was passed elsewhere. On the previous Sunday she had visited Werner for the first time at Küstrin camp, *Wallenstein's Lager, anno* 1915; and her mind was full of the humorous and homely comradeship of the recruits, as she moved among the crowd like any private's wife or sweetheart! She now looked forward to a night in Alt-Drewitz, Wilkersdorf, or Tamsel—to her mere names of which she had barely heard. It would soon be Ascension Day; she could make the excuse of a trip to see the sights of Schwedt on the Oder, for example, or Tangermünde, spend a night away from home again, and be once more a woman. The sap of spring was hot in the world, it had risen mightily since the end of April. These cherries bore witness to its surging energy.

"The good ones in the pot, and the bad ones in the craw, I suppose, Frau Mahnke?" asked Lenore in the words of Cinderella, as she held one of them for a moment between her teeth by the stalk, jerked it neatly into her mouth, twisted it round, and thrust the stalk out from her lips.

Frau Mahnke laughed gleefully all over her brown face, until her cheeks, under the slanted Wendish eyes, were seamed with myriad wrinkles. She loved the young lady who went to the university, understood Latin, and could reckon by heathenish signs like young Master David—and yet came and helped to bottle cherries, as though she were still the little Lena, with the doll Lottchen clasped firmly under her right arm, bare-kneed and ten years old. "Lord, Fräulein, if a Count could see you so, or blessed Prince Friedrich Karl that was, in his red Hussar uniform—he'd have swung you into the saddle and galloped off with you. But men can't tell a good thing when they see it, these days. You take an old woman's word, no one knows whom they're going to marry, nor why, not Peter nor the Apostles nor even Mary Magdalene, who must have understood something about menfolk in her time."

Lenore smiled, and sighed. How refreshingly cool it was in that kitchen. The heap of cherries before her recalled the avenues of Polling, and that glorious summer from whose dreams the war had flung them forth—the war that roared and seethed and ravened far away upon the edges of the world, and here, in the reality of this pleasant room, faded into little more than an idea, were it not for the multitudes from all parties and all ranks, from Potsdam, from Berlin, and all the land of Germany, who had gone forth to work that miracle in dust and heat; so that there was war and there was peace—war without, and peace here beside Frau Mahnke's, or rather Frau Wahl's, placid hearth.

It was good to stand and dream, bite into a great cherry charged with summer and with sweetness, and neatly spit the stone through the window into the garden, where Boll, the yellow hound, sat licking himself gravely and snapping at flies.

"Why are we bottling so much this year?" said Frau Mahnke, emerging from her silent thoughts, as she picked the stalks off the cherries with unwearied fingers. "Because there's going to be trouble over sugar. They're going to deal it out by tickets, like bread. I should have thought there was enough beet growing in all Germany. But the mistress knows what she's about; so we're starting now, without waiting for the sugar cards."

Lenore nodded; that was her mother all over; careful in all little things, full of understanding in the house, but as blind as all parents are in her children's affairs. How gladly would Lenore have seen Werner welcomed in her parents' house, and celebrated an engagement in the old-fashioned way, just the sort of thing the parents would have loved. But in this she had completely failed. They did not like Werner, they disliked him, in fact—and so she had to pursue her way in secret, guided by her star. In this union she was truly at home, at the side of one who, in the past two years, had always praised and justified her life—a life that she had led, by some dim insistent urge, in conflict with her environment, her friends, her school, and the parental house, mainly in the matter of her feelings, thoughts, and aspirations, in her taste in dress, in her attitude to the impressions that crowded into her receptive mind from earliest girlhood. Who was it that had thundered so wrathfully against some teacher or governess who wanted to make her do her hair or think in the approved fashion; and had sworn to put the whole pack of them into a novel, so that all this torment should not be altogether wasted? Who had praised her fight for independence, for a little freedom to develop the entity that her parents had produced in the person of Lenore Wahl, and who had swept away her doubts, her agonized self-questionings, with the emphatic words: "You are right, and they are wrong"? Nowhere else had she found so much eager affection, so much regard and sympathy and love. Now he looked altered; but his heart, unaltered, was with her still. Indeed, she had a fresh proof of it; twelve poems for the seventeenth of May, which he had destined for her some while ago. By a stupid mischance she had not received them yet. Paula, unaccountable as ever, had been suddenly haled away by her master on a concert-trip to Denmark and through the whole of Sweden, which he had undertaken at the request of the Foreign Ministry, to lead the music of the German barbarians to victory. She wrote ecstatic postcards; in the first she had made some apologetic reference to a yellow envelope—an allusion which Werner had explained to her at Küstrin—"but I couldn't give up my lessons and such a lovely spring trip which would not cost me a penny. You will be just as glad to have the present when I get back." Of

course she would, and glad to keep it always. She would certainly be with him over Ascensiontide.

A secret smile stole over her face, and Frau Mahnke, with a sidelong glance said, still busy with her cherries, that it was a pity that the young man who had come to dinner that day when there had been pike and parsley, and saddle of vension with Cumberland sauce, had had to go away: "But never mind, he'll be back again one day."

"Look, I've got three red stains on my apron, Frau Mahnke."

"Why, Fräuleinchen, it's just like in the fairy-tale, where the knights always saw three drops of blood in the snow and could not move because they were thinking of their lady. I'll put a little borax on at once, and there won't be a speck on it when it comes back from the wash."

Chapter 6

RECONSTRUCTION

There are awakening states after a deep sleep that encompass a man for endless seconds in impenetrable dream-illusions. No longer asleep, but utterly oblivious of his present existence, on the day before Ascension Day Werner lay on the great goose-feather mattress in his billet at Frau Jerichow's farm. He heard the cock crow through the closed double windows, for there was a huge dung-heap in the yard; and he thought it was Herr Kampfeneder's cock at Polling near Munich, which had so often awakened him to work. There he was, lying in his attic room, with its windows looking out on to the meadows and the forest; he only needed to open his eyes to see the deer wandering over the grass in the unreal light of morning, where later on the village sheep would appear and graze, like moving stones. He had just come noiselessly from Lenore, having left her arms to begin his work again. Already on the way back from her room his face had changed; the red silk dressing-gown, which he wore with a white girdle—it had originally been the lining of a cloak of Lenore's, who had then passed it on to him to wear as carnival fancy-dress—gave a sort of monkish air to his clean-shaven, rather bony face and neck. With bare feet thrust into canvas slippers, he noiselessly paced up and down Frau Kampfeneder's gaily coloured drugget from one wall of the attic to the other. The open manuscript volume on the table at which he both ate and wrote fixed and held his eyes. His pen lay between the pages, he felt between his fingers the squared penholder that he had himself cut from a Bavarian elder tree, and dipped his English nib in indelible ink. From the inmost depths of him came words, the necessity of which he did not realize, and the force of which he did not understand, until they covered the paper in black script. He was working again upon his drama *The Great Bishop and His Enemy,* and was making mighty progress in those enchanted nights. Beyond the table faces hovered: the Bishop's passionate face, and the stern, bearded face of the great teacher, nor did he yet recognize the former as his own, but more exalted, as he would have liked to look; the nose more curved, the chin stronger, and the eyes larger and more full of fire; nor the other as his father's face, rustic but kind, and touched with the decisive power and privilege of procreation. They moved their lips in argument and spoke their minds. He was conscious of a vision, and a vision all his own, into the profundities of his peoples' souls. He would sit down again, with half-closed eyes and parted lips, and his feet perched one above the other on the crossbar of the polished table, with the tense expression of a man who is waiting for the stream to flow. It was a joy to write at such dictation from within. Then came men in cowls and vestments. They moved in a spiritual room that flooded through the walls, and melted into the outer air and the dim light beyond the sloping attic roof. He often came to a halt, and stared absently into vacancy; against the darkness of the night behind the open windows he could see more than moving bars of moonlight. Mist and light fused into facts and presences that peopled the mysterious stage in the writer's mind. He saw them hovering at the foot of the bishop's bed, and while his nib scratched its way across the grained, rough-edged paper, he heard and wrote down the quiet utterances of a contemptuous voice that seemed to find its way into his very soul. The words with which his Bishop, upright in his bed under the heavy brocade baldachin, answered his enemy—shaken by fear, and pain, because the answer came from the man himself, from the sepulchres of his very soul—would serve to carry him over into the labour of the morrow. Bertin's heart beat in long slow strokes. Obstacles that had so constantly risen like a miasma between the word and himself had now been swept aside. He would get up, stretch his arms, pace up and down the quivering floor-boards of the little attic, and peer into the future; his play printed, acted, and—perhaps—a vast success. If he could only throw off the paralysis that lay so hot upon him. Why was the quilt suddenly too heavy?

Suddenly a dull thudding sound burst upon his ears, his heart leapt, and he started up in bed with staring eyes. For another instant he sat thus in an alien world, breathless, encompassed by unknown forms. Then, abruptly, this dim room sprang to life in all its sharp-cut clarity, and brought him back to the real world; he was sitting in Widow Jerichow's bed, outside lay the village of Alt-Drewitz in the morning sunshine, his bedroom was on the ground floor, and the time was spring of 1915. He, a private in the Army Service Corps, had been awakened by someone hammering on the shutters. His watch showed half-past five, in a quarter of an hour there would be coffee, and at six he would go on duty in drill trousers, vest, and tunic, and with boots upon his feet. Alas, he was no longer a monk in a red silk cowl; and as for the play that he so longed to see upon the stage, the agent who was to act for him had kept obstinately silent for a week past. He was a soldier—he who now leaped out of bed, flung off his night-shirt, and washed himself in the cold water that he had carried up from the well the day before. Nor had he slept with his lady; he had done yesterday exactly what he would do today: the whole morning he had worked hard with his hands, his shoulders, and his whole body, he and hundreds of his comrades. In the hot fragrance of drying pine timber, they sweated in those days among the roots and trunks of the great fir forest that the Governor of the fortress of Küstrin had had cut down to a height of about six feet against a possible advance by the Russians. They were working with saws, hatchets, and picks, to make some use of what could still be saved; short round logs for timbered paths and trench props, whole trunks and branches, and roots, which were very hard to unearth. When the tough gnarled roots were attacked with spade or axe, he loved to watch the white of the wood spurt from the brown veins. But first came the march through the sand of Brandenburg, over the green meadows, and into the forest before it grew too hot. Their arms and legs poured with sweat as they trudged along, and stories were told that would have appalled Shakespeare, and might well have shocked Rabelais; the Berlin bricklayer's story for instance, of the birth of his little daughter, which he related with gleams of fanatic humour in his eyes. It ceased to be disgusting, it so far exceeded all common usage that one could not but roar with laughter at it, and at the freckled, red-haired fellow who told it. No time to shave? Never mind, tomorrow was Ascension Day, tomorrow Lenore was coming, it was then that he would need a soft skin to press against her cheeks. She would find a friend who was growing gradually younger and stronger; she would find a man. He banished the foolish fear that something might happen when they slept together. One can't be always tormenting oneself with anxieties and precautions. A soldier trusted his star, or he might as well get himself put into a coffin and buried at once. And a woman who loved him, trusted him, was not too curious as to such precautions. How on earth, in this remote place, was he to buy what every chemist had for sale in town?

Gaily swinging his tin saucepan, a white-clad private in the Army Service Corps clattered downstairs and dashed out of the doorway of Widow Jerichow's house. Viewed from behind, there was nothing to distinguish him from his fellows.

BOOK TWO

LENORE

Chapter 1

FURLOUGH

In those days the people of Germany felt exalted and united by the common experience of that great time. News that brought joy or mourning flashed like an electric current through the barriers between them, the barriers of usage, of caste, and the Nordic fear of laying bare the soul. They felt they were members of one body, a nation, born to succour each other by sympathy, kindness, and common impulses of the heart. So when a neighbour's son came home on leave, it concerned not merely his parents, his brothers and sisters, and the servants, but, almost to the same extent, people unrelated to him who lived nearby and had watched him grow up, laughed at his pranks, and complained of the noise he made. Of course, they became more quickly accustomed to his presence and his changed appearance; only in exceptional cases were they stirred to more than a passing interest that give birth to thoughts and hopes and plans.

In early June, when starlings and swallows were watching over their brooding mates, Gerhard von Ducherow came home on convalescent leave to the villa whose garden adjoined that of the Wahl family. He had broken several ribs in a fall from his horse, he still wore a bandage under his coat, and his chest was thickly covered with plaster. The broken bones had almost healed, the gunshot wound over the left ear had not damaged the bone; and he was doing very well indeed. And yet his deepest self was in a turmoil, and this was reflected from time to time in his helpless wandering gaze. His brain functioned slowly, and important matters took a long while to sink into his mind. His father, Geheimrat von Ducherow, had contemptuously reconciled himself to the possession of a stupid son, and among his friends the youth was regarded as more than ever of a fool. The shrewder of his teachers suspected his more serious abilities. Now, at home again after an absence of ten months, he viewed the world with altered eyes; and the fact that he had no one here to talk to made him almost ill. At Potsdam, he found himself walking in an atmosphere of glory, tainted by a musty odour of school celebrations, of newly painted flagstaffs. He told, of course, the stories that were expected of him; how they had swept through Belgium; how here and there they had had some unpleasant little encounters, sometimes with civilians, so that the Saxon infantry, with whom they kept more or less in touch, had to shoot some hostages as a penalty for attacks by *francs-tireurs*. Later on they rode southwards and eastwards, on turning movements that no one could understand, beyond the Marne and back to it. In Poland a dragoon's life was equally unpleasant in autumn, winter and spring—the roads were fearful. The French had got what was coming to them, the Russians would not last much longer; by Christmas there would be peace. Such was his talk: but, when he was alone, he would shake his head. The gay and cheerful notion of war implanted in his mind at school was little like the damnable reality. It was swimming in a pool, as against a conflict with North Sea rollers: and in that conflict they must live and endure. All experience outstripped the words that were meant to cover it. In August, for example, hundreds of people were shot as *francs-tireurs*. And yet, in those nights there had been hot disputes between the officers of the dragoons and the Saxon infantry as to whether these mysterious bullets might not have been fired from carbines or rifles with slipped safety catches—that is, by Saxon infantry or by dragoons. Of course, one had to shoot at crowds of civilians, men, women and children, all alike, when the order was given. There was no time to make much inquiry. Man and beast, officer and private, cavalry and infantry, were all a mass of quivering nerves, worn out by railway journeys, sleepless nights, badly cooked and bolted food, thirst and dust and heat, weary of riding they knew not whither, exasperated by warnings to beware of ambuscades of peasants shooting from the fields, or roofs, or cellars, and by incessant orders "to advance at all costs."

And what was the real truth about the Russians? It was, of course, a fact that their generals were incompetent, their army organization rotten, their commissariat corrupt, their tinned provisions mainly chalk; and the men rushed like fools upon their fate. Against such an army, observed the beery citizen at home, war was child's play. Well, well! But he could not rid himself of the impression, since they had been flung from the West into the East, that first at Lodz and Lowicz, then at Mlava—Prasznysz, and during the savage fighting in the Augustovo forest, in the matter of leadership there was little to choose; and in the array of battle, so far as he understood it, the Russians were quite equal to their adversaries; they were quick to see the turn of the fight, and always extricated themselves by the steady valour of their men; and then, retaliated, confound them, by outflanking us in their turn. Had he not been shot from his horse among the guns of a German battery, embedded in the vast snowfields of the Masurian country, in its retreat before the Russian cavalry. And if his comrades had not picked him up with broken ribs and carried him off, would he not have been captured with the guns and clapped in a Russian prison, like many another who had certainly behaved in no more cowardly or feeble a fashion than himself? But to these Potsdam people all battles had to end in German victories. Had he felt heroic when he crashed down from his horse as the bullet grazed his skull, a bullet that, if it had gone a fraction further to the right, would have made a corpse of him, long since mouldered into odourless dust? A corpse—like many a man of his own and other squadrons, torn by shells, riddled by machine-gun fire, or neatly punctured by rifle bullets, and tipped out of the saddle. He could hear them cry "Mother!" as they fell, just as though his tall dragoons had been suddenly transformed into lost ill-treated children. . . . Well, however it might be, he could not stay here. At the front he could carry on. There he was encompassed by a consistent world in which a man always knew his whereabouts. Here, too, he was set down in a consistent world, but it did not in any way accord with the other; place them side by side, the cleavage still remained. It was true that from the way his mother often looked at him, and stroked his hair gently as she passed, he guessed that she understood him—but, alas, she did not speak. The others, however, his father included, knew all there was to know. Their newspapers depicted the world as it should have been, and he, a simple lieutenant of twenty, with the Iron Cross and the Saxon Distinguished Service Order, so recently snubbed by his father, was not as convincing as many, many hundred thousand printed pages.

Fortunately he fell in with an old schoolfellow one morning in the peaceful garden of Sanssouci, a tall officer by the name of Wintrich, sitting in a corner and drawing circles on the gravel with a crutch.

"Are you a hero, too?" asked Wintrich, his meagre form bent over his crutch.

"Oh, shut up," said Ducherow irritably; "at least it's quiet here."

And they listened to the birds above them in the tree-tops fluttering and twittering among the fresh green foliage. Nearby, among the darting butterflies, a white marble goddess, half-unclothed, displayed a comely back.

"Sit down here, and give me a cigarette," Wintrich said. And they watched the blue cloudlets of smoke rise into the lovely spring air.

Wintrich, too, came from the Eastern front. He had heard the whistle of his first bullets at Hohenstein, when Samsonov's three crack Corps, tall fair-haired Russians, dashed like wild beasts into the trap and tried to force a way out at Osterode; before that he had been at Stallupönen during the advance against Rennenkampf, when they all grew hoarse with dust and the mad excitement of the battle. So inexplicably broken off, as it then seemed; though not when the secret became known. After that, he was knocked over in the Angerapp sector by a shell splinter that struck him just above the knee, and lay placidly waiting for nearly a whole day until the Russians should come and finish him off with a bayonet—which was what the Prussians said they did. Of course that was nonsense; the only thing that wasn't nonsense was the fact that the Germans had won, and that the Russians had been killed in such masses that his ears still rang with the sounds of that slaughter.

By God, it was an odd sort of war that had to be learned and studied so assiduously in these days. The two young officers were not very articulate at first; they were naturally afraid of appearing critical or supercilious. They talked, with a sort of disgusted admiration, of machine-guns and their devastating effect on an assault. If the men behind them only kept their heads, sluiced the barrels with cold water, and didn't foul the cartridge belts—well, there wasn't a chance for the lads opposite. Unless they signalled to the artillery, though artillery was often damnably unresponsive when it was wanted. Then, of course! Never before could the man of other arms have seen the stripped gunners serve and fire their great thunderous weapons with a frantic energy that quite eclipsed the simpler handiwork of death. The trouble was that they depended very much on ammunition supplies. When there was any really hot fighting somewhere, fighting that went on day and night, the shells ran out and half the army congested the roads; then the gun-barrels could be very well used for baking pancakes, but not for much else. Cold steel was the final implement of war, as it had been with Hannibal at Zama.

"How do you find the people here?" asked Wintrich, after they had sat smoking for a while, exchanging observations of this sort.

"I'm getting away as soon as I can," answered Ducherow.

Friedrich Karl Wintrich, who was stationed at Königsberg, but came from Potsdam, felt something like pity for stupid little Ducherow. As if anyone in his right senses would carry on in such a place, inhabited by purely comic personages—male comedians in frock-coats, females in corsets; the latter, however, when they were young and pretty, were not unamusing in bed. Here was a likely case, he thought cynically, surveying the other with cool appraising eyes. "When our bones are healed, we shall know

where we belong. The receipted bill will appear after peace is made. There are good times coming for the likes of you and me. But until then . . . Do they run after you, too? Can't you manage to keep out of their way?"

Gerhard von Ducherow blushed. He had the Iron Cross, and there had been four or five occasions on which he had shown that he deserved it. But as an officer he was too young to possess the other's equanimity, which he was painfully conscious was beyond his reach. Of course he had noticed that the women made eyes at him, but he had not been long home, and had not gone much into society. He had talked across the hedge to the little Wahl girl, who years before had had something the matter with her lungs or bronchial tubes—or whatever the confounded organs were called that one heard so much about these days—and consequently couldn't stay and nurse with the Red Cross like his sister Else. How charming she looked as she stood there among the sprays of guelder rose and flowering jasmine, wearing a summer dress cut low round her clear-skinned throat; and at her side her great hound, so oddly named Boll. She had spoken to him and invited him to the house. Her hand, still soft as a child's lay for a moment in his own. They both had to stretch a little to reach over the bridge, which was nearly as tall as themselves. What eyes the girl had, he thought, as he met Lenore's friendly gaze. They spoke like old-acquainted neighbours' children, though separated by a difference of caste, and a certain embarrassment made him venturesome. Suddenly they were conscious that someone was looking down at them, a violet-hued figure among the plants in the conservatory. And indeed Frau Wahl, in her silk morning wrap, was standing motionless behind the palms, pressing her hand to her bosom and conjuring up a future that she dreamed of. . . .

No, he admitted, he had not yet had much to do with women. How could one in this respectable town?

Wintrich roared with laughter and clapped his long bony hand on his unwounded knee. "Look here, you come along with me; when we're back again the memory of it will warm our stomachs like a drop of *schnapps.*" He abruptly aped a mincing feminine voice: "No, really, darling, did you shoot him? How marvellous! Tell me exactly how it happened!"

"Where can one find girls in these parts?" asked Ducherow unsuspectingly, as they got up.

Wintrich laid his hand on Ducherow's shoulder. He had too much respect for that small youthful face to lay his hand on the lad's head, as he might easily have done. "Girls," he said sympathetically. "God bless your simple heart. I'm taking you into good society. Heroes are welcome everywhere, and they have always had a taste for females of good family, ever since Helen slept with Paris, while Major Menelaus was making such a nuisance of himself some distance behind the front."

After lunch it was Frau Wahl's habit to sleep; just a little nap of twenty minutes refreshed her until late in the evening. This time an unquiet mind soon aroused her. She was still stirred by what she had seen early that morning—two handsome slim young creatures shaking hands across a hedge. Frau Wahl, as an educated woman, well understood such symbols. Was not the spirit of the time, a comradeship that rose above all barriers, beautifully expressed in that group? She wished it could have been perpetuated beyond that transient moment, and displayed to all Potsdam. And what, after all, stood in the way of such perpetuation? Not, as she had conceived it in the first few moments, cast in bronze and erected on a pedestal in the square between the Church of St. Nicholas and the Castle; but was not the idea that had assailed her mind that morning also a sort of perpetuation, and in better fashion? She could not stay quietly in bed while there were still so many important matters to be looked into; whether, for instance, there was any obstacle to her scheme, any connexions of her daughter's that might be well enough for a girl student at the university, but must soon be dispelled by contact with the reality which was life in Potsdam. In two words: she must find out whether that objectionable young man, Bertin, was still to the fore in Lenore's imagination.

She could never break herself of the abominable habit of turning a door-handle very softly and going into a room without knocking. Children should have no secrets, however much they fought to keep them. In Lenore's bright room there was a pleasant fragrance of feminine tresses and eau-de-Cologne. (It was the only means of getting rid of the smell of tobacco which Lenore was annoyed to find still hung about her. She combed and brushed, and aired the place as best she could.) "Dry your hair downstairs in the conservatory while I'm dusting the glass, and tell me what's been happening in your little world." Frau Mathilde Wahl asked her question with the friendly insistence with which she had now to conceal her maternal curiosity.

Lenore got up like an obedient child; she was glad of the distraction. While she had been away yesterday (with Bertin), something unlooked for had happened, a painful incident from which she had only just recovered. She must think of something else and forget it. On the staircase she asked whether her mother would not like her to read aloud while she polished the Meissner shepherd groups, and those ornate goblets from which no one ever dared to drink.

"Make fun of them if you like," laughed Frau Mathilde; "I wish I were presenting them to you as part of your dowry."

"I would not have them in the house," protested the daughter, as she sat down on a grey divan, turning her back and her fleece of hair towards the sunlight. She felt that Frau Mathilde had something in her mind; the sudden transition to the subject of her dowry looked too deliberate.

Had she heard anything lately from this Herr Bertin whom Papa unfortunately disliked so much?

"No," said Lenore, "except that he has been called up and doesn't come to lectures any more."

This was good news for Frau Mathilde. "Ah! The army will soon cure him of his wild opinions. Do you correspond with him?"

"Oh well—" answered the daughter. "You wouldn't mind my exchanging affectionate postcards with one of our Field Greys."

"With any of our brave fellows," said the mother, "but not with him. A young man of no position—or rather of such a position as his—and with his views. He is well enough in a Munich café, but not in our house. Not that I should mind, dear child," she said, lying, and Lenore knew that she lied. "Papa is delighted that you've been so good about it. By the way, if you want to play tennis or read a book with your young friend, let me know and I will suggest something suitable. The Geheimrätin would certainly be grateful to you. The poor fellow won't be well of his wounds for a long time."

Young friend? Lenore searched her thoughts for a moment. Poor little Mamma! So she had really been looking out from the conservatory and seen her saying good-morning to the freckled young lieutenant of Dragoons, Ducherow. They had often squabbled and snowballed each other in early days. So she was now expected to flirt with him, with a view to marriage. How strange it was that parents clearly knew less of their children than an Australian black knew of the opposite side of the globe. "Excellent, Mamma; I'll start a little reading circle with him. I suggest Goethe's *Elective Affinities,* or *Hans von Bredow's Trousers.*"

Her mother almost giggled. Both books were classics, but hardly cheerful reading. "You bad little girl," she said, "that's another of your grandpapa's jokes." And she pulled affectionately at her daughter's plaits. Let her grow up a bit, and she would be more like her parents than they had ever expected.

Lenore watched her mother walk into the house with the self-assurance of one belonging to an eternally valid social order. Then she let her gaze wander between the palms, the bright dwarf limes, the lovely shining leaves of the India-rubber tree, into the sunlit garden, which only the broad curve of the road divided from the leafy tree-top world of the park. If only Werner had spared her that brutality.

Yesterday afternoon, Ascension Sunday, they had gone for a walk in the country through the fields, where the yellow stamens of the potato blossoms stood up to the sun. Their talk of peace, their hopes for the future, and the joy of each other's company as they walked arm in arm made them feel light-hearted. In a clearing among the short grey-green pines they lay down upon the mossy grass. Suddenly, without warning, Bertin had wanted to possess her as a woman; but under that blue sky that shone so softly through the branches of the little pines, her maidenhood revolted. She thrust him away. Then, for the first time in her life, he gripped her savagely by the shoulders, snarled at her to do as she was told, and mastered her by force. In a fear and shame that banished all delight, she let him have his will. They made their way back in silence; indeed it took her some time to recover. . . . Before she went home he had certainly tried to excuse himself; he had caressed and kissed her, won back her confidence and been forgiven; to dispel the whole thing as a joke, he described a rustic lad who had crept up to them in the clearing, in order to extend his boyish experience by nature study. But, he had frightened the boy away by grinding his teeth and shaking his fist at him. He mimicked himself doing so, to try and make her laugh; well, she must realize what a devil she would marry in Werner Bertin. Better had it not happened. But—and she drew a deep breath—it was with him and him alone that she was concerned; his was the world in which alone she felt at home. Her life, stretched like a gay pennon in a rushing wind, dropped slackly down when the image of this man grew dark within her. Well, it would soon grow bright again; she would not be found wanting.

Chapter 2

UNREST

On the Friday before she went to her lectures, Lenore turned over the leaves of her little calendar; she had certainly been due to be unwell the day before. Calmly she packed into her portfolio some cut bread and butter and a little fruit. That meant nothing. She had often been late in the early days of their love, merely because two hearts had so anxiously and eagerly waited for the event. It was lucky that she would be able to get a swim today when it was so hot; half humorously and half in disgust, as she sat in the train later on, she meditated on the connexion between her expectant and mysterious sex, and the ebb and flow, the rise and fall of fertility upon the earth—as tribute for the passage of life through her body. In the afternoon the swimming bath had smelt familiarly of wet wood; the tepid water soaked pleasantly through her black bathing suit. As she floated on her back, she noticed a fragment of moon hanging in the blue like a little fleck of cloud. How would female creatures have been able to manage their affairs down here, if old mother earth hadn't tied this pock-marked offspring to her apron strings? She waved at it gaily with a dripping hand: "Thank you, Moon."

She did not say it again on the two following days. A pall of disquiet lay upon her heart, though she loosened its oppression by deep quiet breathing. She must not fall into a panic; nothing had happened. Her body was taking a rest. Many girls were as much as five days late; and occasionally they were not unwell at all. And to quench these inner murmurs, she made no mention of it in her letter to Bertin, who, as his custom was, had sent her an affectionate note to the post office early that morning. She sat in thought before her sheet of paper with her fountain pen in her hand. Was there a shadow of a chance that anything had happened as a result of that detestable scene in the wood at Wilkersdorf? The pressure that rose from her heart into her throat made her dumb. Her hands remained paralysed and lay like alien objects on the table. Dread and inevitable, fate itself seemed to be clutching at her. She turned her head fearfully to look behind her; there was nothing there, no grasping hand or claw, and she turned with a sigh of relief, pressed her hand under her left breast, and bade herself be calm and sensible.

Was the structure of a woman such that she could conceive in such a brief and rough encounter? Did the eagerness with which she looked at a peasant woman's little girl on her journey home mean an outburst of the maternal impulse? Never before had she so longed to pick up and kiss a strange child. No, no, all this was hysteria, senseless cowardice and folly that quickly brought its own reward.

Next day she took a hot bath. She used this harmless word to signify a bath that was almost boiling; the strain on her heart made her feel sick; she almost fainted and was scarcely able to get out. With chattering teeth she sat in the bath-towel; her condition was unchanged. It was early on a Sunday morning, she could have gone to see Bertin. But she decided not to worry him. Certainty would indeed have been worth a railway journey; Potsdam, Berlin, Küstrin, Tamsel, Wilkersdorf, and the pine wood—as though she and Bertin would find the truth where they had left it, like a lost ring. Then she put both hands to her head. It was surely panic that prompted such folly. She went to the telegraph office; she would wire to Werner that she could not get away for family reasons. Wearing a broad-brimmed, flowered Florentine hat, she hurried along the streets in her light-coloured shoes, the very picture of health; a woman, said she to herself, who felt so gloriously well, could not be carrying the devil in her belly. As a soldier's lady she felt justified in using such expressions.

On Tuesday she wrote a cheerful letter to say that she could come to him on Saturday afternoon and stay over the Sunday. She wondered if she should add the fateful question in a postscript, and in her mind struck out what she had not, in fact, yet written down. She could surely control her anxieties until Saturday evening.

In the course of this week she learnt one thing; physically she felt magnificent. A flowering meadow could feel no otherwise. But as soon as she thought of her condition, the black wall rose up in front of her; her body was sealed and stoppered. She secretly searched a medical handbook belonging to her mother, a thick volume printed on coarse paper, and all other such books as she could find. She clenched her hands; just commonplace twaddle. None of them dared give a definite hint or suggestion. The reason soon became evident; under the dreadful word "abortion" were set forth a number of strange terms, and details of legal pains and penalties in every country. Lenore was still too inexperienced to realize with what stratum of the social order she was here in contact; she was merely sensible of something of an electric shock as she grasped that it would be dangerous. . . . And so, alas, she did not venture to ask a doctor.

To whom, indeed, could she confess that she was a woman, and had been so for a long while? Besides, at present it was merely a question of a stoppage; it was folly to imagine anything else. There were means of dealing with such a state. It was true that hot baths had been no use; bicycling and long hours of gymnastics had been no use either. However, she could not have conceived, for everywhere she read of weakness, sickness, and fainting-fits as signs of this condition. But often and again she caught herself listening to an inner voice, hoarse with anxiety, that said: "Until Saturday, then."

On Saturday evening about half-past six, after an ecstatic welcome from Bertin, she sat on Frau Jerichow's red plush sofa, and watched him while he slid the razor over his thin brown cheeks. He told her of the marches they had done, all of their exercises and activities. They had corded together great bundles of logs from the felled forest and used them to build a pathway across a marshy piece of meadow, up to their ankles in water.

But the boots they wore were admirable if properly greased; for the first time in his life he had something on his feet that really kept water out. The trench-digging of the previous month, which had been so suddenly suspended, had been, so it was said, the result of a friendly understanding with the bailiff of a certain nobleman's estate, to which the meadow belonged. It meant a nice little present for Herr Boost, better hay for the Count, and work for the Army Service Corps company that was not exactly provided for in the programme; and now they were all wondering what would happen.

Lenore was tapping the point of her shoe on the sanded, scrubbed floor-boards. This was all very interesting, no doubt. But she must say what she had come to say. While he was washing the soap off his cheeks with cold water, she at last opened her mouth: "Do you think it possible that something happened that time?"

At first he did not understand.

She explained that she had not been unwell; she was a whole week late, or, to be more exact, nine days.

Slowly raising his head he looked at her and grew pale; the tan on his keen face turned to a despairing yellowish grey. For a few moments the great flies from the neighbouring cow-shed buzzed unheeded, and their buzzing was the only sound in that room of many ornaments. Bertin's gaze rested on the latter, as he sat there open-mouthed—a china dwarf, a red wooden toadstool, a little pig with real grass growing on its back, and a shell inscribed: "Greetings from Rügen." Lenore was not a girl for idle words. "Have you tried everything?" he asked.

"I've taken hot baths, swum, done gymnastics, skipped, and gone for long runs."

He was sitting in the chair opposite her, under the mirror. His back grew bent, his head sank forward, and his hands hung limply down. Then he moved to her side. His slippered feet stepped as heavily as though they had been in boots. A whirl of fragmentary thoughts circled in his brain; and guilt was in every one of them. Then he put his arm round her and drew her to him.

She could feel that he was shaken; there was not a shadow of grievance against him in her heart. She was not a maid deceived; she had borne him company as a woman, and carried her share of the inevitable.

He sat, and could not speak, he found no words. And yet he must confess what a brute he was. The risk had occurred to him in that very room exactly a fortnight ago. He longed to pour forth his guilt, and certain muscles in his stomach were contracting convulsively; but he was silent, and merely pressed his hands against his eyes. What was to be done, he asked himself helplessly, still trembling, for he very well knew what was to be done: "You must have it taken away."

"Yes," she said simply.

"When?"

"Later, when it's quite certain."

He, too, in spite of all his assumed knowledge of the world, was much too inexperienced to know that then was the time to go to the doctor, in any case, whether it was certain or not.

"Where shall I find a doctor?"

He stammered out a name. The man was reliable, he had helped a friend of Bertin's last November.

She heaved a sigh of relief. "Then all is well. Write me down his address. It will cost money," she added thoughtfully after a moment or two of silence.

The word "money" seemed to strike him under the ribs with a sensation of physical pain; he had no money. The instant he was called up, his student's allowance had ceased. In Berlin he did not know a single person to whom he could apply. There was no news from publisher or agent. Suddenly he realized that there was really no difference between himself and a stonemason or a plumber called up to join the army; thirty-three pfennigs a day. "I'll raise some money somehow," he said, confidently.

"We can pay it back out of my dowry later on."

He laid his face against her hand as it rested on the red plush cover of Frau Jerichow's sofa. Who would give several hundred marks advance on stories lying in a trunk in Kreuzburg? A whirl of difficulties paralysed his mind, and made him long for a peaceful way out.

"Suppose we married," he asked, "and had it?" By "it" he meant that uncertain, perhaps even as yet unformed, electric cell-existence, with which fate, strange and dæmonic, threatened to strike at the centre of her being.

"Impossible," she said decisively.

"But before it is born," he said reflectively; "next February there will be peace."

She shook her head impatiently. Who could be sure? She could not fight for her family's consent to the marriage in the face of abuse for her misconduct, or by a process of blackmail. But how could she go away and have the child without any money? And where should she go? And how avoid notice? In a little place like Potsdam? What parents would forgive their daughter such a scandal? Besides, she said softly, was he sure of staying permanently at Küstrin? "Oh dear, how lovely life looked ten days ago. . . ." Her voice broke; her eyes quivered, and a few large tears rolled down her cheek. "Suppose something happens to you. What should I do? I can't yet face people by myself. So it seems that even such a ruffian as you is good for something." She smiled again, and powdered her nose. "If you don't survive the war, I should give up. A child would only make things worse." At present, she said in a level voice, it was no more than a little scrap of flesh that could be clipped off like a fingernail. In times like these one must be always ready to make a move without much luggage.

Bertin listened to her in dumb amazement. It would be hard to deserve the love of such a woman. In her spoke a force of decision unused and untouched through many generations. He kissed her on the lips; and he told her how he admired her. He would never forget what she had said to him that day. They agreed to wait until she was next due to be unwell, before taking any steps—until midnight of June 28th.

Equipped with the vast energy of unexplored life-forces, the male seed dashes, comet-like, upon the expectant female cell. The egg thus impregnated, no larger than a grain of dust, hangs loosely upon the wall of the mother's womb, divides and grows, and can in those first few days be easily removed; thus are avoided all the complications produced in a hidebound social organism by an unwanted child. It can no longer destroy its mother's existence, ruin her scheme of life, or wreck the foundations that she must have beneath her feet in order first to fulfil herself before she reproduces life. But if the tiny germ is allowed time to take root, to put forth threads and veins into the mother-walls that enclose it, and to become a living expanding entity within her, then what was simple enough calls for an operation none too easy for one who is unprepared.

Lenore Wahl, a girl belonging to the age of peace, was not in the least prepared. She was, of course, ready to acknowledge all obligations that she undertook of her own free will, to treat ideas and emotions seriously; she had a horror of prejudices and viewed the world of her parents with a critical eye. Like her friend Bertin, she overestimated the completeness of this world, its claim to endure, and the right and reason of its system. Like him, she thought the time had come when, by the passionate worship of beauty, by art and literature, humanity had been raised to a higher level. The war had as yet taught them no lessons. But as certain good specimens of our species are not permitted to persist in error, formative forces now began to lay hand on them—forces that they could not fail to understand.

Chapter 3

THE MOUSE

Early one morning Lenore awoke at half-past three; her heart was throbbing and she was damp with sweat. Sitting up in bed naked—she had had to take off her night-gown—she pressed her face into her hands and tried to think. An awful terror of her childhood had once more come upon her; once again had Professor Groll, in his gleaming spectacles and white smock, snipped out her tonsils, gripping her between his knees, while the assistant held her hands behind her back. It had been a sharp and short affair, without even a local anæsthetic—and the shock of it, the sobbing child, all the blood and mess, had been effaced only from the surface of her mind; now it came before her vision once again in all its terror, the outrage upon her inmost self had never been made good. No, there was no more room for hope. How red and menacing the moon had looked last night as she rose from among the tree-trunks; thus must she look when she lures the lost children in the magic forest to the witches' house. No one can foretell at what a cost one must fight one's way forward on this earth where the laws of life hold so stern a sway.

No, she could no longer sleep. She dipped her face in cold water in the bathroom, put on some light garments, beckoned to Boll, who shook his great collar, got out her bicycle, and glided away. The great park was breathing under a pale sky of unearthly clarity; the sun had not yet risen. In the tallest tree-tops early thrushes were heralding the day. In the east, a low line of red lay like a rim of faintly smouldering fire along the horizon. The town was silent. Never had its houses seemed such solid and sharp-sided cubes. Vegetable carts and milk trucks were rattling in from the countryside. She slipped past the horses' clattering hoofs, and Boll, from a sense of duty and from habit, bayed at the great beasts. All down the long street stood sleeping houses and villas. At the end of an avenue, through four rows of trees, could be seen a glimpse of Charlottenhof Castle, and beyond it the red and resplendent edifice of the New Palace. And at last her tires rasped faintly over the gravel of a country road. Among tall pines and birches, noiseless before the morning breeze had risen, she got off her bicycle and sat on a bench; her breathing was soft and calm. From her mind, too, the shadow had passed; she felt composed and high of heart to face what was to come. The time of marvels lay far away—behind her, in the land of childhood. She must silence the insistent voices that pleaded for its return. Destiny, like a great eye from somewhither, had marked her. It would be greedy to expect the years of youth to contain nothing but good days. One must be ready to pay the full price without dispute, and the full price would be demanded. The way led inexorably onwards; she rose, still pondering, and wheeled her bicycle between the dew-soaked grass and bushes, while Boll snuffed eagerly at smells that had not tickled his nose so unmistakably for a very long while—smells that portended rabbits, hedgehogs, and mice. The way led inexorably downwards. At the end of the next stage would be—the pronouncement of a sentence; then probably an operating table, white and nickelled—she forced herself to look no further. All her energies were needed for the immediate task, nothing else should be considered now. Her heart beat eagerly; she could feel its soothing rhythm throbbing down her body to the hollows of her knees; and it beat in sympathy for her. But flinging her long plaits behind her—she had not done her hair before she came out—she pulled herself up sharply. At that very moment thousands of soldiers were facing worse than this. Black guns thundered between Ostend and Alsace, between Libau and Czernowitz; the early morning, here a paradise of pearly freshness, was there torn by the rattle of machine-guns, so familiar to her from the practice drill of the Guards, the explosion of shrapnel, the columns of earth flung up by bursting shells, the vast upheavals of the mine-war with the English in the Wytschaete sector, all that the Official Bulletin hammered into the consciousness of those who read it—there it stood for reality, as real a reality as this smoothed path between the silent tree-trunks, on which large dignified woodpeckers had now begun to tap. She noticed a group of three of them busily engaged in impaling beetles underneath the bark. Thus were men picked out of trenches and dug-outs, and impaled; and the baying hound, Boll, who dashed like a mad thing over the meadows, and put the shrilly protesting woodpeckers to flight, was there replaced by the roar of artillery and anti-aircraft guns, every whit as real as he. But she must not let her imagination run away with her, as the doctor would say. Endurance was, and always had been, women's form of action, and she would endure as much as a woman might.

Absorbed, and oblivious of herself, she leaned against her bicycle, and looked down the path along which Boll was trotting back to her, still soaking from his gallop in the dew; suddenly he stopped, sniffing and pawing in the tall, now dawn-lit herbage at the edge of the path, whence came a faint squeaking. He had caught a mouse and crushed it over and over; but it could no longer hear his thunderous baying. Boll raised his head to his mistress, looking for her praise, and lay down humbly beside his victim. Lenore thought of the tiny mice, for whose sake the mother had probably ventured out into the meadow, and her eyes suddenly grew moist. Her little child, if indeed there was now one forming within her! She must give it up; it must not be born, it was never to lie in her arms or drink at her breasts. Could this really be? Were there forces—the Family, Society—that compelled her to submit to such a horror? Oh, to be an animal, to creep into a thicket, scrape a hole for herself, there drop her young one when the time came, press her teats into its mouth, nourish it with her own sap and blood, and tear the eyes out of any that might come to do it hurt; a cat, savage for her kitten. She pressed her arms against her breast, which at once began to hurt her, and stared along the path with set and dreaming sightless eyes; oblivious of the present, she had plunged back into past ages in her longing to be a naked savage, and to know no other home than the wild forest; that would-be ecstasy, ultimate fulfilment, the Islands of the Blest. She yearned to shield her child from the sun with her own hair, with her own body from the rain, to play with him all the day long on his bed of leaves, tease him with cherries and watch his laughter. The animals would not fear him, neither the deer, nor the old mother hares with their brood of young . . . what a glorious life it would be. . . . A surge of physical pleasure swept through her breast and her womb. . . .

But she must pull herself up, this would never do; she must not dream away the strength that she needed for action. Here there was no expanse of southern sea, and an age of gold, lit with the rosy radiance of dream; here reigned the newest Age, the cold authority of convention, the ordered life of teeming cities, provisions and precepts for everything in law and custom. And a child would mean suicide, a child would mean the wreck of all she meant to do, the destruction of her life with Bertin, if he survived the war, or a barren and hopeless future if anything befell him and she could not follow. She was torn between her primitive wild impulse, and her knowledge, equally intense, that she must break the bonds that gripped her; in such a trap, in such a prison was she caught and held. It was no more than the common complex of man's life today—she laughed abruptly at the thought—was it not all the better suited to the manifestations of the Almighty Mother Nature, who had but lately beckoned to her? Did Nature not feed upon herself—mice on plants, plants on salts, small beasts of prey on mice, while man took tribute from them all? And now she, in the fullness of her strength and youth, must go down and offer up to fate, the vast impassive feline deity, the lovely vigour of her soul, the thrill of resistance, and that savour of torment that has ever been the most acceptable sacrifice to the gods.

No, no—for God's sake. She shuddered at the thought of probes and knives! How she longed to go forward with the stream of wholesome growth, to preserve her body from the shears of reason. That alone was why, in the confusion of her fear, she had listened to the persuasive counsels of delay; that alone was why she hoped for the twenty-eighth of June, and the miracle. If only she could have flung herself on her knees before a crucifix or the Mother of God, and prayed that she might escape once more—just this once more! But for her there was no comforter, no faith, only the empty heaven of the ordered universe. So, until the twenty-eighth, there would be a respite!

Her two plaits of hair made her look like a girl of eighteen, as she got into the saddle again and rode through the park-like country between the great banks of foliage, with the hound cantering at her side. The willow-herbs were already blossoming, and the tall thistles with their violet crowns stood up rigid from their grey encirclement of spear-pointed leaves.

Chapter 4

JUNE 28th, BEFORE MIDNIGHT

The last hot weeks of the radiant early summer moved over the North German plain; and early ripeness made the raspberries sweet. The freshness of the nights began to be already welcome.

On the terrace of the Wahl villa, looking towards the garden, sat two old gentlemen over a bottle of old burgundy, which cast a long dark shadow across the table in the reflection of the lamp. The smoke from their cigars kept off the flies and curled up towards the house, into which the coolness of the night flooded through the open windows. One of the pair, Justizrat Obstfelder, his coat over the back of his chair and a dark blue cummerbund round his portly person, sat stroking his broad grey beard; the hand holding his cigar hung loosely at his side. As he sat thus at ease, his gaze wandered over the black edge of his glasses up to the sky, away beyond the tree-tops. A faint warm wind rustled through the poplars down to the Havel, which spreads round Potsdam like a lake. The other, Markus Wahl, host for the time being, as Herr Hugo Wahl and his wife had had to take the cure at Karlsbad, war or no war, clasped his bony chin in his hand. He was wearing a yellow suit of undyed silk, and his white hair, shaven close round the bald patch, shone like a stone or a bit of birch bark. From his little black eyes he shot a quick bright glance, like that of a listening bird, at his friend's bearded lips: "Will you read me that paper of yours now?" he said.

Justizrat Obstfelder raised his right hand to where the pocket of his coat would have been, but let it fall again; and he frowned, enjoining silence.

From the windows behind them came the sound of music, on two pianos: Schumann, piano concerto in A minor.

In the music Justizrat Obstfelder felt he could hear the dead marching. He loved music and he had ears for the music of the world, the inextricable confusion of conflict and reconciliation. From what dark tumultuous struggles had been born the genius of Germany! There, in that music, was the spirit of his country, as it had moved through the centuries, and might now for many year be silenced—one with the night and air, the earth and trees and stars. For today his country spoke, not the voice of Schumann, but the voice of German generals. A year ago that day a fanatic youth at Serajevo fired a pistol, and the crack of that shot was a signal that, with their war-lords at their back, they could hardly miss. In celebration of that day, on which everything began, the two friends had sat down here at the garden table; they felt a need to talk over the situation. For they began to be uneasy. The pronouncements that had once filled the newspapers were now less self-assured; the outlines of the picture had grown a little blurred. There were many voices now, and they did not agree—the first sign of approach to life and to reality.

There the trees rustled, there streamed the music through the air that gave it birth, reflected Justizrat Obstfelder; and in the meantime Pomeranian Grenadiers and English infantrymen were shooting each other down at Ypres, and French and Germans bayoneting each other in Champagne. We have given our lords supreme power over war and peace, and we may not complain; we are old, and we let the young pay for us. It has always been so, and it will always be so, and with that we appease our consciences.

Yes, thought old Wahl, things are going marvellously well; it pays to be a grandfather and look on. They would have to keep an eye on that lad indoors, with his passion for music and his confounded impudence. And Fräulein Cohn . . . He did not like the looks of her. Still, she was but a setting—and what a setting! —for the jewel of her music. He was reminded of the words of the ugly Rabbi Akiba to the Emperor's daughter. "Was not your father rich enough to store his wine in golden jars? And yet he put it into paltry earthenware pitchers. Thus did God with me." Thus had God done with her. It was a pity that Lenore had gone to bed; the child looked so radiant as she went about, and when father and mother were away one could see what a pearl of a housewife she would make; he could not help envying the coxcomb who would get her one day. What splendid music that was of Schumann's! A last soaring rush of notes, and the music echoed into silence.

Justizrat Obstfelder drank a deep draught of wine, flicking a moth away from his glass. "Yes, I'll read it to you now." And fumbling for a sheet of newspaper, printed on one side in two narrow columns, in the pocket of his coat behind his back, he began to read in the husky voice of the inveterate cigar smoker, interjecting a few dry comments as he went along. "A Last Warning," ran the heading; and beneath it, with an assumed aspect of indifference, the announcement of disaster upon disaster. The compositor's stamp showed the date 7.30.14; the sheet was almost eleven months old. Markus Wahl knew what it was; this was to have been the leading article for the Sunday number of the most widely read paper in Berlin, the paper of the small folk who were not consulted, and whose voice—since the daily round kept them close to life—uttered the real feeling of the nations; and that was fear.

It began by maintaining that England would not remain neutral, but would join France, either at once, or when the country was in difficulties. On the other hand, those who acclaimed Japan would find themselves sorely deceived; Japan would not attack Russia, but would not improbably attack Germany, as a direct result of the Peace of Shimonoseki, by which we had, without the smallest reason, cheated her out of her victory over China. Nagasaki, Tokyo, and Kyoto would march; but Rome, Naples, and Milan would not march. The Triple Alliance had ceased to exist. If Italy moved, it would be against Austria, which was still in occupation of Italian soil in the Trentino.

"The prophets are still with us," stammered Markus Wahl, for at the beginning of that month Italy had in fact declared war. "Our people have not lost the gift. Did he write all that last year before the mobilization?"

Without a word, Obstfelder held out the proof sheet with its date stamp clearly marked. "Yes," he growled uneasily, "Dr. Bernstein knows something about politics, and we were all idiots in those days. However, if you're going to interrupt me all the time, read it yourself."

Markus Wahl glanced over the sheet with his long-sighted eyes, holding it close to the light. He read as follows: no one knew whether Austria-Hungary was strong enough to carry through a war which would last between three and five years; a revolution in Russia could only break out as the result of Russian defeats; the violation of Belgian neutrality would bring in England, and with England the whole civilized world against us; and America, Holland, and Denmark would indeed supply us with what they could do without, but the influence in those countries would be British and not German. The old gentleman was now sitting in quite a different attitude, bent stiffly forward, with his thin hands on the table, and his cigar between his teeth. Between three and five years? What this journalist had prophesied eleven months before, had since been, point by point, fulfilled. There would be no peace then this year, nor the next year, nor the next after that; it took a man's breath away.

Lenore was walking noiselessly up and down her half-lit room, with slippers on her feet, and wearing only a thin shift, on account of the heat. She had tried to sleep, but could not. It was not the Schumann Concerto that had disturbed her; she knew it by heart —bar for bar—that rhapsody of self-surrender, in which David and Hilde Cohn were taking part. All the doors stood open for the sake of air, and the sound of their playing floated up the staircase to her room. Sharp and distinct, in dark intensity the conflict between the two groups of notes rose and fell, through the night and through her heart. The silver voice of the grand piano, cadenced lamentations that passed in yearning to the ultimate deliverance—that was she: and her heart spoke too in the menacing tumult of the orchestra—David and his "pianino," which only he knew how to handle; under his fingers the ancient ivory keys rattled like enchanted drums. She did not know whether music was good for her or not, but without its distraction, she might well have torn her flesh with her nails until she bled. For today was her last day; the time was half-past eleven; and no change had come. The decision was at hand. Eighteen days of glorious well-being had merely played her false. She could no longer wait for Werner and his money. She still had fourteen marks, but on the first of the month her grandfather would pay her the allowance which her parents had increased before they went away; it would suffice for immediate needs. Tomorrow she would go and see the doctor, and as Paula Weber, with money in hand for the first time in her life, had scarcely returned before she went off again to Hirschberg, Lenore would go alone. A woman who went her own way could not be surprised if there was no one to stand by her when trouble came. Of course she could not visit this doctor dressed as a girl in good society. In order to awaken his sympathy, she must look like the daughter of a small official, and pose as a postal assistant or a telephone girl, whose whole existence would be wrecked if she had an illegitimate child. She laughed mockingly at herself as she stood before her mirror in the darkness. What a dubious member of the family was Lenore Wahl. Seduced by a poor but clever student in his attic, and now carrying her shame about with her. When her mother read a story in which matters were described as they invariably befell, and as they had now befallen her, she would think she was reading the story of depravity itself. Such a girl must, of course, finally go to the bad. Strange it was, and even comic, that she did not feel in the least degraded, and not for one moment did she regret that she had abandoned the world of parents and of propriety, in which one is safe from such experiences as this—at the price of not living her own life. For compared with the sensation of existing, of facing the claims of her little world and meeting them, as she had done every minute of the last two years, all else was flat and dull.

She began to rummage in her shoe shelves, and she laid out stockings, underlinen, a skirt and blouse to match it, and last of all, gloves. She shivered. She wrapped herself in a kimono, sat down in a wicker chair by the window, and looked up at the starry sky; striding mightily with slanted girdle the hunter Orion stood over against the south in the hot darkness of the night. The pianos began once more.

A heart, young and irresolute, communed with itself. Rising doubts, light disharmonies, eased the tense terror of the prelude, and burst forth into deliverance: life remained, placid and indestructible, sweeping steadily and gently onwards, all-embracing and victorious, as the sun mounts the sky.

The music echoed through the empty rooms. The servants, before going for their holiday, had carefully enveloped the furniture in coverings of faded chintz, and wrapped huge sheets of paper round the electric candlelamps on the walls. The lustres, with their prisms and lilies of Venetian glass, encased in muslin, hung in the air like huge white deep-sea beasts, trapped in nets.

Obstfelder bent down with a groan, picked up the sheet which his friend had let fall from the table, and read the conclusion. In a few days (said the author) no one would be allowed to write the truth. Our diplomats were well aware of the position; but the threats of the Pan-Germans and militarists, who did not shrink from the basest methods, reduced them to silence. In any case, responsible politicians never had a say in Germany when the military began to speak. The only victor in this war would be England; the result would be a million dead, two million disabled, and fifty billions of debts, and nothing else.

As the husky voice ceased, around him in silence lay a garden, the foliage of many other gardens, a park, a town, the night sky, and Germany.

"And was it never published?" asked Markus Wahl.

Obstfelder twisted his half-smoked cigar over the lamp. "Never," he said. "It is just a proof that was left about in the printing works. No newspaper wants to be suspended these days."

Markus Wahl went on obstinately: "If that were known, people would have something to say."

Justizrat Obstfelder twisted his broad grey beard, raised his melancholy heavy-lidded eyes, and said: "People have had a great deal to say in the months that followed, both at the front and at home: the press—some of it—has had its say, and the widows of dead soldiers have not been silent. It is no pleasure to go to prison, even for a Social Democrat. But we are plain citizens, and every publishing house wants to earn money; we say nothing." An anxious look came over his face as he folded up the sheet and handed it to his host. "Put it in your collection. It will look well beside the special edition of the *Lokalanzeiger* that forced on the mobilization, when it was still hardly thought of." It was a pity that Lenore had gone to bed so early. When his son, the doctor, came back from the war—at the moment he was at a dressing-station near Arras and under fire daily—he must marry the girl, if she would have him. She had had some dealings with a young author—hadn't he read the man's name yesterday afternoon in a contract which Bauch, the agent, wanted to draw up with the Deutsches Theater? His play would probably be acted as soon as the censorship came to an end—after the war presumably.

He interrupted Markus Wahl, who was telling him about the other items in his collection, and asked him about the young man whom Lenore had met in Munich, and who had lunched at the house on one occasion. Wasn't his name Bertin? An author? Rather modern? He would be famous one day. Tomorrow he would be able to buy six hundred marks' worth of Second War Loan. Wasn't the Wahl banking house disposed to earn the gratitude of the Fatherland?

Jests of this kind usually precede departure. Tornow, fortunately too old to be called up, would take the Herr Justizrat and Fräulein Hilde Cohn back to Berlin; a pleasant journey past the lakes and parks and woods, and through the sleeping outskirts of the city.

Like a white ghost on noiseless feet, Markus Wahl perambulated the house to see whether all the doors were shut, the chains up, the dog Boll in the garden, and all the lights out. Meditatively he walked up the stairs flashing his pocket lamp before him. He was right; that careless lad David had forgotten to turn off the piano lamps. So Herr Bertin was not unknown. No one was less surprised at this than Markus Wahl. He had marked him—his fine forehead, and his independent opinions. She would not be likely to fall for a fool. Little Lene was very much his grandchild. He had been thinking of her as the daughter of her parents, and had not expected to be shown so soon that he was wrong. He knocked gently at her bedroom door.

A startled voice, very much awake, cried: "Is that you, David? Come in."

Markus Wahl opened the door, put his head into the room, and spoke in the direction of the bed, a grey shadow in the general darkness. "I don't know whether it interests you, my child, but this Herr Bertin has every prospect of getting his play acted when the war is over. Obstfelder was consulted about the contract yesterday. As they're paying six hundred marks advance, the theatre people are taking it seriously."

Lenore gasped. Here was the money she needed! A white fluttering form leapt out of the bed, and two bare arms encircled Markus Wahl; and warm lips were laid on his.

Markus Wahl climbed up to his turret room, and undressed himself sighing. Old age was a bore.

Chapter 5

THE PHYSICIAN

Poor little post-office girl, thought Dr. Wismarski, sympathetically, as Lenore got up and dressed. Her fear enhanced the pallor of her face, and in her rather long and delicate features there was a look of the hunger-years that were to come. The doctor sat at his writing-table, wearing a white smock, fair, full-cheeked, quietly surveying the girl with his blue eyes. "There is no doubt, Fräulein, that you are pregnant, all the symptoms are present." Outside, the asphalt was molten under the fierce heat of that summer day. Most of the traffic between Charlottenburg and the centre of the city rattled and rumbled past the windows. An ice-seller was crying his wares—five syllables: *Ice, fruit-ice, fruit-ice!* in a melodic cadence. Dr. Wismarski who, like most doctors, was musical, listened for a moment to the ice-merchant's call, before he pronounced judgment:

"You must make up your mind to have the baby, Fräulein. You won't find anyone to help you."

Lenore did not understand. She had explained that she could not have it, that she was the daughter of a postal official from Brandenburg on the Havel, engaged to a second lieutenant, now at the front in Champagne country; and he was the father of the child that she might have conceived. She sat up very stiff in her chair. Perhaps she had been wrong in pretending to be still more of a novice in such matters than she really was. In her anxiety that the doctor should not think there was any risk because she looked delicate, she had answered his leading questions with rather blank and stupid negatives. No, she had had no hæmorrhages nor coughs, there was no tuberculosis in her family, neither her father nor her fiancé drank to excess; she had not suffered from chlorosis, and all her periods had been regular. At the moment she felt stronger than she had ever done before, and in these last few weeks she had done constant exercises, and swum and bicycled a great deal. In a tone of imploring innocence, she said: "You needn't have any fears, Doctor; it wouldn't be long before I'm on my legs again, would it?"

Wismarski thought to himself: "Poor little fool, but you wouldn't hold your tongue, and then we should both be in a mess. I shall probably have been called up before that, which would make things particularly nasty. They haven't been able to make use of me until now; but that was how Felix came to grief, the tenor violin of our quartet, and an excellent musician." "No, Fräulein," he said gently, as they faced each other in that stuffy consulting-room. "Go home quietly, tell your parents, and you will be glad in the end; your fiancé will marry you—see that you get him home in good time on marriage leave. It would be a shame not to bring the child into the world. And the Emperor will want soldiers later on," he added in a sad and bitter tone that went but ill with his red cheeks and fair hair. "Anyhow, I can't do it for you."

Lenore looked at him with candid innocence. She was mastered for the moment by the part that she had played so carefully, by this simplified and false description of the situation. In that minute she really thought: Why indeed should I have it taken away? We'll have a war wedding, all will be well, and Papa and Mamma will be glad after all.

"What can we doctors do, little Fräulein? Every day someone comes to us as you have done. Prison isn't a cheerful prospect, you know."

Yes, thought Lenore submissively, the prospect of prison is certainly no joke. Between her and the doctor's words there was a strange abyss. She heard them, and immediately conceived them as her own opinions. "That is true," something answered from within her; "but you also have obligations towards young people."

Suddenly the reality of her position flashed through her mind; had she not thought over all this many times already? "But Herr Doktor, it will be so awful," she stammered. "Isn't there any chance of your helping me . . . ?" And her staring eyes were wet with tears.

"Alas, alas, my beauty was my ruin," he quoted to himself, as he involuntarily edged behind his chair, which served as a support and a protection from the poor girl's distress. Goethe had been a man of understanding. "No, no, my child, it's no use," he said to himself. "Even if you could scrape the fee together—not that that matters much—one day I should have an unpleasant visit from a father or a fiancé. I don't fancy this little Gretchen will venture on a secret abortion. What was always a nasty job, now, in time of war, with the casualty lists what they are, is simply suicide. No one can ask it of me."

Lenore had indeed dressed herself in very provincial style; white skirt and white shoes, but grey stockings and a grey summer blouse with a high collar, and her hair stiffly knotted behind her ears. This examination had been the first in all her life; it had called for much self-mastery to let these strange hands touch her; was it to be all in vain?

"You can't let me go like this, Herr Doktor," she implored, as she dried her eyes. But even in her torment, there was not the suggestion of a threat in her entreaties. "But you helped Fräulein So-and-So from Kreuzburg, last November. Oh, you must, Herr Doktor."

Wismarski, with a glance at the clock on his writing-table, began to grow annoyed, but he controlled himself.

"No," he said decisively, "you must go. If you had come to me during the first month, I dare say something might have been managed. You are now at about the end of the second month; during the third, the embryo often becomes detached through physical disturbances. You can tell that by a hæmorrhage, Fräulein. Then, of course, there will have to be an operation at once, to avoid the risk of septic poisoning." In the tone he used for his popular discourses, he flung her a sort of life-line. If she were in a position to catch it, he might still have a chance to fish her out of her sea of misery.

"In that case ring me up at once. So all is not lost yet. But now you must go home, there are patients waiting for me outside."

Lenore was indeed aware that a haggard-looking grey-haired woman and two ladies were in the waiting-room. She stood up, and found that her feet would actually carry her. Once more she implored him softly: "Herr Doktor—please . . ."

But he led her to the white-painted door into the passage. "There is not a doctor in all Berlin who would give other advice. I do not mention the fact that you are asking us to break the law, or I should speak to you quite differently. Good-bye, Fräulein Peter."

As the door clicked behind Lenore, he thought how unjust life was, and how stupid was the structure of society, that made these pretty creatures suffer when they fulfilled the purpose of their creation. Then he opened the door of the waiting-room, and asked the wife of Kranz, the builder, to come in.

Chapter 6

BROTHER AND SISTER

When Lenore came home, the afternoon coffee, carefully covered with a cosy, stood upon the table; it was rather weak, as Frau Wahl's alliance between her patriotism and her housewifely ambition persisted in her absence.

David Wahl, a fifth-form boy of sixteen, looked up frowning from his book, Stevenson's *Treasure Island,* over which he sat absorbed, chewing vigorously the while, and greeted his sister with the words: "Tomorrow I shall apply for war-relief for this family. We can't afford to buy coffee. You just taste."

Lenore laughed, nodded to him, and sat down to the table ravenously hungry; in her heart was despair, which she had had to control and conceal the moment she reached the steps of her home. Before her inner gaze rose the huge social machine against which she must pit her strength, with the sole aid of a private in the Army Service Corps called Bertin, and there was but little that he was free to do. It was odd, though, how good the food tasted. She ate quickly, and as she was disposing of a roll made of grey war flour, she felt a sudden twinge in a back tooth in the right lower jaw. In those last weeks she had read enough to know what that meant; the little growing ghost within her was absorbing the lime from her teeth. How long could it be postponed? And in her fear she groaned aloud. She stared terror-struck at the rapids towards which she was being carried. She felt like someone standing by the rail of a torpedoed steamer, far above the grey sea, who must leap in, though he can hardly swim, if he is not to be sucked down by the sinking iron berg.

"Why, what's the matter with you?" asked the lad, looking up quickly from the exciting passage where Jim Hawkins in the apple barrel listens to the conversation of the pirate crew.

"Toothache," she answered with a wry grimace, putting her hand up to her cheek.

"Toothache . . . You?" He observed his sister with an appraising look. Had she let it get as far as hurting her? It was scarcely credible. She looked altered. Her eyes had lost the usual confident expression of a fine vigorous young girl. In spite of the enclosed and alien worlds in which brothers and sisters usually live, she had often let him talk to her when she helped her little brother over the solution of an equation or the composition of an essay. The little brother closed his book with a bang, tearing off a bit of the paper napkin to serve as a bookmark. "Listen, my dear girl," he said, "what's up with your young man?" (My dear girl, indeed!)

"How did you get such an idea into your head?" she asked, surveying her brother's fresh brown face.

"Well," he replied, "a good deal can be gathered from the envelopes that you throw into the waste-paper basket. Küstrin, my dear, is only a base camp. Have they bundled him off to the front already? . . ."

Lenore looked at him. A brother's emergence from boyhood betrays itself at first in changes that are often trifling, such as a look or an intonation; then the realization comes with the effect of a series of shocks. True, for months past, many such schoolboys who had joined as volunteers had been lying in grey ranks and heaps out yonder, dead.

"You want to marry, eh? And Mother's making a fuss? Do you want some really sound advice?" David went on soberly. "Grandfather said this morning that all sensible people thought that the war would last for two or even three years more. Just imagine it! The beastly bloodthirsty folly of the thing!" He almost groaned.

Lenore nodded gloomily. The world outside her was full of misery too. This lad was not afraid to listen and to utter what he thought. "David," she whispered, wide-eyed, "one day they'll come and fetch you too!"

"I won't go," he cried, "I won't take a hand in such butchery. I was born to play concertos, not to handle rifles."

"One is never asked what one was born to do," sighed Lenore. The whole world reeked of force, and blood, and iron.

"Perhaps," David went on more calmly, "I had better change myself into a girl when the time comes. Then I shall need your help; clothes and stockings and corsets and so on, and you'll have to show me how you do up your confounded little hooks and eyes. Better be a nursemaid in a South German family than cannon-fodder in a Prussian infantry regiment. Do you want someone to clean and grease your bicycle? For prompt and efficient service, this is the firm."

Lenore stirred her cup slowly. Should she speak? The tremendous venture hovered for a moment between her tongue and teeth; then she spoke.

"If you are serious," she said, "I really do need someone's help." And she added in a lighter tone: "I am going to have a child; I must have it removed, and no one will tell me how to set about getting this done."

The fifth-form boy looked up and said nothing. Then he whistled a tune in descending thirds. "Well, every girl's in for it some time. I suppose it's Herr Bertin," he said, in a noncommittal tone, drawing curves among the crumbs on the tablecloth. "I've read his novel; it isn't up to much, but there was something in his opinions. If I were in his position I should appear in the missing list of my unit next day. It isn't quite impossible to deceive a Prussian officer, my girl. Forgive me, but I know how to deal with that sort of fellow. Don't mind what I say, you can trust me not to let you down. Now tell me what you've done up till now."

In the afternoon silence of that veranda, he listened to what she had to say; and she spoke to him, not like an elder sister to a young brother, but with the childlike relief of a woman speaking to a man who is better acquainted with the technique of life than herself. Then he said: "Well, I'll see what can be done. How about money?"

To this she replied: "Bertin will soon be getting six hundred marks advance on a contract."

"First rate," answered David Wahl. "I've got five hundred and fifty marks in the savings bank, and a private credit in our Papa's books of two hundred and seventy-two marks, with which he proposes to buy me a war loan. I wasn't such a fool as to put all my money in the family firm. Very well, then, it's an awkward business, but we've got to go through with it. In the words of our respected master, Buffke"—and he continued in the pompous tones of that pedagogue—"when once the phalanx of the hoplites was set in motion, it never stopped until the resistance of the enemy was completely broken down." He added in his natural voice: "Kindly translate that into Greek."

Lenore could not help laughing. She laughed so long and so heartily that she nearly choked, not so much at her brother's drollery, but because she had found help so near at hand, and where she had least of all expected to find it. "No," she said, still laughing, "I would sooner translate the following sentence into Latin: 'I have found help near at hand, and where I least of all expected it.' "

Chapter 7

KLIEM

The lad David Wahl had an older friend whom he consulted on all difficult and serious matters that called for experience; Herr Kliem, his swimming master, who, when he was a boy of eight, had initiated him into the frog-like antics of human beings in water, holding him first by a sort of huge fishing-rod, and then by a rope that was gradually slacked, as the skinny little creature wriggled his way round the tepid water of the swimming bath. As, in young people, every exercise of the body becomes a habit, Herr Kliem saw the lad through all the stages of boyhood and adolescence until his present state of fifth-form schoolboyhood. He kept on easy terms with the lad, and talked to him with the superiority that was naturally more easily acquired by one who had first been a sergeant in the Sappers, then a hand on a Havel steamer, and finally a bathing attendant and swimming master, than by the son of a banker at a time when boys are almost born with starched collars round their necks; and he delighted the lad with sage counsel and stories, such as how he had lost his left hand one Sunday on his steamer, and how he had gradually learned to use a hook instead. For his left arm ended in a steel hook.

Herr Kliem, when not on duty, lived on the Kiewitt, a secluded strip of river bank, the name of which was perhaps an imitation of the plover's cry. Behind a pile of timber near the water stood a shed, full of all manner of implements and oddments, beside a dilapidated landing-stage, at which a ferry-boat put in from time to time, and brought or took away passengers, mostly bicyclists. In the evenings—the swimming baths were shut at seven—it was

Herr Kliem's custom to sit on this river bank and fish. Peacefully he dangled a spitted form in the water, hoping to hook a pike or perch, and drag it by its horny jaws into the choking element of air. It was a soft evening of July, a little after eight o'clock, and still pleasantly light; among the meadows the flies found many an opportunity of drinking human blood, as the dried earth round Germany was doing at the moment, though they retreated from time to time before the smoke of a pipe with which Herr Kliem repelled the attacks of their tiny squadrons.

David Wahl got off his bicycle, greeted Kliem with a brief nod, lit a cigarette, and waited until the brown-haired angler with the fair moustache and shaven head should choose to notice him. Kliem carefully lifted his rod; only a little dab of mud dangled from the hook—Kliem wiped it clean, and said: "Nothing again. And yet they ought to be biting like mad. But there's no relying on fish nowadays."

David pointed with a smile at the large wash-tub, in which four or five fair-sized fish lay motionless in water. "That? Oh, that's as good as nothing. When you've baited for a pike, a perch isn't much to console yourself with."

"Oh well, if you won't look at anything less than a pike . . ."

But Kliem, having put a fresh bait on his hook and flung it far out into the smoothly gliding greenish-blue stream, explained that he wanted the pike for a little business of exchange; a box of good cigars had been promised him in return for one, and in any case it was well worth a pike to keep on good terms with Dame Bimst, the owner of the little local shop. "Not what you think, my lad," said Herr Kliem. "I know what dirty dogs you schoolboys are; but food later on. Flour is going to be short—you mark my words; and we shall see a good many strange things before the war's over. Fortunately, I'm forty-two, and a man who has done his service in the Sappers of the Guard, has been through most things, and knows all about the blasted Prussians."

The Socialist Deputy Karl Liebknecht was member for the Potsdam constituency, and in point of fact he owed a few of his votes to Kliem, into whose blood military drill had injected moral indignation and a taste for politics.

"Ah well," said David, "I dare say respectable citizens would call us both dirty dogs, wouldn't they? But you ought to think kindly of me this evening," and he produced a little packet of tobacco from his pocket and handed it to the other. Kliem surveyed it sceptically in the late twilight. "Marakaibo-canister" he spelled out, peering closely at the label. "Thank the Lord," he added, as he felt the tobacco carefully with his finger-tips: "That's the stuff all right. It isn't the rubbish that's thought good enough for our Field Greys—Mossrose, or Conqueror Kluck, they call it, and dried cabbage is what it's made of. There's some people ought to be stoned for taking the soldiers' good money for the muck they sell them. And yet," he added with a sigh, "war is war, and it doesn't come every day. Profits is written with a capital P these days."

David Wahl abruptly swung the conversation round to what was in his mind. "Perhaps you weren't far off the truth when you talked of dirty dogs, Herr Kliem. What would you do if you had sprung a baby on a girl and didn't want it to see the light of this lovely world?"

Kliem whistled through his teeth and said knowingly: "You young blackguard. A baby, says you? Nonsense. Why, it won't be bigger than a tadpole. You haven't let it go for very long, have you? You'd hardly be asking my advice otherwise, I suppose. When did it start?"

"Two months," said David, "or two and half months, at most."

"And what do you expect me to do, you little ruffian? Am I to go and see the parents, or throw the young woman into the Havel? You don't know much about Kliem. Wilhelm needs soldiers, and if he doesn't, his successors will. Anyhow, if I help you, I'm as much in it as you are. I don't want to find myself in jail, thank you."

"It won't be quite as bad as that. I want to know how to find a reliable midwife."

Kliem swung up his line, on the end of which hung a meagre little pike three or four inches long. Its long pointed head stood out against the lighter-coloured sky.

"Better to wait until the storm's over," said Kliem, by way of encouraging himself, as he carefully detached the little brigand fish from the hook, and flung it far out into the water. "You wait till you're a year older. There isn't a war on here, we don't need you before you're grown up. I'll give it up for today; or perhaps I'll try again about eleven, if I'm awake."

He rolled the line round the long bamboo rod, propped it against some osier branches, sat down on his stool with his back to the tree-trunk, cleaned out his pipe, and filled it with his new tobacco. In the flare of the match David could see the face of his friend, whom he trusted more than any man he knew, looking at him intently.

"Midwife," he murmured, puffing at his pipe. "Midwives aren't in my line. That just shows you how stupid educated people are. No, no, my son, although this tobacco tastes first-rate, a bathing attendant isn't able to supply midwives. How would it be, though," he went on, unconcernedly surveying his stockingless feet in their brown canvas shoes, "how would it be to look at a few advertisements in the daily papers? They're headed 'Discreet,' or 'Assistance even in the most difficult cases,' which goes a little further; or, 'Conscientious Advice,' and so on. The first word always printed in thick letters; that's the way you notice them. If it says 'Conscientious,' I should let it go; 'Advice and Help' is much more promising. Such women must live, and they're usually pretty well in with a doctor. 'Advice and Help,' or, 'Experienced Midwife,' or just—'So-and-so, Midwife.' I shouldn't be inclined to have anything to do with 'Discreet' or 'Reliable.' When anyone writes on a shop sign what goes without saying, it always makes me a little suspicious. And the district, too, is some sort of a guide. The West wouldn't be much good, but a woman of that kind with a decent clientele would be likely to live somewhere round the Halle gate. Last of all," he said, sniffing at his own smoke clouds with an air of great enjoyment, "I should remember to play up like a decent lad. If I was with the girl when it was all gay and jolly, I should stand by her when she's got to go through it. Don't forget. A man has the authority; women by themselves treat each other like brutes."

David heaved a great sigh, and realized what a load had lain upon his heart until the last few minutes. He would like to have seized his friend's great brawny fist and shaken it with both his hands. But this would not have been in accordance with the terms of their relationship, which was based on the exclusion of all expression of feeling. So he merely contented himself with thanking his friend, and saying that this was just exactly what he wanted to know.

"Yes," observed Herr Kliem, puffing vigorously at his pipe, "I don't know much; but if you get a proletarian girl in the family way again, I'll kick you as hard as if you had gone off with my new life-belt. You wait, my lads," he went on, with a menacing look at the landscape in general. "It will be different one of these days, and that before very long. I dare say people will learn something from the war; Liebknecht will tell them what. They've had to give him leave from the Army Service Corps—that's where they put him, did you know? So that they could make him hold his tongue, and keep him out of their way. But they won't do *him* down like the others, you mark my words."

"Ah, Comrade Kliem," replied David uneasily, for he felt the deep feeling behind the man's words, "you'll find me on the right side. And now I must go home to supper."

"Thanks for the tobacco," Kliem answered, shaking him by the hand.

The pure silvery sound of the chimes from the Garrison Church echoed through the evening air, pealing forth in halting intervals the sweet old-fashioned air, "Serve ye Truth and Honesty," to mark the hour of nine.

Chapter 8

NO CONNEXION

Along the road from Wilkersdorf to Tamsel, on a sultry afternoon of high summer, a man was hurrying—a young man, burdensomely clad for such a day, in heavy boots, and a thick grey jacket, and on his head he wore a flat, brimless cap, which served no purpose but to make him sweat. Sweat ran down between his eyes and under the horn-rimmed spectacles along his nose; sweat ran from his skull down his neck and into the hollow of his back; and when he unhooked the collar of his tunic, a sour reek of sweat rose up into his face. The man had a bold and finely moulded forehead, shaven hair, and prominent ears. He trudged through the dust, which smelt strongly of chocolate; on his right a slope and ditch covered with powdered herbage, in which the kilometre stones were barely visible; on his left, at the furthest edge of his field of vision, lowered, blue-grey, and faintly flickering with lightning flashes, a summer storm, one of those storms that roll up slowly over the flat river landscape. He would certainly get wet on the way back, but he did not mind. If he had learnt to ride a bicycle when he was a boy instead of reading Shakespeare, he would have been better off now. Yes, if he could only have exchanged that stupid serge tunic for his light drill jacket, and worn string-soled shoes on his feet, he would now be standing in the post office at Tamsel. "Well," he thought to himself smiling, "there are some disadvantages in learning to ride a bicycle in one's youth; a lad who minds his books is more likely to get a play acted, for instance. . . . Six hundred marks! And the money's actually there—what a weight it would be off Lenore's mind. We must discuss how I can make it possible for her to draw the money." There were so many important things to talk about, since even yesterday. His first idea, of course, was to carry the news to the beloved himself, and he applied for leave to Berlin from Saturday afternoon to Monday morning. But in the meantime certain trifling events had occurred that had shifted the situation and altered his prospects, and made it essential for him to get in touch with her at once in view of the changes that now threatened—but the post office shut at six. . . . And that was why Private Bertin of the Army Service Corps was panting heavily along the road on a hot summer afternoon. If he was in luck, he might be overtaken by a cart being driven fast through Tamsel to Küstrin to avoid the storm. If not, then he must walk and think, walk and torment himself with thinking. His lips, which he kept moistening with his tongue, moved with the words and sentences that poured from his brain. He had been on duty that day from about six until eleven, and again from two until five. From six until eleven—and his arms and hands were still quivering from toil—they had been building a causeway of roughly hewn pine-stems through what had once been forest to a place where an ammunition dump was to be constructed. In the afternoon there was practice in saluting, under the added discomfort of the then scorching heat, and, in the shade of a small pine wood, instruction in the badges worn by the officers of the German and Allied armies; and last of all, physical exercise, intended, presumably, to loosen the men's muscles. In the course of these, the lanky sergeant, Boost by name, had taken occasion to give them the broadest hints of events to come, which had in itself been sufficient to send Private Bertin on his walk to Tamsel. Moreover, he had already received, when the post was handed out, a short letter containing some equally explosive intelligence. What, Bertin was reflecting, could be done? By which he meant, how could he reconcile the two facts between which he was now torn. She had to undergo an operation, and they were going back again to Küstrin; she was risking her life, and they were to get no more leave; she had to face her ordeal with all its possible consequences, and they were being sent off to the war . . . perhaps to garrison duty in Warsaw or Lille. It was not yet decided where, said Boost, but it had been definitely decided that they were to go. Such being the case, it was essential that he should see Lenore; she must visit him at Küstrin before she made up her mind to take this risk. Of course, he would not use the word risk, but he could not view the affair very differently; and it was his fault. Well, he must face what lay before them; eyes front!

A column of dust whirled along the road behind him, and the wind seemed to grasp at his neck, hot and light like a feverish hand. No cart appeared that might have shortened his journey and preserved him from the tumult of his feelings. As he approached Tamsel, the road grew more populous. In the shade of the tall acacias, under which Frederick the Second, when fate was against him, had perhaps ridden in days gone by, many soldiers were coming and going; and as Bertin was inferior in rank to everyone, even to the lance-corporals, with only one copper button on their collars, he had to keep his eyes pretty wide open to avoid unpleasant encounters. But as he blindly saluted everyone who looked as if he had a claim to such attention, he succeeded in making his way through a throng of soldiers who were bound in the same direction, and past a column of five transport lorries, to the post office, which, like every post office in the neighbourhood, reeked of stale tobacco smoke. Behind a partition of wood and opaque glass, approachable only through a small window, laboured a harassed postal official. Eight men were waiting; two of them wanted to send money to their wives, one had come to telegraph, two to fetch letters, one to buy stamps, and two to telephone. When Bertin's turn at last came—when the hoarse official told him his call was through to Potsdam, and he, quivering with agitation, pressed the receiver, on its short and twisted strand of cord, to his ear, the time by the post office clock was already a quarter past six. He heard a faint crackling on the line as Küstrin spoke to Potsdam, while his eyes wandered over the dull brown walls and dirty floor-boards of the shabby building. He heard Potsdam 189 announce itself just as the thunder began to roll in the distance. But as the instrument, the only one in the town, was not fixed in a sound-proof box, but stood between the two windows of the main office room, where soldiers in heavy nailed boots came and went incessantly over the creaking floor, shouted to each other, or talked to the official; it was hardly to be expected that a place so distant as Potsdam should express itself very clearly to Bertin's one listening ear. He heard some words he could not make out, some indistinguishable brief staccato noises. Eagerly he asked whether Fräulein So-and-so was speaking—Fräulein Lenore. And amid the laughter of the waiting soldiers, he once more repeated the name of his friend, reddening with shame at having to do so: "Is that you, Lenore? Please speak louder, I can't hear a word." But although sweat ran into his ears again, this time from excitement, although the thick atmosphere of the room and the strain of the conversation brought him near to choking—yes, though he concentrated his whole soul in his ear, he still could not make out who was speaking at the other end. The current available, now that the storm, too, was approaching, was far too feeble for an insignificant little station like Tamsel. . . . There stood Bertin, agonizing at the end of that short twist of cord, bursting with important news, and eager to ask the most urgent questions—in vain; until at last an elderly soldier clapped him on the back and said: "That'll do, my lad; your girl can't understand you, and I must talk to my old mother."

Full of shame and fury, utterly cast down and weary, Bertin looked up from the desk at which he had been glaring all this time, and recoiled into what was now his world, cut off from that larger world in which he could assert himself as a man, instead of being a mere number among a thousand others like unto himself; and he dropped the receiver with a click into its place.

At the other end of the line David Wahl, with a shake of his head, laid down his receiver also. Thanks to his much better instrument he had heard Bertin without difficulty, and had also been aware of Bertin's fruitless efforts. A queer sort of lover who, in his fear that he might be speaking to someone who did not know the facts, insisted on spending three whole minutes asking whether Fräulein Lenore was there. He told his sister about it in the evening, as she, looking meditative and certainly a little pale, was putting out what she would need for her journey "to Wismar, to study the brick Gothic of the North"; tomorrow she was launching into the unknown.

"Never mind," she said. "He need not know. When it's all over, he can come and see me. You can go to Küstrin first and tell him all about it."

David burst into a sudden laugh. "You can't think how comic he sounded as he kept on asking for 'Fräulein.'. I should think he must have got hold of the first and original telephone apparatus. Sleep well, my daughter, I'm going to see Kliem."

Lenore Wahl was a girl behind whose imperious brow dwelt many thoughts, strange and all her own. But this time she drew a deep breath and told herself that it was good that there were Bertins in the world, but that it was at least equally good that there were men like Kliem not far away.

BOOK THREE

AN EVERYDAY OCCURRENCE

Chapter 1

FRAU NOCKS

Families always remain true to type, and their habits and manners are not altered by an ice age or a war. Fathers fight against the fat that begins to accumulate on the inside of their bellies, and for that purpose their wives accompany them to watering-places where other and strange gentlemen are taking the cure, and allow these ladies to discover that even a woman of forty-three can still be desirable. Children speed along the paths that are to lead them to the heights or to the depths of life, like small new stars in the human universe. Grandfathers—but here the picture changes. Grandfathers are people who are not now swayed by impulses alone—impulses that serve and shape creation; and apart from a certain leaning towards parsimony, they are ruled by experience and reason. Thus, perhaps, they are filled with anger at the confusion of the times; they are furious that the war should have so inopportunely revived the ancient feud of Austria and Italy, and unloosed fresh hymns of hate in the usual terms—murder and savagery glorified by a now abdicated intellect. Their newspapers and almanacs provide them with much patriotic poetry of hate; and they busily cut out and arrange material for a collection of extracts to illustrate "The Spirit of the Times." Grandfathers anxiously observe the apparently increasing prosperity of the war profiteers, which is left untouched by taxes, because the authorities do not want to discourage patriotism among patriots. Grandfathers live in an atmosphere of large events, and have little time for smaller ones. Grandfathers listen abstractedly and approve when granddaughters suggest a trip to Wismar or Mecklenburg to study the monuments of antiquity in those cities.

A small suitcase; a journey to Berlin; a swaying, grinding train. Past the window of the cushioned compartment sped the familiar and ever lovely landscape of lake and foliage, bright painted houses and flat countryside. Green, dimmed by a haze of heat, the tops of the pines quivered against the blue of the sky. Lenore leaned against the cushions and looked at them—she was a little excited, but betrayed no visible disquiet. Nothing proclaimed to her that she had crossed a ridge or pass of her existence which led into a domain full of astonishing events. Only the fingers of her hand, as it lay on the arm-rest of her seat, contracted involuntarily from time to time, like the legs of a dog just about to make a spring.

Beside her David buried himself in the adventures of the crew of the *Hispaniola,* which had now landed on the Treasure Island, and of the boy who, unknowing, brought those adventures to a happy ending. He silently admired his sister's composure; he, on the contrary, felt very uncomfortable at the prospect of what lay before them. He wished it were already evening.

The suburban train between Potsdam and Berlin no longer stopped after Neubabelsberg, to the annoyance of those who lived in the Western suburbs. It thundered over the remaining section like a real long-distance train, and the arrogant rhythm of its wheels disguised the fact that, compared with genuine flyers and D-trains, it played a very humble part indeed. It makes a difference to a locomotive whether it spends the forty thousand kilometres of its lifetime between Potsdam and Berlin, or between Berlin and the Central Station at Cologne.

Lenore Wahl loved travelling in trains or in her father's great car. One could never think so well as when driven smoothly through a cheerful landscape; and thinking, the light inflow of ideas, was one of the most notable joys of life. As the train rumbled on its way through the outskirts of the vast city of Berlin, and forest gave place to houses and fields began to be dotted with factories, she set herself to estimate the enterprise to which she was now pledged. Like many young people of that time, she felt at intervals the need of a ruthless clarification of her position, just as a captain on the open sea had to take his bearings every day in accordance with the time and the position of the sun. The only important things in the world were spiritual; they came to fruition independently of all material conditions, and radiated all the forces of creation. Bodies brought the sensation of happiness; they were matter instinct with soul, instruments of character, love, health, and work, and portals to that lovely world of sense experience, which is the securest source of all our knowledge. But if the physical element got the upper hand, it had to be thrust back into its place, just as Papa and Mamma were now busy doing at Karlsbad. Something like that was now to happen to her today—thanks to an outworn social code; and it would be a rather more dangerous process than a Karlsbad cure. She would soon get it over. She was a young woman who, deliberately and of her own free will, proposed to set her personal affairs in order, with every prospect of success. In her inmost heart there was probably a deeper fear, but for that no one was responsible. All possible inquiries and arrangements had been made, and with all proper circumspection. David had already been to see Frau Nocks, and even the doctor whom she had recommended (which he had better not have done, as will appear). Dr. Karl Umleit had questioned him gravely and had made a good impression on him. Now for an effort of will, and all would soon be over.

Berlin was already sweltering though it was not yet midday. The newspaper women were too exhausted to do more than gasp out their cries. Along the pavements stood barrows covered with heaps of cherries, red and yellow and black, and luxuriant flowers. Lenore eagerly absorbed that picture of the busy life of everyday, to try and drown certain undertones, a disquiet of the body and the mind, that now arose within her. She felt soothed by the sight of the flushed faces of the women under their large hats, and the girls astride upon their speeding bicycles, as she and her brother moved through the busy scene on the black leather seat of an open cab, which was actually too hot to touch. The horse's brown ears, beset by flies, nodded through two slits in a yellow straw hat.

The house stood on the Möckern bridge; a narrow dark entry in front, and beyond, a dim passage leading to an invisible staircase. The place smelt of dust and of stale food. There was no carpet on the stairs, and the worn banisters, that twisted upwards in a narrow zigzag, looked endless. Lenore's knees suddenly refused to carry her. Half-way up she had to sit down. Her face, damp with sweat, looked pale in the light of the yellow and green panes of glass. Her teeth chattered audibly as she tried to excuse herself to David. The boy put his arm awkwardly round her shoulders, and sat down beside her on the bare staircase that had once been painted red. With his large grey handkerchief he dried her forehead and her face under her eyes. Against his calmly beating heart Lenore regained her strength, and was able to listen to the shrill tinkle of the bell in the flat of Marie Nocks, Midwife.

At the same hour a column of thirsty men, who were shifting quarters, toiled on their way from Tamsel to the fortress of Küstrin, seventy-five men of the Army Service Corps, and at their head, Corporals Näglein and Kowarzik. They were not singing, hardly anyone was talking. They were too conscious of the weight of their heavy uniforms, their packs, and their rolled-up overcoats; in a flat haze of dust they panted along the burning road with drooping heads. A peasant cart, piled high with blanket-bundles, cardboard boxes, and wooden chests, followed them; Sergeant Boost had hired it at the charges of the company so that no one might collapse by the way. Not far away Frau Boost and a few other wives trotted along. Uncertainty brooded over all those heads, from which the sweat dripped in salty streams. Thus the grey human serpent clanked along, between ripening corn and far-flung meadows, with the rhythmic swing of many limbs, and the reddish-yellow planes of the faces sharp-cut against the brown planes of the packs. Thus, in the years to come, would it wind along many a road on the round terrestrial globe. Sergeant

Boost meditated rather gloomily on his prospects; and yet he was not cast down for long. It was his fault that the grand days of Pompeii were now at an end, there was no manner of doubt about that; and it was pretty galling to be reduced to corporal again. But apart from that—did it really matter where he strolled about so long as his men did the work? How was he to know that it would be near Fort Bondues in the neighbourhood of Lille that one of a myriad shrapnel bullets, fired from an aeroplane, would split his skull beneath his cap and make a dead man of him? Abruptly he shouted to the men to sing. Song is good against the heat of July, and song burst forth from those parched throats. They "shot the stag in the wild wood, and the doe in the leafy brake; the eagle in his craggy lair, and the duck upon the lake." Some sixty mouths sang those lines, and almost seventy admitted that "though their hearts were hard they also had felt love." This led to the "Wood and the Heath," and they finished up with "Lützow's Ride."

No more stifling heat, no fear of the unknown. The packs had lightened, a fresh breeze blew into the loosened collars of their tunics. Here marched soldiers of a great army from their training camp, elderly men and young men, and each and all of them felt heartened. They knew what they meant to do; they meant to bear themselves like men, and march like soldiers when they came to towns and houses. And among the most cheerful of the singers could be heard the voice of Private Bertin. He had thrust his sweat-beclouded spectacles between the buttons of his tunic, and sang out lustily, though the choruses were little more than a vague and vigorous roar. His practised ear led him to construct a second part, an accompanying alto, of thirds and fourths, in which a few others also joined; this gave fullness to the singing, and a sense of musical completeness. Who knew what was to become of them, the gods were still taking counsel, but the next few months would be a gay and adventurous time; in the dust of that country road they could smell the odour of strange and distant lands. Foreign lands would make a man of him, if he were ever to become one. The past must not hang about his neck,

indeed it did so no longer. Lenore's business would be over; and —for this now came to the surface of his mind—it was for her sake that he was coming to maturity.

A sheet was spread upon a black oilcloth sofa; near it moved Fate, in the person of Frau Nocks, with the thin mouthpiece of a syringe in her hand. She was stout, and she waddled as she walked; her watery blue eyes and her soothing speech could not dispel the impression that she was about to impale her victim. But Frau Nocks said:

"All absolutely antiseptic, little Fräulein, I know what's proper. The best ladies come here—Potsdam and the highest aristocracy. But you must keep quite still; I shan't hurt you a little bit."

Lenore compelled herself to look at the tin wash-bucket that hung from the window-bolt. Then an incredible sensation shot through her. The pain forced a shriek out of her—a shriek that she tried frantically to stifle. It struck at her most secret soul, at life itself—it was more than she could bear. Then followed a sensation that she was floating. The pain was gone—she had often suffered more at the dentist—but was the sofa sinking slowly into the floor, head first?

"There, there," said Frau Nocks in her good-humoured voice, "that's all over. That was just to open it up, Fräulein, and it's better done from the outside with a syringe, than six or seven months later by the little head of a newcomer to this earth."

Lenore clutched at the sofa. "It's nothing," she said to herself, "I'm all right." The window frame yonder looked quite black in the darkness, in the grey dim light. A surge of weakness made her heart shrink. She grew pale, and then yellow.

"Come now, pull yourself together, little Fräulein," she heard Frau Nocks whisper, "it's all over."

A woman who appeared to be clad in oilcloth moved towards her like a cloud. A waft of methylated spirit floated pleasantly into her consciousness, and a sudden coolness made her face and temples smart. A white bird seemed to be flapping kindly wings above her. Yonder was the cloud-woman waving a towel in the air. Ah, now she began to see more clearly, she must just be patient for a little; the midwife had said it was all over, peace poured into her with the drawing of her breath. . . . Through her half-closed eyes she could see the ghost moving about the room, putting various things away, and washing her hands.

"If only my ladies would calm down a bit before they get here, there wouldn't be any trouble at all." Lenore began to feel like an individual once more; with every beat of her pulse the deafness in her ears grew less. The broad dialect of Berlin seemed to fall from the shoulders of a white apron on to a young woman far below, who lay there exactly as though she were giving birth to a child, or conceiving one. "There's no sense in torturing themselves like ladies usually do. It's all very well to go straight at a paper wall in a circus, but a real brick wall, Fräulein, you've got to get over or under, as Wilhelm said. And so it is with the War, Fräulein. It's very hard for the likes of us to understand. The Lord God isn't outside the world. And if you want to find out all about it, now that you've got to lie up for a time, you try the Apocalypse. You'll find it all there, and in the prophet Daniel, too. No parson can get me to believe that our Lord Jesus would now be a sapper with the job of cutting barbed wire. We seemingly can't make fools of ourselves without making a fool of the good God too, eh? What did Jesus say? I am the Alpha and the Omega, the beginning and the end. He didn't say, I'm doing all I know to help you in the war. Again: I saw a woman seated on the dragon, and the woman's raiment was crimson, and she had three heads and three crowns, and the woman's aspect was fearful and the Kings of the earth had committed whoredoms with her."

Lenore in her distraught state hardly heard all this. She must get up, put her clothes straight, make certain necessary arrangements, and go. She was utterly bewildered by this demoniac outburst.

"Next Sunday I'm going to try the Adventists. Perhaps they have the right spirit. When Christian men, Fräulein, begin to throw bombs and burning oil at each other, it looks as if the last day wasn't very far off—and I've no use for a parson who says that it's all right."

In the other room David looked up from his book. The black shadows under his sister's eyes and her yellowish pallor made him clench his fists. He longed to have the handling of the arrogant brute who had let her in for this.

Frau Nocks peered very carefully at the new ten- and twenty-mark notes before putting them away in the pocket of her apron. "There are cabs at the corner, young man. No. 6 Heinrich Heinestrasse. Dr. Umleit is expecting you. I could have sent you to a Professor, but Dr. Umleit is better. He's a dear man. Good luck."

Brother and sister expressed their thanks. On the stairs Lenore smiled a rather wry smile and said: "My dear, now I know where the soul grows—at least in women."

Chapter 2

GETHSEMANE

This second staircase had to be surmounted as though it were the steep rock-face of the last ordeal before Paradise. Windows on the landings opened on to the courtyard at the back, a circle of grass, dotted with shady trees. Men were lying on stretchers smoking cigarettes; and some were sitting with thickly bandaged legs in wheeled chairs, reading. A very young one, with an arm in a sling, was staring up at the sky. The two lower floors of the broad rear wing of the building were filled with wounded men; it was Professor Mondstein's surgical clinic.

Dr. Umleit got up from behind his small writing-table, came two steps forward, and shook hands with his two visitors. "You were introduced here as Frau Werner, Fräulein Wahl," he said. "Anyone with a brother like yours needn't be quite so careful as all that. Now just sit down here a moment—nothing's going to happen to you. Will you stand by the window, young man?" And after a pause: "All in excellent order. Herr Wahl told me I must be very gentle because he obviously regarded us doctors as cannibals."

A defiant look came over David's face. This was a good beginning, he thought, straining his ears to listen. Of course, one had to explain everything to these people.

Tilted backwards in a white, polished examination chair, with her legs supported at the back of the knees, she hung rather than lay, defenceless and ashamed. Her heart fluttered wildly; what was going to happen now? Too abruptly had she been flung from the domain where young ladies lived into the savage nakedness of such a chair as this. . . . Then she felt vaguely that someone was dabbing her with wadding; and her gratitude melted away her fears.

Dr. Umleit washed his hands in running water. Then he drew up an arm-chair for her to rest for a few minutes. Over a reddish moustache steady eyes peered through the glasses of his spectacles—the eyes of a man who cannot look at the sufferings of the world without sharing them. "The lords of creation have got all their own way now," he said. "Put a man in a tunic, and he's a savage who can only shout and crack a whip. A fine type of man the war will leave us. Well, God be with us, and indeed with us alone. Now I will call the sister, you must go and see your room, and this afternoon we shall meet again."

When Sister Vilma, fair-haired and lively, had had a good look at young Frau Werner, and had also observed her engagement ring on her right hand, she said: "Now we had better get comfortably into bed, Fräulein, and begin to think about lunch." Her confident smile commanded the situation.

Lenore looked at her wide-eyed, blushed, and dropped her head shamefully. Although the intertwined letters L.W. on her linen agreed with the name under which she had come, this fellow-conspirator meant she should understand that no such subterfuges were needed, and that bad conscience was at a discount here. Alas, she was plunging more and more deeply into the secret places of life. . . . Well, she must bear this, too. For the moment it all seemed quite indifferent. She lay in bed; she could stretch herself on the cool pillows and look out at the blue sky, the pure morning blue of a year that was near its zenith. After a tremendous exertion of all her energies, like a rower who is rowed completely out, she had reached a harbour where she could rest at last. The world might pass her over with its cheap contempt; she, with a faint smile upon her lips, merely thought of the ancient verse that she had learned in her history lesson at school, and which acquired a new quaint connotation from her presence in that place and in that bed: "Wanderer, if you go to Sparta, tell them that you have seen us lying here, as the law commanded." Sparta stood for Berlin, or Potsdam, and the law might lay different commands on different people. . . . At peace, with limbs relaxed, she fell into a doze, barely moving her head once or twice from side to side. Dreams came over her; her parents, walking with red sunshades along the avenues of Karlsbad, and carrying in their fingers odd objects made of glass, at which they were sucking. . . .

She awoke much refreshed, with a strange sound of singing in her ears. Yes, it came from beyond the tree tops, very high-pitched and expressive; except that she did not know what it expressed. Suddenly it changed into a shrill howl of torment, that made her get out of bed to close the window. "Sister, Sister, I'm going to jump out of the window," came the voice from without. And the sister answered soothingly, with an undertone of malice: "That's just the labour coming on, my child, you must make up your mind to bear it." Hurriedly Lenore closed the window-catches. Just for a little pain in the stomach, she thought bitterly. No such sound should be heard from her in that house.

Dr. Umleit sent for the operations sister. Sister Anneliese appeared, young and pretty, with thoughtful eyes set widely in a sun-tanned face. After more intimate relations as man and woman, they now looked upon each other with friendly respect; in hours of work, indeed, they were no more than Sister and Physician.

"Are you off duty any time today?"

"I've got a friend coming for me at four, Herr Doktor."

"Still the Swede? Ah, Swedes are very faithful. But before you go I want to start on Room No. 3."

A cloud came over Sister Anneliese's face. The anæsthetic would take more time than she could spare. "Sister Vilma can take my place perfectly well."

"I'm afraid not. Don't worry, I shan't be using an anæsthetic."

Sister Anneliese raised her eyebrows. "It hurts, Herr Doktor."

Dr. Umleit nodded. "That's why I shall want you, and Mieze, too, with her strong arms. It isn't going to be any pleasure to me. Anyone can see she's sensitive."

"Sensitive and tough. They're the sort to bear it." (Sister Anneliese spoke from her own bitter experience.)

"Just so. Our young friend told us to be careful of her heart."

"Yes, a kindly lad with all his wits about him—the sort I like. By the way, the sapper downstairs, the one with the gunshot wound in the leg . . . "

"The lad who played the harmonica?"

"That's the one; went off early this morning, quite suddenly. Embolism."

"Ah . . . We shall want Frau Werner fit and strong for the operation tomorrow. We can't let her off today." And he sighed.

Sister Anneliese looked at him curiously. Was he already in love with the new patient? Not more than a good woman's doctor has to be, she reminded herself. Such sympathy was a gift; not everyone possessed it. "At what time?" she asked.

"Let us say half-past three. When it's over, veronal in discreet doses."

Such misunderstandings come from affectionate but untimely interference by younger brothers; here was the result of David's first visit. His urgency had aroused in Dr. Umleit suspicions of the soundness of Lenore's heart—suspicions that were quite unjustified. Now the centre of acutest pain in a pregnant woman is the inner aperture of the womb where the passage narrows almost to a needlepoint. It can indeed be extended to the width of a baby's head. In order to be able to use an instrument of reasonable size during the operation, the doctor widens it by means of an expanding implement of wood, which in the course of a day renders this preliminary process clean and automatic. But when an anxious brother has represented his sister as delicate and sensitive, the doctor is liable to take this as referring to her capacity to stand chloroform or ether, and make him nervous that her pulse may give out, or her heart stop. And as he wants subsequently to save the patient's life unhampered by any such anxiety, he prefers to give her, quite deliberately, a great deal of pain at the first encounter.

Lenore, outstretched on the examination chair, uttered no more than a sharp gasping moan as she clutched its metal edges. On each side of her a sister held down her arms and shoulders with dragoon-like fists. The violence of the onslaught almost deprived her of consciousness. Her heart seemed to change into an organ sensitive to pain, and she felt as though it were splitting within her breast; an engulfing surge of torment swept over her forehead and temples. "She's very brave, very brave indeed," muttered Dr. Umleit, with real admiration, as he had her lifted on to a sofa. Poor creatures, they always had to pay the bill. The man was an author, he had heard, and not without talent, and would marry her—but what a careless brute he must have been! This long-legged narrow-hipped young woman seemed, on the other hand, a highly finished human specimen. How smoothly her broad shoulders passed into the graceful arms, and how smoothly the little breasts curved up from her rounded chest. Her soul, too, was stiffened by a backbone of resolve, self-control, and courage. After all, courage is everything, thought Dr. Umleit, as he rubbed her forehead and temples with eau-de-Cologne, and told her to breathe deeply. "She comes of good stock; she'll get through all right—and she would get through worse than this. I should like to see more of her later on."

She lay, or sat, her head bent over her shoulder and a wry smile on her lips; what seemed to her like a foretaste of the shrieks of Hell slowly died away within her. Dr. Umleit, in his white smock, stood and surveyed her. "There, that's better, isn't it?" And after a few whispered words to the sister: "The worst is over now. Tomorrow you'll be out of your troubles. But promise me, little lady: later on you'll make up for this by having three babies—one after the other." He thrust out his lower lip, sucked in his moustache, and added: "What do you imagine is going on in other places? The men certainly make more fuss when they have to bear pain, but a gun-shot wound in the lower jaw is no trifle, you know."

Lenore, with her eyes turned trustfully towards him, nodded.

That was true. There were much worse things. And she certainly would have babies; later on, after the war.

Lying in her bed a little while afterwards, she longed to shriek, and go on shrieking, uncontrolled. How insensate the blue sky looked through the window-panes. How lunatic it was to lie there and suffer these hellish tortures, in the very bloom of her youth and health. Why didn't she jump out of bed and lay about her, and wreck it all: this mouldering social order that imposed such horrors; the war, that brutalized humanity; this crass intensification of suffering on the planet. Ah yes, at her college lectures she had listened to wise saws on the value of pain. When life was easy, such fine philosophizing was well enough. All that was nonsense; the merest palliation of a world that contained nothing better than abortions, wars, wounds, and murders.

An afternoon, filled with such thoughts as these, went very slowly by. Then Sister Vilma remembered the doctor's instruction, and at last brought her some soothing tablets.

By the early morning the rending accesses of pain had passed into a regular ebb and flow. Pause, and a new onset, growing more intense; it was beyond endurance, it had reached its height—it could go no higher; but it could. Then a faint whistling breath, as the heart strains under all the forces of the will and of the soul, and the great wave of pain seemed to crash and ebb, subsiding into a throb that shook her whole body, which for a moment relaxed, while her hair lay damp and matted against her forehead and her temples. Food? There was none, and Lenore thought of none. She only begged to be taken at once, but Sister Vilma said: "No, Frau Werner, that wouldn't do." ("Ah," thought Lenore in the midst of her agony, "Dr. Umleit must have given her a hint.") "The lady next door hasn't been to sleep as you have."

So passed a morning without end. Every three or four minutes the woman fought this surging onslaught. Had it been worth while? asked the voice of reason within her. Was it worth while

—that brief encounter between the sexes, even when there was more pleasure in it than there had been in the Wilkersdorf wood? No, it was not worth while. But since men flung us aside when we did not let them have their way, what could women do? Love, she thought, love is really something quite different. For us who belong to this year nineteen hundred and fourteen, love is mainly a fusion of souls, two streams of life that flow side by side. (Feverishly she groped after what she knew, until a fresh wave of pain bore down upon her and engulfed her spirit.) Certainly love dealt in the pleasures of the body, but they were not the whole of love. Under the shield of society it was possible to reach some sort of compromise; but to turn one's back upon society, and creep into a clinic, meant a descent into a vale of desolation.

When Sister Vilma at last came to fetch her, she clenched her teeth. There was no one to carry her, no one to take her by the hand; no one even to lift her on to the operating-table—she had to climb on it by herself, with that dreadful implement still in her body. This would be a nightmare all her life, she thought, and so thinking, she lay down; if her grandfather only knew what was happening to her, his heart would burst within him. Her imploring eyes sought the doctor. At the moment he had his back turned towards her and was busy soaping his hands. All the appurtenances stood ready on the glass tables; the place reeked of ether. . . . "The mask, Sister. Count, please." The capable look came over Sister Anneliese's intent features. Her breast now rose and fell, and she knew the horror of inhaling something that could not be breathed—something that smelt sweet and had a burning taste, at once unpleasant and alluring. Then she began to suffocate—she could breathe no more; try as she would, she could not breathe. Tong . . . tong . . . tong: the sound of an incessant dripping upon metal, and a murmur like the murmur in a seashell. She forced her eyes open, but already she was blind; she could not see, she could only hear. Whispering, far away, and very clear; the doctor and the sisters. Surely they were not going to begin? She wanted to scream out that she could feel everything

—but she could no longer scream. Oh the terror of that counting voice! The room vanished, time vanished, and with them vanished a girl called Lenore Wahl; all that remained was something that counted, a spark of energy that sped from a bright centre-point of life into a hollow that contained teeth, and a tongue, which, by the agency of vocal chords, clicked against those teeth and uttered figures: "Seventeen, eighteen, nineteen, twen . . . "

She came to; slowly she became aware of air and walls. Her self, her consciousness returned. What was this that ran down her nose? Tears? She was indeed crying; her left cheek was buried in her pillow and her chin felt unpleasantly wet. Like a piece of paper crumpled up and flung into a corner she found herself back once more in her room. She really ought not to have been left alone for a moment; accidents may happen after the use of anæsthetics; but in this place the staff took a generous view of their duties. The bell, however, had been put under her hand; she just managed to move three fingers.

It was not the formidable Sister Vilma, but another with gentler face and sympathetic eyes: "My name is Sister Mieze," she said. "Dear, dear, Frau Werner, how very sick we've been."

It was the awful reek of the anæsthetic; the after-effect of the fumes on an empty stomach. In her mouth was still the acrid taste of bile.

Sister Mieze held tepid water to her lips, cleaned her chin and neck with a wisp of soft paper, dried her eyes, and tidied her hair. A hot fear that she might have babbled while under the anæsthetic gave Lenore no peace. She moved her leaden jaws to ask. But Sister Mieze reassured her: "No, Frau Werner, you said nothing," and she added with convincing friendliness: "Many talk a great deal, but you were quite quiet."

Lenore breathed a deep breath of relief. She was glad that a whiff of ether had not extinguished a woman's will. "Is it all over now?" she stammered in the crystalline voice of a child. And Sister Mieze replied in the same motherly tone: "Yes, Frau Werner, it's all out now."

A sudden smile came over Lenore's face, a pitiful parody of a laugh; she felt like a goose which had been drawn. Here she lay like some bird, which her mother or Frau Mahnke had so often spread out on the kitchen table, before taking out the intestines, liver, stomach, gall—this called for the most care—and last of all the heart. The ovaries with their pretty yellow yolks had always impressed her most of all. . . . "There, it's all out now," was the phrase then used. Yes, it was all out now. The fear of the months to come, the shame, the snare in which she had been caught by destiny, all out and over; and the rending agonies as well. If she had not been too weak to raise her arms, and if she had been vain enough to ask for a mirror, she would not have been spared one discovery; her face had changed. Her eyes, especially, and her mouth were touched with a look of horror, which had also found expression in the high clear tones of her faint small voice. Perhaps this would disappear later on, but in the meantime it laid bare the truth; how a rasping five-pronged devil's hand had ripped from her soul the sense of inviolacy, the courage of youth, the innocent acceptance of life, all the play of doubt and mystery, her unquestioning confidence in the future, all the gay *décor* of life with which the will to live veils the reality. On those pillows she lay and dozed, the mere frail and empty envelope, the outer husk, of Lenore Wahl. A magician had taken away her maiden heart, and replaced it by the wise heart of a woman now mature; the magician "Reality" with his ragged coat and his indifferent eyes.

Then the door opened and Sister Mieze entered with a tray, from which rose a very appetizing smell. "This will put some courage into you again, Fräulein; a drop of lovely pigeon broth. And then a glass of red wine with an egg and some sugar beaten up in it—and we'll have those red cheeks back again by the time your husband comes."

Ah, Werner! True, he existed; and he would come.

The trouble was, he could not. In his absence came a succession of letters, full of confused information, written with a copying pencil on bluish paper, which it made her tired to read. So much, however, she gathered; something was happening which the young man had not foreseen—some transfer of troops that had destroyed his plan. One sentence surprised her: "I constantly find reason to admire your foresight." Very kind of him, but what did he mean? She had had much opportunity to exercise that gift in the last few weeks. . . .

So he did not come. In his stead came David and spread the fear of the Lord about the place. He and Sister Vilma had some sharp passages one day, when he twitted her for taking so long to say good-bye to her soldier-friend downstairs that she had had to be rung for several times, as usual. He had confidential talks with Dr. Umleit about the way to deal with nurses who neglected their charges, and he was very short with the matron when he settled the weekly account—all behind Lenore's back. To her, he took a mother's place, and filled it completely. Who put her pillows straight for her? Who kept her supplied with iced fruit-juice? Who read to her? Who disappeared at the slightest sign that she was growing tired, and came in, with a bunch of flowers under his arm, when she felt like company? He was very lazy at writing, like most youngsters of his age, but he wrote letters to the parents that made Lenore laugh, long letters, so that she only needed to scrawl a few lines at the end. He reported everything that happened. He had now got on to Brahms—it was the chamber music that had captivated him, the finest he had ever come across. (It is hardly necessary to observe that everything for David was either "Bosh!" or "Glorious"; he had no intermediate terms.) But he had not been able to play these masterpieces with Hilde Cohn. She had lately gone from the Alt-Jacobstrasse to an Auxiliary Hospital. Yes, in defiance of the objections from certain quarters, she had at last found some sort of a job in a hospital, David did not quite know what; in any case she now played no more Schumann sonatas in A-flat, she was performing with plates in Mariampol, Lithuania, and from her letters she appeared very happy indeed. The dog, Boll, had stolen a raw cutlet from the kitchen, bolted it, spat it up in the garden, and then buried it. "He doesn't trust us; he hides about the place as if he hadn't got a home." Grandpapa had got hold of a book in several volumes; Delbrück's *Art of War.*

"He made Tornow dig my old lead soldiers out of my lumber-room, and yesterday night, he and old Obstfelder and I did the Battle of Cannae—lunatic, I call it. Hannibal's Semitic blood has come out in us all. He sat on his chair as if it had been a stuffed elephant, and we destroyed the Roman army. He would have it that generals had really learnt nothing since that battle." Kliem had pulled Else Ducherow out of the Havel—she had swum out too far (he had merely remarked: "They always do these silly things on a holiday"), and Frau Mahnke had written from Oldenburg, where she was spending her holidays at home, that she was bringing back a whole goose and a good address for future supplies of butter, "and honey in the comb for Fräulein Lene." Yes, he radiated life in that sickroom, where, indeed the patient was no longer ill. David, her good genius, thought Lenore, when he left her, expressing all his affection in a look and a light word; he would only allow himself to be kissed, with reluctance, on the cheek. How fortunate that she had him, and that these were his holidays. When one day he produced from the depths of her wardrobe at home a photograph of the good Empress, framed and signed with her own hand, "Augusta Viktoria Imp. Reg." awarded to that model pupil, Lenore Wahl, on the occasion of her leaving the Potsdam High School, she turned her face to the wall and wept. She could hardly bear to recall those placid days of childhood. . . . But David persuaded her to let him stand the photograph on the little table at her bedside. "You wait and see what a good effect it will have." And indeed, it worked wonders—the portrait of that kindly lady with the high frontal of hair and the large pearls; the sisters suddenly became assiduously attentive to Lenore. Then Werner wrote that he was definitely coming, he would get leave for Berlin at the end of the week. "Some more of Augusta's magic," remarked David dryly.

But Werner's leave was not the result of the Empress's photograph. Quite other forces were at work yonder in the garrison town of Küstrin.

Chapter 3

THE VOLUNTEER

On a broad stretch of exercise ground, the Küstrin Reserve Army Service Corps company, Garrison section, formed the three sides of a hollow square, under a blazing July sun. The time was getting on for eleven o'clock; the men had been standing there since half-past nine. It was not Bertin's first experience, as a soldier, of time idiotically wasted, nor would it be the last. The soldier, it has been said, spends a good half of his life waiting for what never happens. But in this case something did happen, as Captain Laab, who commanded the whole battalion, appeared at last to have come to some decision. In any case, he went up to the company commander. Acting-Officer Federich, who was portentously parading up and down for the benefit of Sergeant Mielenz and the two corporals.

Along the three grey lines there was much furtive whispering over the bad news that had been current that morning when coffee was served out; the rumours were two, and apparently in conflict. The company was standing at ease; in that appalling heat one or other of the older men might well have collapsed on to that trampled earth. No notice was taken of the whispered disputes or surreptitious gestures. "Mark my words, we're in for a mud-bath in Flanders. . . . " "Rubbish! It's Warsaw. I got it from the Orderly Room, and they know."

"Company! Eyes right! 'Tention! Eyes—front!"

The lines stiffened into a semblance of three walls of an unfinished house: Captain Laab and his adjutant stepped into the centre of the open space; Herr Federich rapped out the designation of the company and its strength. The captain surveyed the array before him with the professional eye of one who regarded man solely from his military aspect; who looked for order, drill, and smartness, and, if he did not find them, demanded an explanation in no measured terms. And yet he imagined that he saw those men through and through, as he passed from the first line to the second, and then finished his leisurely inspection at the third. Thanks to the training of the last few months, several hundred faces turned, as though drawn by a magnet, and followed his progress. "A sound and healthy lot," thought he. "Look almost like soldiers. Needn't be ashamed to show 'em to that old soaker, the major."

He passed Bertin, unheeding. But Bertin saw Captain Laab. He saw him with the understanding eye of the good soldier. Military training tends to make intelligent men stupid, but it also makes stupid men brighter, it quenches or transmutes ambition, but stimulates the idle into energy; and Bertin's goodwill and earnestness had made his military education a success. It was war-time. Earth, speech, intellect, and living men, were fused into a great unity—the Fatherland. So Bertin did not observe Laab's round belly, nor the creases of crimson fat above his collar, and he was not disturbed by Lieutenant Wolkwitz's arrogant aloofness; before his mind was the idea of a vast articulated and coherent structure of values and duties, the spirit that was Germany, expressing in the valiance of the German armies how much more nearly it achieved the great purpose of the world than the genius of France, England, or Russia; which was precisely what he was intended to think. But that, incidentally, he did not know.

"Company, at ease!"

The officers beckoned to Sergeant Mielenz to join them, and with an air of slightly condescending affability discussed with him and Herr Federich the steps that were now to be taken. The conflicting rumours of the early morning proved both to be justified. The cities of Warsaw and Lille were to be garrisoned from the forces there present, which were to be divided. Those for the West were to go first; they, with others, were to join the first company of the new A.S.C. battalion shortly to be formed, X/20, under the command of Major Jansch. For this unit, handworkers were especially needed; a list of the trades in question was produced—and in any case, men who could speak French. The men for the East would choose the better part. Large administrative bodies would be "established"—for it seemed unlikely that the Russians would ever see those provinces again—and the abler and more adaptable of the garrison troops would soon find themselves transformed into officials—such as foresters, teachers, clerks in banks and law courts, sugar-refiners, distillers, tobacconists—and uncommonly hard-worked for fifty-three pfennigs a day; but there would be prospects of civilian jobs later on. The others, those who were to be pushed off first, would be drafted to a great city in Northern France, with shops and pastry-cooks, clean stone houses, and alluring ladies. Still, the West is the West, it lies inexorably near a district in which men are daily smashed to atoms, and it would be dangerous to predict what might be the final destination of troops stationed in the West.

Acting-Officer Federich, in civil life secretary to the municipal gas-workers at Küstrin, saluted the officers with proper rigidity, and they hurriedly withdrew into the shade of their cool room. For an Acting-Officer is—as his name implies—an officer, but merely a very exalted non-commissioned officer, and must be made to feel it, even if he does not grasp it for himself. For that reason he was glad to see the two officers' backs, as he was now left in command of the field, and could take his stand in the centre of the open square.

Men drawn up in ranks must only think when they are asked to think; otherwise they must obey. He therefore gave no explanation of the command: "Men of the following trades stand out by the right!" Those in question realized that they were to run down the ranks outside and form a new front on the fourth side of the yard closing up by the right. Once more he rasped out:

"Painters, stand out by the right! Bakers, barbers, builders, stand out by the right!"

With much clatter of nailed boots, those indicated detached

themselves from the three sides of the square, and gathered in the left free corner. "Printers, stand out!" The whole proceeding aroused a most undeniable disquiet among those who remained. Everything that happens in the army, every movement that is made or omitted, may be fatal to a man. Which would be sent to the West—those who had been called out, or the rest? A rumour gradually spread through the ranks of these latter, a rumour that originated with the Barber Niklas. A shave cost ten or fifteen pfennigs in the city, N.C.O.s and clerks were glad to save a penny and liked to pay with useful tips on service matters. And so yesterday Wilms, the clerk said as he lit a cigarette: "If any man's a barber tomorrow, it's all up with him. They want barbers in the West, so that the men can tell when it's Sunday. But anyone who's had a job at a swimming bath or a hospital had better speak up. There's a lot of men wanted for the new de-lousing establishments, civil and military, in Poland." Since then Barber Niklas had realized that his real profession was that of bathing attendant; he would stay in the ranks and go East. From that moment those who had been called out turned a shade paler where they stood. Those who remained behind suddenly found it far less hot; they were aware of a gently cooling breeze.

Not all of them, of course. Educated faces, and among them those that wore spectacles, exchanged frowns of understanding; the budding barristers Bertin and Glücksmann, Rosenthal, who was in business, and Dr. Nahmann, the lawyer. The East presented difficulties especially for Israelites, owing to the large numbers of their co-religionists in those parts. There, smartness and good conduct would be of little service to a Jewish soldier. He would have to stand by while his superiors or his fellow-soldiers cursed the Jews, and have to protest or else say nothing —both alternatives being equally painful, which it would be better to avoid. In the West were Lille, Gothic Churches, educated people; in the East, filth, poverty, vermin, interminable autumns and winters. And as they had learnt French and even English at school. . . .

"Tool-makers stand out!"

Bertin's neighbour, young Holzer, an excellent fellow, a good workman and something of a politician, faced about, dashed out of the line, and reappeared in front on the left. Bertin marked his quizzical grin.

"Cigar-makers stand out!"

Krause, his left-hand neighbour, vanished. He would be confoundedly lonely without his usual comrades. There were now few human activities unaccounted for. "Number off from the right," rapped out Federich. Bertin's new neighbours were—on the right, Kröhling, the engineer, and on the left, Strauss, who travelled in furs, and beyond him, young Rosenthal, his handsome bored face gazing into vacancy; he was heir to an important dress-shop in the aristocratic quarter in Berlin.

"Are you going to the East?" whispered Bertin to him. "Not such a fool," answered Rosenthal; "lousy hole."

But Strauss, who was better able to look after himself than any of them, observed: "Wait a bit, they want men who can speak French."

Bertin, both in his life and work, was very far from being ashamed of his Jewish origin; indeed, he had taken every opportunity to lay stress on it, as could be seen from his writings. But in the deeper currents of his mind there were other elements than those mirrored in its surface, and his love of certain great Frenchmen, and more especially the sparkling eloquence with which Nietzsche, the idol of his youth, had acclaimed the clarity of the West, its gaiety, its spiritual freedom, the pre-eminence of its culture as against the superstition of the East—all this stood for a great deal that determined his decisions.

Kröhling, the engineer, alone observed the proceedings with complete detachment. He was resolved that he would be sent neither to the East nor to the West. He was waiting to be applied for by the drawing-office of the motor-works where he had been previously employed. This application was on the way; and he was very well aware that everything had to be suitably paid for. He had accordingly paid a visit to a cheap and carefully selected prostitute, the consequences of which would become apparent at the next examination before drafts were sent on active service. As he was neither a Jew nor a working man, but the son of respectable parents, he could direct his affairs without reference to sentiment. But the others were merely waiting to show how unjustly they had hitherto been judged by the military authorities and the bearers of the national conscience; they would heartily despise Kröhling, and it would be years before they had become so adapted to the war world as he was by the end of July 1915.

The new unit as yet contained only ninety-eight men; it was to consist of a hundred and ten. Here was the chance for all those young gentlemen who were too fastidious to come into contact with the East. Strauss, the traveller in fur, made a beginning. His black eyes twinkled as he turned, with military correctness, to his corporal. He asked to be allowed to volunteer for the West.

Corporal Näglein stared at him with bewildered eyes. Was the man out of his mind? Even if his home *was* in the Moselle valley—the poor fool! And he motioned Strauss to get back and hold his tongue.

But Federich, whose eyes saw everything, asked in a rasping nasal voice what that man there wanted. Landsturmmann Strauss asked to be posted to the West because he spoke French well, and his parents lived in the Moselle valley? Excellent! What the fellow wanted, that he should have, in God's name. Did any other gentleman want to volunteer? He had no need to ask, for fifteen men stepped out of the three columns, among them eight Hebrews, who preferred the West to the East because they spoke French.

One of them was called Werner Bertin. He came, indeed, from Upper Silesia, knew a little Polish, and, moreover, had learnt Russian at school for two years on his own account, so that with a little practice he would be able to conduct a simple conversation. But he had completely forgotten all this at the moment under the impulse of his anxiety to get to the West. And he failed to realize that it would take less time to get to Berlin on leave from Warsaw or Suvalki than from Lille; he heard no still voice warning him that there was a young woman lying in a clinic who had claims on his company, or at any rate called for some consideration; he flung himself blindly into the adventure. So, with his squat blue shadow before him, he stood among the fifteen; his choice was made.

Acting-Officer Federich smiled, a half relieved and half sardonic smile, and with a silent gesture swept the fifteen towards the rest. Their comrades who remained behind grinned, shrugged their shoulders, and nudged each other. As he now had three too many, Federich withdrew from the consignment for the West three men who could speak Polish. The clock struck half-past eleven. The unpleasant business was at an end.

For years afterwards the chime of that clock reverberated in Bertin's ear—two strokes of a leaden clapper on an iron bell. It was like the sharp melancholy clink of the switch in a railway signal-box when the points are shifted.

This was the last time that he used his own free will to impel himself to action.

Chapter 4

THE VISIT

From Sunday morning until early on Monday the men of the new unit I/X/20 were given leave to Berlin to put their affairs in order before their transfer in the following week. The railway carriages were thronged with soldiers on the same errand. It was a dismal journey in the heat, through plain and meadowland, rough thick heath, and Brandenburg sand. In his corner seat, buried in an epic novel by Tolstoy, Private Bertin managed to efface for the time being the unpleasant apprehensions awakened by the meeting that he had so soon to face. Closing his ears to his own inner voice, he was much more ready to listen to the gay talk of the soldiers, who—("just once more before I'm killed, Fräulein")—were to take their pleasure with women before they departed for the unknown. The man whose eyes were so steadily fixed upon his book turned uneasily from such thoughts as these, so much so that a shadow of his ill-humour fell upon the woman who, ten days before, had had to suffer through him and that all-powerful impulse. He must now stand in her presence; he must now answer for what he had so lightly brought about—and, moreover, he must tell her that he was going away, to the West, whither he had volunteered. It was something of an ordeal; and he was glad, by the aid of the great Russian, to escape for a time into a larger world; a certain Prince Andrey had at the moment more attraction for him than the image of the woman whom he loved. The grey-clad soldiers' jokes, their crude talk, their unabashed joys of anticipation, no longer distressed him; they disgusted him that day. From time to time the vision of a sum of money slipped across the printed page, six hundred marks, the largest sum that he had ever possessed, and one which, even so, only belonged to him in name. So he hid himself from the unfriendly world between the pages of *War and Peace*. And now and again he sighed.

On the fourth floor of the clinic, he stopped and drew a deep breath. For even a wounded sergeant was still a sergeant, and had a claim to salutation and respect from his inferiors, though there had been no instruction as to the marks of rank on hospital jackets. Such were the forces that now pursued a man right up to the threshold of his intimate life, to the threshold of a door, whitewashed and numbered, behind which lay a bridge to the past existence of Bertin, the student; along it he could walk back without a pause as far as his earliest days. But he felt no pain and anger at this intrusive military world; he had only a vague feeling that he had to run away from it. None the less he hesitated for a moment before knocking, and summoned all his strength of heart and soul; for he was to need them.

A faint hoarse voice replied: "Come in."

The door opened inwards. Against the opposite wall of the white room, in a white bed, in a white shift, sat a strange girl. Her thin face was spanned by a mouth that seemed strangely wide and bloodless. To the right and left of her eyes was a deep groove of shadow, and another from her nostrils to her chin. After all the strain that had been put upon her, the body was labouring to rid itself of that "whiff of ether," the poison in her nerve-fibres and cells. Dr. Umleit, who knew his business, could not understand why Frau Werner was always so sleepy, why she did not seem fresher and look better; but his instructions fell upon deaf ears. No one waked the patient all day; no one made her breathe deeply, and move the muscles of her arms; no one massaged the skin of her breast and back to loosen the pores again. A sleeping patient makes very little work; and sleep, after all, would do her so much good.

Only her thick brown plaits of hair and the steady eyes under the curved brows gave her visitor a familiar greeting. He stopped near the door with his right thumb in his new belt. In his left hand he held a great bunch of roses.

Sister Vilma had looked forward to this meeting, and she got up from the end of the bed, a wholesome summer-like figure, rosy and buxom. She had drawn a mental picture of the man in question; he was to be a private soldier. And so he was; but that brown, spectacled face yonder, clean-shaven, menacing, seemed to drive her from the room. She passed him with a shy, respectful "good morning"; his eyes seemed to look through her. And she went, to spread the news in the sister's room.

Bertin suddenly found himself on his knees by Lenore's bed, with his head against her poor thin body, which he could feel so clearly beneath the coverlet; and he felt his fingers clench. He tried so hard to hold back the tears that brimmed into his eyes; he fought and agonized, but at last he broke down and wept.

Lenore, exultant, and ecstatic, radiant with love, was caught up into the infinities of emotion. And yet tears, too, came into her eyes, tears of self-pity, and tears of gentle reproach; but the beloved, prostrate there at her side, made up for much. Dear lad—dear, dear wild lad.

She stroked his hair; it felt like a soft brush. Each caressing movement spoke of pardon. Now all was well.

"Don't cry. It's all right now. You are with me . . . don't worry any more." She had some difficulty in finding her words; what she felt and loved to feel was that this stage of the journey was now over. The merest gesture from him had disposed of Sister Vilma, and now he would keep her safe from all plagues and torments. Man and woman were surely two parts that made a whole. With a faint childish gurgle she smiled up at him, where he now sat on the edge of the bed; she let herself slide down on to her back, said: "I must sleep for a little while," laid her head happily against the pillows, and slipped away into a glow of deliverance. There was time before them; she saw before her a companionship without a break—today, tomorrow, always.

Bertin looked at his sleeping lady as he had done in very early days, when his still lonely self struggled with the visions of the mind. Music, the sweet, sad cadences of Schubert quartets, flooded his inner consciousness. Just as, at a certain level of talent, pain and effort are the marks of the artist, and must follow the first fine outburst of success, so they, who each suffered in their several ways, first came through suffering into a deeper intimacy. Must he once more convince her how utterly he was hers? She had never been prodigal of her feelings. But there she lay and slept, with him at her side; this was surely the most ardent declaration of love that a woman could make to a man, when she had suffered so grievously at his hands. He must now help her in every way he could. The surest way, which was to be with her—was, alas, out of his power; he must, indeed, make clear to her that they were to part. . . . The homely destinies of old days were then so constantly repeated. The man went off to war and left the woman that he loved in misery. But they would soon meet again; and when he was not there, she could live at home in peace and take care of herself. That story of the bad sausage at Wismar had served its purpose well; of his own part, the lure of the West that had made him volunteer for service there, he might, he thought, say nothing. Sleep, dear child, sleep, frail vessel of love; draw strength from sleep, and let me speak of what is past. We are living quickly now, we the generation of 1914. Deeds that must be done assail us like a storm, and out yonder there are worse still to be accomplished. We are not of those that think of themselves when the great ship Fatherland is caught in a hurricane; we are seized and swept onwards. You have suffered many horrors; but the earth, shaken by agonies far more horrible, is giving birth to a new world-consciousness, vast new soaring forces of creation. Aloof and alone we may no longer stand.

Those who have greatly suffered draw strength from sympathies near at hand. Words of regret and sorrow, when another hand has dealt the blow, pour balsam into the soul; for beyond all sense and reason the soul feels shattered and humbled, cowering beneath the judgment of angry gods, and gentle speech touches the most delicate fibres of her being, inspirits her, and gives her a new impulse towards recovery. For within each one of us today there is a child and a wild animal, and they are especially alert at times of weakness and distress.

As she awoke, Lenore felt the presence of her friend like a soothing magnetic influence. All she needed was that he should be there beside her to be looked at, and to look at her again. She peered at him through her thick lashes and pretended to be still asleep. She longed to dwindle into a bird and nestle in his hollowed hands. How steadfastly he gazed through the window at the blue sky! The line from his ear to the point of his chin had surely stiffened, and he was well shaved—as he had not always been. She must make him sit in his shirt-sleeves—the unfamiliar coarse serge offended her eyes. She laid her hand on his and said: "I'm awake, dear. It's so good to be with you. We'll have some lunch soon, I've ordered some for you. But take your tunic off."

He laughed. So she did not like a soldier in the room. He hung up his belt and tunic on a hook by the door. From a little distance the garment with the red squares on the collar and the blue shoulder-straps, had a queer and clumsy air in that sickroom. The scarf had to come off too—uniform must be worn complete or not at all. He then turned the corners of his shirt collar inwards, and sat just as he used to do on summer days, his adam's apple prominent above the hollow of his neck; now, all was well.

But all was not well. Had Werner always been as talkative as this, or was it that she had not noticed it? He told her about his journey to Berlin, made fun of himself and his own incompetence and experience, which made his new life so baffling sometimes. But his old life, his life as a writer for his living, though now in suspense, was flourishing; his, or rather their, fortunes were in the ascendant. One of his comrades, little Rosenthal, was reading the paper one day, when he asked: "Is this you that's mentioned here? You look like doing pretty well." He had begged Rosenthal to say nothing about it, and had brought the paper for her to see. He wanted to remain Private So-and-so of the Army Service Corps; he didn't want a fuss made about him.

To Lenore all this seemed tedious and strained; indeed it got on her nerves. She wanted to be cheered up; if he was going to talk, then let him talk to soothe her mind. He ought to say how sorry he was for his behaviour that day, and for all the needless troubles he had brought upon her. She would reply that it hadn't been so bad, and after all it had been partly her own fault; he mustn't worry about it. But first it must be clear that he was, in fact, worrying. And as she stroked his hand abstractedly, she wondered why he didn't take her in his arms and kiss her. Why did he go on like this? It was dreadful. But she forced herself to say: "Don't talk for a while; I'm getting a little tired. Darling—" She raised a frail arm from her nightdress, drew him down, closed his eyes with her fingers, and kissed him.

The day was long, and even between these two there was a certain awkwardness to be surmounted. The moment was not yet; but the moment would certainly come.

It did not come during lunch, nor did it come soon afterwards. The food, daintily prepared and served, was very welcome to Private Bertin; and he ate up what she left. Prussian rations did not include chicken, butter sauce, new potatoes, or stewed apricots. She was delighted to see his eager appetite, ordered some coffee for him, and told him to smoke. The fragrant atmosphere of a cigar was an aid to serious talk; she then could tell him from her heart what she had endured in these long weeks of her life. Cautiously she felt her way; didn't he want to hear how it had all happened; how lucky she and David had been, and how everything had gone well until now; and all that she had learnt?

But he held his hands to his ears. No, he would not listen to anything of the kind. One day, in peace and quiet, he would hear all that she had gone through for his sake; he would not shirk that story. But now his little girl must live in the future, be brave and go on loving him, even if he was not here. For he would not be here. She had always said that he wouldn't stay in Küstrin;

she had always been the brightest and the more foreseeing of the two of them. But she need not be afraid; it meant little more than a change of scene. The company was being transferred to Lille for garrison duty, and they were to move this very week, perhaps Wednesday, perhaps Thursday. Yes, so soon. But today he could sit at her side once more, and look at her and love her. It was only a few months' parting, scarcely longer than the long holidays of the year before. They would see each other again at least by the end of October, for in the autumn there would be peace. No one would dare call upon the troops for another winter campaign.

Lenore's eyes opened very wide. She turned right over on her pillows. "You're leaving me—you want to leave me!" She saw in a flash, like one about to drown, that this was why he had talked so incessantly before, and that he knew no defence against this blow. "You always told me not to talk nonsense when I told you this would happen," she added in almost a whisper, speaking to the wall so that he should not see that she was crying; "but you're so silly." What a poor wretch he was. She wanted to breathe in the warmth of his heart, and, with him beside her, to recover her energy and courage. Instead, he was going away. This was the end.

Sister Vilma appeared. She carried off the tray, and said that the Herr Doktor must now run away for an hour and let the little patient sleep according to the doctor's orders, so that she might soon get well and strong again. Sadly he left her.

He spent the hour in a neighbouring tea-shop. The Sunday afternoon silence of the empty rooms, with their marble tables, flies, and rows of cakes on glass shelves, recalled his slow empty holidays at home. He turned over the pages of various gaily coloured periodicals, which presented the war as an entertainment, or paid professional prophets to pronounce their blessing on this great epoch. What he read was but little to the credit of the writers. He, Bertin, would write nothing more until he had experienced something worthy to report. Now, he would soon be at the wars, but, alas, at the wrong moment. He felt honestly unhappy about it. The girl needed him as she needed water for her drinking, and he was to be torn from her side. He felt moved to poetry about it; but only six lines would come. He then realized that it would be well to leave in her hands a list of his short stories and articles; and he found he remembered them all.

At the stroke of half-past two he stopped. As he paid, the white-aproned waitress touched his hand; she had soft brown eyes, but he did not notice her. He found Lenore awake and sitting up in bed, with cushions at her back. Rosy of face and with shining eyes, she greeted him as he came in. Her brother David was ambling about the room in radiant good humour.

All was going splendidly at home; no one had the slightest suspicion, the picture postcards sent by his school friend Peter Prinz, from Mecklenberg, had produced the desired effect. The parents, too, had written; they would arrive at the Anhalt station at five o'clock on the evening of the 28th; a week later, Lene could be sent away again to recover from this wretched attack of sausage-poisoning—to some quiet watering-place, where there would be few distractions as the long holidays were nearly over. "This must be the end of trips to Wismar and the study of brick Gothic, my child," Mamma would say in a tone of mild reproof; and her housewifely heart might inspire a letter to the Editor of the local Potsdam paper to warn the public of the perils of indulging in sausages in the height of summer, more especially in Pomerania and Mecklenburg. Lenore could not help laughing, and it hurt her to laugh. "Tell him, David, how you thought he could manage to stay with me."

David set his youthful countenance into an impressive frown. "You will just have to disappear for a few days, Bertin."

Bertin looked at him with an uncomprehending air; what could David be thinking of? It was quite out of the question. A sort of fear possessed him; such a device might be tried, but it would bring him into conflict with all the powers that ruled his present existence. The idea was that he should not go back that night, but lie hidden for a few days in civilian clothes (provided by David) until his troop train had departed. If David could get one of his acquaintances, a lad called Albert Loth, to take a hand in the venture, some kind of nervous breakdown could be arranged and reported to his company commander. Private Bertin had had a breakdown on the journey, or something of the kind. He could then come and seen Lenore three or four times until she was well on the mend; then the doctor would report him as fit to travel, he could return to Küstrin and join his company in due course. Yes, and be marked down as a coward; and torn from the pleasant companionship of the company to which he belonged, which had accepted him almost as a club accepts a new member, and where he now had thirty or more very good friends. . . . With these men he had worked, eaten, slept, and lived in close association for thirteen weeks; as they worked, he talked to them and told them stories—of the life of Friedrich Schiller, and the solitary Lessing, the structure of the universe, the bewildering physical facts that first made possible the existence of life upon the earth; he remembered expounding to them that water was not at its heaviest at zero but at four degrees above, so that the sea could never freeze from the bottom upwards. Was he now to spoil all this, and find himself thrust into a position of doubtful prominence, or be attached to another unit and sent away with it? Or, at the worst, get himself court-martialled, with the result that Lenore's illness might conceivably become known. Not a bit of it, and he laughed David's proposals aside. He was too old to play Indians, and the army authorities were not distinguished by a sense of humour.

Upon which the boy replied curtly that he should have thought of all that before. It was now his duty to think of his lady as well.

Bertin answered in a mild and deprecating tone; common sense was at his back; but the boy insisted that he could not go, he wasn't a loaf of bread or a railway truck, he had a will and a head of his own; he must definitely stay in Berlin, or it would be difficult to get the lady into good shape and on her legs again.

Bertin appealed for help to Lenore, who was looking anxiously from one young man to the other. These two must not quarrel. Werner's reasons, as he now explained them, threw light on his attitude. He must not run into danger on her account. Against so mighty an engine as the German army the individual was really powerless. She would soon reconcile herself to the inevitable, and if she went to the Baltic or somewhere of the kind to convalesce, she would make an effort to get gradually well even though he was not there.

David observed the other as though he had been some strange beast from distant forests. They had certainly beaten him into shape, if indeed much of that process had been necessary. "It is sweet and noble to make others die for the Fatherland," he reflected, adapting the Horatian tag in such frequent use for school essays. And when Bertin thanked the lad indulgently for all he had done for his sister and himself, which, indeed, gave him the right to speak as he liked, David blew out his nostrils. "There's a slight mistake there, sir, I did nothing for *you.*" And turned away. And each thought the other a fool.

David soon departed. Brother and sister merely exchanged a long silent glance.

Left alone, the lovers had much, and nothing, to say to each other. Old times were talked over, and hopes warmed up afresh for times to come. Bertin showed Lenore the little photographs of her that he always carried with him. A certain yellow envelope was not yet in her hands; which showed how chances may shift with the purposes of men. They knew each other now too well for any illusion to disturb the essential bond between them. "You should have asked," she interjected once, and he: "I can't bear it now," as he had said before. He read her the six lines he had written and she thought them good. Her eyes burned into him, and his eyes learned her face by heart, her neck, the soft lines of her shoulders, and her bare arms. Love means torment, and the acceptance of that torment. While life exists, nothing is final, he had said at the decisive moments of his youthful novel.

And, afternoon faded, the light grew more golden, the green hue of evening slid across the sky, twilight filled the room, and in the corners already lurked the fear of solitude; then it was eight o'clock, and supper came; and then it was nine.

When the arc lamps began to glow in the streets below, Bertin took leave of Lenore, not much more vehemently than at Küstrin or Wilkersdorf. He held her in his arms, as she leaned weakly against him, felt her hands folded round his neck, and kissed her damp face. "Nothing's going to happen to me, I belong to you—so that I can try to make up for it all," he stammered.

This awful parting! She felt as though, with him, a piece of flesh had been taken from her breast. "Come back to me safe," she said, and then their fingers loosened.

He backed towards the door, her eyes caught and held him with their agonized entreaty, the more compelling in the half darkness. He had to catch a particular train, and there was a two hours' journey before him. This he said to himself at the end of the corridor; but he could not go, he turned and tiptoed clumsily along the passage and burst once more into her room.

She was still sitting upright, her arms outstretched upon the bed, her wide eyes and parted lips raised to meet the brightness of the evening sky.

"You," he cried. "You!"

She thrust out her arms and gripped him by the shoulders, "You," she answered.

A wild surge of longing strained them against each other's hearts.

That night, just about the time he was leaving Küstrin station and showing his leave warrant, she sat up and looked about the darkened room with a sensation of awful sickness. This man had gone away, asked no questions, and had let himself be loaded like a sheep on to a truck; it must have turned her stomach to think of it as she lay and dreamed. She wanted to change her soaked and clinging nightdress, and she wanted a cold compress for her forehead. She pressed the bell, but no one came. It was Sunday night, in high summer; even sisters are human beings, and must go off duty some time.

Chapter 5

SEPARATION

In the dim places of the soul, life is often kindled from defiance. "This won't do," she calls to her possessor. "Come, is not mobilization the order of the day? Summon your hosts and send them forth. Let us see whether this departing gentleman is to have the triumph of defeating you." It is not a wholesome energy that is thus stimulated, and some kind of reaction will surely follow. But for the time being one does not trouble about such prospects, which is very wise. For he who would extract and use only what is good in the chemical processes of human decisions and achievements, would be far too deeply occupied.

From the hour of Bertin's departure, Lenore Wahl pulled herself together. She slept less during the day, she exercised the muscles of her arms, calmly demanded massage, and asked Dr. Umleit how she could most quickly recover her strength. With David's help she stood up for the first time, though indeed she at once collapsed on to the bed. She practised walking; after her first tottering attempts, the same sort of faintness came over her that she had experienced in the room of Marie Nocks; no matter. No matter—it was her favourite phrase. It came from Kleist, her favourite author, and expressed a veiled defiance, freedom, and indifference in the face of destiny. She began to read again; his *Marquise von O* to begin with, *The Earthquake in Chile* and other short tales. Then she sent for *Mathilde Möhring* and drew courage and good humour from the pages of this little masterpiece, which had been found in Theodor Fontane's writing-table after he was dead. Later, ten or fifteen years later, she often thought that she would have got well quicker with the help of gramophones and wireless, but Mathilde's life and example, her obstinate Berlin courage, her kindly progress to prosperity, and her redescent into misfortune, borne with such demure composure, her marvellous adaptability—all this, and the crystal clarity of the prose, would not have thus impressed itself upon her, so deeply that the recollection would never fade. One could read oneself well, just as one could read oneself ill, she reflected, as she laid the book, when the time came, on the night table. Her room was expensive, the clinic cost money—there the money lay in her trunk; Bertin's advance against future success. She was pleased when David showed her the banknotes that he came to fetch; what delighted her was not that they were there, but that they were growing fewer. She thought much about Bertin, and in a kindly spirit; but there was a touch of bitterness within her that stirred her against him, presented him as ridiculous, and stigmatized his cowardice. Hardly had she fallen asleep when she began to hate him in her dreams; she forgot it when she awoke, but ever thinner grew the film which divided that bitterness from her consciousness. The sham wedding ring on the thin finger of her right hand became for her a symbol; she talked affectionate nonsense to it, full of perilous undertones of pardon. As the day approached on which she would have to leave the clinic, though she was not really fit to go, her indignation burst forth at last: not against her parents on whose account she had to leave, but against Bertin.

He sent her a photograph of his half-section, ten men with packs complete, picturesquely grouped round Sergeant Schwerdtlein; field-caps, great-coats rolled up above their packs, slung with bread-bags, water-bottles, drinking-cups, all in high boots, and complete with a slate inscribed in chalk: "Good-bye! 11th half-sect. 1st comp. A.S.C. battalion X/20." And dated: "Day before entrainment, Küstrin." She reckoned rapidly, with the absurd picture in her hands; then, at that very hour, the train was perhaps making its way round Berlin, or even across the city, on its journey to the West. "It's too bad," she cried, to the open windows, as she became aware of angry tears between her eyelids. He insulted her with this scrap of shiny paper; his expression looked resolute and martial, his departure for the West seemed to her only a continuation of that process of escape by which he kept his ears closed against the brutality of life—he could not even bring himself to hear what she had had to suffer in her own body. He could hardly have got himself omitted from that friendly group—but this she would not admit. "Good-bye, Herr Werner," she said, ripped the photograph across, and tore one of the two halves into small pieces. Later on, when, to avoid attracting attention, she picked up the bits and looked at them again, she found Werner undamaged on the untorn half, and put him in the Fontane book—between the pages, as it happened, on which Mathilde descants mockingly on men.

To recover her freshness, she needed one week more of rest and recuperation; the weakness of her back, her knee-joints, and of her fluttering heart, cried out for it. But that week, spent away from home, would mean discovery and ruin, for in the course of it her now rejuvenated parents with tanned cheeks and beaming faces were to arrive at the Anhalt station. So Lenore had to get up and pack her belongings, though no one believed that she had the strength to do it, and she least of all. Besides which she could not feel much better until the tooth, that raging grinding pain in her cheek, had ceased to rob her of a part of her energy. Moreover, these last three days did not prove very restorative. She tossed from side to side in bed—(How often did she hear: "You *must* lie still, Frau Werner!")—clutched at the coverlet, struck nervously at every fly, meaning only to chase away her thoughts—or rather, her one thought, that seemed to buzz about her and settle on her skin and suck her blood; and this thought was—Now he has gone, now the coward has really gone. . . .

Many hundred thousand soldiers pull themselves together better than I, she thought, as she went downstairs on David's arm to Dr. Umleit's room, to say good-bye.

From the clinical point of view, the doctor could let her go without hesitation; but humanly speaking, he viewed his patient with fatherly concern. "Still a bit shaky, Fräulein Wahl," he said as he held her hand between his warm palms, dry from incessant washing. "Will you be able to look after yourself?"

Lenore nodded without speaking, sturdily disavowing the gloom that possessed her heart. She was filled with horror at the prospect of going forth again into the hot summer tumult of existence; but she was filled with no less horror at the strong and gross life-impulses that burst into being where the sisters came into contact with the more lightly wounded men, amid a reek of carbolic and bandages, and clouds of buzzing flies. She longed to find a cave and crawl into it; but behind all her inner visions she saw a train speeding westwards, in a compartment of which sat a small clear-cut figure, Private Bertin, a doll carved from the substance of her thoughts. A thread, woven of the most delicate nerve-fibre, stretched between him and her; it grew longer and longer, and drained away her courage. "I should take my burden upon me," his voice suddenly rung in her ear, an illusive echo of his words at Dr. Lederer's round table those many months ago; even his faint Silesian accent.

Liar, what a liar!

This gave her a shock and she gripped the arms of her chair.

Dr. Umleit blew out his cheeks sympathetically as he fingered his short moustache. "That's only weakness," he said confidently; "and we'll soon deal with that." And he wrote out a tonic for Lenore, small doses of a blood-forming specific, mixed with iron and arsenic. Antidote against love's poison, he thought, as he added his clear and legible signature in the corner of the prescription. He was inwardly recalling a passage in *Tristan und Isolde* where the confusion of poison and antidote in affairs of love had, with Isolde's voice, so haunted him in his Munich days.

Once more David Wahl had to think of everything. He asked the Doctor for a second prescription against sudden attacks of faintness, so that Lenore might seem in good health during her first week at home.

Dr. Umleit nodded approvingly. "That's thoughtful of you, Herr Wahl," he said, as he wrote out a second prescription. He really wanted to say something even more complimentary, but he did not, as he thought that David would probably resent it. "In good health, eh? For the parents' benefit?" he asked, with his eyes tactfully turned to the paper, while Lenore sat between the round arms of the chair beside the writing-table, with but the faintest flush of colour in her face. "But we can't help looking a little pale, can we?"

Lenore pulled a wry face. "I'll buy some rouge," she said. "I'll carry through my part like any other actress." "I am taking my burden upon me," she said inaudibly to a point moving into the far distance.

Dr. Umleit smiled. When life looked like crushing them, these delicate women had to circumvent it with their little arts and devices, but for that very reason they would defeat it. In the event of any further trouble he gave her a little bottle of dark syrupy substance, a very ancient specific, ergot, made up in the latest fashion. He said he thought it might be awkward for either of them to ask for the drug in a Potsdam chemist's shop.

David had already been to the office and paid the account, the amount of which was not unreasonable, though it made a large inroad on their resources. No mention was made of Dr. Umleit's professional services, in case of any unwelcome attentions on the part of the public prosecutor.

Then Lenore got up out of her chair; she had come here to mark the end of an episode, the lowest point that her line of life had touched, and to emerge once again out of the peril from which this white-clad man had rescued her. She gave him her hand again. "Thank you very much, Herr Doktor, for everything," she said. Everything? That, in this case, meant a great deal; skill, knowledge—well and truly learned, and human kindliness, without which the earth would have long since been depopulated, and the race of men have perished. Such an experience stirred responsive forces, and among them, gratitude; to these, her grave voice, her long look into the doctor's eyes, bore witness.

He held her frail fingers, though his mind was already elsewhere, as an urgent case was awaiting him in Room No. 4, and he only heard Lenore's words: "In such a difficult time. . . . But one always seems to find the right person."

"One does what one can," he answered. "Good-bye."

And in that moment both felt their courage renewed.

Then, with a faint smile, she looked about her once again and, on David's arm, left the white room and the white-clad man within it.

The padded baize door closed between them; Dr. Umleit turned to wash his hands for the twentieth time that morning; Lenore walked slowly, step by step, down the stairs into the tree-shaded courtyard, flecked with the harsh dark blue shadows of high summer. Both thought of each other with real sympathy, and both knew that, however near at hand their lives might pass, they would never meet again.

Lenore did not turn. She heard a bitter voice within her say: I have taken my burden upon me. What was left? The man invented phrases and then went off to France. Something that held us together, Herr Bertin, disappeared here in a bucket. Sister Mieze had said that it was about the size of a cherry.

It is a common experience that all pain vanishes in a dentist's anteroom; but a sensible person sees through these subconscious illusions, and sits, quivering inwardly, in the martyr's chair with the little gurgling basin at his left.

Lenore cautiously touched the ailing tooth with her finger. "This one refuses to take its burden upon it," she said with a wry expression, washing her mouth out once again. "Please take it out."

Dr. Samson tapped the tooth, which held firm. "That would be a pity," he said, manipulating his mirror. "With a little patience we can save it. If we took teeth out in that way, the human race soon wouldn't have any teeth at all."

"I've wasted enough patience on it," answered Lenore, "and I want to be rid of it at last." But she trembled, as she had never done when she had been a girl of seven.

Brother and sister were very much at home in their dentist's consulting-room. David, pacing up and down, and admiring Dr. Samson's new instruments, especially the electric drill, explained that his sister had been poisoned by a bad sausage while travelling and that was why she was sitting there in that nervous apprehensive state.

Dr. Samson, his firm and gentle fingers already holding the instrument at Lenore's lips, listened inattentively. There were two lines of gloom and bitterness at the corners of his closed mouth, which gave his erect figure a look of age. He found the trouble, painted the tooth with a local anæsthetic, and began to drill it carefully, stopping constantly to ease the pain.

Her sweat of fear and throbbing heart she could not control; with a deep breath Lenore marked the end of the ordeal. When should she come again, asked David, rightly interpreting the looks and sounds that came from her as she washed her mouth out.

"Not to me in any case," answered Dr. Samson. "I must hand you over to my deputy or successor. I have to report for service tomorrow."

"Good God!" cried David Wahl.

And the dentist, one of the most famous in Berlin, nodded ironically. He had been called up before his time to join the artillery as an N.C.O. He had made the mistake of calling at the Ministry of War about three weeks ago, to urge the establishment of an army dental service, his pockets full of scientific material demonstrating the damaging effect of bad teeth on the fighting power of large formations, especially as the food of the rank and file was often indigestible. But he had gone, it seemed, to just the wrong place. He had been confronted with the corpse of a major behind a writing-table, whose jaws, however, still functioned, and were soon rasping out contempt of his proposal; that wouldn't do at all, they knew very well who were trying to fix up soft jobs for themselves, and they would not forget *him*. As a result of which he had found the familiar yellow form, appropriately filled up, among his morning post the day before.

"That's what you get for being patriotic," said Dr. Samson. "They're responsible for the people's health, and they'll make a nice mess of it. I don't much mind for myself," he added grimly; "it will be a pleasant change to look at something other than my respected patients' jaws and gums, and to smell different smells. But who will suffer if people like us are to be used for sitting on gun limbers? But you'll be well looked after by Fräulein Dr. Slonsky." He was a solid figure, with short hair already going grey, and a calm and steady face grotesquely distorted at the moment in the glittering mirror attached to his drill.

"Now for the hairdresser; my hair is all sticky with sweat."

On the blue-covered back seat of the rattling cab, brother and sister gazed down the great thoroughfare that stretched away to the Underground station in the distance. The driver was muttering curses to himself, not unmixed with threats. He, too, had received his calling-up notice that morning, and had torn it up in his fury, though he had subsequently collected the bits and put them in his pocket; his orders were to report to the same artillery regiment as Dr. Samson, in front of whose house he was accustomed to stand; and neither of them knew that Fate intended to bring them into close connexion, and finally to carry them both back to Berlin. Angrily he glared at the black-white-red colours with which assiduous home-warriors had decked their windows in honour of the latest victories; the Germans had taken Ivangorod, Novogeogievsk, and Warsaw, and into the latter city, as the report stated, Prince Leopold of Bavaria, after breaking through the outer and the inner forts, had made a triumphal entry. "Breaking through?" sneered Gieske, cab-driver, of the Gossowstrasse, with a grim smile. "It was others that did the breaking through; they lie quiet now and hold their tongues. And he drives into Warsaw in his fifty horse-power car. Pah! What a filthy world it is." So saying he spat upon the pavement, and he had to check his right arm sharply as it was about to bring the whip across the hindquarters of the faithful old brown horse Viktoria, as she jogged unweariedly along in front of the cab. "No, Viki, no," he said. "It isn't your fault. You didn't want the war either."

A young lady with a high colour and red lips, her hair carefully combed and puffed and waved, but with weary eyes and movements, left the hairdressing establishment of one Amalie Gannaz, whose husband had been called up ten weeks before, and was also in the Army Service Corps at Küstrin.

"Potsdam station," said the young man, with a glance at the clock on the taximeter. But the red-faced driver had been honest, turned off the ticking meter while he was waiting.

BOOK FOUR

BY THE BITTER WATERS

Chapter 1

STOCKTAKING

A little dog, just saved from drowning by his master's fist, and flung into the boat, will not be very fastidious about his accommodation. It is enough that he has been snatched from that engulfing substance that yields so treacherously beneath his paws, and in some mysterious fashion grips and yet eludes him; he is content to lie down somewhere, and feel the air, and peace, and safety. Not until a little while has passed will he get up and wag his tail, shake his dripping coat, and gratefully lick the hand that grabbed him just in time.

It was thus that Fräulein Wahl buried herself in the sand of the fishing village called Tramsin. The beach was a vista of deserted digging operations; the little builders of all the walls and trenches were once more back in their schools and nurseries, dreaming perhaps of their masterly erections of sand. In a especially lofty castle, that promised protection from the world outside, Fräulein Wahl had found a refuge—she lay curled up in the sun, let the gritty powder run through her fingers, and shook it over her breast and knees. She tried not to think, but only to exist, to feel the warm air against her body, and to breathe.

Far better to have gone to the mountains of central Germany. There, the warm breath of sunlit forest soil, the sharp air of mountain peaks and gorges, would have sent her home content and sane in a few weeks. But the sea, best of all playgrounds for the healthy, has in such cases as hers just the opposite effect. The dampness of the atmosphere relaxes the nerves, and the prevailing mood is one of strain and melancholy; like a burning-glass, the glaring waste of waters concentrates its dark radiance on to the enfeebled body; the incessant murmur of the ocean, its infinite circumference, its unchanging imprint upon the sea-shore, are but too apt a setting for nerves and sadness and depression, especially when a human soul is inwardly mourning for a little child. Then thoughts and feelings brood upon that injury, that squandering of youth, "tædium vitæ," the corrosion of life, stands written on the horizon. How shall the salt-laden air, or the breath of the bitter waters in which life was born, contend against such melancholy? She might not swim—the chill of sea water was forbidden. This was another blow at her peace of mind. In other days she had loved to plunge into the water and wave a defiant hand at the moon. Now, after so small a matter—("Why, you'll be on your legs in a week, or at most ten days.")—she was deprived of these delights. She was deprived, too, of the long walks, to which the limitless distances might well have tempted her. She was only allowed short stretches, with frequent rests; like her old Aunt Minchen. For her knees were rather inclined to be weak; she sometimes felt suddenly giddy and faint, and it would have been disagreeable to collapse on the beach of Tramsin and lie there like a derelict seal. So she took her walks in the cheerful company of the trees.

Forest? Yes, there was forest. From the heart of that country it surged forward on to the steep cliff west of the estuary, where the Slav fishermen of Tramsin had planted their little settlement. A vast array of beeches with great gnarled roots lay like an encamped host on the white flint-scattered cliff slope. It was marvellous to gaze through the grey-flecked stems; there was a faint breeze in the translucent air, below lay the expanse of murmurous blue-green waters; and after the dazzling glitter outside, the shadow-roof of the tree-tops was a rest and a relief. It was only strange that, here, the joy of the forest lasted such a little while. A pressure upon the heart made breathing difficult. Fräulein Wahl walked painfully; her back hurt her. In search of sympathy she stroked Boll's brown head, as he stared gravely upwards at the shining sky. Yonder, at the edge of a clearing, it was pleasant to sit on a bench and read, or do nothing. But her restlessness drove her onwards, along narrow paths between tall ferns, further and further into the forest. It was haunted, even in broad daylight. Bearded dwarfs, in the form of lichens and mosses, swung from the branches like pendant corpses. Above, the forest was never silent; trunks and branches groaned, dry twigs snapped and fell. Her feet stirred odours of decay, fungous exhalations from damp mouldering leaves.

In open spaces, with the sun full upon her, beads of sweat stood out upon her skin, the air was heavy with heat and moisture. But no sooner had she passed into the half-light of the cooler places than she was overcome with fear of the great citadels of the ants, their black and red marching columns, and the sharp pincers of their soldiers. No fallen tree and no stump was safe from their onslaught. Their heaps rise up in the untrodden wilderness like termites' hills. And between the tree-trunks loathsome cobwebs, full a yard across, float out of the twilight on filmy cables that no eye can see. Shuddering at the thought that such a glistening weft might touch her face, she would fly to the sunlight and the open.

A fortnight of solitude gives everyone a chance to test what survives after a cataclysm of all values. On what could she now rely? The current of events in which she had been moving flung up bubbles into her consciousness, gleams and reflections that gave the girl new insight into Bertin, as she sat throwing sticks into the water for her dog. She observed, while sauntering down the plank walk to the beach, that she had been retracing in her mind the events of the past few weeks, and suddenly she started at the sight of a thistle. "That," she thought, "is I." It so happened that a foolish passerby had beheaded it with his stick; none the less, the truncated end still bloomed, its blue and lilac corona still attracted small blue butterflies, and through its parched yellow and grey-green fibres the sap of life still flowed. Thistles were much in favour with donkeys, she recalled in mocking allusion to someone who wore a grey uniform, and it is their proper destiny to be dealt with in this fashion.

There lay the sea, vast steadfast, passive like a woman; wave upon wave sweeps up the beach, leaves its imprint, and is no more. The sea, so constantly vexed by the violence of the wind, has little profit from that steadfastness. Even so, the male element plunges down upon the woman's womb, leaves its seed, and departs. But the glory of life is embodied in that onslaught; and where fear of it prevails, life dwindles into a stagnant pool, serving only to mirror the passing birds or gather up the scattered drops of rain. We may weep, we may clench our little fists, but in the depths of us we feel the same surging force of life that courses through the bruised veins of that broken thistle.

Her fellow-guests in the Pension, more particularly a white-haired building contractor from Rostock, who was partial to his bottle of claret, were well disposed to a pretty young creature of good family, slim and tanned, agreeably taciturn, and certainly not inclined for adventures. She took warm sea baths, lay a great deal in the sun, and had plainly been through some ordeal, as indeed was clear from the grave lines round her eyes and pallid lips. She received many letters, all in the same handwriting, through the field post. The old contractor thought respectfully of what these little women had to endure at that time; it was a bad time for young blood, but, please God, great times would soon be here. It was fortunate that the young lady could find comfort in such solid books as she took down to the beach.

But she found difficulty in reading. She could not, indeed, bring herself to read poetry at all. Half a page of Jakob Burckhardt—and between her and the buildings of the Piræus rose the vision of a gigantic Frau Nocks, waving a white towel, or kind Dr. Umleit with his dreadful instrument, Sister Vilma trying to humiliate her, or Sister Mieze saying softly: "It's all out now." She would close the book with a shiver and fall to drawing circles in the sand. . . . What was the use of her now? What should she do with herself? How, in God's name should she shake off all this? She smoothed the hair back from her forehead, sat down, and plaited it into two plaits, gazed at the peaceful shore about her, the smoke of passing steamers, infinitesimal on the far horizon, and the warships that practised gun-fire at night; those who heard them started up in bed, their hearts stood still, and plaster pattered down from the walls. Was there anything now to distinguish her, Lenore Wahl, from those working women who had seemed so utterly alien to her, when she sat among them in her Sunday best in Büderling's garden at Küstrin? Nothing; except her parents' wealth that provided the padding for her life—her parents, whom she conciliated, or deceived. If she failed, if anything was discovered of what she had been through in those last months, she would find herself in far worse case than a girl of the people. The great red barrack of the prison-house began to assume a crass reality, and crushed her like a fly. Her thoughts went further: could Herr Bertin protect her if Wahl the banker, of Parkring II, Potsdam, declined to continue to support her, because he no longer approved of her mode of life? Would that kindly old gentleman, Herr Berthold Bertin, of Kreuzburg, offer her shelter because his son had got her into trouble, now that she was no longer a distinguished and desirable connexion, but portionless and desolate? Not a bit of it, Fräulein Wahl, you may not close your eyes to the facts. Defy society, and society will expel you; you must fend for yourself as best you can. Fräulein Wahl had allowed herself to be educated, to be turned into an attractive young lady whose destiny was marriage, an agreeable husband, agreeable children, and an agreeable life. Instead of which she had gone her own way, a strange and rather painful way, and she must now face the just consequences of her acts. Alas, this was in fact beyond her. A girl's brain, weakened by loss of blood, cannot generalize from her own position, and forthwith recognize as allies the unknown multitudes, who are defenceless and dependent on the mighty Wahls of this world. Still, one day it might be otherwise. The wise are never defeated, and he whom the gods love need no more than one stroke of the lash.

Yes, so it was . . . but this helped her little—here and now. How was she to order her life when she was well and went back home? She had founded her existence on the companionship of a man of mind, on her efforts to help him in his work, on her powers of criticism, on her pleasure in watching over him from the background, delighting in his successes, which were her successes also. But now that she wanted to hear of him no more, this dream had lost its value. Everywhere she looked she saw only her own shadow, and the hated form of one whom she had loved. He had turned out a poor creature; and the judgment fell. All that she had learned and dreamed and planned and suffered had gone for nothing; that she had to admit, and therewith her utter bankruptcy. And by a wretched chance, he had done his best to exasperate her wrath by a letter which she had found against her coffee-pot that morning, stamped with the field postmark of the Fourth Army.

Chapter 2

LETTER-GUIDE FOR LOVERS

When sleep has gone and will not return, it is easy to be up early and carry a heavy heart through the stillness of the dawn. Grey lies the sea, rippling faintly against the pale sand; from the sun, hidden behind forest and village, comes a wan heralding glory—it is going to be very hot today. Then, along the great stretch of resilient sand, which the dews of night have made more firm, accompanied by her dog, wanders a slim figure in a white skirt and a white woollen jacket—the only perpendicular object to be seen. The tireless gurgling trill of the lark's song goes with her.

This veiled clarity, the light in which life was born, one creature certainly found little to his liking: Boll. Where was the wind that so gloriously stirred the sea, and the white-crested waves into which a dog could plunge like a winged thing, and come up, with a bewilderment that never failed, spluttering the foam out of his jaws? And then dash along by the water's edge, scaring every sea-gull, leaping over every stone, and fighting gigantic battles with every washed-up log. This morning there was only the Fräulein, and Boll felt bored. Suddenly she tapped him on the nose, as though inviting him to a race, and his little stump of tail quivered with anticipatory joy. Then she started; but she only ran a few steps for appearance's sake, before she fell back with a rueful laugh. But Boll put his head down between his forepaws and let the coiled muscles beneath his gleaming skin race on alone. Lenore watched him, and recalled a day when she too had dashed off on such a wild career, one Sunday to Küstrin and Tamsel.

Away ahead, where the dunes almost reached the sea, they met once more, Boll waiting gravely until she whom it was his duty to protect had come up with him again. There were shadows now, sky and sea shone forth in many colours, the great orb was moving upwards. . . .

Thus, in due order, the day began. In her bedroom the tub was filled with warm sea-water. She looked almost as she used to do, except that the appearance was deceptive, she ate her roll and butter and honey and drank her good brown coffee with a healthy appetite, though she really ought to have been careful about the coffee, which had a depressing effect on her. And there, insistent on the breakfast table, propped against the blue-patterned jug, stood a letter or a postcard from Bertin, and the paralysing present had hold of her again. Every day, or every other day, he sent four affectionate closely written pages. She opened every one of them with a thrill which even she felt to be pathetic. Had such a thing ever happened before? For two whole years this man had been involved in the most trifling incidents of her life. There was not a book, nor a dress, hardly even a pair of shoes that she bought without consulting him: whether he was near by, or during the holidays, far away at his home, his mind was always with her in all her affairs, he supported her against parental inhibitions, strengthened her own impulses, set her right when she went astray, and all in gentleness and kindness. Now he was shamming dead. Anyone can run away from things, he used to say in condemnation of those who did so, and what was he doing now? He was sacrificing to his own self-respect like the meanest and most conventional citizen. What did not suit him simply did not exist. Had he grown insensitive? By no means. His letters proved how unweariedly he noticed all the little things of every-day. Only of her affairs he would not speak, he locked his heart against the sense of guilt. It was no doubt very encouraging for her to know that he was employed as an interpreter and visited farms to borrow implements, which he was very careful to return; and how he talked on friendly terms with the woman and children; and how, for want of better tools, they had spent days cutting the wheat out of the wire entanglements with pocket knives. This, no doubt, was the sort of news to send a lady whom he had left in all her miseries to depart for France. He descanted on the various ways of fortifying positions—by a framework of wicker, timber balks, or by cutting transverse canals through the ashen subsoil; all of which devices might have to be undone when the sergeant, or even the lieutenant or the captain took over from the sapper corporal. He told her about the fighting in the air, and assured her that very little damage was done by the bursting shrapnel. Did he suppose that all this interested her? Let him stay shut up in Fort Bondues, eating wooden cheese and mouldy bread. It was always himself, nothing but himself; what moved and struck him, what went through his head, what made him glad, or restless, or despondent. In one letter he announced complacently that he had discovered humanity. In the company of English prisoners, Belgian workmen, and French townsmen, he had become truly aware that humanity was one; the differences were only on the surface. The humanity about which he had heard so often in the lectures at the university was no more than an artificial concept, an instrument of thought—that he now realized. The unity of the human race had suddenly impressed itself upon him in bodily guise, when he grasped that there was no cleavage between himself and these so-called foreigners; only a common life, and a deeply rooted understanding. Excellent, Herr Bertin; why not work it all out in detail for the benefit of a lady to whom you have no more important news to offer. And when he wrote in the language of love—that, indeed, was worse still. Then he became positively fatuous. He acted as if nothing had happened. He could not conceive her changed. She loved him, she was dependent on him, she belonged to him, no matter what he had inflicted on her. "Fool," she thought bitterly, as she put away his letter (still unopened) in her white enamelled chest of drawers; "try some more advice; tell me to be strong, implore me to forget and to live in the future. Oh, you will soon see what has come of it all—you and your fine promises to make up to me for what I have endured. What are you, after all? A passing acquaintance now grown so tiresome that I had better strike this page out of my life; a man who gives a girl a child and then goes away. To the war, it is true; that sounds well, no doubt, but it is really no more than an excuse. If you had liked, you could have taken the risk and disappeared that day you came to see me at the clinic. Was there anything to prevent your staying behind, and spending ten days with people you knew, among the many millions in that great city? In ten days you could have emerged and taken your punishment, if you could not get them to believe that you had fallen sick, or sprained your ankle or something of the kind. Then I should have known that you still loved me, that you valued my affection; and your cruelty would have been passed over with a laugh and forgiven. My brother David at such a moment would have jumped out of a moving train. But you, my friend, slipped away to the war like a coward, and had not even the sense to see what you were doing. Well"—and she gripped the salt grass with angry hands, and tore up the tough stalks by the roots—"well, you will be surprised. This time you will not have your way; we have finished with each other, as you will soon find out."

One evening, sick beyond endurance of the brief friendly notes with which she usually put him off, and for which she made weakness her excuse, she poured her heart out. On the thick dark grey paper that she then used, with the letters L.W. in the top left-hand corner, she let her fury loose. Page after page, sixteen in all before she had finished. She addressed him formally as "You" and "Herr Bertin"; thus and thus you did to me, and thus and thus I feel about what you have done. She seized him by the hair, as she used to do with her doll Lottchen in other days, shook him, and flung him into a corner to be thrown away. Hurriedly she addressed the envelope in a large indignant script. Then her hands sank down exhausted; she went to bed. For a long time she lay awake, while her heart ebbed slowly towards rest. She became aware of terrifying noises all about her. Like the gnawing of some devilish rat, the death-watch beetle ticked in a piece of furniture. In the coolness of the night, timber that had grown dry in the heat of day, cracked as though heavy footsteps were moving over the planking; like porters carrying sacks full of wasted hours and murdered hopes. The wind whined venomously round the corner of the house, and through the open windows flies buzzed shrilly against the gauze curtains, the sea rustled and murmured like a marsh that gurgles as it sucks its victims down. Thus, as she at last fell asleep with tear-stained face, lonely as she had never been since she was born, the threads that led from her to the man Bertin grew slack and tangled. The searchlights of home-coming ships moved through the darkness across her sleeping form.

Next morning she again held those four sheets in her hand. On her way to the shore below, the letter-box awaited her; she had but to raise the blue envelope and drop it in. Yes, it was her duty to make a clean sweep and send it now. And yet her conscience bade her think once more before she did so. Two years of youthful comradeship could not be severed like a cucumber from its stalk. Today the satisfaction in the deed had gone from out of her; Boll snuffed impatiently at her side, gave her his paw, got up on his hind legs and pulled at her arm, to make her put down the letter and take him at last for his morning walk; she had slept longer than ever before. Very well; a suitable hour would come when she could take up these barbed sentences again, and brace herself for the conflict. For the present she would put it in a drawer and go.

A day passed like many that had gone before. She bathed, read, walked, and rested in the sand. Lunch was large and good; Tramsin was at the edge of a very fertile province, and beside a sea that swarmed with fish. Then she undressed, lay on her bed, and slept. Tea in the afternoon freshened her again, she was glad to saunter between the sea and the woods. For dinner she changed into a light frock, and sipped a little soft red wine, which the doctor had recommended, and the old building contractor chosen for her. Then she wandered forth once more into the green evening, still postponing the moment when she should look once more at certain grey sheets of notepaper. It was good to have written down her fury, bitterness, and just hatred, with ink that did not fade, and on paper that would hold it safe. Whenever Herr Bertin received this letter, he would feel a shock at the knee-joints; his little eyes would goggle with amazement and his great ears wag with desperation. It was pleasant to imagine all this; but the realization had better be postponed. Perhaps he would grow more sensitive and more observant, when bad times came upon him too; he might be transferred from Lille, just as he had only stayed a few months in Küstrin. He was having a hard time at present; his work lasted all day, it was dull and monotonous, so was the food, he hated the daily round of duty in the gaunt barrack where he lived—weeks would come, weeks of rain, winter, darkness, in which he would cling the more fervently to his earlier life, that glorious life of love and work, embodied in the girl Lenore Wahl, and to dreams of peace. . . . But if he started with lamentations about himself, a pitiful catalogue of selfish plaints, then all was at an end, once and for ever.

Beneath the veranda in the half-light stretched the vast expanse of sea, flecked with steel-blue shadows. The sun, red fruit of the warm day, sank rayless into a bank of cloud. Lenore Wahl, standing or sitting with her back against a door post, gave herself over to a riot of hatred, and listened to an inner voice, of her lacerated being, that bewailed her slaughtered love, and the malignant forces by which life was ruled.

Chapter 3

DAVID GIVES IN

Then, almost unannounced, David Wahl appeared in the middle of term, bored, as he said, by the whole swindle. For the last four days of the week his class had been assigned to two large estates to help in the harvest. The family doctor had forbidden him in a written certificate to undertake any heavy work in the hot sunshine, as he was beginning to grow again, and his lanky person was liable to lose weight very quickly. He told Lenore that he was uncommonly glad to have got off and to be with her. His enthusiasm seemed at first a little strained, and it was not until he had had a second swim in the afternoon that he talked more quietly. His arrival meant the beginning of a great time for Boll, whom he accused of being fat and lazy. In the morning he ran with him to the end of the visible world, along the shore under the steep cliffs; then he undressed quickly to enjoy the luxury of a bathe without a swimming suit. Out through the shallows that whirled round his thighs, into the deep water, where he was transformed into a leaping fish. Boll, like an Egyptian stone image, watched beside his clothes and the rolled-up towel, whining faintly, his eyes bursting from his head, for he was responsible for his adored young master who seemed so perilously far away. Then, from out yonder, a whistle; barking and yelping he plunged into the waves. Sea water was always unpleasant, a dog had to strain his neck to keep his head above it, so that the disgusting salt should not get into his nostrils. But a self-respecting dog knows his duty; if his master was to drown he would listen to no orders, but drown with him. However, even a man comes to his senses in time; at last both boy and dog reached the shore on all fours, fell full length and lay prone in the sunlight, letting the water trickle off their skin and dry upon them. In gratitude Boll licked David's knees.

As the result of this, David's face recovered its accustomed freshness, though there was still an unwonted line between his eyes. On the second evening, after dinner and a walk by the sea, he came through the door between their two rooms, as Lenore lay in bed, and sat down on the edge of that faintly creaking article of furniture. Might he smoke a last cigarette with her? The twilight glimmered through, although, to gain daylight and save coal, the clocks had been put forward in the spring by a whole hour. Lenore lay and watched him, as he sat with his hands behind his head, his face lit up from time to time by the glow from the cigarette which he smoked in rapid puffs.

"Well?" said she, turning back to what they had been saying on the first evening. "What has happened?"

"I shall have to volunteer for service," answered David Wahl.

Lenore raised her eyebrows and felt a slight catch at her breath. "You?" This tall fifth-form boy usually meant what he said.

"The fact is," he went on, "no one can hold out any more at school. The masters treat a fellow with open contempt. There are now only eight left in the Lower Sixth, all the others have given in. The worst of it is that they themselves can hardly expect to be taken. Three of our lot went yesterday, two of them shorter and weaker than I am. The Bedbug honoured them with a funeral oration, which contained sundry hidden threats and allusions to certain football players and swimmers who would do well to take a lesson from those departing." (The Bedbug was the master who took the Upper Fifth, and instructed them in German, history, and geography.) The mental image of this gentleman diverted David for a short time from his theme. A loathsome fellow—so uncertain of himself that he felt he had to be just a little more patriotic than the Potsdam aristocracy. "Do you know," he proceeded, "our population is increasing so fast that we are bursting through our frontiers? So the Bedbug keeps on telling us.

Bismarck ought to have been in our class. We want new land in the East, of course without the native population, as well as Antwerp, including the territory inland; Liége is also needed, for security, and if, in addition to the Polish industrial area to round off Upper Silesia, we don't get the ore deposits of Briey and Longwy, within two years after the conclusion of peace we shall die like mice in a cement house. In geography, my dear, you may learn that the key to Germany's future lies in Baghdad, because we must get our own petroleum from Persia. Full stop. So you see we are fighting a war of defence and are ready at any time to make an honourable peace."

Lenore raised her frail hand—she felt quite oppressed by all this boyish cynicism. "What do you propose, if this is serious?"

"It has been serious for a long time, my child. As soon as I pass out of the Fifth, I shall have to give my name in as a volunteer. If I don't I shall be in for a very bad six months. And if I try to get out of it when the time comes—well, I couldn't defend that, of course, as you can see for yourself. The outside pressure is simply more than a fellow can stand."

"But it was your idea to get out of it," she said, "and dress up as a girl."

David bent down and looked at her with troubled eyes. The cigarette had long been thrown out of the window. "That was just hot air, Fräulein," he answered impenitently, "nothing more. I'm much too cowardly, and that's a fact. You can't go against seventy millions. It needs less courage to bend to the storm than to put one's head up all alone. I've been talking a great deal to Kliem. He thinks as I do, but he can't work miracles either. I say," he suddenly grew lively; "he's a great fellow, Kliem is. He suggested I should apply to his old unit, the Sappers of the Guard; he said he would then ask if he could join up again, though he has lost a hand. Only one hand is needed for the hand-grenades—the right one, and there are always several men to serve a minenwerfer. Then I shouldn't feel so lost and should have someone who would put me up to things a bit. And until spring 1916, he thought, they would be able to make damned good use of an otherwise healthy N.C.O., a trained regular soldier, and then very likely, if he really pressed for it, they would discharge him. If I get my stripes first, I'll be out of the worst of it, and there'll be two of us."

"He is something like a friend."

"Isn't he just!"

Lenore contemplated the ceiling meditatively, the centre of which was adorned with a garland of roses. A certain Bertin had no such friend as this to help him on his journey as a private soldier between Küstrin and Fort Bondues. The poor fellow had in fact dropped out of his caste, which is good for no man. His ability and education entitled him to advancement; among the Prussians he would certainly have been promoted to sergeant, and more sensible nations would have quickly made him an officer and even more quickly got him killed. (No, she didn't want that to happen to him yet.) But such promotion was dependent on training with a definite aim, and attachment to a proper unit; a private in the A.S.C. remained, without hope, in the status of a coolie. These reflections suggested a juster view of his letters as well as of his conduct as a whole. She did not want him to have an easy time—of that there was no question, but she did not want to be unjust. It would be wise to put that venomous grey letter away for the time being. "Listen," she began after a silence; "things aren't going well between Bertin and me, as you can imagine. He's writing me the most absurd letters—a sort of sentimental journey in Northern France."

"Yes, I *can* imagine," came a grim answer from the darkness.

"I've written him a letter—it's over there in the cupboard—but you're not to read it."

"All right, I won't," said her brother quizzically.

"But I want to get rid of it for a little while," she went on.

"The fellow's in Lille, isn't he?"

"Listen; I want you to take the letter and give it me back when I ask for it. It's rather venomous."

"You ought to fire it off, then. That lad deserves anything

that's coming to him. To write it and then not send it is a poor sort of thing to do, my dear girl."

But Lenore slapped him lightly on his still downy cheeks, and said: "Don't talk nonsense, and give me a kiss. Good night."

Outside the windows the white rays of the searchlights swept over the coast and across the walls of the room.

As he went out, David glanced affectionately at her profile, darkly silhouetted against the bluish background: delicate nose, resolute round chin, and firm brow. "She'll be all right," he thought, opened the cupboard, and put the thick envelope in the inner pocket of his jacket.

Chapter 4

WIDOW BUNGE

When Lenore, two days later, received a telegram signed Paula, asking her to book a room for that same day, she was glad. Paula could have easily come during those weeks when there had been no David to relieve her loneliness, but so it always happened: pleasant events, like unpleasant ones, always came in twos or threes. If Paula brought no friend with her, thought Lenore with a smile, as she waited at the place where the post-car stopped, watching the sleepy afternoon activities of the little village, and all the chattering women who sat outside their houses knitting, then it was all up with our David. He would fall completely for this entrancing person; and Paula would undertake his knightly education. And as she nibbled cheerfully at little local plums that she took out of a bag, she called up the image of the elegant Paula Weber who, all fresh and rosy in her light grey costume and a small severe straw hat, would be one of the first to spring out of the car. But, as the old omnibus quickly emptied, the grey costume indeed appeared, but not the hat; from beneath a black straw cloche a strange face looked out at her. Pale and haggard, with reddened nose and reddened eyes, and lustreless hair—thus had Paula's eldest sister looked when she visited Berlin last year: the wife of a police court official in Strassburg and the mother of three. Lenore stood before her for a moment in dismay, and then took her by the arm. Something had happened to her parents in Alsace, she thought, and her sensitive heart began to dread the prospect of revelations. The elderly porter at the Pension took her handbag, and her luggage ticket; the brief line of houses opened on to the sea. Vast and lovely, like the joys of life itself, the great expanse, gently ruffled by the wind, stretched away into the haze of afternoon.

Paula broke out at once in her husky voice: "How fine you're looking, Lenore—so brown. I wish you wouldn't look at me. Let me be ugly if I like—André is dead." Without her appearing to notice it a few tears trickled down her nose. "They've murdered him." Then she lifted her veil and wiped her eyes with a flowered white handkerchief.

Lenore stood still.

Andreas Bunge, student of economics from his earliest childhood, had had to have treatment for a weakness of the right ear, which inclined towards catarrh. His two months' labours in the A.S.C. during the preceding October and September had not diminished this tendency. His training at Hirschberg, exposed as he had been to mountain winds and sharp rises and falls of temperature, had brought on a catarrh in the aural passage, the symptoms of which he knew very well. He reported himself at the morning medical inspection. The battalion doctor, accustomed to dealing with Silesian peasants and sons of cottagers, snarled at him contemptuously, and after a very cursory examination wrote him down as fit for service. The fever which had been at 37 degrees Centigrade on the second day, rose on the third day to 39, upon which Andreas Bunge insisted on being brought before this experienced physician once more, who now bit his lower lip in agitation, but his aspirin and hydrogen peroxide now came too late. The catarrh had made good use of the opportunity to spread inwards; and when his betrothed was summoned by telegram to the hospital, she found the final agony was not far off.

"It was minutes before he recognized me, Lenore. Just imagine how the poor boy must have suffered. Then we talked about getting married. 'Go home,' he said, 'I'm done for.' From time to time he screamed, and I held my ears until they gave him opium. It went on for twenty-four hours. They wouldn't let me be with him, Lenore. Perhaps you wonder," she said later on, "that I'm not wearing mourning. I know I ought to, but I can't walk about as a war widow, when it was the doctors that killed him. Perhaps I ought to have spared you all this misery," she said, when she had grown a little more composed, "but one wants to live. Lenore, in spite of everything, and what could I do at home where every cushion reminds me of André, or with friends who were also his friends and are walking about alive and well. In your company I can at any rate cry. Your man is in France, and he was a friend of André's. One of the Jägers, a Breslau student, helped me a bit; and so I got home again. To comfort me, he told me a proverb that they had made up in Latin, Lenore: 'The knacker knocked us on the head in the little garrison town.' And he laughed; not a nice laugh, Lenore, but it helped me. When my papers are examined and stamped and all the rest of it, I shall be allowed to go to my parents in Alsace. They are in the war zone in Altweiler, and after the war, if I am still alive, I shall go to France. I'm not a Prussian, dumb heroism isn't in my line, all this talk of Spartan endurance makes me sick." And she flung herself full length on the sand, and sobbed, with her eyes against her forearms, until Lenore soothed her at last by stroking her quivering shoulders. An aural catarrh, she thought, a childish ailment; and the lively Andreas Bunge. And she saw his thin high-bred face with the kindly eyes and humorous mouth, one of those clever young Germans who had trained himself by study and self-discipline to serve the Fatherland in his maturity; and now he lay in a cemetery in the Riesengebirge, nor was it a bullet or an illness that had put him there. Naturally she thought, too, of Private Bertin; his health was not of the soundest, as he also had a tendency to catarrh of the throat that might well develop into a mortal illness, and he was certainly no better looked after in the forts of Lille.

Personal news gets about in places like Tramsin in a subterranean fashion, through the talk of servants. They meet after work is over, bathe in the sea like the visitors, but in moonlight or twilight, and tell each other the events of the day, who has come and who has gone, and the fates of each and all of them.

In the forest at the back of the village, behind an unobtrusive enclosure, hidden away among the pines and facing a cleared stretch of ground, stood the large convalescent home of Tramsin, which now housed seriously wounded soldiers. On her walks nearby, Lenore had already avoided the sight of blue striped smocks, stretchers, crutches, and open-air shelters for the sick men. One evening a visiting-card was brought in to the two friends; on it was printed—Sophie von Gorse. In the summer uniform of the nursing service, with a short cape and a white hood, a girl awaited them in the drawing-room among the wicker chairs, with a steady grave expression in her eyes. She gladly agreed to sit with them out of doors, on the upturned beach chair in Lenore's castle, and talk.

The stars were coming out; slowly they flickered forth through the gradually deepening twilight. The sea heaved gently and mirrored the moon as it rose above the forest. Sister Sophie was a young woman who had grown up on a large estate, very reserved, and an object of sympathy among the hearty self-satisfied male members of her own class. Two summers ago, a professor of painting from Berlin, a favourite of the Emperor, had been invited to paint, in their natural haunts, goats and deer for a hunting-lodge belonging to his illustrious master. He had a favourite pupil with him, a slim and rather haggard youth, but a talented artist with an assured career. He loved to contemplate the dreaming pools among the mossy pines of Alt-Gorse; to him, art came before anything. Although he was of the middle class, they became engaged in the last autumn of peace. A long time would have to pass before they could marry, she and Walter Brinkel; but a delightful future seemed at last to open out before her. Then the war broke out; all Gorse was emptied; the father, the brothers, and she herself, went to their various posts. Walter, who was delicate, was shielded by the professor, so long as it was practicable; he took him to Kiel, where he was painting pictures of torpedo-boats, and there he hoped to find a refuge for his pupil. "God alone knows how delicate Walter's lungs were. He has always lived carefully, spent the winters studying in Rome or Florence. But he *was* called up. I was on service at the time. At the beginning of September we were all taken prisoner, when that extraordinary retreat happened. We had already been picturing ourselves in a magnificent hospital in Paris in one of the great hotels. However, we had to stick by our field dressing-station; and then the French advanced, further and further. I hated the French doctors, but the English nurses were very nice. It was some time before we were exchanged. At last when I was in Switzerland I got news of Walter; he was in a hospital in Heidelberg and very anxious for me to go and see him. The card had been waiting for ten days, and I could not go at once. But at last I found myself in a great hospital ward, and went from bed to bed looking for Walter—in vain. However, the head orderly assured me that he was here. I read the names on the lists and discovered Walter Brinkel, written over a frightful fever curve. There he lay, with a great nose and hollow eyes and round his mouth the line that one can never misunderstand. His voice was quite changed. 'Bear up,' he said, and that was all. He went out the same night, quite gently, he had only been waiting for me. He was treated as a malingerer, too. When he got into hospital at last, only one of his lungs was working."

Lenore looked at the girl's slim figure, sitting there so straight, gazing out towards the horizon at the gun-flashes from the warships at firing practice, while the dull thunder of the detonations rolled across the waters; and in the rooms the plaster flaked off the walls, "And you tell us all this so calmly, Sister Sophie," she said. "I should be screaming and ripping the wicker seat to pieces."

"That wouldn't bring him to life again," came the girl's answer through the warm night air in her clipped North German speech. Moreover, Sister Sophie had seen so many horrors that she was now, as she said, but little stirred by her own trouble. On a certain French railway station, where the German nurses had had to wait a long time while being sent to the rear, she had seen a number of badly wounded Germans, who had been given no water for days. The French sister in charge had forbidden them to have any. Why? She was really out of her mind and ought to have been under restraint, as hardly ten days before, her own son had been brought back blinded in both eyes as the result of a hand-to-hand fight. The German sisters could do nothing, nor could the English nurses in a hospital train on another line; it was a wounded French officer who rounded on the woman and had water brought to the unhappy men. "I have seen so much heroism, so much sacrifice, and so many horrors, that my own loss seems little enough now. But I had some bad times because I kept it shut up inside myself. Today when the kitchen sister told me what had happened to you, I felt I must come. Thank you for letting me talk."

Lenore sat beside the two women's side in a whirl of hurrying emotions. "They oughtn't to treat our men so," she whispered; "they ought to be kept safe against the peace. What are the standards by which great epochs are judged? Not by casualty lists; by the achievements of architects, artists, and writers, by the works of the intellect. It's bad enough when they have to sacrifice themselves in defence of their country; with us they are simply thrown away."

"Because in our country there is an age-long hatred of clever men," said Paula Bunge, in a voice that came from deep down within her breast. "Fools like to crush them to revenge themselves for their own inferiority."

This was beyond Sister Sophie, as she admitted, and anyhow her time was up. She had only leave of absence for the evening and had to be back by ten o'clock.

The two young women walked with her through the dark forest. They gladly promised to return her visit, and suggested that they might read or play to the wounded men, if a fiddle could be found anywhere.

Sister Sophie knew of no fiddle. She thought that anyone coming to convalesce at Tramsin would do well to keep away from the hospital. There was a man with a wound in his back the size of a plate, another without hands, another whose heart could be seen beating through a wound in his chest, one whose hip bones had been crushed into a pulp, and one without a chin. "It is unimaginable," said Sister Sophie softly, "what these men will endure; no honour and no gratitude will ever be enough to repay their heroism. We? We are simply serving, which is all that we can do."

Her gay-coloured dress vanished between the grey tree-trunks.

Fräulein Lenore Wahl wandered thoughtfully home, with her hands behind her back. At her side, defiantly gnawing her lips, walked her friend, with the white handkerchief still at her eyes.

Thenceforward the folly of the world became a torment to Lenore. The impressions of the darkness, Sister Sophie's quiet words, ebbed away; but the reflections that they brought, did not depart. In the vast noon silences she envisaged with horror the planet earth, this star upon which its denizens were locked in so terrible a struggle. In the guise of a swollen and pregnant belly it hurtled through the universe, fertilized ever and anon by evil and mysterious radiances, and by the light that rushes through the spaces of the ether. Mother Earth conceived continually, discharging a stream of creatures from her womb, and swallowing them again, sucking them down into the abysm of the tomb; for earth was a sepulchre as well as a womb. True, this frenzy of impregnation, birth, and ravening destruction, was the law of life, and the war, which now filled such myriads of graves, did but lend headlong speed to a process that would otherwise have continued, but more slowly. The war was merely the most intensified form of human society. This open war among men did but obscure the fact that there had been an age-long war between men and women, rich and poor, the country and the town, the healthy and the sick. Today, indeed, it was a war of the sick against the healthy, for in these days death and disablement came nearer to him who walked about safe and sound upon his legs.

From this certain consequences must be drawn. She could not take up her old idle life again, as she now described her studies. The idea of new friendships, of relations with other men, made her feel quite sick. Research work at the university might do; but that had ceased. If only she could make great discoveries that would benefit humanity. But she was only a woman, a creature of feeling, predestined, as it were, for companionship, and little suited to any other role. She could not work in hospitals; her sensitive imagination would have unbalanced her mind; she would inevitably have been careless and rebellious, filled with a wild desire to wreck the monotonous routine.

It was David who, on the day of his departure, pointed to a possible solution. "You wouldn't believe it, but schoolmasters are being called up by the hundred, and if they leave their Homer behind and learn to enjoy a pipe of tobacco, they'll make quite decent soldiers. In the meantime what's going to happen to us, the poor orphaned youth of Germany? Who's to examine us in Greek grammar, correct our German essays in red ink, read the *Bride of Messina* and Cicero's letters with us? You're an educated woman. Why don't you learn a bit more, and help by teaching in the schools? And if you come to realize how much more sensible it would be to improve the virgin minds of workmen's and peasants' children instead of operating on insolent young louts like us, you will at any rate have gained something. Think it over."

It was not a violently alluring project, but it was worth thinking of; and in the course of the last week it made its way into her mind. She came back from her walks more and more resolved, with the salt of the spray bitter on her lips. She understood young people, and she might thus shake off the oppression of what had happened to her; it could never be effaced, though much more horrible events turned every minute of that time into a silent shriek of torment. There was so much that the younger generation ought to know. They were being deprived of knowledge which bold spirits of the nineteenth century had conquered for their disciples, Germans, French, and English. What was commonly taught was mere froth upon the surface; the whole of history, which made so brave a spectacle, was a brief and recent epoch of some three hundred thousand years. And even that was distorted to exemplify the apologues, sometimes hardly literate, of fatuous old teachers of philosophy and science; the supremacy of the male, the superiority of his understanding and his muscles, and the inferiority of the female. But look a little below the surface and how the aspect of things changes! A sun-god, Moloch, ruled the earth, but only since the dethronement of the women, daughters of the moon goddess. In the burial chambers of wise and ancient peoples there are still traces of her sovereignty, and the myths are full of lamentations for the deposed Mother. The leagues of young men had placed the world under the sign of the sword and laid their yoke upon the women until they did no more than bear and suckle children—they, who had discovered agriculture, founded cities, invented weaving, taught how to plait with reeds, moulded vessels, cooked, and brought up the children. Since then the ear of corn and the spinner's star had been displaced on the armorial bearings of humanity by the bull, the lion, and the eagle, which fed upon living flesh. And since then wars had never ceased. . . . Further than this she would not allow her thoughts to go. Enough that in her mind there was a stir of purposes, a confusing urge to take hand in the conflict and fight the evil forces as she might. Before a class, before those young faces and attentive eyes, the right words would be given to her. The man who had brought her forth from the half-light of her girlhood would thus slowly pass out of her mind. For a long while she had ceased to maintain the illusion by which he was permitted to write affectionate gossip, as though nothing had happened between them. One day he would realize that something had perhaps happened between Küstrin and Tramsin; and she would have liked to be there when he did.

So, curled in her fastness of warm sand, Lenore Wahl slipped into a cold and frozen solitude, like a little planet, whose elliptic was whirling her away from the focus of life. Far below her, infinitesimal, like a busy ant crawling among countless others of its kind in France, somewhere between Lille and the front, she saw and looked with disfavour at one Werner Bertin, her lover and her foe.

BOOK FIVE

A BRANCH CAUGHT IN THE CURRENT

Chapter 1

DUCHEROW

In those days life worked very far-flung and surprising patterns into the web of human destinies; remote events conjoined to bring forth consequences that persisted into a distant future. If the English or the Germans in Flanders exploded their mines in the Wytschaete sector, not merely did they transform human bodies into scattered food for vermin; they also transformed spoilt young women in London or Breslau into indigent survivors, dependent on the charity of relatives, or on the labour of their hands. Children escaped from school too soon, and learned to be chauffeurs or electricians; girls became cinema attendants—and existence revealed to them much unsuspected cruelty and kindness. Widows, now that their men were dead, saw hopeless years before them; hordes of children found themselves suddenly freed from their fathers' guidance, support, and—possibly—tyranny. They discovered a life of their own, and led it in defiance of their mothers; some grew bold and some shrank back; some made their way, and others came to ruin. Plans were wrecked, obstacles were swept away, the ill-luck of one was the good fortune of another; in those days the threads of the Norns were strangely intertwined and loosed. An incident of this kind changed, quite unremarked, the course of Lenore's future, like the wave of a magician's rod.

There were very few in Germany who then realized how dangerous the alliance with Austria-Hungary might prove to all three nations. In every German beer-house men sat and jeered at these feeble allies, and the increasing reinforcements that they called for—which now amounted to entire German armies. Still, in the Carpathians, the Bukovina, and on other fronts, these armies were indeed defending the Fatherland, and at its most vulnerable point. For the Hungarian plain uncovered Germany's open flank. If Russian troops crossed the Carpathian passes, the way lay open to Munich, through Budapest, Pressburg, and Vienna, or through Prague to Dresden. In both cases German armies would be taken in the rear, and the lie of the land and the railways was such that no sufficient forces could be sent to fight and hold them. To secure this flank, it was decided to lengthen it, to destroy Serbia, to establish railway connexion with Turkey, and to rest one wing of the united front on the Sea of Marmora, while the other reached to the North Sea. Then Bulgaria would be forced to come into the war, while Rumania would be finally frightened from doing so; Germany's access to the East would be secured, together with supplies of Rumanian wheat and Rumanian oil. Thus, at last, it seemed possible to conquer Egypt, and to strike at England on the Suez Canal, if the Straits of Dover proved impregnable.

On the seventh of October, 1915, German, Austrian, and Hungarian armies attacked Belgrade and Semendria. Within twelve days not a single Serbian soldier was fighting on his native soil. The best infantry in the Balkans could not stand up against the huge guns that were this time brought against them. Most of the survivors, and their young sons, whom they took with them, perished in the agonies of that murderous retreat through Albania; and yet a Serbian army still clung to the soil of Southern Macedonia and Greece, until the English and the French came to strengthen and relieve them. The main object of the undertaking was thus frustrated. The struggle had been fierce: many German fighting men had found graves in Serbia, and one of them was Gerhard von Ducherow.

He had been as delighted as a boy with the secret entrainment to Southern Hungary, and all the various incidents of the journey. He loved the cheering throngs of pretty girls at the railway barriers, brown-skinned girls, with sparkling teeth and eyes, laden with grapes, and food, and cigarettes. With beating heart he had watched the operations of the engineers, the passage of the river, the heavy street fighting that followed the thunderous hurricane of the bombardment; the squadrons of cavalry clattering across the bridge, the hammering hooves of the German dragoons before Belgrade. He was reminded of the song of "Prinz Eugen der edler Ritter," under whom men of Brandenburg had also won fame. The stony land opened out before them; river valleys, planted with maize, tobacco, and vines, narrowed into gorges; and above them stretched the barren ridges of the Planina. In bivouac, under the glitter of stars more southern than any he yet had known, he lay down content; here at last was something new and strange, the horizon of adventure was approaching, every day a fresh vision met his eyes. The van of the army, the point of the great wedge, drove onwards. They were under rifle-fire all day from dawn until darkness fell; on every side there were nests of Serbian infantry, either cut off, and trying to fight their way out, or rear-guards left behind to die where they stood. On one such early morning, when they had but just mounted and trotted out of camp, a bullet from a lynx-eyed sniper among the crags struck him in the forehead, and flung him for ever from his saddle, and from the dreams of boyhood. A field battery that galloped up and began scattering shells, served but to help him to his grave.

The lamentations of a mother who is also what is called a lady are not heard by neighbours through double windows and closed doors. But even before the cold proud words that announce a soldier's death have appeared, topped by the iron cross, in the left corner of a local paper and of another in Berlin, the servants round about have spread the news. Even before lunch, Frau Mahnke, all disordered, had rushed in to tell the gracious lady.

Frau Mathilde's eyes filled with tears. She was truly and quite unselfishly touched by the loss that had stricken the mother near at hand. Not until after lunch did she realize that all her dreams had vanished into cold air as suddenly as the stem of a plant is snapped. There she stood, arranging late roses and deep purple dahlias in a jug, which later on she would make up into a spray and send across with a card of sympathy; her eyes were wet, she was baffled by a prospect that seemed so blank and so inexorable.

In the early twilight, she made Lenore sit with her at the coffee table, under the glazed veranda, where the lights had not yet needed to be lit. How the child had grown, she thought, as she glanced at her daughter's face, which looked more troubled than she remembered ever to have seen it. "Poor child," she said suddenly, full of heart-felt sympathy.

The daughter's heart at first responded with a thrill of affection; then she bade herself be careful. "Do you find me especially in need of sympathy today?"

"How they are all dying—these young men of ours. It is terrible."

Lenore nodded gloomily. Out of the small circle of her acquaintance, almost ten, if she included Bertin's friends at Göttingen and Kreuzburg, who from his enthusiastic descriptions of them were more familiar to her than many men she met at tennis, or sailing on the Havel. The young man in Lille had always been a loyal friend.

"And now Gerhard from next door. Why, Tornow was always telling us, and he ought to know, that the cavalry never came under fire in this war. His nephew in the Gardes-du-Corps hasn't so much as heard a shot, except our own, of course."

Lenore sighed. "I can't bear to think of Frau von Ducherow. What will she make of her life now? You mothers don't set much store by daughters. Supposing something happened to our David? Suppose he never came back, and we never heard his footsteps above our heads any more?"

Both women were silent. From the tall chestnut tree to the right of the garden great golden leaves floated past the windows. Frau Mathilde grew pale as she sat in her basket chair, and her hands lay lifeless on the arm-rests. She must first settle Lenore's affair—and then concentrate all her maternal forces upon the boy.

"You shouldn't try to suppress your grief, Lenore. It will only be worse for you in the end."

Lenore surveyed Frau Mathilde Wahl, who lived upon another planet. This poor childlike creature had really dreamed of her marriage with young Ducherow. What on earth could she say? "Thank you, Mamma," she answered quietly.

"Well," went on Frau Mathilde, "the younger generation aren't like us. We just wanted to cry our eyes out on our mothers' necks. But you say nothing and you try yourselves too hard."

If she only knew. "There are limits, Mamma."

Frau Wahl sighed the sigh of a woman who has seen much of life. "There's a limit to everything whether you bear it in silence, or whether you cry till you can cry no more. Life goes on."

What could be in her mother's mind?

"But a child should show a little confidence and have her letters sent, not to the post office, but to her home."

Lenore pricked up her ears.

"It often can't be helped. Something might get into Papa's mail, and then there would be trouble."

Frau Wahl was delighted; here spoke her daughter. Peace in the house was more essential than a good dinner. This offered some prospect of an understanding. "That can be arranged," she said lightly, "I think I could answer for Papa—now."

"And for yourself?" asked her daughter softly, smoothing a strand of hair from her forehead. "I'm thinking of times past."

Mothers find it hard to learn to respect their children's cupboards and diaries. "The past is past," said Frau Wahl, with a blush. "You needn't be afraid now, you suspicious girl; you're a true granddaughter of Markus Wahl. Get that little iron box from the attic, and stop going to the post office, dear. Leave Papa to me. Do you ever hear from Herr Bertin?"

"Not often," said her daughter untruthfully. "His battalion is in Lille at the moment."

"There have been some good accounts of his work lately, by influential people, so Grandpapa says."

But that was nothing to Lenore; her heart, alas, was frozen.

"Do you think he would like a parcel?"

What could all this be about? "Any soldier would. But of course they can buy a great many things in Lille"—(if they've got enough money, she added to herself)—"except good cigars." She did not forget that a certain sum had been considerably reduced and not by him. . . .

"I thought he might care for a smoked sausage—ours are better than any." Frau Wahl got up. "When you write to him next you might send him a few small presents, just to show we don't bear any grudge," she added, pensively. "Who knows what may happen to anyone these days?" She turned as though to go through the curtains into the next room, and paused.

How poetic, thought Lenore, and how ironical it would be to send him presents after all that had passed. If only her mother knew how little she needed to worry about him. That sententious youth was safe enough, even if not too comfortable, at the base. However, it was pleasanter to stay at home in bad weather. She would certainly have her letters brought by the postman. (Bertin had carefully refrained from telling her that the A.S.C. companies had had casualties from the moment they arrived; and she would hardly have remembered the genial Sergeant Boost, who, for three weeks past had been sleeping—so the phrase went—in the La Madeleine cemetery.)

Then the mother turned, and there was a new brightness in her eyes. "I don't know what you feel, my child, but I feel much more cheerful for this talk," she said. Lenore looked up. To her mother, she seemed uplifted and transfigured by grief. Dear child, thought Frau Wahl, as she bent across the corner of the table and kissed her daughter on the forehead.

"Perhaps I'll write tomorrow," answered Lenore. Suddenly, to her own surprise, she found her lips were pressed against Frau Mathilde's soft hand.

Chapter 2

LITTLE ACORNS

At a window opposite the cathedral of St. Maurice, black and grey stone Gothic of the fifteenth century, stood two men in uniform, surveying the portal, and the statues on the carved pediment above it. There, every Sunday, certain soldiers played church music; they were musicians by profession, privates or N.C.O.s, and poured out their hearts in music. Anyone who longed to hear great music—a sonata by Handel, a Bach prelude, a motet by Heinrich Schütz, was to be found, if he could leave, in the dark-pillared aisles of the lofty church, whose netted windows shed such dim rich radiance within. There were always men from No. X/20 Company at these concerts, like convicts who are allowed exercise once or twice a month.

"I told Dimpfel to pick me out as clever a lad as he could, one with spectacles."

The A.S.C. captain turned to the major of artillery, whose billet it was, and who commanded many batteries of heavy guns to the north and west of the city: "That's all very well. But how are you going to use an A.S.C. private against his own major?"

The Bavarian artilleryman turned a wrinkled smiling face towards the Württemberger, and laid a hand on his shoulder. "My boy, I fancy you'll find it stated in your Field Service Orders that the essential thing for a soldier is to seize an opportunity that may never come again. Mackensen is attacking in Serbia, and Gallwitz under him. And as we have already sent them Brandenburgers, Alpine troops, and a quantity of Magdeburg artillery, they are now asking for more. That's Prussian logic. This time they want A.S.C. battalions for road construction. I've got the whole list here, because I've been sending some batteries of my own. And now I come to think of it, I noticed yesterday my Army Service Corps battalion is on the list—XI/21, Captain Friedrichsen, with the men from Hamburg and Altona."

"Ah, a good fellow."

"Yes, it's a pity, I agree. Why didn't they take that swine from Berlin, who makes the club uninhabitable, and destroys all decent conversation with his damned swagger?"

"Do you know what he did yesterday? I was in the same tram-car with him; there were a number of soldiers in the car, and some other people. I was saying what I thought about the slaughter that's going on now——"

"For God's sake don't shout about it."

"And I was a bit lit up with the wine I'd had for lunch. I asked the infantry captain, Prinziger, what we were doing here, and whether we were going to stick here for ever. I said I thought we'd better get out while the going was good. The French people nodded, they've got some sense—they know we can't carry on for ever."

"And Jansch?"

The major opened the window, and looked out into the wreathing mist. The organ, faintly audible, boomed to a triumphant close. People were leaving the church, black-clad burghers, and old women.

"He talked about getting me court-martialled—it was treason to talk like that in public. He'd report me to the authorities. We had to hold on to Lille, and the whole of Northern France. And he maundered about Germany's high destiny, the right of the victorious sword, and all the rest of it."

"Yes, but the victories were won, not by the likes of him, but by his men. And those beastly newspapers will keep the war going until the English kick us out next winter."

"And the usual stuff about Bernhardi and Treitschke and Wotan and the soul of Germany, and all the rest of it."

"And its name is Jansch, its height is five feet four; arrogant little beast."

"I'm sick and tired of being told that Dante was a German, that Michael Angelo came from Berlin, that the Mark of Brandenburg was occupied by the Ostro-Goths and the Order by the Lombards, but that Paradise, where civilization began, was in Mecklenburg, and if I hear much more of it I won't be responsible for what I might do to the little brute. Well, I've had an idea. To-morrow I have to see the Old Man about the units to be sent East. I shall want your concurrence. We both say that XI/21 is indispensable; X/20, Major Jansch, can be spared and may be released unconditionally. Major Jansch, too, we'll tell him, wants to distinguish himself. He is not popular among his brother officers, being much given to political argument and abuse of the Chancellor and the Foreign Department."

"Good. That will fetch the Old Man."

"We all know that H.R.H. will send off any troops the Old Man suggests, and he'd sooner send Berliners than men from the Baltic. That's why I got Dimpfel to send up a man from X/20, so that I could ask him a few questions about his company."

All manner of units were here employed under the general command of a major of Garrison Artillery; but the internal economy of the A.S.C. was their own affair. No inquiries were encouraged, and indeed any information on the subject would be remarkably hard to come by.

Bertin did not at all like his position. It was never to a private's advantage to be sent for by officers. Besides, he had been hoping to get a little peace and quiet in a café, to write a long letter to Lenore, away from his noisy comrades, who loved to roar "Lights Out," when he was reading in the night. They did their best to rob him of his poor remnant of seclusion; indeed, as the weeks passed, it melted slowly like an ice-block in a thaw.

The orderly relieved his mind; there was no trouble ahead, and the major was a man to be trusted.

"Yes, but he can't make my Sunday any longer. I've got to be out at Bondues about eight, and it's five now."

"What are you doing out there?" asked the orderly.

"Shovelling shit," answered Bertin grimly.

This was no more than the truth. It was not an agreeable task to clean out the fort latrines after many years of French occupation, a process that involved raking out the excrement and digging it into the soil. The platoons engaged upon this were ungratefully indignant, especially as those detailed for the job happened to consist largely of professional and business men. Their attitude was a source of much amusement to a bearded sergeant named Wachler, at home a petty mechanic, but here a man having authority.

The officers looked up; they saw a man of obvious education, looking rather ill at ease in his uniform. He gave his name; the officers nodded and asked him to sit down.

Did he know French? asked the major. "Fairly well." Could he translate a document for them that seemed of some importance?

Bertin saw his letter vanish. It was very bad luck to be called upon like this, on a Sunday afternoon, too. He replied that he would, if it was not too long. He still had to write a letter home, and was only free until eight o'clock.

But didn't he get time off in the evening in his company?

Bertin said that he, at any rate, had never had evening leave. He would have often liked to go to a concert, or see Agnes Sorma in *Minna von Barnhelm*. But perhaps such entertainments were thought to be above the heads of the A.S.C. at Bondues.

The captain laughed; what was he doing at the moment?

At the moment, answered Bertin, they were engaged under the orders of the Württemberg Sappers in digging infantry positions on the grass slopes of the casemates of the fort.

"Ah!" said the captain. It was his own area, and these men were under his own command. He might have asked after them before; he would look into all this at once.

His Swabian accent made Bertin scent some reason for the question. So he did not add that these positions were probably intended to draw the fire of the English airmen.

Here, said the major, was the text, putting before him a printed sheet: *"Instructions concernant la défense des fortifications."* He observed that it was fairly short.

Could he have a dictionary? A dictionary was produced. "Go and sit in the next room—I'll have some coffee sent in to you—and bring me the thing in German. What's your job in civil life?"

Bertin looked at his interlocutor, a man of middle age, with a well-shaped Roman head, possibly a professor in a technical high school, and told him he was a university student and an author.

"That's very fortunate," said the major promptly. "But why aren't you working on the newspaper here? There are a lot of men in your battalion seconded for civilian jobs, aren't there?"

"Yes," said Bertin, "a hundred and ten men out of our company alone. But no one wants people like me. A certain prejudice against educated men has to be allowed for," he ventured to add.

"A hundred and ten men," repeated the major reflectively. This was the real point of his colloquy with the A.S.C. private. He might find a hundred and eleventh place. What were all these men doing?

Bertin did not know exactly; except that men of his own company were employed in various factories on military account; others drove trams, paved the streets, laid cables, cast railway lines; barbers, too, and tailors had been released. And now might he go to his work, as time was getting short?

Major Reinhardt agreed, and so did Captain Lauber. They established Bertin in an adjoining room, beside a large and elegant French bed inlaid with metal, at a claw-footed table on which Bertin spread out his papers and began to write. He was soon enthralled by the clear compact brevity of the French text. Dimpfel brought in coffee and two cigars.

The two officers talked in low tones, from opposite corners of a curved high-backed sofa.

"A hundred and ten men from No. 1 Company alone. You can't possibly send it. It's a damned shame, and if Jansch makes a fuss—as he certainly will, since he knows we want to get rid of him—your scheme's a washout."

Major Reinhardt filled a fresh pipe. "The ways of the Lord are wonderful. How would it be if we left the thing as it stands, and sent X/20 after all?"

The captain shook his head. "You have to get them released—good Lord, what an infernal affair."

"No, I shall transfer them."

"How do you mean?"

"Don't you think that if Captain Friedrichsen is allowed to stay here with the rest of his men, he will be quite ready to hand over a hundred and ten men to 1/X/20, and take on these hundred and ten Berliners employed in this city? Friedrichsen would give his hand not to be sent off to a lousy hole like Serbia, where he would have to scramble about the mountains all the winter making roads."

Captain Lauber sat up and stared blankly into his friend's eyes. "You mean to put a hundred and ten Hamburgers into a Berlin battalion, and a hundred and ten Berliners into a Hamburg one? Have you taken leave of your senses?"

Major Reinhardt broke into a burst of deep laughter: "So you see the point, you silly old Swabian. That's what I call putting the Imperial idea into practice. One heart and one flag, you know."

"Do you think it'll come off? We'll have the best bottle of Chambertin we can get if Jansch is shifted."

"He will be, mark my words; unless, of course, the swine gets wise to anything too soon."

"Right. That little man next door must have finished translating that stuff by now."

"He's to leave his name—remind me, will you? We mustn't let him go off with his unit. Shall we have a game of chess? You owe me two revenges."

They pushed a small table between them, set up the men, and immersed in their game, forgot Bertin.

He puffed at his cigar, and turned over the pages; all went well, and in barely an hour he had finished. The silence of the lofty bedroom released a much profounder current of feeling for Lenore than a crowded café might have done. He pulled out his pocketbook and wrote.

"My dear Heart: I happen this moment to be sitting in an officer's billet, beside a large empty bed. which would well suit the two of us, and thinking longingly of you. If you had been here yesterday when your letter came, I should have fallen on your neck with joy. It is very clever of you, darling, to have managed to have your letters sent to your house at last. How did you do it? Well, our policy of trying to wear down that grim old parent of yours seems to be succeeding after all. While I was busy today on the stupid and disgusting jobs that fill our life here, I declared this Saturday a double anniversary. This makes me all the more distressed at what you tell me about your present plans. I can't see you as a teacher—trying to manage a class of unruly third-form boys. Dear heart, it won't do. You have no notion what you are letting yourself in for. The masters won't be able to help falling in love with you, the women teachers will hate you, and the boys will do all they know to make things impossible. The Fifth and Sixth Forms would be better; we would have made eyes at you and worked hard, just so that you should think well of us. But for the higher forms you would have to learn a lot; and besides, though you may not believe me, you would be paralysed by the atmosphere of one of those awful institutions, and your health would suffer. Anyhow, there is bound to be peace this winter. The land road to Constantinople is in our hands, the alliance with Bulgaria will secure it for good. The advance on Egypt is now only a question of time. The English are much too sensible to wait until we reach the Suez Canal and carry the Holy War to India. And we shall be married before you have time to get a job. Think it over—I am sure you will give up the idea.

"I have just been hearing some music, rather a moderate sort of performance, but in a cathedral, which makes even an amateur rendering of Bach (the flute sonata in E minor) rather thrilling."

And he became so immersed in his feelings, in that scrap of music that he had just heard, faint shadow of a glory that had once illumined and transfigured his whole life, that as he mechanically switched on the electric light to finish his letter to Lenore, he heard a clock strike seven. Hurriedly he stopped, gave his finished work to Dimpfel, said he must get back at once to

Bondues, and tiptoed out of the building and down the stone stairs. He hurried through the darkened streets, at almost a trot, waited at the tram stop, and got in; there he sat, amid all the unpleasant smoke and noise of a throng of soldiers going home. And as the car rattled and rumbled on its way, no one in it guessed, neither he nor any other man belonging to I/X/20, that this movement was only destined to come to rest in far-off Macedonia.

Chapter 3

A BARBED HINT

Lenore thrust out her underlip, and laid this letter with the rest. He advised her against it—and her intention was confirmed. She wanted to be independent in every direction, and of every person; that was something worth while working for. She was surrounded by piles of schoolbooks, her room became a hermitage, and outside the rain poured down. In those weeks all news from Bertin suddenly ceased; this did not distress her much, at least not noticeably. Letters or postcards were often held up at the sorting stations by a block in the post; and then half a dozen all arrived at once. He was, in fact, in a hard-seated, rocking troop-train, rumbling towards Munich. They had made their way down the Rhine; they were to strike the Danube at Rosenheim, and thence look down on the monastery of Melk, Vienna, and the plains of Hungary. Unshaved and dirty he lay asleep, with large sheets of newspaper spread under him, on the floor of a central corridor with his head on a folded tunic and an air-cushion, covered with blankets. Not until later was he to make the discovery that brought so much relief and solace to him and in time to many others who were to make that agonizing journey—eight men in an uncushioned third-class carriage, for six days and six nights; the device of stretching the ground-sheet, served out to every soldier on leaving for the front, like a hammock from the luggage nets, so that four men could travel comfortably above and four below.

She had to bring up her knowledge of several languages, ancient and modern, to the required standard; some subjects she felt confident that she could manage by herself; but for Greek she thought she would need extra help. David recommended a certain Fräulein Hannes, who lived in Steglitz. When she revealed her intention of damping the warlike ardour of her future pupils by getting them to think, he observed dryly: "Congratulations. Have you thought which prison you would prefer; or do you think that Papa's connexions will save you from arrest? You'll be lucky to find yourself in no worse place than a lunatic asylum." And he told her about the woman Deputy Rosa Luxemburg, a highly educated Socialist, who was now serving a year's imprisonment for some harmless utterance made before the war.

Lenore shrugged her shoulders; she had worse than that behind her, and was not to be frightened. In point of fact she did not believe a word of it.

Just then, one Sergeant Leo Brümmer, of the Trade Section of the Governor-General's Department in Brussels, came home to visit his family; it was an alleged duty trip, in order to comply with the leave regulations. On the second day he had reached Potsdam and announced his arrival to Herr Wahl. Herr Hugo Wahl was glad to see a man who owed him his advancement and his comfortable post, and who knew it; and he asked him various questions. What Belgian factories were now idle? Under what conditions could they be worked for German account? What view did the foreign representatives and journalists take of these matters, and did he think anything could be accomplished by capital alone? Herr Wahl listened composedly to answers that were not too encouraging, observed with an assumption of envy that Brümmer had grown thinner, and that the war appeared to have done him as much good as a cure at a spa; he praised the fit of his sergeant's tunic, which had been made for him, twitted him on his military moustache and tanned cheeks, and as his visitor left the banker's sanctum in the great black building by the church of St. Nicholas, Herr Wahl wished him a good leave, and incidentally, asked him to type out five or six copies of a statement of his views on the possibility of employing Belgian labour in German concerns, with special reference to the Fleming question. A matter in which two great industrial magnates in Berlin and on the Ruhr were then much interested.

At that moment, on an afternoon in late autumn, Lenore arrived to fetch her grandfather. She put up her forehead for her father to kiss, shook hands with Herr Brümmer, and sat down in her red linen frock, crossing her feet like a caller who does not propose to stay long. But it was written that she should rise a sadder and wiser woman from that waxed-cloth white-nailed office chair. Markus Wahl leaned back where he sat, a thin bright-eyed figure with his red hands laid upon his thighs, and the corner of the writing-table between him and Herr Brümmer. When the slamming of many doors had indicated the departure of Herr Hugo Wahl, a silence fell—that silence that heralds the event. A faint ticking of the clock on the wall was the only sound; and outside the window-bars the walls of the church stretched prison-like along the street.

"Well, and what about peace?" asked Markus Wahl, who did not trouble to be punctilious in his speech to his protégé.

The visitor threw him a deprecatory glance, and raised his right hand from his thigh as though to say: We can't talk about that here. The reference was to Lenore.

Markus Wahl swept aside his apprehensions. "Don't be ridiculous, Brümmer. The girl knows how to keep her mouth shut much better than we do."

Sergeant Leo Brümmer felt a desperate need to unburden himself to someone; and it had not taken him long to realize that he must not talk to his wife. "Peace?" he repeated. "I'm afraid, Herr Wahl, that we shall have to wait for that. The English don't want it, by all appearances, and England is not merely paying the cost of the war, as we are often told, they also provide a sort of moral backbone for the French."

Markus Wahl nodded: "Is that a bad thing? England had more sense than the whole crowd of them. No other country has enough authority to open up negotiations. Haven't you seen how excited the *Norddeutsche Allgemeine Zeitung* became about peace rumours last October, and every six months since?"

"This October, too? Have you got a copy?"

Markus Wahl pondered; he could not remember that he had noticed it this month, but October was not yet over.

Sergeant Leo Brümmer shook his cropped head. "You won't notice it this year, Herr Wahl, nor next April. We have made bitter enemies of the English at last."

"How is that?"

"Wasn't there anything in the German papers about Miss Cavell? Or in the *Zürcher Zeitung?*"

Markus Wahl drew up his knees and clasped them with his arms, hunching himself into his chair with the air of an emaciated bird. In the last fortnight a few numbers of the Swiss paper had got lost in the post. What had happened?

"Wait a moment," said Lenore intently; "I remember reading something about it. Wasn't that the name of a female spy who was condemned to death in Brussels? Was she English?"

Sergeant Brümmer loosened his collar. "We shall have to pay for that girl's blood, and it will take a great many lives to avenge it. They tell me that the English newspapers are wild about it. Why were these people allowed to shoot a brave young woman because she helped prisoners to escape over the frontier. And after all it didn't matter very much if they did join the French or Belgian army. We shan't lose the war on that account."

"Was that why she was shot?" asked Lenore, and there was fear in her voice.

"She wasn't just an ordinary girl, she was a nurse, Fräulein Wahl. And she worked in a hospital where she had looked after a great many of our men, both officers and rank and file. I needn't tell you the story in detail, but it's the talk of all Belgium, and indeed the whole world just now. And I tell you it has raised a storm that will bring many hundreds of our Field Greys into their graves."

Lenore sat with wandering eyes, ready for flight. She remembered the Archduchess, the first victim of this war. Shot in Serajevo; and now another, and a woman too—shot in Brussels. Had not all the thinkers in Germany, and indeed in all the world, conferred on women their charter of humanity? Couldn't she have been pardoned, or even imprisoned? This was too much. . . .

Then Sergeant Brümmer told his tale. His source of information was unquestionable: orderlies, clerks, chauffeurs, telephonists, all the more passive agents of the military administration. Miss Cavell had taken the whole affair upon herself, admitted and confessed to every detail. She, and one or two other women had, in a certain sense, fought against Germany, and were guilty of treason; but no woman, no German woman, would have acted otherwise. The court-martial had an easy task; the sentence was, and had to be, death; though they recognized her high motives and her woman's feelings.

"You know," said Brümmer, standing up, and beginning to pace up and down the banker's narrow room, "we didn't believe that they would dare to do it; there were too many interests involved. For the execution of this woman, as we all understood, was worse than a crime, it was a folly of the very first order."

Markus Wahl banged his fist on the table: "Don't say what you can't answer for. A crime is a crime, and no folly can be worse than a crime."

"Oh, very well," said Brümmer uneasily, "but the world thinks otherwise. The world ignores crimes, but it avenges follies through their consequences."

The old man's face grew flushed and blotched like the face of a sick man. "Brümmer," he shouted, "I forbid you to talk such nonsense. Every crime, whatever else it is, is something that is beyond all sense and reason. You are a young man," he went on, calming down a little, "and you haven't seen much of the world yet. One day you will learn the truth of the words—He visits the sins of the fathers upon the children, unto the third and fourth generation, among those that hate Him. We are all guilty; and we cannot expect to escape."

Lenore crushed her handkerchief in her right hand, which she held behind her back. She said nothing.

"The Governor-General was on leave, and that was the beginning of the trouble. The courts-martial for espionage are under the military authorities—which meant, for the time being, the Governor of Brussels, a General, who could act on his own responsibility. The German Government and the Foreign Ministry are represented in Brussels by the P.D.—Political Department—just as in a branch of a business there is always a confidential man to look after the interests of the head office. This is in charge of a diplomat, a Baron, a man of sense and education, and he has a voice in everything that concerns policy. He knew exactly what was at stake in this matter; he realized that this would be a red rag to the English, and to the Americans too. Nor did he have to fight alone—the neutral Ambassadors helped him. The American was in bed, ill, but he sent his secretary; the Spaniard jumped up from a dinner party when the news came, left his guests, and rushed off to the Baron. That very night they wrote out a petition for mercy—it's not yet a fortnight ago; they urged that the sentence should not be carried out until the real ruler of the land came back from leave. Then they drove in the Baron's car to the General's house, and the Spaniard waited outside for what he was sure would be a favourable answer. The Baron returned after a few minutes, looking pale and shaken. His car was a good one with a very silent engine, and the chauffeur, who told me the story, kept his ears open, and only his eyes on the slippery street. The General, you will understand, swept the petition off the table without so much as looking at it. The Baron was rather taken aback, but he controlled his feelings, bent down, picked up the paper, and laid it on the table again, keeping his hand on it this time. And now listen to this, Herr Wahl. It was nearly twelve o'clock, and the General wanted to go to bed, so he told the Baron pretty sharply that he did not receive communications from a major. Do you understand? The representative of the Empire, of the Chancellor, and of all us taxpayers, was only a major; and our employee, to whom we pay a couple of thousand marks a month to look after our affairs in Belgium, was a General, and could get his own back. Well, there was nothing more to be done. The Baron told him that the woman's blood would be upon his own and his children's heads. But the General was a man of iron. 'I was trained to take responsibility, Herr Major,' he said triumphantly, and went to bed. Well, if that's responsibility, I want to hear no more of it. Then came the dawn, the last walk to the execution yard, the rifle-shots, and a grave. She did not complain, she did not cry, she knew how to face her end, and as none of us interfered, we shall all have to share the burden of what was done."

Fräulein Wahl suddenly noticed that she had bitten her underlip almost till it bled. "Herr Brümmer," she said, "what an awful story, and oh, how much we ought to learn from it. But it makes one want to burst into tears."

"Yes," said Markus Wahl, "and it's a pity there should be things we can't talk about until someone else has left the room."

Both listeners stopped suddenly, and all three looked with troubled eyes at the floor. Each in their own way loved Herr Hugo Wahl.

"Shall we take Herr Brümmer to the station, Grandpapa? There's fog on the bridges, and I think it's freezing."

Markus Wahl got up. "Well, we must put up the shutters over our hearts, let everything in and nothing out, and wait for the end. This is the iron time, of which it has been written." Indeed a time for silence, thought Lenore Wahl.

Chapter 4

THE GODS DECIDE

Herr Hugo Wahl said good-night to Tornow outside the front door. The next day he proposed to spend at home in Potsdam; he began to find the constant journeys to Berlin too great a strain. He must have a rest at Christmas and the New Year; Harzburg would do, or, if not, Oberhof. And his wife would then be quite ready for ten days' snow and sun, and Lenore, too, not to mention David. Rain pattered on the roof of the limousine, the lamps at the corners of the Parkring flickered with a turbid greenish radiance. There was a light in his father's room in the turret; Markus Wahl was sitting over his books. "We'll have our sleep out tomorrow, Tornow, we're neither of us youngsters. And the good God has partly washed the car for you."

"He's washed the roof, sir, but not the underneath; I shall have to take the garden-hose to that."

Herr Wahl laughed wearily, nodded, told Tornow to come round next morning at a quarter to eleven, and disappeared into the house.

In the study, he took the cigars, as his habit was, out of his case and put them in the cabinet, so that they should not get dry. He did not turn on the light; it would have been odd if he had not known every handle in the house after twenty years. A man is only master of his house when he can find his way about it without help in such times as these.

He stood there in his evening clothes, a massive figure, his chin gripped in the opening of his collar above the thin black tie, and his fists in the pockets of his dinner-jacket. No, he preferred not to go up and see his father. Old people were never good house companions, they always knew better than everyone else; but during the last week Markus had been almost unbearable. Just about the time that Brümmer had arrived, it had ceased to be possible to exchange a reasonable word with him. Probably his old-fashioned ideas and opinions had become a little confused owing to certain events in Belgium and in Turkey; the Turks, as it seemed, had not shown themselves exactly tolerant of the Armenians. It was indeed, fortunate that he had confined his furious protestations to the mute walls of the office and his own room.

Herr Hugo Wahl put his key-ring in his pocket and made ready to go upstairs. A reflection from the dimly lit street glimmered into the room. The electric light would have hurt Herr Wahl's eyes. Thoughts still circled in his still restless brain, though his body felt heavy. And yet if he lay down now, the red wine he had drunk and the cigars he had smoked would certainly keep sleep at bay for a long while.

He lowered himself into the deep arm-chair, thrust his legs out in front of him and relaxed his whole body, leaning his head against the back of the chair. His neck was too fat behind, he must really begin to have massages.

Herr Hugo Wahl was just over fifty-two and, with the exception of a slight fatty congestion of the heart, in tolerable condition; with his thick moustache and double chin, he looked impressive enough, even without the imperious glitter in his searching beady eyes. A round belly, adorned with a neat iron watch-chain, was a not uncommon complaint—but all things considered, the total effect was that of a solid stable man, in full control of himself and his affairs.

But all was not well. In matters of business there was scarcely anything to depress him. Trade was slight in these times. Too many possibilities of business were cut off; foreign countries had confiscated German property, and Germany had done the same. Of course, when peace came, this would be put right. The enemy would have to release our property, and compensate their own nationals for what, on grounds that might be good or bad, we might decide to withhold. The status or the shares of this or that industry or undertaking might indeed fluctuate; but the economic structure of the country as a whole was sound. Trade was based on, and bound up with, the war, and a spiral diagram could have been drawn showing how raw materials and production, distribution and retail trade, were grouped in concentric gradations according to their importance for the war. Hence, and within the financial compass of our enclosed economic life, it was only possible to give one's customers relatively modest hints. Absolutely safe investments? War loan, of course. Excellent interest and the highest guarantee in the world. The entire property of England, France, and Russia was pledged for the quiet sleep of those who chose this security for their old age or their children's future. But productive capital found its way, where possible, into steel works, coal mines, the timber trade, and textile factories. Old iron was much in request for smelting. Some bright intellect devised the utilization of slag heaps, containing supplies of semi-metals and other matters that were growing rarer and had suddenly become valuable. Copper was almost worth its weight in gold. Investors were fortunate who could secure an interest in chemical works in Thuringia or Bavaria, on the Rhine or the lake of Constance. If there was an explosion anywhere, it was anxiously kept secret, but the effect on business was slight, for it was not the shareholders who were blown up, only the workwomen, and the shares remained steady.

Herr Wahl yawned. A banker troubled as little about his money as a writer about his sentences, or a musician about his notes. It was the means to his end, the stone that built the structure. Money could be made out of everything—out of waste-paper, for instance. Indeed, the more venturesome were taking up more and more shares in factories that manufactured artificial thread and paper in substitution for wool and cotton, though this was regarded by many as absurd. All depended on how long the war went on.

Here, trade trenched on politics and indirectly on the military sphere. Since his conversation with Colonel Schieffenzahn, Herr

Wahl knew that with such men the conduct of the war was in the right hands. Small circles of sensible men in Unter Den Linden, or the Wilhelmstrasse, had never doubted that there might be anxious times, but such anxieties need not be published in the press. Trade was ready to back the financiers, and expected them to appreciate its own difficulties. We could carry on the war for a long while. A progressing concern like the German Empire, with such unusually strong credit assets, must, judged on the basis of any other such concern, show a profit on balance, and reward its directors, shareholders, and its loyal workmen, in accordance with the deserts of each. That meant visible spoils at the end of the war, in the form of annexations, cash indemnities, increase of power and population.

In all these matters he was at one with the Lords of the Berlin, Rhenish, and Silesian industry. The Landlords of the Mark of Brandenburg, his more especial customers, on whose confidence his father had built up the business, thought exactly in this fashion. The victory in Serbia, the steady advance of the Field-Marshal and his Generals, made everyone feel cheerful.

There was no sense in sitting in this chair; he could get no rest with his boots on. Herr Wahl walked softly up the stairs, a beautifully designed curved structure of yellow oak, reaching right up to the glass skylight. Someone would now be wandering about the Ducherow's house also—a mother. Poor youth, who had sealed with his blood the victory of the German arms. Geheimrat von Ducherow's manner betrayed nothing. He bore his loss with dry composure; only the line between his eyes had deepened. And it was said that his temper had grown worse.

Herr Hugo Wahl, too, was inclined to irritability in spite of his corpulence; but for a long time, indeed for months past, no angry word had been heard from him. There was a rift in his inner consciousness that paralysed him.

In the dressing-room he also avoided turning on the light. Latterly, Mathilde had been sleeping so lightly that she was awakened by the click of the switch. He could manage in the dark; breathing heavily, Herr Wahl found his slippers by the door; he could hang his coat over the back of a chair, and leave his trousers for one night out of the press. His stiff collar and shirt-front creaked obstinately as he took them off. The bathroom was next door. There his pyjamas and dressing-gown were waiting for him, and he would have to turn on the light.

As a politician and banker he could not but believe in the victory of our arms; compared with that, the duration of the war was a matter of indifference to him. As a father, his heavy jaw often dropped as he looked at the great clock in his office, or the calendar leaves on his writing-table, two unequal heaps, pierced and held by metal rings. The section for the past months of the year grew larger and larger. The new year was steadily approaching, and at Easter David would have to offer himself as a volunteer. Of course, a miracle might happen; France might suddenly collapse, or the Tsar lose heart at the losses that awaited him in the East. But it had to be admitted that the endurance of the French and the energy of the Russians had been undervalued. The Cavell case had now aroused an outburst in England, where there was now a general call for universal service. And he was dismayed to observe the skilful anti-German propaganda in America; and confidential reports from the Embassy there admitted a disquieting change of feeling.

Herr Wahl brushed his teeth, slowly and thoroughly; he did not like yesterday's taste in his mouth when he woke up. Then he washed in tepid water, and sluiced some over his head. That did him good. Then he freshened himself by rubbing his head with a rough towel, and dried his hair and moustache.

With any luck, David would be rejected as undeveloped; he was sinewy but too thin, with oversensitive artist's nerves, active brain, and lanky limbs. Please God he would be put back for six months—then one could breathe again. At that point, Herr Wahl conceded, still enveloped in a towel, his process of direct thought came to a halt. He had been among the very first who had flung all that they had and were into the will to victory; his savage confidence in Germany's military and economic strength drove his energetic temperament forwards and held him on his course. But from this point he was torn this way and that by a contradiction. The war must be carried on so long as Germany's greatness made it necessary; but his David . . . Of course, David must become a soldier, the very next day if it were possible. He must go to the front, and bear his burden; he must distinguish himself and be wounded—a wound that would not be dangerous and would take a long time to heal, and of course not in either of his hands. Only with the certainty that David would come back, could he carry on at all; and yet . . . and yet . . . he was shocked to think that he was making reservations for his son. It was true that one worked in order to work; but the prospect that the lad would bring artistic glory on the name of Wahl made Herr Hugo Wahl's heart beat faster. One must have a son, so that visible life might continue.

Herr Hugo Wahl weighed a hundred and eighty pounds, or rather more, but he could walk softly; he loved well-oiled door-hinges, and a bed that made no noise. The faint melody of the spring mattress did not count.

Recumbent thoughts differ from sedentary ones: the panorama of images passes more smoothly behind closed eyes. The Wahl family had no one in the field; and that was a sting and a reproach. The contrast with the house next door had now grown acute. After Board or Committee meetings he was often asked casually: "I think you are so fortunate as to have no one at the front, Herr Wahl?" And it cost Herr Wahl some effort to reply composedly: "Not at the moment, Herr Ministerialrat, but my boy is only waiting to go." Lenore would have removed all these difficulties if she had been engaged to poor Gerhard, or to some-one at the front. His wife had been lately referring a good deal to this Herr Bertin, who had been sent to Serbia not long ago.

Perhaps it would be a good thing to take a couple of soothing drops. The valerian root deserves a place of honour among the domestic herbs. He felt about cautiously on the little table by his bedside.

"Why don't you turn the light on, Hugo?"

There is always something startling about an unexpected human voice in the night. Husband and wife greeted each other; Frau

Mathilde was sorry for Herr Wahl, who was kept so late on business. It must be half-past one in the morning. Still, it was pleasant to have someone to talk to when one was bored with one's own thoughts.

But why wasn't she asleep?

Frau Wahl had indeed been asleep, but she had woken up again; Lenore would be twenty-three in December.

"Strange—or perhaps it isn't—that you should be thinking of that, too. A son-in-law would be a blessing for all of us."

"For David, too."

"For him, too," answered Herr Wahl.

"She's so self-centred now. Her last idea is to become a schoolmistress, and take the place of a master in a public school; she sits over her books, and smokes, and hardly talks at all. I haven't had a sensible word from her for a month. Dr. Matthias said the other day that for a girl of twenty-three a home of her own was a physical necessity. He always expresses himself so tactfully."

Herr Wahl gave a snort indicative of a short laugh. "The average girl spares her parents such anxieties. But men avoid her; they're afraid of those cold eyes of hers."

"Herr Bertin isn't."

"I don't like him," said Herr Wahl emphatically.

Frau Mathilde snatched irritably at the silk eiderdown; such a man was really too stupid. She, too, would have preferred another son-in-law, but one had to look facts in the face. All her welfare work for soldiers' dependants, her committees, all her labours among the poor who were afraid of accepting relief—all this went for nothing, so long as the Wahl family stood aloof, and was not rooted in the common destiny with its own flesh and blood. The attention of the world must be diverted from David. In the spring he would pass into the Sixth, volunteer for service, and be put back; that must be managed somehow, she did not yet know how. A fiancé at the front must be provided for Lenore before that. Why not the one that the girl had in her mind?

"Engagements are often broken," she added after a pause, "unforeseen circumstances, you know——"

"A prospective son-in-law at the front," said Herr Wahl meditatively, "that's an idea."

"And you'll soon see how the child will cheer up," said Frau Wahl, pursuing her train of thought.

"So you think she's in love with him?"

"I know it," said Frau Wahl, triumphantly, remembering an occasion when Bertin had kissed her daughter's hand; also, Herr Wahl had not kissed ners for many, many years.

"Well, really!" said Herr Wahl, thinking it necessary to make some show of indignation.

But Frau Wahl was not to be put down. "He'll be a famous man one day—you ask your father."

Herr Wahl shook himself. He did not want his father's views on these matters. A strange feeling of relief came over him. "A clever wife is a pearl of Solomon," he said, trying to quote an ancient proverb. "One proviso I must make; as long as the man is not a beggar, I won't oppose it at first."

"Silly," simpered Frau Mathilde. This was excellent. She would thus have her heart free to see about David. The engagement could be announced at Christmas or the New Year, with the added note: "At present with Mackensen's Army Group." That would avert all questioning looks, and silence all innocent inquiries. There was only Hugo's stipulation to be considered. She felt for the bed beside her, and touched Herr Wahl's shaved cheek. "What do you understand by a beggar, my dear? Everybody hasn't got a safe as full as yours, of course."

Herr Wahl could not help laughing. His wife's admiration tickled him all over, like the touch of her fingers on his chin. "Let him produce a bankbook; he must have a little money of his own—say, five thousand marks." He put his arm under Frau Mathilde's neck. She snuggled up to him. He became aware of the warmth of her body, the fragrance of her skin; and her hair brushed across his face. "Thilde," he murmured.

Chapter 5

BELATED DELIVERY

Bertha came in and announced that a woman wished to speak to the gracious Fräulein.

Lenore looked up from Cicero's letters—the orator was just then telling Tullia to see that the bathroom in the Tusculan villa was clean, as he was bringing guests. "Take the lady into the grey room." The likeness of the Roman world to our own delighted her. In those days, too, there were constant wars between the peoples of the North and West and mostly in France.

Bertha remained standing in the doorway. "It isn't a lady, gracious Fräulein, it's a woman in a shawl and a bonnet."

Lenore bent down to pick up her cigarette case: "All right, I'll come down at once."

The secret was out; the blow was about to fall. Too many people knew about it. One mouth had not been kept shut. Frau Nocks? Sister Vilma? Now the blackmail was beginning. A woman of the people in a shawl and bonnet would, if she were harmless, be asking for Frau Wahl, never for Fräulein Wahl. How much money had she? Not much. But she would soon earn some. When she got a post, she would be able to satisfy this envoy of complicity. None the less, she had to grip the banisters as hard as she had done in her worst days at the clinic, and a hysterical laugh was very near her lips.

The house was comfortably warmed. Many women whose husbands were agonizing at the front would have given something for a living-room as pleasant as this staircase in the Wahl house. Lenore knew this. The poor people were much worse off this winter than they had been in the previous one. What, to them, was the use of the government maximum prices, and lavish supplies in the shops, when the monthly wage hardly sufficed for bread, potatoes, and rent, a little sugar, lard, malt coffee, and milk? She must be careful not to make a mistake. She must listen to the blackmailer with all her wits about her, and, if she must, pay tribute for what she had suffered. Indignation would be no good. The patience, she reflected, of the poor, was as the patience of God. Their multitudes were groaning under the burden of the War. By ill luck a little of the reckoning had been presented to Lenore. She entered the familiar room with its light grey silk upholstery. There, with her back towards her, sat the strange woman who had come to levy tribute from one who had so sorely suffered; perhaps to buy butter for her children. Bowed shoulders, and grey hair secured by steel hairpins.

Then her heart leapt like a bursting bud. Frau Groschka. Paula Weber's—no, Paula Bunge's—charwoman. All was well; she breathed, and walked, and talked like her own self, and laughed Lenore Wahl's gentle laugh.

For a few moments Frau Groschka did not succeed in announcing the object of her visit. Her mind was still oppressed by the splendour of the room. Lenore was touched to hear her praises of what had been in the best taste at the beginning of the century: the Venetian lamps, their clicking prisms glittering faintly in the chill November sunshine, the gilt picture frames, the carved legs of the heavily upholstered chairs. Such matters were the ambition of small folk; the silver filigree of the three-tiered card-tray on the table, the gilt bronze flower-vases, the Chinese storks on the stove; all the splendour of a castle in the home.

Paula Bunge had gone back to her parents. She had been in a poor state since her young gentleman had died so sadly (". . . and so unnecessarily, Fräulein, he must have been a bit soft in the head"). Since she had come back from the Baltic, she distrusted, it appeared, all the public services. She maintained that one was overheard at the telephone; everything was lost in the post, and there were too many accidents on the railways. A friend of hers, a young man in the Foreign Ministry, was taking important papers by car to Strassburg and she had seized the opportunity to go with him. She was starting some time yesterday or today, although it was more uncomfortable, took longer, and she could carry less luggage.

"She'll get over it in time," said Frau Groschka encouragingly, "but she's still in a bad way." She had brought a letter for the gracious Fräulein—a large yellow object, inscribed "To be delivered by hand," as indeed her young lady had impressed on her. So here she was, and she had never seen such lovely gardenias in her life.

It cost Lenore an effort not to embrace her. She took the large envelope, warm from the contact with Frau Groschka's arm and bosom; the address was written in Werner Bertin's hand. Not now, not now. . . . She wanted to hear first how Frau Groschka was getting on, and what was the news from Paula's lodgings.

Frau Groschka had three jobs, at three different places, all in the morning; the lodging was to be sub-let, as Frau Bunge did not want to give it up. Some foreigners might be found to take it; Frau Groschka hoped to get another job, round about midday, since foreigners got up late. She had taken three hours on this trip, but Frau Bunge had paid her fare. She also went out and did washing, afternoon and evening. Her husband was driving a transport truck in Poland. And now she must go away before it got dark; daylight didn't last long these days.

Lenore pressed a five-mark note upon her, shook her hand, which felt hard within and cracked without, and took her down for a cup of hot coffee on the ground floor, in Frau Mahnke's warm well-lit domain. She was clutching the large yellow envelope tightly between her arm and breast.

She was conscious of her longing to open the letter, and to see at once what was inside its thin enclosure. It came from Bertin, and therefore it must be put aside in favour of her work. Alas, the time had passed when she tore open his letters the instant they arrived. She wanted to be well prepared for the Latin class tomorrow; her own affairs could wait.

Late that night, when the house was quite still, she began by opening Paula's letter. Her friend's sprawling script brought back a breath of the past. She had not been able to say good-bye; Frau Groschka would explain. She ought to have delivered the enclosed papers personally, on May 17th, as she had been instructed to do, "but I forgot, you know very well why. I am sure you will forgive the slight delay." (Slight delay, thought Lenore with an indulgent smile; she loved exactitude in all obligations.) "I hope you will soon get over your caprices, and all your old moods and opinions of those days in Tramsin. Women like us always find men. But, believe me, Lenore, only the man predestined; and when you have him, keep him. I think you are being obstinate, just to hurt him and yourself."

Lenore was shaken. Was she indeed taking vengeance on herself, she wondered, pacing up and down the room? And it was with no good conscience that she stifled the answer she could hear within her.

Thus pondering, she took Bertin's belated package into the light of her lamp. Poems: addressed to her, a little too fluent, in scanned metres, innocent of the modern angularities of speech and form; but adoration thrilled in every word. At the end of them she found another envelope inscribed: "Testamentary Disposition." She read the first sentences and the tears came into her eyes. Great round drops fell through her fingers on to the pages. Why had he behaved thus, and made her suffer so? Why never a word of understanding or sympathy, and no plea for forgiveness? But it was long since she had felt her heart go out towards the youth whom she still saw as he had been in Polling, with the fair hair and thin cheekbones of a boy. So the unhappy lad had made her his heir; she smiled, and her eyes were wet. What had he to leave? But that evening her sorrow was very sweet to her. She was, after all, just a young and foolish creature of three-and-twenty.

Frau Wahl was an anxious and attentive parent. She listened to her daughter, and asked tactful questions. Herr Wahl talked to Lenore paternally, without, at present, mentioning his proviso.

David was in favour of the engagement, and said so; he did not, indeed, much like owning such a fellow as his sister's fiancé, but she could break it off later on. Lenore, almost indifferent to this miracle, and in any case outwardly quite unmoved, said that she had no objection; her engagement with Bertin could be announced for the New Year. She hoped, from her very soul, that he would come back for it. When her mother brought the news, which she had obtained from various official sources, that an engagement was not at present regarded as a valid excuse for leave from the Balkans, she set her lips for a moment. Of course it wasn't. Well, the engagement should take place without him.

One night, about this time, she had the most absurd dream. In it was laughter and rejoicing, southern landscape, vistas of railway lines, locomotives and trains rumbling towards her and vanishing into tunnels. (Serbia, she thought in her dream.) The brave chief Great Snake had succeeded in escaping from the martyr's stake, and was wearing at his belt the flaxen scalp of Lottchen, the doll. Unfortunately little Lottchen had had to die. Her murderer was pale and bearden (so she dreamed the word—not bearded); but at the end there were great scenes of reconciliation; it had rained, a seven-hued rainbow arched the heavens like a gateway, and through it glimmered the gods bringing victory and peace; there was music, long-linked repeated harmonies, trumpets, the cadenced sweep of violins, and the softer notes of horns. She stood by the bitter waters, and threw into them grains of glass, like honey, amber pearls, clear as gold, clinking faintly as they fell. This was some fleeting memory from opera—against a background of scenery, the great Manitou pointed to the constellation of Edith Cavell; it hung in the firmament between Andromeda and Cassiopeia, and sang the great Amen.

Chapter 6

THE NIGHT AND THE DAY

On the flat South Hungarian plain, between fields of harvested maize and the brown Pussta, stood, like a tall crooked gallows, the draw-well by which the field kitchen of 1/X/20 had halted. It and the little truck with the post bags were the centre of a throng of men, as the company rested for an hour at midday, and letters were given out. The vast void bowl of heaven swung over that company of field-grey men, who, severed for weeks past from every connexion with their own troops, now stood with their great-coats flung open, spattered from head to foot with mud, balancing parcels in their hands and tearing open letters. Here and thus Private Bertin learned that his engagement to Fräulein Lenore Wahl would be announced on January 1st in three newspapers, one in Berlin, one in Potsdam, and one in Kreuzburg. Owing to the bad communications in Serbia, where railways are few, he read the news very little earlier than the rest of the world, namely on the last day but one of the year 1915, which, according to the arithmeticians and prophets of the army, was also to have been the last year of the war. He sat for the moment on the handle of his shovel, which he leaned against the parapet of the well. Then, in spite of his aching feet, he hobbled down into the maize field with clods of earth still sticking to his boots, broke off five or six thick maize stems, lay down on them and stared up into the cloudless blue, now washed clean of all the rain of yesterday. A miracle. It was not to be grasped, nor questioned; it was to be accepted, for it had most unmistakably befallen him.

The company was engaged in repairing a road to Kevevara,

the road being a sort of sluggish stream of clay. To make it practicable for the removal of heavy guns to Germany, the men groped with their hands in the miry mass for stones to fill up the chasms in the foundation of the road; the clay was then shovelled away and heaped into yard-high walls of dirt on either side of it. After fearful weeks of rain, a warm December sun had now appeared to dry these toil-worn labourers. Yesterday they had finished a section of this appalling highway, only to have to shoulder their packs again early this morning and move on to fresh labour, fresh desolation, and fresh hunger. Three of them, Willms, Holzer, and Bertin, had bidden a friendly farewell to the Serbian with whom they had been billeted, a young peasant in the Serbian quarter of a village in which there was also a Saxon, Rumanian, and Hungarian quarter. They spoke Austro-German in those parts; their host produced a good atlas and showed them where they were. The three Berliners were astonished at their first Serbian acquaintances, man and woman; it seemed to Bertin that their profiles might well have figured on the gems and coins of another Balkan land to the southwards—a land called Attica.

Slowly the company trudged through that fertile land—through the six-foot jungle of the maize-fields, the stretches of wheat-stubble, as they neared the Danube. Beyond, towards the south, a blue delicate line of mountains rose into the sky. Every dawn they were awakened by a sudden storm of cock-crows from the trees and roof-tops; stern discipline had preserved the peasant's farmyard.

The evening before his engagement Bertin spent in a baker's oven. The farm to which they had been assigned was already swarming with angry men from the head of the column; evading such disputes Holzer came upon the top of the great curved clay chamber, into which they could creep by bending double; the chimney of it was large enough for a corpse to have fallen down it, as happened in the fairy-tale. All three dragged some straw out of the barn, and made themselves comfortable, though they had to be careful not to knock their heads against the sooty roof;

there they were able to sit at their ease, and chew some pieces of very hard bread, a thin strip of bacon, and a little roasted pumpkin. With the soldier's heedlessness they warmed their tea, a sugary and somewhat dubious drink, at a little open fire. Bertin lay back comfortably and smiled at the Hansel and Gretel bake-oven to which he had been consigned by the spells of stepmother Fate. In his pocket he could hear the crackle of the letter sending soft electric currents through all his being. Tomorrow, his own and the Wahl parents would duly celebrate the betrothal—the union between himself and Lenore that had seemed so utterly impossible. The two families were to meet at Schreiberhau, half-way, in the beloved mountains of his home, which, for purposes of this meeting, Herr Wahl had finally preferred to Oberhof and Harzburg. The fairy-tale suffered some slight alteration; the Prince had indeed been lucky enough to win the Princess, but he was still sitting in a bake-oven or even humbler places wondering how he should get out. Three tired soldiers lay snoring in the harsh reek of the stale soot, and among the tickling wheat straw.

On the following day at noon, on a steam pontoon, the company crossed the Danube, a vast clay-yellow stream that dashed in leaping eddies against the sides of the vessel. A wind had sprung up, a cold mountain wind, and the little steamer laboured heavily across. On their left rose the crenellated walls of the Turkish citadel of Semendria; up the slope of the hill clambered the first Serbian town, neat white houses, embowered in vineyards; and yonder stood the wreckage of a graceful little church tower. The company was billeted in an outlying street, and told to keep as quiet as they could; the Inspector-General of Communications was in the place and his people were always down on A.S.C. men. They all scattered among the neighbouring streets; and Noglisch, Russ, and Holzer soon came upon an excellent spot: a deserted ironmonger's shop, which, though it was heavily shuttered, they were able to enter from the back. They collected frying-pans, nails, tools, and some little stew-pots. Thus, within the compass of human strength—for they had to carry all this themselves—they were provided against all emergencies. Bertin was attracted by the white cubed mass of the church. In the tumult of devastation beams and fragments of beams lay in confusion on the floor; great liturgical books, inscribed with square notes of music, had been scattered in torn sheets before the altar; and the bells hung in the sacristy beneath the open sky. The young man clambered meditatively out into the air once more. He took with him a scrap of yellow brocade, embroidered in red upon a gold ground, a fragment from a tattered altar-cloth, intending to send it to his fiancée for her betrothal. Today, on New Year's Eve, she would be sitting there, so lovely, her sensitive face perhaps pensive and sad, perhaps turned in sweet vivacious interest towards his parents. She would gradually make friends with them, and come to love his mother's shy kindness, and the formal courtesy of his father, who would certainly fall in love with her—Bertin could see his face at that moment, with its myriad little wrinkles at the corners of the eyes. And on New Year's Day they would drink wine in Silesian crystal goblets and clink them in celebration of this alliance. He sighed, but he admitted that any complaint against this unimaginable stroke of luck would be the crassest ingratitude against his destiny. Indeed, the main feeling in his mind that evening could be embodied in the words: Marvellous girl, how did you contrive this also?

However, it was fated that he too should celebrate this evening with wine, though he was to drink it from tin or aluminum. There was much whispering going on among the men. Willms had spoken to a sentry who was tramping back and forwards round the corner of the street, a Bavarian infantryman. He was guarding some sort of establishment where wine was kept; below in the garden stood great barrels of fresh fermenting must. A sensible sentry; his instructions were to march up and down his beat, and what happened in the meantime behind his back was no concern of his. Holzer, Willms, little Winkler, each with two saucepans, hurriedly disappeared. The others stretched themselves out upon their blankets; a jolly night was before them. The three spies came back from the Promised Land with their grapes in liquid form; in the darkened streets they had met many grey figures in overcoats and field caps, cautiously bearing water-flasks and saucepans.

Hoffman Georg, publican, and a man of weight by virtue of his self-possession and his Berlin speech, took charge. Bertin tasted cautiously; yes, it was must, not yet fermented, calculated to overthrow the strongest, and only to be used convivially in the strictest moderation. He allowed himself a quarter litre to toast his betrothal. It was not usual to warn grown men if they thought fit to plunge into an unexplored adventure. None the less he did tell the others that this stuff made a man very quickly drunk. Roars of contemptuous protest from all sides echoed from the kitchen. Did he think that Berlin workmen couldn't stand their drop? This thin muck wasn't going to do them any harm. In secret, Werner Bertin raised an aluminum cup in that bare room, and drank to his beloved, a thousand miles away, beyond many rivers, plains, and lakes. Over great cities, Budapest, Vienna, Prague, his thoughts flew northwards through the night mists and over humming telegraph wires, white and swooping like a carrier pigeon, crossed the snowy ridge of the Silesian mountains, and alighted in the brightly lit guest-room of the "Three Ravens" hotel, on a lovely young woman's bare shoulder. A silvery tinkle in Lenore's ear announced his arrival; she heard, laid down her fish knife and cried: "That's Werner; he is thinking of us; let us all drink his health." In that moment she quite forgot that she hated him; she was just his betrothed, who had overcome the opposition of the world; sadly she stretched out her bare arm and raised her glass, while her gaze swept through and far beyond those walls before her.

Near a stump of candle Bertin was smoking his last cigar but one, and slowly sipping his drink. A sort of boyish gaiety thrilled within him; he was dreaming contentedly of what the future held in store. Alas, the page was turned. A man of the first platoon suddenly burst in, in overcoat and pack, and slung with clattering utensils. "Come on now! Fall in! We're off again." Great Heaven! They had all begun to sing in chorus, and were toasting the drink, the New Year, and the peace. It was ghastly to have to tumble out again. But discipline beckoned with iron finger; there was a general rush for the door. Here difficulties arose. The room turned round in the most malignant fashion, the floor heaved, and a man saw several packs where he looked to find his own. It is not easy to force a foot with the left boot on it, into the right boot as well. Hoffmann Georg, dripping with sweat, a gigantic figure with furrowed brows and great grim nose, tried to sober himself by the force of will. A feebler character, little Winkler, for example, sat on the hearth in the kitchen and refused to budge. Jensen crouched over the fireplace and roared out that he had been poisoned. "My lad," said Holzer to Bertin, "I'm very glad I took your advice. Now help me to get the brutes out; they'll sober up in the open air."

Outside on the cobbled street men from the various platoons crashed and clattered and stumbled, looking for their fellows. Lit up by the glare of pitch torches, the alcoholic throng at last straightened into the swaying semblance of a line, with neither head nor tail, leaderless and bewildered, surely the drunkest company in the whole array of Prussia; and upon that shameful spectacle, the house-walls of the conquered town silently looked down. Staggering N.C.O.s stammered out the names of their men; many of them saw double, and many could hardly see at all. This went on for some time, until the Sergeant-Major, one Barkopp, was aware of something like a line of men in front of him. He had stiffened himself by fixing his rifle under his pack, after the fashion of the peg that keeps toy soldiers upright. The corporals did likewise. Orders were rapped out in broad Hamburg dialect and the clipped speech of Berlin, amid much clamouring and laughter, until at last the Sergeant-Major roared: "Number off from the right!" Usually the numbers ran like a sharp staccato through the ranks, but that night, though no one actually missed, there was much choking and spluttering and stammering, as each man took up the tale.

Private Bertin, certainly the only sober man in the company, from his place between Holzer and Willms, surveyed this Witches'

Sabbath, these New Year antics, and thought them an excellent omen for the great times of peace that were soon, he believed, to come. Suddenly his eyes fell on Acting-Sergeant-Major Glinsky who had abruptly appeared behind Sergeant Barkopp and was dryly observing the scene. He too had drunk nothing; perhaps company business had kept him out of the carouse. Sergeant-Major Wachler, with the long beard, had been attached, owing to his special knowledge, as liaison officer to the Constructions Section of the Line of Communications, and had gone on to Jagodina; Glinsky, by rank and age Barkopp's junior, was in charge of the company. "Look out, my boy," said Bertin to Holzer; the latter asked whether he was dreaming, or whether that was Glinsky who had just appeared from the void. Fear made him alert. There was certainly something up. It was known that Wachler had sent in to Berlin an application for transfer, because he could never become an Acting-Officer in that company. On strictly service grounds, Barkopp's was the better claim to the succession, but Glinsky, a typical go-between and bully, would have suited the officers much better. The spectacle of a snake eating up the frog, Barkopp, might then have been observed. Bertin saw Glinsky's cold eyes fixed upon the sergeant: "Stand aside, please, and get along to your platoon."

At any other time Sergeant Barkopp would have grasped that any sort of misconduct would lose him all chance of promotion or the Iron Cross, and ensure his being put to the most unpleasant jobs available. But he felt so utterly in the right, and in such remarkably good humour. What? He, Barkopp, not fit to lead his section? And to be told so by a swine from Berlin, who had no feeling for the men and thought only of his own promotion! He snorted, pulled his rifle out from under his pack, swung it on to his shoulder, and swayed menacingly towards the enemy; and he roared out that he would command his section drunk, just as well as Glinsky sober. He wasn't going to take any orders from *him*.

"You heard," said Glinsky, in a tone of ominous composure, to Corporal Bohne and Lance-Corporal Näglein. "Refusal of duty under arms, and in the presence of the rank and file. You will have to give evidence."

"You go to hell, my lad," shouted Sergeant Barkopp with great cheerfulness. "These are my men, and under my orders. 'Tention! By the right—Turn!"

"That's enough," said Glinsky in a tone of contemptuous disgust, looking over the head of the drunken man. "That's more than enough." And, in fact, no more was needed. "Company! Attention!" His voice cut sharply into the night air; and the company swung stumbling by the right into the main street where in the glare of torches the transport of 1/X/20 stood waiting. And in a storm of shouts, and songs, and cat-calls, the long column swung through the silent streets of Semendria to the railway station. It was about twelve o'clock; and as the hour struck, the roars of greeting to the New Year and curses on the Old Year next day impelled the Inspector-General of Communications, a very irritable nobleman, to inquire what sort of revolution had broken out during the night.

Werner Bertin walked along beside his wagon, pondering as he went. Barkopp was done for. (A fortnight later he was, in fact, given several days' field punishment, and deprived of all good-conduct marks.) Glinsky was now to be the man; he, Bertin, must keep out of the way, and take care not to get into his power. There was time and enough to impress this on his mind. An icy New Year wind swept across from the Danube. Sobered and very cold, the men crawled up the sloping approaches to the station. Here and there stood braziers, which gave but little warmth. Thus broke the New Year of 1916, over many aching heads. About four o'clock, they at last all crowded into a line of freight cars, and lay, crouching close and shivering under their blankets, while the train rumbled southwards into Serbia.

Chapter 7

FRÄULEIN HANNES

A young lady, very bright and brisk, her small nose, rosy from the cold, pressed against her muff, is hurrying down the steps of the Potsdam railway station. Her eyes under her fur cap are clear and shining, she grasps her portfolio of papers firmly under her arm, and her hair glitters as she climbs into the omnibus. Unquestionably, Fräulein Lenore Wahl.

After Christmas she had done a cure which must have been very effective; she had been tumbling about in the snow in vain attempts to slide down a hill on skis; and her many companions, officers on leave from the ski-battalion at Hirschberg, unwearyingly picked her up, brushed the snow off her, and thought her very pretty. An engagement ring on her left hand, which Herr Berthold Bertin had put on her finger with charming Silesian compliments—only older men can really appreciate a girl—must certainly be gifted with electric force, apart from all the good fairies of the climate. University holidays last longer than school holidays; but the Wahl ladies, with the father and brother, have come early back to Potsdam. Frau Mathilde, perched on a sleigh and a trifle bewildered, had let herself be steered down a hill by her daughter, so fast that she could hardly see or hear, and the snow whirled up her puttees. The folk of Schreiberhau prided themselves so ingenuously upon their mountains, their pines, their high and wholesome air, as though they had produced them all; and the food on the hotel tables might well have suggested that the villagers themselves had enough to eat, which they had not. Lenore knew that she felt disgracefully well. Secretly she sent half her monthly allowance to the collecting station, to provide a plate of milk soup for the schoolchildren every morning.

She was full of grateful feelings when she got into the train to come home. As they passed through Hirschberg, her thoughts went out for a moment towards the soldiers' cemetery, where, above a snowy mound could be read "Andreas Bunge, Jäger." Since she had passed through a little while before, a wreath of laurel, holly, and mistletoe had been hung on the cross.

She now began to enjoy her work more than ever. How easy it was to learn Greek, especially under so able a teacher as Fräulein Hannes. She was a tall East Prussian girl, with shapely limbs, strong hands, yellow braided hair, and eyes of cornflower blue. Her face dimpled when she laughed, and her parted lips showed white and shining teeth; then, in an instant, from that grown woman flashed forth a lovely village lass, one to win and hold men's hearts.

"Every official must be replaced by a woman sooner or later," observed Fräulein Hannes in her broad Prussian speech, as she strode up and down Lenore's room. Every morning she went to the local secondary school, where she was a temporary teacher, lined up the fifth- and even the six-form boys in the corridor, and drilled them, as she had learnt to do from watching the manœuvres on the parade-grounds of her home. "Eyes right! Eyes front! . . . By the right—turn! By the left—turn! Forward march!" and "Company!—Right about wheel! That," she said, "is such good exercise for the mind. A few knee-bends are better than a declension. And it keeps the little ruffians in hand." In the later mornings she taught Latin and Greek, and on four afternoons a week she came to Lenore. They liked each other. Each thought the other her superior. Fräulein Hannes felt a sympathetic admiration for Lenore's graceful cleverness, her luxurious setting, and her aloofness from life; Lenore found in Fräulein Hannes a purposeful and cultivated woman, facing what she had to face, and determined never to give way. She often spoke of delightful experiences with a friend of hers, a well-known painter called Fritz Niehoff-Barmen, to whom she was, indeed, engaged, though they did not at present want to get married. He had been called up eight months before, and he too was in the Army Service Corps, on the Western front. Fräulein Hannes, when she had heard Lenore's vocabularies, introduced her to a new conjugation or taught her some simple mysteries of syntax, was always glad to stay to supper with the Wahls—as this meant an addition to her fee, and helped her to make her rations last out.

By that time bread, meat, potatoes, vegetables, milk, and eggs, were all subject to a detailed system of regulations, which the Germans had to obey or take much trouble to evade. The constant production of food cards stamped the purchaser as the inferior of the seller; it was always with a gasp of relief that women emerged from the shops. The monthly distribution of the cards at the magistrates' offices became an exercise of force, transforming a crowd of once humble employees into unrelenting masters.

Fräulein Hannes did not object. She was a Prussian from Königsberg, and thus "doubly dyed in the wool," in the old phrase; the main thing was that we should win the War. "What we have conquered," she said, rolling the *r*, "we should be fools ever to give back. Our enemies will finish the War a good deal less well off than they started it." From time to time she spoke of her friend, with reserve, but there was fondness in her eyes. On one occasion she brought a large sketch-book full of water-colour studies of the Courland sandhills; and some studies of the nude, in which Lenore recognized Fräulein Hannes's vigorous and lovely form; both much more talented than the picture of his that she had seen more formally displayed in an exhibition. Fritz Niehoff had talent; something, however, must be done to stop him from working up these bold and lovely inspirations into academic oil paintings. "Now," said Fräulein Hannes with shining eyes, "he is serving the Fatherland. But afterwards, when the war is over, he will produce something great, real German art from the Rhineland."

Lenore was rather taken aback to find herself comparing Private Niehoff of the A.S.C., and Private Bertin of the A.S.C. In the latter, too, there was more than his present "work" suggested. He, also, was now serving his Fatherland; if he came back, he, too, she hoped, had stored up the stuff and energy for great designs and great achievements. But she, Lenore, had gone through more than this frank and sensuous creature had ever dreamed of. She wished she had talked candidly to Bertin.

"We've both of us got husbands in the A.S.C.," Fräulein Hannes would often say with a laugh, "except that we don't get any separation allowance. I don't suppose you've lived like a nun either." Her man was in Flanders busy building gun-positions and dug-outs, in that awful water-logged land. "If he only doesn't get rheumatism in his legs—a painter must be able to stand and walk about."

David, too, made use of Fräulein Hannes's visits. She was much better than his toothless old usher at explaining a passage of prose, or disentangling the grammar of a line of poetry. He was fond of sitting down beside the two girls after supper; and late in the evening he would bring into his sister's room some point that puzzled him, if he saw her light was still burning. What particularly annoyed him was that her relations with Bertin had not improved. He wanted to see Lenore cheerful and full of energy as the time came near for him to make his own decisions. Now and again came a postcard from happy little Hilde Cohn, who was working in a dressing-station far away behind the lines in Poland, and was inclined to sentimentalize over the heroic times and her own hard work. "When are you joining us?" she wrote. "Come out into the great world and grow into a man." "Silly little fool," observed David; "fancies herself as the bride of a hero. Has your young man written again? What is he really doing in Serbia?"

"He isn't having too good a time," said Lenore evasively; "after all, he'll soon have been at it for six months, and it's hardly his job."

"He hasn't once been home on leave," growled David, rummaging in Lenore's bookshelves. "You're becoming very learned, Lene; I shall soon be getting you to coach me."

"Oh, indeed! But coaching is not to be had for nothing. You ask Fräulein Hannes."

"And then," said David, kissing her on the neck, "I'll see if something can't be done for your young man."

"No use," said Lenore with a sad smile, "he is a thousand miles away as the crow flies, and a private in the A.S.C., more insignificant even than one of the little infantrymen that march round the corner every morning."

"You wait and see," said David, with an air of mysterious triumph. "Leave me a free hand, don't ask questions, and don't be rude to your little brother."

"As if my little brother minded what I said to him."

That evening David Wahl carried a thick letter to the post. It contained only the briefest message from himself; he had merely taken some grey sheets of paper in a grey envelope from a secure hiding-place and "shot them off," as he described it, to his sister's young man, so that the latter might reflect whether, war or no war, he had not urgent duties awaiting him at home. For, thought David on his way back from the post, with his hands in his great-coat pockets—a damp, chill, bitter wind was shrieking through the streets—though this was war-time, the war would sometime end. But if the views of the older and more foolish generation were right, it would never end at all. As his idiotic ushers were accustomed to observe in their speeches on the Emperor's birthday, the day of idleness and peace was past. Germany would have to guard for half a century the conquests she was now imposing on the world. Today cohorts of new Romans tramped again along the roads of the old world, holding their triumphant eagles against the wind. The day of triumph—whenever it did arrive—would find upon the earth a conquering race, inured to hardship, and the true frontiers of the Holy Roman Empire thrust down to Milan, and as far north as the Eider; Pax Germaniæ, victory and peace. So—let us look upwards at this hour. . . . (Cheers!)

As he was on his way to his room, Lenore's door opened. "Come in if you aren't too tired. I feel lonely and I can't sleep."

There was a shudder in her voice. What had happened? Something had happened that day, and something so fearful that her mother's news of her father's stipulation that Bertin must prove himself possessed of not less than five thousand marks before marriage could be thought of, had quite vanished from her mind, and she sat there at half-past eleven, writing.

Fräulein Hannes had appeared at her usual hour—a flickering ghost of her, with parted lips and staring eyes. She saw Plato's *Phædo* on the table, snatched it up and shook it savagely, and cried: "Plato is a lying hound! He said that to die was to get up silently and depart to ampler regions, like a sentinel who has been relieved. Despicable rubbish!" And she hurled the book against the wall; it dropped to the floor and lay, with outspread pages, like a dead butterfly. Her man, Niehoff, had been killed; the War had got him at last. "They put him to manage a canteen," she sobbed, with a handkerchief between her teeth, "behind the Flanders front. He had to sell beer and groceries to the men." Five days before, the English had shot the canteen to bits with railway guns, and both Niehoff's hands had been torn off just as he was cutting up a length of soap. He had soon bled to death, and now lay buried in a watery grave in the cemetery at Hollebeke. And that was the end of him. "They're beasts," shrieked Fräulein Hannes; "the War's driven them crazy—you can't treat human beings like this."

Gone was the glory of the War; she ceased to look for victory. She was no longer a girl; she had shared her life with one who had now been reft from her. "I shan't get over this," she said, with trembling lips. "I'm finished."

And Lenore saw that she might go on living, but that she would now never change. She had not had imagination enough to enter into the lives of others; but character she did possess, and what struck at herself, she was far too candid to disguise as sacrifice. The saddest thing about it, she went on, now grown calmer, was the cemetery of Hollebeke. In July 1912, on a holiday in Flanders, he had stood with her by the cemetery at Hollebeke—they had been to see his parents at Barmen, not far away. "How lovely," he had then said to her. She had heard him with her own ears, she had not dreamed or imagined it. "I should like to be buried here." Where did he now lie? Perhaps in the very spot on which his eyes had rested, as he had stood there with his hands on the cemetery railing.

Strange things grew stranger when the teller of them had such haunted eyes. She pondered. Men had mysterious forebodings, that was certain. When the rhythm of the soul grew slower and man sank into the recesses of his self and ceased to think, he could dimly see the curves of destiny.

Men of the Army Service Corps behind the Western front had no easy time. It warmed her heart to think of Bertin in his bake-oven or in a Serbian pig-sty. If only he came back safe and sound. He was bound to be rather damaged by the hardships of his present life, but she would soon make up for it and put him right.

David listened with lowered eyes. "I have just sent him the grey letter, the one from Tramsin, you remember." As she rose quickly and stood before him in a flush of fear, he held up his hand. "You told me to do as I thought best. Now he'll try his hardest to get sent back here, and you will be your old self again."

Lenore looked at him, and in her eyes was a deep-seated doubt. "Who knows what you have done? I don't think I shall be able to sleep tonight." But then she suddenly raised her shoulders, drew a deep breath and said: "Yes, you were right, I shall sleep tonight."

When David had gone, she knelt down by the little yellow-covered *Phædo,* and fixed it with needles into the cracks of the flooring. To make sure it would not be touched, she drew a warning circle round it in chalk. Bertha, the housemaid, would then understand. For a few days she would leave it so; the graveyard of Plato and his consolations, that are of no avail when the red blood of the beloved spurts on to the tent-walls, and a man goes down to meet those dogs from which there is not return.

Chapter 8

A BRANCH CAUGHT IN THE CURRENT

Werner Bertin, in deep contentment, strolled from Üsküb station up to the town. Among clouds of pink-glowing peach and almond trees, cubed honeycomb-like, gaily painted houses climbed both banks of the river; above them towered the ramparts of the Turkish citadel. In the breast pocket of his tunic he carried the grey letter. Behrend the post-orderly having, with the best of intentions, handed it to his comrade early that morning before he started for Üsküb with Sergeant Bohne to fetch some new field-kitchens. The winter was over; it had only lasted two months. After some hard marching up and down the sides of mountains, they had at last reached Nish, where they had clambered on to the roofs of freight cars and rumbled through many tunnels to Vranje, which was to be their headquarters for many weeks. They kept the roads to Kumanovo in condition, just as they had previously repaired the Semendria-Nish road; and their work was done with skill and energy, under severe privations. Bertin had learned a great deal. Always in close touch with the inhabitants of the country, both peasants and townsmen, he had come to think that the newspapers had libelled Serbia in a manner very hard to understand. In the mountain villages the house doors were never locked; they were barely closed by wooden bolts, and clean with the cleanliness that goes with poverty alone. He had made friends with Bulgarians and exchanged presents with them; and he had watched Serbian peasants, carried off by the Landsturm, taking a dumb and heartrending farewell of their wives and children. These men of the Balkans were certainly not less human than the readers of the newspapers, who believed all the rousing propaganda that was printed. He was often surprised to find how well he felt, in spite of short rations and continual toil, without Sundays and holidays. He had never before spent a whole winter, and a spring that came so quickly, at a height of three thousand feet in the latitude of Florence. In that clear air he had to protect his eyes with dark glasses; otherwise no precautions were needed. The long marches back and forwards before the dawn and in the twilight made and kept him fit; and the spring soon scattered primulas and plum-blossom over the slopes of Vranje. In the noontide hours weasels darted in and out of dead horses' skulls; a few paces from the roads the country was a desolation of ravines and thorn bushes, and undergrowth now turning green; and a Turkish castle above the town provided a peaceful refuge in which to write a poem and escape the attentions of the redoubtable Glinsky, who would not, for so much as a quarter of an hour, allow anyone under his command to feel at ease.

In those days a feeling of confidence in a speedy peace was rife in all the armies of the Central Powers. At the headquarters of the local command in Vranje, the war reports were eagerly awaited: German armies had attacked Verdun, and success after success had been announced. "Now the whole bloody show will soon be over!" shouted a young Hussar lieutenant beside Bertin, when the fall of Douaumont went up on the board, and all the bystanders, including the bespectacled Bertin, thought and shouted "Hurrah!"

Bertin loved the new town. Almost a dozen minarets rose like white smoke columns turned to stone in the immaculate blue of the morning sky. There was time to stroll about; he loved to wander in the streets, and contemplate the mosques with their grey and shining cupolas, and their snow-white walls embowered in jasmine, lilac, and roses. He ceased to be a soldier. As the minutes passed, the man that he had been rose from the buried levels of his soul, thrilled within him, and looked out of his eyes. An eager traveller, open to all the trivial experiences that the passing hour might bring, suddenly found himself in the East, and drank in all the new impressions that poured from every corner, from the long stone walls, and the narrow cobbled alleyways of a little Turkish town. Macedonians in baggy-seated breeches, Turks in their turbans and red girdles, and black-veiled women walked across the bridge, which was guarded by helmeted sentries; it spanned the Vardar on several stone arches, and was perhaps of Roman construction. In an open grey car, with much hooting of the horn, the Field-Marshal, looking like a white-haired panther, drove across the bridge, and at his side, the thin insignificant figure of an Imperial Prince, who was spending the war at Üsküb. Austrian officers in slim tunics, red-breeched Hungarian cavalrymen with corded dolmans, shaggy dromedaries, peasant women with water jugs upon their heads as in the days of Alexander the Great, filled the scene. A street of Spanish goldsmiths, with their signs in Hebrew characters, fascinated Bertin. He marvelled at the smoke-yellow amber, from drops and blocks of which they fashioned ornaments: pipe-mouthpieces, necklaces and hairpin-heads. He longed to buy a piece of silver-work or an amber pendant for Lenore, but his money would not run so far. A penniless author with an income of fifteen marks ninety a month must think of some more modest gift. The far-flung walls of the citadel tempted him up the road to the upper town. Here he was encompassed by the Orient; in the noontide hours, between the arches and the windowless house-fronts with their filigreed Moorish portals, the light was dim and magical. Suddenly the alley opened on to a broad square; at the further end of it the great house of Allah held him spellbound with its broad and dignified façades, broken only by two small windows, and above them the great smooth dome like a curving breast. Could he get inside? An old man with a broad grey beard approached him, impressively turbaned, dark-faced, bright-eyed, and arrayed in a long red-girdled robe—perhaps the Mullah of the Mosque.

"Parlez-vous Arabe?" he asked abruptly, raising his hand slightly as if in salutation.

Did he speak Arabic? In a flash Bertin thought of his beard.

A growth of shining black hair covered his cheeks and lips; since the end of the previous year he had not had an hour's daylight in which to shave himself. He understood; the man thought him an Oriental, probably of Jewish extraction. He smiled as he answered in French; unfortunately, no, he was a German soldier. Might he be allowed to see over this wonderful church?

The Mullah surveyed him in silence, motioned him through a door and a curtain beyond it, signed to him to take off his boots and withdrew.

He stood in a great chamber, the chill of which struck suddenly against him, lofty and void, rough-cast in reddish brown, the floor quite covered with carpets. Never had Bertin seen such stuffs. Woven marvels from Persia, parrot-green and pink, under the sandals he had put on in the anteroom. The incenseless air was still faintly odorous of wax. From a dais came a monotonous murmur of prayer or instruction that recalled the ancient melodies of the synagogue. In three rows, crouching crossed-legged under the lofty vault, sat schoolboys in lambskin caps repeating stanzas, and swaying rhythmically back and forward. He realized that this was the way in which the Koran was learnt; and he did not want to disturb them. The sun burned steeply down upon the dust-coloured square, and his shadow grew shorter. Hunger drove him back into the more populous quarters of the town, and he had to ask someone to direct him to the privates' mess where he was to get his dinner that day. But he was not anxious to sink once more into the Prussian private, so he thought he would still pretend to be on a holiday. He sat down on a metal chair, warm from the sunshine, outside a little café, drank Turkish coffee made with sugared water in small copper jugs, and nibbled little horns of almonds pounded up with rose-water. Men passed with great skin bottles on their backs or loaded on to donkeys, and chanted the praises of their *oka,* a refreshing drink, light brown in colour and made of fermented milk. Bertin tried a cup of it. He longed to disappear, change his clothes in yonder corner, and emerge as a dignified Spanish Jew in lambswool cap, sitting all day long in a little shop selling tobacco, honey, or goldsmith's work. At last he lit a cigar, preparatory to opening the thick grey envelope in the shady quiet of that place. At once the scene around him vanished—the Orient, the little town, and one Private Bertin. A savage tirade struck him in the face: accusations and reproaches and insult. She addressed him formally, called him a coward, a deserter, who brought about disaster, and then with cheap excuses went his way. She said she was done with him, and would never see him again. Just as she had had to manage her little "affair" by herself, so she would manage her life alone—without him, his arrogant pedantry, and all the qualities she so despised.

Werner Bertin, when he read this, was a man still young, quick to anger, who had been ten months a soldier. Regarded without any mitigating prejudice, he had fallen into the lowest stratum of human society—except that he himself had not really become aware of the fact. He could neither go nor come as he wished; his clothes were prescribed for him down to the smallest detail. He had to submit to the most intimate handling of his person when it was the will of his superiors, he had to eat his food with spoons out of tin saucepans, he had to satisfy the needs of nature, in company with many others, perched on a horizontal bar; he had at all times to subject his will. He had to learn to estimate everything that came within his purview in accordance with the claims of the commonest needs of life; did it satisfy hunger, provide warmth or shelter from the rain, or contribute to the improvement of his lodging? He was thus on a level with very small children, convicts, and conscripted labourers, who have no earnings. But he had left a sphere full of difficult human relations, the life of an imaginative artist, who could feel his way into the future. A writer who was to divine and vivify the new and ardent ways of love, that plunged youth into fresh understandings and fresh conflicts, must indeed be such a man. It now became clear that ten months cannot change the centre-point of being. In the terrible weeks of Jabukovac, Pojate, and Razani he might perhaps have given way to panic; now, he drew a deep breath, and though the colour left his face, he calmly scanned the incredible document. It was undoubtedly Lenore's handwriting, and her style; the date, "Tramsin, August 15," explained everything. It was only too natural that she should then have hated him, fresh as she was from those dreadful weeks. But why now, after the engagement, did she rekindle the ancient grudge. In the envelope he discovered a small card, covered with a small sloping script, angular, but very clear. "My dear future Brother-in-Law," wrote David Wahl. "Many of us find your descriptions of the painted Serbian marriage carts rather tactless, especially when there is one of us with an account against you that you have not met. So I enclose, without further comment, this letter, which I have not read." (The "not" was twice underlined.) "Perhaps this will induce you to cut short your country holiday, though the prospect of your return is not very agreeable to, yours sincerely, David Wahl." Bertin burst out laughing. Passersby must have thought that he was reading something entertaining. But this nervous laughter came from the man's heart. Stupid boy! As if every soldier in the army did not carry with him the unspoken question: "When shall I get leave?" But leave had just been closed for his company. Of course, he must see Lenore and relieve her mind. But how could that be managed? In two months he would have been in the army for a year; he could plead urgent business that needed his attention at home. His soldiering would end sometime, but marriage endured; he was a soldier by accident, his feeling for Lenore was the very essence of himself. He was glad to have received this blow in Üsküb; he could deal with it at once. He must try and work some leave by pleading exceptional circumstances; for this purpose he would certainly need expert information from more exalted quarters than the A.S.C. In the kitchen of the headquarters one was likely to meet with knowledgeable persons—men attached to the Staff, or clerks.

The kitchen was situated in the ground-floor rooms of a large building looking on to an inner yard. A capacious ladle filled Bertin's bowl with fragrant bean soup containing small bits of pork. N.C.O.s and men were still coming and going. One of them, with a clever, smoothly shaven face, his hands clasped behind his back stood and surveyed Bertin's black-bearded features. Their eyes met in a look of recognition; both of them were Jews.

They fell into talk when Bertin had shaken out his dregs into a bucket set aside for that purpose, and was carefully scrubbing his bowl with a wisp of straw. That would not make it *kosher,* observed the sergeant in the speech of Frankfurt. Bertin retorted that this was not his purpose. He supposed that the sergeant took him for a pious Jew, just as a man in a turban had lately taken him for a pious Arab. He was a plain private in the A.S.C., and he wanted to find out what were the prospects of leave in Macedonia.

"Bad," said the sergeant, with a laugh, "as you might imagine. But if you're free, come and have a cup of coffee at my place. I'm interpreter in Bulgarian to the minenwerfer school, and thank God every day for my old father's inspiration of starting an export trade to the Balkans."

They made their way across various yards, under arched doorways, and over a tract of waste ground.

The sergeant, a Berlin business man, born in Offenbach, proved a very friendly person. They entered a clay-walled shed, clambered up a ladder and through a trapdoor; it was an airy and pleasant abode, though perhaps a trifle hot. The coffee saucepan was bubbling on a little stove, the iron pipe peered drolly through the window, and a sudden uprush of sparks might well have set fire to the roof. Swallows twittered under the high rafters, and a sharp eye might have discerned pendent bats behind them. Bertin sat on a flat chest, and his host on a stool opposite him.

"Yes, leave," and he sighed.

For a married man with a much-loved wife and two charming little children at home, this question, of course, came first, after the question of peace. In this place, a man was as good as cut off from the world, since the Balkan express was not allowed to be used by the rank and file. Moreover, it sometimes happened that leave men went to hell in Budapest, or pleaded that they had not been able to make the connexion in Vienna.

"If they get ten days, and stay away for twenty or twenty-five . . . " he stopped, and his silence was eloquent. "How long have you been in the field?"

"Since last August," answered Bertin.

The Offenbacher chuckled sympathetically. In that case Bertin would be well advised to keep his mouth shut. No man had any claim to leave until he had been a year in the field, or what was called a year.

Bertin reflected calmly; a year. In that case he had better not make himself unpopular. If this was the general pretext for refusal, no application in higher quarters, whether on the ground of university affairs, or family troubles, would be of the least avail. Lenore: well, she must now show whether she had come to her senses and was his friend as she had been before.

The sunshine slanted through the attic window; time to go. It was pleasant to have met in this strange land and to have come to so quick an understanding. Bertin thanked his host for his good coffee, his excellent cigar, and for his guidance to a point whence he could not miss his way to the railway station.

Sergeant Bohne had long since disposed of his field-kitchens; his two other companions came upon him exactly on the stroke of four. They boasted of dark but agreeable encounters.

"I hope you haven't caught anything, you swine," he inquired with a grin. "The responsibility's on me."

Bertin laughed softly. "No fear of that, Sergeant. We all know our duty to 1/X/20."

When they reported themselves about eight o'clock, Corporal Diehl was alone in the writing-room beside a candle, bent over a letter. The four men were given their post of that morning; they were told to go out quietly, as Glinsky's quarters were just across the passage. Diehl, a taciturn man with cropped black hair, an elementary-school teacher from Hamburg, surprised Bertin by the expression in his eyes. He decided to stay for a few minutes, sat down on the edge of the bed, mechanically stuffed tobacco into his light meerschaum pipe, on which the fine Macedonian tobacco first conferred its proper dignity, and waited.

"Did you have a good day?" asked Diehl.

"A change of air, anyway," said Bertin. "What's been happening here?"

The writer stared into the candle. Then he addressed his letter and folded it—one of those letter-cards at that time in common use.

"When are we likely to get any leave?" asked Bertin, with an air of indifference, still busy with his pipe.

"You'll soon be on the move," said Diehl.

Bertin threw his head back. "How do you know that I wanted to get back?"

The other smiled darkly. "We shall all be on the move. The battalion is to be transferred. Make the most of life; we're for Verdun."

Bertin looked at him attentively. He saw no grounds for depression. He heard an inner voice say—At last! He had not left all that he had and was merely to mend the roads of Macedonia. He was much more anxious to show that he was equal to the fate that now fell upon every individual. Thank God—Verdun, he thought, in a flush of excitement. That will be something to have gone through.

"But that's between ourselves," Diehl went on. "I tell you because you get a lot of letters from people with good handwritings. Especially one lady, who is always writing to you. Ah, that's a hand with character, if you like."

Bertin said good-night. "I did not know that you were a graphologist." He concealed his irony; he regarded handwriting experts with contempt, which was the view usually taken of them in those days.

"What does one man know about another?" answered the man, engulfed in the egg-shaped shadow thrown by his long skull on to the wall of the hut. "The post will soon be stopped; just give a hint to your people, but don't talk too much."

"When shall we start?" asked Bertin from the doorway.

The other shrugged his shoulders. "Good-night," he said.

Bertin made his way to his quarters. The night glowed between the poplars, and in the winding alleyways of the outer town. At the bridge over the stream a sentry challenged him, and asked for his pass. Bertin said he had none, and was returning off duty.

The sentry, a Bavarian Jäger, surveyed him mistrustfully and then let him go. There was war between the Bavarians and the Bulgars on account of certain mysterious shooting that had lately taken place under cover of darkness.

Vast in the majestic blackness of the firmament burned the constellations of the South. Bertin drew a deep breath and asked them where his destiny would lead him. Then he lay down beside his three sleeping companions on a pallet of maize straw and a blanket that in the course of many weeks had been flattened into the semblance of a mat. Tomorrow he would write to Lenore. He would tell her that he would more easily get leave from Verdun, simply because it was not so far away. And he went to sleep with the image of the mosque before his eyes, the placid four-square chamber, the carpet, parrot-green and pink, and the Mullah, whose hand, thin and brown, he suddenly saw before his inner vision.

It is good for sleeping people, who as yet know little of life, to plunge into beneficent delusions. A branch, flung at first into smooth shore water, floats fitfully downstream, and is often caught and held; when it really will begin to move, whither the yellow surges of time will carry it, and whether the vortex that has engulfed it from afar will ever release it—who can tell?

BOOK SIX

THE TIME APPROACHES

Chapter 1

LETTERS

The most important events of men's lives in those days passed to and fro in letters, in the eighteen million or so postal packets which the Field Post dealt with daily. The Imperial Posts had sent more than ninety thousand employees to the war, and engaged a large force of women in their place. Postwomen in uniform, with caps on their bobbed hair, hurried up staircases, and rang at bells, unperturbed by their monthly visitations, and an insufficient diet of potato bread, barley coffee, bad dripping, and thin milk. All the emotions were poured out in written script, disguised or declared, blurted forth or adorned with all the phrase of sentiment. Wives, mothers, sweethearts, mistresses, friends, and children, all wrote. To all of them the postwoman brought an answer, in Berlin, Magdeburg, Stolp, Aschaffenburg, and Constance. All the reality of the life of peace-time, of life as it truly is, went to and fro, embodied on sheets of paper; it was related how another assistant had been called up, that the landlord was making trouble about the rent, that Otto was constantly being sick, that the winter had been mild, that business was excellent, that the children at school had been forced to subscribe to the war loan, that the butter was being adulterated, that the jam was largely turnips, that the ladies in the welfare bureau had been so kind and helpful, that the Christmas parcel would have to be the last for the present, that the children were getting so wild, that they might be taking another foster-child into the house—the child of Plotz, the bookbinder, whose wife had kidney disease and was dying; all this was metamorphosed into handwriting by the agency of ink, copying pencil, or black lead, in characters expressive or indifferent; it was taken out of sacks, sorted by women into other sacks, loaded on to trains by men, and carried through Cologne, Frankfurt, Strassburg, Munich, Passau, Prague, Oderberg, Kattowitz, Thorn, Insterburg, Eydtkuhnen, Stettin, Kiel, Wilhemshaven. From all directions of the compass, on postcards mostly and on letter-cards came a reply; comfort, wise counsel, anger, resignation, bewilderment, and threats. Women were told to be patient, economical, brave, to hold out, and not to forget their men.

In terms deliberately disguised to defeat the inquisitive, Lenore read that Bertin was gong to Verdun, with lengthy adjurations that she must not worry. She saw before her eyes only Niehoff-Barmen's bleeding wrists and his blood spurting on to the tarpaulin roof of the tent, over the stick of soap that he was just about to sell. Panic fell upon her; she leapt out of bed with the speed of a whiplash. Looking very like a boy in her pyjama trousers, she stood in the middle of the room and trembled; her eyes wandered past the bookshelves, past the pictures to the window, and the clouded sky. O God. O darkly brooding God!

The lad had stood for much in her life, among other things he had made her into a women—he had revealed to her the domains of thought and of self-fulfilment. But from him had come much evil too. No matter, he must be got out of this, and got out quickly. Thousands were now reading his book, it was surely of some consequence to get him into safety. In such a case, a man had to be "applied for" in the language of the time. Werner Bertin must be applied for, and she must see about getting it done.

For a whole day she went about in restless efforts to find some access to the military world, which towered like a walled fortress, smooth and steep, above common folk, and by them unapproachable. No one in ordinary life knew the laws that held sway behind barrack doors. At last she thought of the man who once before had uttered the word of deliverance. After dinner she knocked at David's door and went in.

He looked up holding a manual of mathematics, with a display of geometrical figures, circles, and quotations, open in his hand.

"My child, I must work. We've got our mathematics exam tomorrow. What is it?"

"How is a man applied for in the army? Talk to Kliem about it. He knows everything."

The onslaught on Verdun had lasted a month. The expectations of the first weeks seemed still unfulfilled. No one knew what the prospects were. The newspapers were full of rhetoric, but gave no real view of the situation. After the first joy over an advance at last, the little flags on the war maps moved only about a millimetre forward. New names, small places—but this time it was better realized that they represented blood, corpses, horror, stark heroic courage, and unmeasured sacrifice. Douaumont, Vaux, Fleury, the Meuse heights called "304," and the "Mort Homme," were burned into German memory, and into the memory of the world. Once more with bent head and bayonet at the ready, the French and German infantry faced and fought, the hand-grenades hurtled back and forward, men strove for clumps of trees, strips of meadow, and hill-tops, engulfed in myriads of shells and groping in a fog of gas. Men and women who talked habitually in terms of sweeping victories had indeed revised their expectations. It was a victory when some small position or supporting point, or even a battery, had been wrested from the French. And there were rumours of terrible losses on both sides.

But Kliem, what did he say? He first expressed his satisfaction because twenty Deputies of his Party had at last found the courage to turn their backs in no unmistakable manner on the sycophants and nincompoops and wiseacres that populated parliament. It was really too insolent of the Junkers to go on defending the three-class electoral law. "My lad," said he, "if we go on winning, and they can behave as they please, people like me will have to get off the pavement into the gutter, and stand to attention when they see a foreman, and anyone who didn't fight in the war will be lucky if he gets a bread card. Don't you believe," he went on, frowning darkly, with his chin in his hand and his elbow on the table—he was sitting in his kitchen, odorous of charcoal and pipe tobacco, "that we shall all be able to buy bread as we like when the war's over. Where's it coming from? Where's the corn to grow? On the battlefields? My friend Ilde, who's with the Sappers, tells me that they take pretty good care that there shan't be any ploughing where the war's been. The peasants'll have to live on the dud shells they dig up, I suppose." And he went on in a lower tone, as though he thought there were no one in the cottage but himself: "I'm doing no good here now. I wish I could chuck it all up, and get back to my battalion. For why? Because they live better out there than we do. And there's plenty of trouble coming to us here. Besides, how am I to know that they won't call me up one day and send me where I don't want to go? But there are certain claims, my lad, like what you read about in the storybooks, that tie a man's leg to the table and won't let him go."

Certain claims? thought David. And what might they be, Comrade Kliem? And then he asked outright what was the best method of getting a man seconded out of the army.

Kliem, of course, knew how that could be done without the least trouble. An industry of national importance—and what was not of national importance in these days?—notified the Home Command that such and such a man was needed for the punctual delivery of the last army contracts; by profession a moulder, machine-tool maker, chemist, or whatever it might be. The man was fit for garrison duty only; in his place, So-and-So, who was fit for active service, could be bundled off to the front. "After a few weeks, if it comes off, the order goes through to the regiment, and your man clears out, first to the reserve battalion, then to the District Command, and so back to his master, who shakes him by the hand and says he's very glad to see him; and the war's over as far as he's concerned, if he knows how to keep quiet, of course. Is your man fit for garrison duty only?"

That was so. There were three grades recognized in those days; fit for active service, for garrison duty, or for work of national duty, or for work of national importance, and after a medical examination in Serbia, the army doctors had assigned Bertin to the second grade, so that there was no formal obstacle to his recall. But when Kliem heard that the gentleman in question was a writer, he scratched his ears and spat into the ashes. He knew little about such people, indeed he hardly distinguished them from compositors or printers. But, after all, there must be someone to write in the papers and keep up the spirits of the nation. But that would need some influence; and he shrugged his shoulders.

Next morning brother and sister met at breakfast; large plates of steaming oat-cakes, with tinned milk and a tiny pat of butter, with grey bread and marmalade to follow. By David's place lay his usual little packet of lunch, which Frau Mahnke always prepared with her own hands—six slices of bread spread with goose fat and made into some kind of sandwich. The schoolboy's appetite left nothing to be desired, and David, being a growing lad, was invariably hungry again by the middle of the day. Herr and Frau Wahl breakfasted later. The streets looked grey and dull in the light of a March morning. David gingerly spooned the steaming porridge into his mouth, and as he munched away he told his sister what Kliem had said. Kliem knew his own world thoroughly, but only his own world. Getting a man out of the army was a question of a man's employment; there must be influential people in the writer's profession, and they must be made to move in the matter. This was more in Lenore's line of country; surely she could think of one who would speak for her. So saying, he stuffed his packet of sandwiches into his overcoat pocket—he always arrived at the table ready for the street, so that he could sleep as late as possible in the morning—grabbed his shabby satchel, and dashed out of the house.

Lenore drew her wrap closer round her. In her mind's eye she saw a white-tiled stove and leaning against it a tall angular figure, with gaunt cheeks, thick arched eyebrows, and a pince-nez askew across his nose. That was the man. She would ask Hermann Lorcher, the author, how one could get a friend out of an A.S.C. battalion, when he was doing a navvy's work and completely thrown away.

She had often heard of the Lederers. Dr. Lederer had been called up some time ago and had been given a commission in the

Austrian army. Frau Mela Hartig-Lederer gave Brahms and Beethoven concerts behind the lines, and played for charity in all the cities of Germany and Austria. In the winter she had played five times in Berlin, and five times David had sat in the hall, quite close to the platform, each time more ecstatic than before. What a woman!—said David.

Hermann Lorcher lived on the Nordbahn at Frohnau, a new suburb of small houses with gardens, mainly occupied by literary men, clerks, and the better paid working men. He also possessed a telephone. She rang him up. Hermann Lorcher's voice sounded rather dubious over the line. He mistrusted women who wasted his working time with important interviews. Important for them, no doubt, but not for him. Lenore listened anxiously; and she assured him that nothing was further from her mind than to intrude. She wanted his advice on a matter that perhaps was vital to a young man who might very likely become a great writer. But this did not seem to mollify Hermann Lorcher. The name Fräulein Wahl recalled nothing to his mind. But just at that moment he happened to be writing an article on Leo Tolstoy, in which he praised the Russian author's ready response to appeals for help, as for instance in the case of an unknown French student of the name of Romain Rolland, who had consulted him on matters of conscience. Was it urgent? It was. Very well. The young lady might come, he would keep half an hour free for her on Sunday, about midday.

Lenore Wahl laid the receiver across the hooks and stood for a few seconds motionless in front of the black polished box. Never had she intruded on the solitude of one whose work gave him the right to hold himself aloof. No matter; she must shake off her misgivings, Bertin was on his way to Verdun. She went up to her room, and looked out a well-loved volume by a young contemporary, Franz Werfel, and in the grey morning light read aloud to herself in an undertone the poem that describes how the Saviour, walking with His disciples, comes upon a heap of dead animals, and weaves himself a crown of mouldering life, of dead rats and otters and creeping things.

Chapter 2

VISIT TO AN AUTHOR

Authors easily forget appointments unless they have trained themselves to faith in calendars. Their writing-tables are piled with memoranda, and how on earth are they to find, at the right time, the scrap of paper on which is scribbled, "Sunday 12.00, Fräulein Wahl," especially when on the Saturday they had been surprised by the visit of an old friend on leave? In the evening someone had called up in a strange and yet familiar voice, to say that he was in Berlin for a few days, and wanted to come round as soon as possible. And a meeting had been eagerly fixed for the Sunday morning.

"You can keep Lederer to lunch, I have picked up something good," said Frau Lorcher proudly to her husband, as they sat at their meagre breakfast of peppermint tea, with saccharine, toasted war bread, and turnip marmalade.

Hermann Lorcher frowned. He did not like his wife picking up something good, since that meant getting it by some illicit transaction. He insisted on her managing with the rations that were available for his political friends, the poor. "Good," he said hypocritically, "and what may it be?"

"Six young pigeons," answered the grey-haired lady with a secret twinkle in her eyes, for she knew there would be an outburst.

But there was not. "Three of them will go to the hospital, and three to the elementary school. I wonder you want to put money into the pockets of food profiteers. Anyhow, I shouldn't touch them."

Frau Lorcher stretched out her arms to him across the table, and there were tears and deep affection in her heart. "They're crows, you old stupid, a present from Schmidt the forester. Now will you deign to eat them?"

Hermann Lorcher grinned in mock anger. "Yes, and I'll bite your head off for being too clever for a man like me."

"Ah well! You can laugh or you can cry at everything in the world," sighed Anna Lorcher, reflecting that a man with her husband's brains had, for conscience' sake, to be fed on birds of prey. Then she went off to her kitchen, for no cookery book contained instructions as to how long young crows ought to be boiled.

About ten o'clock Theodor Lederer was sitting on Lorcher's brown wooden balcony on the garden side of the house. Birds were twittering in the bushes and the tree-tops, mostly sparrows, and from below the falsetto crowing of young cocks; all these voices spoke of Sunday. Dr. Theodor Lederer was in no way changed except for the expression of his deep brown eyes and the curve of his fine aquiline nose. For the rest, he looked about twenty years younger, and he felt so. Gone was the long hair and beard, the transparent skin, and the wrinkles in his forehead. From the collar of an Austrian infantry lieutenant's tunic emerged a gaunt head, pitted with scars. In a hand-grenade attack on the front between Asiago and Arsiero the then subaltern had come in for a shower of shell splinters, twenty-three of them, on the back of head, neck, ears, skull, shoulders, and upper arms; not to mention scattered bits of rock. His recovery was one of the countless marvels of this war, which were more particularly manifested in hospitals. Man had no notion of his latent forces of resistance. The descendant of great East Galician rabbis, the expert on the mosaics of Ravenna, the man whose fingers seemed moulded to grasp a Chinese jade carving, rather than a revolver-butt, lived and was cured; and he was to spend the next week inspecting trenches in his native place.

Hermann Lorcher surveyed his friend, half in admiration and half in embarrassment at his own admiration. But Lieutenant Lederer laughed. He was, indeed, twenty years younger, but also about twenty years nearer death, unless there was a prospect of peace. The Russians were preparing a great attack which might have incalculable consequences. What were the possibilities of peace—and peace very soon?

Hermann Lorcher had never surrendered to any illusions about militarism. He had but to turn up past numbers of his little paper called *The League,* for evidence that he always pointed to the war that lurked just below the surface of civilization. For that reason, during the emergency of the war, he would not write on politics, and took refuge in great poetry; he armoured himself against the world about him by lecturing on the great Greeks, and, at the moment, Homer. But he observed events with alert and watchful eyes.

He pulled at his beard. Since the victories at Verdun prospects of peace were more remote than ever. But Lederer waved this aside. The battle of Verdun was certainly not a victory. The attack on this great fortress might have succeeded as a coup-de-main; and for four days this had seemed possible. But since the beginning of March, in the frantic conflicts for every little corner in those forests, the French had shown themselves the equals of the Germans. Even if they evacuated Verdun, nothing would have been gained; but that they would never do. The enlargement of the salient on the right bank of the Meuse was of no advantage, so long as it could be swept by heavy artillery fire from the left bank.

During his long convalescence he had been employed as interpreter in a hospital for officer prisoners, because he spoke Italian as well as he did German, and could make a shift at speaking Polish. There, and later on in Vienna, he had picked up a great deal of information on the relative strength and training of the forces engaged, and on strategical and tactical questions. He had been an excellent soldier; the complete change of environment had done his brain good, and the problems of military science were theoretically less difficult than those of his own profession.

For these reasons, and as a result of his lifelong familiarity with Austria and Germany, he now saw what lay beneath the passage of events. The business of the war had outgrown human control—so much was clear; some effort must be made, or it would proceed indefinitely. The professional soldiers of Europe certainly refused to accept this view; they could not be blamed; no man could be expected to assist in his own abdication. They all embodied the same spirit, they played the game of war in accordance with rules which they held to be irrefragable, feared or despised each other, but paid each other the tribute of mutual respect, and were convinced of the necessity of the war. In every country personal passions and aversions played almost as decisive a part among them as in other professions. The battle of Lemberg, and therewith several of the best Austrian corps, was, for example, lost because a General wanted the Maria-Theresia Order, which is only awarded for a success won on a commander's own initiative. During the past autumn the Austrian Field-Marshal had put before German General Headquarters comprehensive plans for destroying the Italians, or, under the command of Colonel-General von Hindenburg and his colleagues, for delivering a decisive blow against Russia, which might then have forced the Tsar to make peace. But the German Supreme Army Command refused to provide adequate forces for the great encircling battle and the breakthrough that must precede it, because they thought their colleagues on the Eastern front had already been successful enough. The corps which they then maintained that they did not possess were now being broken to pieces before Verdun; a fact which imparted to this battle its special quality of horror, waste, and ultimate unreason.

"We once thought that we could read in the horoscope of history that he who plotted the destruction of another was himself destroyed, and that he only is defenceless who has not understood the means at his disposal. How can this wisdom be made manifest today?"

Hermann Lorcher had not realized what fevered pride in Germany and her greatness burned in his heart. His love for this land and this people could not endure that his friend should describe two years of great achievement as meaningless.

He listened in a kind of paralysis of emotion. The war, he had long known was a deliberate act; it was not an unavoidable natural catastrophe even if the untamed instincts of the white races, their lust for robbery, slaughter, heroism, and glory, were to be credited to nature. He had always opposed the soldiers when they trespassed upon matters, whether political, social, or spiritual, with which they had no concern. But of their skill in their own business he was genuinely convinced. Lederer's calm words disclosed all the concentrated human fallibility, error, carelessness, and selfishness, with which he was so familiar among jealous actors; but with them it was only the success of a theatrical performance that was at stake. He realized with horror that the gods had not changed since Homer, except that they now paraded in bodily form over the fields of slain, and blamed each other to save their own reputations.

"You must surely see," Lederer went on, "that no one in uniform can escape from the vicious circle—from the continuation of the war for its own sake. Someone from the people must stand forth for peace—a civilian. No soldier will ever realize that after two years of daily and hourly destruction, the word 'victory' has become meaningless—on all fronts. An ordinary citizen can see that, and speak."

Lorcher at once grasped that this was an appeal to him. He grew pale, and slowly shrugged his shoulders.

"There is no one—what would be the use? The people cannot speak, and the world cannot hear."

Lederer gazed thoughtfully at the fruit trees against the garden wall: "It is so difficult to get used to this conception of futility, when one has always lived as though life had a meaning."

Hermann felt an anguished impulse to defend himself.

"All active men are in the army and believe in victory. I'm not a crank like Liebknecht, I'm a lonely author with a strong sense of solidarity. I could conceive myself leading a movement, but not a revolution."

Theodor Lederer suddenly grew calm, and almost cheerful. In a flash he saw Germany, Austria, Europe, driving rudderless upon their fate. He remembered a rainy afternoon in his pleasant country house at Steglitz, where a certain somebody had angrily turned upon a young man, because that young man had refused to disobey an order. There were no more spiritual leaders. Henceforward there would be no help except in miracles, great and small. He, for instance, had survived; and this was a miracle. "Wait a bit, and then drink a cup of tea," ran an old Silesian proverb. "You will see some much stranger things than the Conscription Act in free England," he said with a smile.

His tone was no longer intimate, and Hermann Lorcher felt a shock at his heart. "I can write to the President of the United States. He might read what is put before him by an independent man, and take some steps. It's the only chance."

"And to the German Emperor," added Lederer, without irony and without hope.

This gave the other an opening to unburden himself of a feeling of guilt towards his friend and towards the world. For twelve long years in articles and speeches he had inveighed against the prevailing regime and its visible representative, William II, and twice he had been put in prison for so doing. That this man, in all else the very embodiment of supremacy, should not be even capable of making his subordinates mind their business, acted on him like an irritant poison. His fury seemed to flood that Sunday morning, his garden, all the budding trees and flowers that he loved, his large footmarks on the snow-strewn paths and his wife's little ones beside them.

Lederer, in the kindness of his heart, did his best to divert his friend's mind with facts, and so bring the subject to a close. Soberly, as though he were speaking in a debate, he pointed out that Austria, with an army composed of races speaking nine distinct languages, could not withstand a further Russian onslaught. In any case, her assistance was not really an element that counted, because, since the French Revolution, no dynasty in the world could resist the impulse of subject races towards self-determination. And he was proceeding to develop this point when Frau Anna Lorcher appeared, wearing a striped apron. Had Hermann forgotten that he had made an appointment with Fräulein Wahl? Lorcher blushed. One couldn't get any peace even on Sunday. He would soon dispose of the lady. Smilingly Anna Lorcher laid her arm on his shoulder. "Now, sit down, keep calm, and don't make the young lady suffer for the fact that you won't use a calendar."

Then she led Lenore on to the balcony in the warm noonday sunshine. Carefully dressed, with her thick fur collar up to her ears, and a little cap of the same fur pulled down over her forehead, Lenore looked confidingly at Lorcher, and inquiringly at the strange be-ribboned Austrian officer, whose eyes awakened an uncertain recollection. Not until Lederer greeted her cheerily, was she at last able to penetrate his disguise. She felt at once that his presence was fortunate for her. There was a line between Lorcher's thick brows, and his bony fingers tapped with none too friendly a sound upon the table. She had come, she said, to ask Herr Lorcher what possibilities there were of getting her fiancé back from the front, and what steps she ought to take.

"And you want me to manage it for you?" Lorcher burst out, with a feeling of injury he could not himself quite explain. After all this talk of horrors, these hordes of dead, it disgusted him that anyone should trouble him about the fate of an individual. He replied roughly that he would have nothing, absolutely nothing, to do with getting a man out of the army, or any such organized poltroonery. With that he thought the interview at an end, and he half-rose from his chair.

Lenore remained seated. She did not care, she must not let herself be put down by insult. "You want to send me away before you have heard me out," she said bravely. "And yet you write about mutual aid, and the comradeship of the intellect." Enough intellectuals had been killed on the battlefield and behind it; something must be done to make sure that later on, in the wilderness of the money-making world, there shall be monuments of the spirit that may deserve such sacrifices and such endurance. She did not need to name the many that were gone, and now there was Niehoff-Barmen, a better painter than the world realized. And even though Werner Bertin was her fiancé and she now sat there pleading for him, he was a coming writer, and it was worth while making an effort to save him.

"Ah, yes," said Hermann Lorcher, superciliously, "the fellow who talked about Strassburg cathedral and wrote *Love at Last Sight* that now lies by everyone's bedside. Is he your fiancé? I wish you happiness, but I may tell you that a Leipzig bookbinder or a Munich framemaker seems to me just as important as Herr Bertin, and no one thinks of getting them out of the army. I could show you letters from workingmen which, as human documents, are certainly equal to anything your friend has ever written."

"All the more sad that there's no one to look after them, but must Bertin for that reason risk being killed as a private in the A.S.C.? That doesn't seem to me logical."

But Hermann Lorcher was obdurate. "Try the newspapers. Send them some pathetic letters from your friend. . . ."

This was almost too much; but Lenore merely gazed with curiosity at this infuriated personage. Against such unreason she found herself armed with something near to cheerfulness. Of course, Bertin had not written a line that hinted at release, or even thought of it—she knew him well enough for that. She, on her own initiative, had wanted to find out how she could arrange to see him again. From the outset she had known that danger was coming nearer and nearer to him; and her feeling had grown more acute from month to month. Since, as a private in the A.S.C., he would not get leave until he had been a year in the field, not before the beginning of August, she would not and could not wait until then and do nothing. At this point Lieutenant Lederer slipped into the conversation. Since the renewal of his youth as an officer, he had rather taken to these young women, brave and patient creatures, stirred by their instinct to continue the race. The nation must be maintained; races only survived wars because women bore children. "The genius of life wins homage even from the genius of death," he said with a smile. "There is an infallible method of getting your friend back, at least on leave, and one that only you can use."

Lenore looked incredulously at his friendly face. She would not fail, she said with an answering smile; what was it, please?

"You have only got to apply for marriage leave for him. No army in the world refuses to send a young soldier back to a prospective bride. We don't go so far as the Bible," he went on, as he watched a deeper and deeper blush spread over her face, "in which the young newly married man was given a year's leave from service in the army because he embodied the genius of life. But you will get your friend for a few weeks—only you must marry him."

Lenore stood up; her parted lips and urgent eyes asked Lederer whether he was serious. He was quite serious. This was the law. Then she thanked the two men, she now knew what she must do. She would not interrupt their talk a moment longer. She longed to kiss Lederer's hand, but remembered she was a lady, and he no longer wore the beard that would have made the gesture possible.

Lorcher wanted to take her to the door, already half-ashamed of his outburst of bad temper; Lenore shook her head. Anyone who had so much claim on her gratitude need express no regrets. "One day, I am quite sure, you will think otherwise about Bertin, and until then I remain in your debt. Say good-bye to your wife for me, and now—I wish you good-morning."

On the journey home she did not feel the chill of the leather carriage cushions against her back. Gradually the whole project opened out before her inner vision. It warmed her to think that all lay now in her hands. They must speak and speak the truth to each other before she could let Werner run the risk of death; they must once more feel the ties that bound them before they faced what destiny might bring. She would have him with her for a few weeks, and in that time they could again become as one. Had she but spoken to him, shaken him by the shoulders, heard good words from him, and felt his good kisses on her lips—she need not then be left desolate, to mix that quick poison which David would have had to get for her from a butterfly-collector—if fate had willed it so. Then she would not have vainly sacrificed that germ of being, her child; for now she knew, too bitterly she knew, how hopelessly the dull and dreadful life of everyday had power to wear her out and drag her down; without him she was a feckless creature, at home and everywhere she went. Then, if it must be, he could go back to the front, and even—though she shivered at the thought—not return, like Niehoff-Barmen. The oppression lifted from her mind, and she felt once more free. She would marry him.

Chapter 3

QUESTIONS OF FINANCE

"Fantastic," said Herr Wahl, "fantastic. You want to make the buyers responsible for the fact that prices have gone up; that your protégé, Brösecke, was first prepared to deliver his saddles at a hundred and twenty-five marks fifty, and now asks a hundred and seventy-five marks seventy-five?"

Once again father and son faced each other; the old-fashioned office was almost filled by the great desk. Between them, where Herr Brümmer had so recently told the story of Edith Cavell, Lenore sat listening. On her account, and on account of those next door, they lowered their voices. She felt that to be a good sign. How was Werner to put down five thousand marks in a bank, when he possessed nothing but his two hands, and a head, now covered by an A.S.C. private's cap? Anyhow, money was not his business, it was the business of people like the Wahls, and they wanted to implant it in all their connexions.

Herr Hugo Wahl relit his cigar with rather exaggerated deliberation. "Matches are getting dear. We must have a lighter on the table. You might see about it, child."

With senile perversity, as it seemed to Herr Wahl, his father resumed the dispute. He discussed Herr Brösecke's standpoint, explained his motives, and began to grow excited.

In the first months of the War, officers had approached the contractors with a view to buying up supplies, and they had fixed ideas as to the price of what they wanted: bridles, harness, haversacks, and saddles. Brösecke, a saddler in a large way of business —he and Markus Wahl had known each other for more than thirty years—had made his price, delivered his goods, and now had been turned down. But a competitor, a manufacturer in Werder, had got the valuable contract, although his tender was fifty marks higher.

"Borgmeier must have delivered the goods more promptly," said Hugo Wahl.

"He did not, he fixed a date and failed to keep it," burst out the old man shrilly. "Since then, Brösecke has sold at the manufacturers' prices and why not? His goods are better; better leather, yarn, and workmanship. And who bears the loss? The taxpayer. You and I. And that isn't the worst of it," he added mysteriously. "These gentlemen are destroying the wholesome relation between price and value."

"Well," growled Herr Hugo Wahl impatiently, "and what about it?"

"I'll tell you all about it, my boy," said his father. "The war has already lasted for twenty months, and everything is dependent on the war. When merchants do business, they understand something of the goods in which they are dealing, and each one knows what a reasonable price ought to be. He knows the raw materials, the labour involved, the wages and the risk. He takes care that he is not over-reached. But now the officers come along and see Borgmeier asking fifty marks more for his inferior stuff than Brösecke the saddler for first-rate work, and they naturally think that the dearer must be the better, for what do they understand about the goods offered? Merely that they look all right. The facts are found out later on by the Ordnance Departments when they take over the stuff; and money goes for nothing. Thus, with this insensate cry for haste, they destroy the sense of the relation between price and value, and injure the nation where it can least bear injury; and the effects will be seen for thirty years."

Lenore found this much after her own heart. An element of brutality invades public life when people are tempted to take advantage of a nation's extremity, merely because business men are not allowed to handle matters of business. She had lately heard a certain professor deliver a lecture in disfavour of commercial, as compared with military, ethics, with obvious contempt of England

and much laudation of the military system. She would have liked to sit that gentleman down to dinner with her grandfather. Her father had been with her that evening and she had wanted to ask him about it, but she did not; he had seemed for some while set upon other matters.

Herr Wahl pretended to listen. He was more than polite; happiness welled up within him, and no one knew from what deep source it came. He had always felt the stigma that, in the last resort, he was no more than a freedman, whom the lords of the land despised, even when they used him, and, at such a moment, all the more; great families like those of Arnim and Dohna, Kracht and Sparr and Schulenburg. But now the officer caste, as represented by their most able member, asked for and recognized his help. For two days past he had been carrying in his pocket typewritten sheets. On the first of them the Commander-in-Chief of the forces on the Eastern Front invited Herr Hugo Wahl to a conference at Kovno on the twenty-seventh of March at five o'clock. The second postponed this meeting from five until a quarter to six; both communications were signed, Schieffenzahn. "As for myself, Herr Wahl, I have taken special care to remember your name." The proof of it lay here—involuntarily Herr Wahl placed his hand upon his heart where he could feel the faint crackle of the sheets—and made him feel gratified and important. He did not care if his father went on talking about Herr Kuhl's haversacks and Herr Brösecke's saddles. He had been summoned to the Eastern Command to take part in a consultation, together with Obstfelder and Dr. Jonas. The question at issue was probably the new loan-bank for the districts administered by the Eastern Command, which was to be established on the same basis as a bank of issue, to provide the necessary money for the occupied area, without encumbering the German currency. He would do his best, give his whole attention to the problem, stay in Kovno for several weeks if necessary, and leave matters here to manage themselves. His father was always talking about price and value; his daughter was intent upon her marriage—small souls, and shallow heads! Scieffenzahn's invitation had the effect of a bomb among his acquaintances in town. Everyone was suddenly on the spot when he had anything to say; and here in Potsdam, Geheimrat von Ducherow had accepted a lift from the station to his house, the like of which never happened before. This mean alliance with a common soldier, and a private in the A.S.C. at that, belonged to the past. Lenore must be made to realize this by a process of gentle insinuation. She had had enough of dances with youthful lieutenants and lawyers, and after violent disputes with her parents had retired to Munich; and she had been right, as was now clear. She was not meant for a young man; now that her mind was settled she would make an excellent wife for an older man—the sort of man who might help to secure her father in the exalted position which now opened out before him, and which he had achieved by his own ability. Of course the old man felt spiteful about this trip to the Eastern Command. Let him! "Well, we'll settle this together later on," he heard him say, "the child didn't come here for this. She wants to talk about her own affairs. She's your daughter and my granddaughter, and there's a great deal of sense in that little head. Now then, out with it, my dear."

Lenore, with her eyes on the church wall, on which the flying clouds cast alternating light and shadow, explained what was in her mind. She had first thought of a long engagement, but there was now no room for such half measures. Things were now moving so fast that she wanted to marry very soon, and for that purpose marriage-leave must be obtained for her fiancé. But first she wanted to know how matters stood about her dowry. This was not to be regarded as an ordinary sum of money; it was to serve as backing for the work of a writer, which before the war only produced a modest and uncertain income. "Werner will always be able to provide for himself, and in case of need for me too, and very likely with a good deal of comfort," she went on boldly, knowing that she had to deal with her father, "but I don't want to burden him with children, and I would like to have children. I am, as you know, twenty-three years old now, and that is the best time, Mamma says, the physically natural time, and then I should have something to care for when Werner is away again, or if the war, which God forbid, goes on for a long time."

"It *will* go on for a long time," echoed Markus Wahl from his high-backed chair.

"In that case my dowry must be kept for emergencies. The mother bird tears out her feathers to line the nest for the little ones; I only want to tear upon the Wahl money-box! I have always understood I should get eighty thousand marks; the interest on that will make a comfortable addition to our income. But please may I have it in Swiss Government stock?"

Hugo Wahl surveyed his little daughter with amusement. "In Swiss Government stock?" he said with a bland smile. "I suppose industrial shares wouldn't do?"

The child probably missed the irony of his remark. She answered warmly that she did not know what shares were. She had merely thought that of all the neutrals, Switzerland, hemmed in between France, Germany, and Italy, would be the most certain to remain neutral. For that reason she preferred Swiss Government obligations.

"And who put you up to this?" asked Herr Wahl dryly.

Lenore assured him that these were her own ideas.

"Of course they are," cried Markus Wahl, beaming with satisfaction. "Have you no sense? Can't you be proud of your own flesh and blood?"

"Treason!" retorted Herr Hugo Wahl, "economic treason! Anyone who buys foreign bonds today is committing a crime against the Fatherland. You are a little fool, my child, and I shall pass over what you have said. The safest paper in the world is German War Loan. To provide anything else for your dowry would be a disgraceful act. You are only an innocent girl, and nobody expects you to understand where you are wrong; but you don't need to tell me the sort of atmosphere in which such treacheries grow. It is bad enough to realize that I am thus referring to my own father."

Markus Wahl gripped the arms of his chair as though he were about to leap up, but Hugo Wahl had not yet finished. The measure was running over, and he had once and for all to show who was master in this house. "I had reasons for consenting to your engagement, but—you must bear to be told this, my child—perhaps Herr Bertin is a genius, perhaps he is not. More probably not. Geniuses have names like Goethe, or Schiller, or Kleist, and not Bertin or Wahl or Obstfelder. At present he is merely a *bocher*—you know what that is: a young Jew who is still a learner. In short, I must think very carefully whether I can release eighty thousand marks for a *bocher,* even in War Loan."

The "even" was a slip, he realized it at once. It depreciated the paper that he had described as the safest in the world, but fortunately no one took the point.

Lenore, indignant and hurt, did not reply. In her stead, Markus Wahl, who had not moved, made answer. "My dear son," he said, in oddly lifeless tones, "my attitude towards you has been quite mistaken, I admit that at once. I said"—he laid stress on the "I," and his voice fell into that mysterious cadenced rise and fall of the debates in the Talmud schools—"I said that one must understand something about money, and something about the land and the soil. You said that one must understand something of trade and something of industry. I said that a banker must secure free circulation for money, and must be a free trader and a free thinker. You said that the first thing was to develop home industry, and to put on protective tariffs for that purpose. I said: we are Jews, and our freedom is very insecurely based, we must ally ourselves with all who are in like case; and who, except the Junkers and Industrials, is not in our case? We must go with the Catholics and the Social-Democrats. You said: just because our equality is so little established we must go with our masters, and your line is to act as though you were Herr von Gundermann. I referred to Frederick III and his Englishwoman; you referred to William II and his admiral. I have sworn all my life long that war was the greatest disaster that can fall upon a people. You said that war brought life into business, and you made friends with war forthwith. What am I to say to you? You yourself are aware that your attitude was right, and mine was wrong. Your side has flourished and mine has gone steadily down. Even now, in my lifetime, if we were to draw up an account between us, everything belongs to you except the original capital which I inherited from my late father and with which I worked until you entered the firm. I am therefore a defeated man all along the line, and you can if you like use the word *bocher* to hurt my feelings, except that it does not, in fact, hurt my feelings. I mark your purpose to give me pain, you understand, and that does give me pain, not your allusion. For I was just such a *bocher* when I married my Fanny, and if old Cohn had taken five thousand talers off the dowry because my father had been an immigrant from Grodno or Bialystock, which is now occupied by the Germans again, I should never have forgotten it all my life. But if you propose to behave in this way and make a profit on your own daughter; if you are to regard her as of less value because she loves a young man without money and is prepared to stand by him, a writer and a scholar, there is nothing to prevent you doing so. Except that I shall change my will this afternoon, and the sum that you withdraw from the settlement on these two young people, I shall deduct from my legacy to you. Just tell me, my boy, you who are so puffed up above your father: where is the real value to correspond with the price we are paying for this war; tell me frankly—I want none of your rhetoric. For twenty months past people have been murdering each other, and nothing has been accomplished; before this they worked and traded with each other, they took each other's counsel and agreed together. I know, of course, that you are called upon to rule the world. But what if you are mistaken? I have also read that the glory of these sacrifices is a value in itself, which makes Germany immortal. But was Germany mortal before the war? Answer me that, my astute young friend?"

Herr Hugo Wahl was afraid of his father in that moment. The old man glowered across at him, and his wrists quivered in his shirt-cuffs. "Who was responsible for the lie of England's envy of Germany? Only in this country can the people be relied on to forget how England tied her own hands in 1912 and even later, so as to be able to discuss matters reasonably with us, and tried to give us a colonial outlet, and a good share in the trade of the world. What is the use of your military success of today? You don't yet know what the end will be. You have not lived long enough," he went on in less heated tones, "that's what's the matter with you, and with all those who think like you. Although you have seen everything, you don't keep your eyes open. Do you know who it was that swore the English would lose the Boer War? And they won the Boer War. Who was it that swore that Russia, with her huge armies, would win the Japanese War? And Russia lost the Japanese War. That France was so rotten and diseased that she would be at our mercy in three weeks? And France still stands—indeed, France does a good deal more than stand. They will not defeat us and we shall not defeat them. If we can then make a peace on the basis of a *status quo,* we can really say that Germany has won the war. Germany will have held out against the entire world. But if a man had no need to risk his life, is he then so tremendous a hero if he does not perish? People will ask why he did risk his life, and call him lucky. Besides, countless thousands will have been maimed or crippled, there will be countless thousands of widows and orphans, and all at a cost of about fifty billions in gold. Have you calculated the interest on that sum? And where has the value gone, when the goods are blown to atoms? So, from your own point of view also, the war is bad business, the worst business that ever was done. I won't say anything about the growing corruption in this country. Merely this: arrogant and positive as you are, I would not be in your place. The Kaiser has not yet ridden through the Brandenburg Gate with that twin-bearded admiral of his, and his six sons, all safe and sound. I am afraid, I am very much afraid, that what I shall see before I lie down to die will be something very different. Therefore, though you may look bored enough now, when you have been invited to Kovno, and my words taste sweet to you, do not shrink, when the time comes, from swallowing others that may taste very bitter."

Hugo Wahl shut his ears. "Too late," he whispered, "much too late. All that should never be said. And yet I can't order my father to hold his tongue," he went on as though talking to himself. "I would sooner make myself an accessory to high treason. I will deal with this affair another time." So saying, he walked out of the room, with shoulders bent, far otherwise than on that afternoon when he had asked Herr Brümmer about events in Belgium.

Lenore looked timidly at her grandfather. It was strange how David's boyish obstinacy descended from old Wahl's independence of mind. But she had no time to waste on such reflections. The iron was now hot, and she must strike.

With trembling hands the grandfather poured himself out a glass of water from the carafe which had stood on that desk ever since Lenore could remember anything. "Such," he said, "are the rewards of a long life."

"But that's not all," she broke in, "we are here, Grandpapa, and we love you. Without your support I could not marry Bertin. You are the only man on the whole earth who can help us, and you *will* help us—promise me!"

The old man asked faintly what he was to promise.

Lenore sat in front of him on the sloped surface of the desk so that their faces were almost touching, and explained. A banking account of five thousand marks was the condition which her father had attached to their engagement. She had not paid much attention to the point at the time, but her happiness now hung upon it. A writer, while he was making roads or digging trenches, could not earn five thousand marks. But when he came back, his plays would be performed at the theatres; the agents had his contracts, and on the security of these contracts Grandpapa must lend the five thousand marks, without anyone knowing anything at all about it.

Markus Wahl, with his hand over his mouth, stared aghast at this persistent young lady; but he liked the idea of the little deception, and decided in an impulse to agree. "If you had asked for the money as a gift, my child, there would have been difficulties; I am mean, I know; all old people, and especially if they are thin, are mean; but since you are of my blood you will pay me back. I am generous enough to let you off the interest," he added quizzically, unlocked a drawer, took out a cheque-book long unused, and in an old man's sloping script, his spectacles poised in front of his long-sighted eyes, he wrote out clearly the amount: Five Thousand marks. "On the day before your father leaves for the Eastern Command, you will pay this into the Berlin Handelsbank, and start an account in the name of Werner Bertin."

Lenore folded up the precious document, put it away carefully in the front of her dress, then slid down on to Markus Wahl's lap, put her arms round his neck, and kissed him on both cheeks and on the mouth. "Remember, dear kind Grandpapa," she laughed, "this account has existed since last year."

Chapter 4

A MARRIAGE PROPOSAL

The railway station was a platform just outside the ruins of a village, a roofless skeleton patched with wire and planking. The trucks emptied themselves of men, but only the first company formed up on the sloping grassy hollow between surrounding hills. The others had obviously been detrained elsewhere in the night. Yellow with king-cups, blue with forget-me-nots, the meadowland, so new to their eyes, stretched away into the distance; they had set foot upon French soil. But above their heads grey clouds moved across the sky, mists veiled their sight, and brown water oozed from under the edges of their boots, so that they could not sit down. However, they put down their packs, and amused themselves by speculating where they were. Some asserted that they had read the inscription "Vilosnes-Est." What they were waiting for, no one knew. At last a corporal appeared, with his arms full of letters and packages, all of which had been accumulating here in the last ten days, and had now reached them. So they had got to the right spot at last. Indeed, a horse was actually waiting for the company leader, a chestnut with a white forehead. The men all roared with laughter at the prospect of Acting-Officer Grassnick, who was more than a trifle knock-kneed, swinging himself into the saddle. It was to be hoped that his high-crowned cap would not fall off in the process. When he was already astride, Acting-Sergeant-Major Glinsky came running up, his leather leggings tightly buckled round his calves; taken aback for the moment by the unwonted aspect of the company leader, he clicked his heels and stiffly handed him a folded map. Coolly the horseman studied the map, and folded it again with his gloved hands; and the company moved off.

They marched with much creaking and clatter, and the clink of metal. The men toiled under their heavy burdens, which had been increased by the parcels they had received by post; and small packages hung from the straps and cords of their packs. They marched in overcoats, with the lower corners hooked up on each side; they slipped on the damp grass, stumbled against the files in front, and had to help push each other up a slope. Very soon the trampled grassland led on to a road, the good condition of which bore witness to the labours of companies like theirs. Beyond a ridge they looked down upon a brown stream curving gently through wooded hills: the Meuse. Small eddies, and ripples where tufts of herbage caught the current, betrayed its movement. They crossed it on a wooden bridge, marked "To Sivry," proud of their martial tread over the planking. Beyond the bridge there was a fork of several roads and paths. Grassnick, with his eyes on the map, rode ahead. The air was utterly still. Not a sound reached them, only the rhythmic tramping of that company, four hundred and fifty men in files of four, announced the presence of life. Grassnick had profited by his experiences in the Serbian campaign; he now put the third platoon in front of the column, with the twelfth squad at the very head, the smallest men, so that they could set the pace for the long legs of the first platoon. Acting-Officer Pohl, Sergeant Barkopp, Corporal Näglein, and Lance-Corporal Bohne formed the first file. Their way appeared to lead along the edge of a wood, which was to be reached by marching round a hill.

Alert as he had never been in his life marched Bertin, the outside man of his file on the right. His eyes drank in whatever they could see; and what he was looking for was war. The village of Sivry was more of a wreck than anything he had seen in Serbia. But the cellars and the numerous barns were seething with military life; soldiers in shirt-sleeves, who shouted mocking greetings at them, and pointed to unintelligible chalked directions to Headquarters, and wireless sections, and stretcher-bearers. For the time being, he noticed nothing strange, except that they were marching across country. He had received three parcels, one from Kreuzburg, and three from Potsdam, together with two letters from Lenore and two from his mother (his father only sent the barest salutations). Who could tell where they were to spend the night, and whether it would then be still light enough to read the news that he now carried, buttoned against his chest, onwards into France, into the country of the enemy. At last there would be an end of his crass and sleepy labours on the roads, of all the barren monotony, all the drudgery of garrison life, unrelieved by any risk. A man would now be given an opportunity to prove himself, and be able to say to his children, "In those days, when I was before Verdun."

An unwonted clatter roused him abruptly from his meditations. The small men of the first platoons were jumping over a trench that had suddenly opened out before them, a narrow deep cleft right across their path. The slippery edge offered a bad take-off for the jump, and the brown soil stuck to the men's boots. Shortly after, they had to take a long stride over black telegraph wires laid in a ditch cut neatly through the turf. Then a second trench appeared, much broader this time and not so deep; they had to jump down into it and clamber up the other side, where crude steps had been cut for that purpose. By this time the company was pretty well coated in mud. Were they on the right way? Grassnick on his steed seemed to be in no doubt; posed like a statue, with set and expressionless red face; he awaited his company. Bertin in the tenth squad, then near the head of the column, looked behind him, and watched the broad grey line coiling over the hills, and the procession of heavy packs, ground-sheets, and tin utensils, rise into view, and listened to the curses and the laughter; and the clatter of drinking-cups against water-bottles. Suddenly the bushes parted, a man leapt out in a great state of excitement, his faded tunic making him almost invisible, and dashed up to Herr Grassnick. Without the faintest salute, he yelled out in broad Bavarian: "What the hell are you doing here?" Grassnick's blue eyes surveyed this quivering figure in blank amazement; plainly a lunatic. The man's putties were brown with mud, but a hardly recognizable sword-frog on his belt indicated that he had some sort of rank—he was an acting Sergeant-Major as it afterwards appeared. Grassnick, a distinguished figure in his irreproachable tunic, his high waterproof cap, and his open cloak draped over his horse's quarters, tried to defend himself against this onslaught. The leading platoons were soon grouped around the pair. "I don't care a —— who you are," roared the artillery-man (yes, he had black tabs on his tunic); "and if you like to take your men under fire, that's your own lookout; but what the hell do you mean by drawing the French fire right on to our battery? The mist will rise in five minutes, the captive balloon will go up, and then I hope the saints of Prussia will keep you all safe."

Artillery? Gun positions? Grassnick rolled his eyes about him in amazement. Alas, many months had passed since he had seen anything of active warfare in the field with his own Küstrin regiment, when he was wounded, and promoted to this peaceful command. There, indeed, were black pits peering from the under-growth, and in each of them an observant eye might have detected a gun. The A.S.C. men stood huddled in a crowd. Their officer, in all ignorance, was leading them on to a battle-field. Did he think he was still playing at war on the plains of Macedonia? He tried to appease the men by explaining that they had only just detrained, and that such and such a way had been marked for him on the map. The other barely glanced at the sheet, and showed him that he had mistaken the cross-roads. He was now astray among the Bavarian artillery positions, and the French might be dropping heavy stuff on them at any moment. He must get his men at the double to the corner by the edge of the wood, where the road branched off to Consenvoye, and creep into the wood at the point where there were signs hung up: "Out of sight here." The company was very silent. Grassnick cursed the inspiration that had led him to put the shortest men at the head of the column, and drove them along almost at a run. Sweating and panting the long line of men clattered past the artillery positions, jumped once more over the telephone wires, and hurried to the refuge indicated.

They were now grateful for the rain that they had cursed before they set out.

They plunged at last into a forest of tall pines and oaks, on either side of the road, which indeed provided complete protection. Wooden signposts pointed the way to Reville, Etraye. Now they could take breath, as the rear ranks, the giants of the first platoon, swung under cover of the trees; with the gallantry of a real officer, Grassnick sat motionless on his horse until the last file was in safety. He let the men move on a little way and then rode meditatively after them. This had been unfortunate. He must clearly take uncommon care to keep his eyes open. He called back a couple of men from the first platoon, told them to put their packs on the company wagon, and get on ahead to see about billets in Etraye; that, too, had been forgotten. His conscience pricked him; if the distances were correct, owing to this mistake they could not reach this unknown village before dark.

The men now had the feeling that all was well. The spring woods, alive with birds, made them feel cheerful. No shell-hole pitted the broad, curved, gently undulating highway. They all began, Bertin as well, to rummage in their haversacks; the Berliners talked of "chewing oakum" when they ate the dry slabs of army bread, but nearly every man had some sort of relish to help him get it down. Bertin opened one of his parcels, cut some thick slices of mixed sausage, which his neighbours pronounced excellent. The meal was finished with a mouthful of cold thin coffee. He rubbed his hands fairly clean on his breeches, filled his pipe, and drew in a deep draught of smoke, which seemed more agreeable than ever in the aromatic rain-soaked air. "Let me be," he said to his neighbours, who were making a great business of lighting their pipes from his, "I want to read letters from home." After the first fleeting glance, he forgot the presence of Holzer on his right, and Metzler in front.

"My dear boy," wrote Lenore, "to make a long story short, we are going to be married. I can't otherwise get you leave, and before you get too deep into danger, I must have had you with me once again. Write to me whether you agree. If so, you must put in an application to your unit for marriage-leave. I will see to all the rest here. By the way, you are quite well off, in case Mamma should ask you. Papa gave his consent on condition of your producing a bank account of five thousand marks, so that I should not be marrying a beggar; we have in the meantime fulfilled these conditions. How this was done I will explain later on. No more today, except that I hope all is well with you. Any two people who have gone through so much in their youth as we have done, have a claim to some happy years, when this awful time is over. We are all delighted that my brother David, who sends his best regards, has been put back for six months and perhaps a year, because his chest measurements are much too small. He has been moved to the Lower Sixth, and, with the whole class, volunteered for service. Did I tell you that I heard from the Nil Publishing Company that they are printing another edition of your novel? The royalty will be paid to you in the form of a monthly instalment. You might arrange for me to receive it for you? Perhaps I am really bringing you luck as we both of us always hoped. No more now. I am so excited over all sorts of practical matters that will have to be settled. Well, I like the feel of it. The main thing is that each of us will now once more be the half of the other. All my love. L.

"P.S.—Papa is giving me eighty thousand marks' worth of Fourth War Loan. I asked for Swiss paper, but he maintained that you, as a soldier, would certainly insist on War Loan. Besides, it seems to suit him better."

Bertin's legs moved with mechanical alternation. Metzler's pack, with his cooking utensils tied on behind, swung ominously near his spectacles; a surge of joy swept through his heart. In exactly ten days it would have been a year since he was called up. At that time their official union lay far away in the dim future, a star that hung deep beneath the horizon. Now it was rising radiant into the sky. Was there such a girl anywhere on earth? "Well, I'm damned," he muttered to himself, as he stuffed the letter quite absentmindedly into his breast-pocket with the others; by which he referred to this stroke of luck. And leave—leave at last!

Suddenly, as the men who were to go on ahead were passing the foremost ranks, under a volley of chaff and advice to make the best use of their long legs—the earth seemed to quiver. From the wood, a green wilderness of foliage, undergrowth, mighty trunks, and slender saplings, burst a detonating roar, the like of which none of those four hundred and fifty men had ever heard or imagined. In terror they recoiled against each other, a blast of wind struck their faces, and they ceased to breathe. A heavy gun had been fired, nothing more, one of the many hundreds that were lurking in this landscape, in clefts, and behind hills. That awful sound revealed a fury of destruction, a measureless force, which no living being could defy. None spoke. Pale and awestruck, they pointed to the gigantic black howitzer, now visible round a slight curve in the road, its cruel barrel, packed with padding at the base, slanting to the sky. Immediately before Bertin's eyes the second shot went off. A tearing flash, a thunderous roar, and—visible for one instant in the leaping flame—a black body soaring heavenwards. The men were almost deafened, as they marched with their hands over their ears, and with parted lips. But there was no third explosion. They moved on in silence. This was no place for them; they wanted roofs over their heads again. It must still be a long way to the barns of Etraye or Reville. An ominous initiation. Surely the air still reeked of burning gases?

Thus the first company of X/20 entered upon their new domain; the outermost circle of the hell of Verdun. They knew that the days of laughter were now past.

Chapter 5

REASON IS THE HIGHEST PATRIOTISM

Herr Hugo Wahl came back surprisingly soon from the Eastern Command. He said nothing, ate his breakfast in silence, and read the newspaper. He cut short Frau Mathilde's curiosity by pointing without a word to the upper left-hand corner of the invitation, on which was typed: *Secret and Confidential.* He was much more annoyed that his father asked him no question. They were together in the inner office throughout the day; almost nothing had happened in the interval. There were memoranda from industrial combines, which were after lucrative war contracts and wanted financial backing. A certain consortium drew Herr Wahl's attention to a Rumanian oil undertaking, on the board of which were several influential politicians. There was the usual slight rise in all securities, which preceded the fresh war loan now imminent—in short, nothing very startling. Herr Hugo Wahl read the letters, dictated answers, signed them, telephoned, drove several times to Berlin, came back, and smoked cigars incessantly.

Markus Wahl threw sidelong glances at his son, or observed him over the top of his old-fashioned pince-nez, as the latter was busy over columns of figures. The old man knew his Hugo; he had no illusions about him, he was very willing to make fun of him, but he loved him in his own way. And he saw that his son had some burden on his mind. On the Friday afternoon, when the office was shut, and a thick vapour of cigar smoke had collected under the green shades of the hanging lamps, Markus Wahl put away his copy of the *Zürcher Zeitung,* which contained a translation of a very outspoken article from the *London Observer* on the British failure in Gallipoli, took off his pince-nez, and blinked at the figure opposite, which, in a stillness broken only by the ticking of the clock, with tired eyes and sagging mouth, looked an embodiment of disillusion. "Well, Hugo," he said, in a gentle tone, quite innocent of mockery, "and what have you been doing?" And his voice made clear that their latest quarrel had passed, like all the others, from his heart, and had not left a trace behind it.

Herr Hugo Wahl started, stared at his father with a bewildered air, gave a sharp snort of weariness and relief, opened his mouth several times, as though words were trying to make their way into his mouth. Then he made his confession.

All the long way through Eydtkuhnen, Wirballen, to Kovno, that little party of three had been agog with the prospect of being called on to assist the Fatherland with their advice. At the frontier, their passports silenced the curiosity of the railway police; then they rumbled on through a land of forests, hills, and snow-covered plains. At Kovno an affable officer met them in a large car. The railway station, still blackened by fire and patched up with new planking, and the ruins of brick buildings wrecked by artillery fire to the right and left of the road, bore awful witness to the struggle that ended in the capture of the fortress. After some rest and refreshment, they hired a cab, driven by a Jew, to take them through the town, which presented a strange blend of field grey and ordinary life. Doctor Carl Jonas was acquainted with several important Jewish citizens here, and also with the heads of the great Talmud school at Sobodka, across the river, where stood an old synagogue, now wrecked by shell-fire. In 1905, he had worked in close co-operation with Jewish magnates for the relief of the victims of the pogrom, and was left with high admiration for their unselfishness, combined with deep annoyance at their obstinacy. The vast military buildings of the fortress, and an enormous domed church, testified to the Russian element in the city, while the Jews were represented by a multitude of shop-signs, inscribed in bad German in Hebrew characters. In the old town, between the river Niemen and Vilya, there were some fine buildings; churches, white and grey, and little synagogues, on the broad central square. They clattered through the city in much contentment, and greatly interested in all they saw; Jonas indicated the objects of interest, while the coachman, quite without embarrassment, interjected comments here and there. Walking the streets were youths in Russian blouses, and pale young maidens, sisters in the Russian and the German Red Cross. The narrow alleyways swarmed with Jews in black caftans, women in shawls, and gambolling children. Snow, spring wind, and the mighty frozen stream, brought charm and brightness into the sombre picture.

At half-past five, after friendly greetings, the three black-coated civilians took their seats at the green table, which, with foolscap paper and pencils before every place, reminded Herr Wahl of a board meeting; the other members of the conference wore field-grey tunics, rows of ribbons, the Iron Cross of the First Class, and spurred boots. From the head of the table Major-General Schieffenzahn opened the meeting and stated the business before the assemblage. His courteous words, his graceful gestures, did not prevent everyone present recognizing, and respecting, the able ruler of a great country; more especially Herr Wahl.

Food supplies were causing the administration great anxiety. The agricultural produce of the vast area between Windau and Bialystock or Bielsk, ought have been quite adequate to satisfy the needs of the Army of Occupation and the inhabitants—seventeen people to the square kilometre—if the methods of cultivation had not been so out of date. They would be gradually changed; but, for the moment, account had to be taken of them as they existed. The towns were unproductive now, and merely constituted a burden on the land. As in Germany, the traffic in the necessaries of life and in raw materials had been lately placed entirely in charge of War Trade organizations. This had deprived traders, or, in other words, one half of the Jewish inhabitants, of their earnings. But the other half also, the hand-workers, were coming upon bad times. The more prosperous sections of the population had been carried off by the Russians when they evacuated Kovno (forty thousand Jews had been sent away by train), all the factories were dismantled, and work at a standstill. New contracts—as for instance in the building trade—there were none. But as the building trade was the key industry that covered many others, such as carpentry, painting, glazing, plumbing, tinning, heating, and decoration, the military administration had to consider how a famine was to be avoided. The military authorities naturally employed soldiers of the Army of Occupation, German craftsmen and workmen, who were more efficient and much cheaper. As regards the country districts, in requisitioning their products just so much could be left as would support life. The towns, on the other hand, remained a problem which it was hoped the present conference might help to solve. Captain von Wasow would put forward considerations which had been embodied in a scheme that they would now proceed to discuss. A youngish-looking captain, sitting near the Major-General, then got up with a memorandum in his hand. "We three," went on Herr Wahl, "stared at each other in utter bewilderment—Jonas at the end of the table, opposite the Major-General, Obstfelder at his right, and I, the youngest, at his left. This man now controlled the entire structure of an army and a country. To begin with he had won his victory, as the indispensable coadjutor of our great Field-Marshal. Now his day was taken up with a hundred detailed matters—every quarter of an hour of it, as we had seen for ourselves. And yet this man found time to exercise his mind over feeding the Jews in all these little towns. While he was speaking, I thought a great deal about you, father, and wished that you had been there. You have often laughed at my respect for Prussians, and jeered at me when I resented the critical attitude of people like Bertin. No nation in the world can produce such officers, I thought proudly, and I waited like a gun-dog for what the captain might have to say. Obstfelder was the only one of us who was uneasy; you know how he chews at his cigar when things are not going to his liking. The captain began by observing that he had ascertained that every year before the war a certain section of the Jewish population emigrated to America, where, as it seemed, their shortcomings were not so apparent as elsewhere.

I felt myself quiver, and I saw Jonas lower his head ominously and thrust out his moustache. What did this captain know of the vices of such poor people, a population with whom he could not have exchanged ten intelligible words, and for whom potatoes and herrings were a feast. This looked serious, and we soon learned what was to come. What had been the practice in peace-time, was essential now. The military administration of Lithuania therefore proposed that this emigration should be resumed and organized. The suggestion was something of this kind: the superfluous population should be collected into concentration camps, put on shipboard at Libau, and sent out into the Baltic, where they would be met and escorted on their way by American vessels. The navy had been very willing to place captured merchant ships with adequate freight room at their disposal for this purpose, and huts for the lodgement of the emigrants could be easily constructed by local labour under German direction. Materials would be provided by the Government of Courland free of charge. Can you imagine it?" said Herr Hugo Wahl to his father.

Markus Wahl stood beside his son, with his arms resting on the table, he looked down at the upturned face, in which every fold of the skin seemed flushed with blood. His head, on its long skinny neck, recalled that of a great bird of prey. "I can," he answered softly.

"Then you think more quickly than I do. For a whole minute I could not grasp a word. Why should not the Jews be helped to travel to free America? Did not their households here all live on the few dollars which an industrious emigrant sent home? A large number of them would certainly seize the opportunity of turning their backs on Russia without expense to themselves. At this point Schieffenzahn asked whether one of their guests from Berlin desired to make any comment. We had asked Jonas to act as spokesman. Obstfelder, as you know, has a hasty temper and doesn't mind what he says, while I am better at accounts than speech-making. Jonas got up. I wondered why he looked so sickly and pale; and I found myself thinking he would look like that on his death-bed, with his white moustache, his bushy eyebrows, and the stubbly hair on the top of his head. I was really the only one of us who produced an at all Jewish effect; if Jonas had put on a uniform or a green shooting coat, everyone would have taken him for Herr von Jonas, while Obstfelder with his democratic beard—well, you know him. Jonas cleared his throat and asked whether it was suggested that the emigration should be voluntary or compulsory. The captain replied courteously that only voluntary emigration had been contemplated in the first instance. The advantages of these proposals would be made known as widely as possible; but in the event of insufficient applications forcible measures might have to be considered. What was the position, Jonas asked, with regard to the consent of the American Government? To secure this, answered the captain, would be the task of the emigrants' co-religionists, who would also have to arrange for the reception, housing, and care of the newcomers.—What would happen if Washington refused its consent?—That, said the captain, they could not consider.—But at such a time of the year, the end of winter, and early spring, a sea voyage might be very dangerous for women, old people, and children?—The captain merely shrugged his shoulders.—Were there not mine-barriers in the Gulf of Libau and elsewhere?—At a sign from Major-General Schieffenzahn, a naval officer in a long blue coat took up the tale. Yes, there were certainly mines, German, Russian, and English.—Who then would guarantee that these emigrant ships would escape the mines? Who would get them across in safety?—With an air of faint astonishment the officer replied that, of course, no one could give any guarantee.

"The atmosphere in the great room, hung with portraits of Russian monarchs, had suddenly grown denser. These awkward questions made it perfectly clear how delighted they had all been with the idea of getting rid of so many Jews. They had sent for us so that we might bear a part of the responsibility, and all the odium. They—educated Germans—were tempted by the example of Russia. It was only the lamentable Jews of Eastern Europe that came into question. They would be bundled on board ship, and sent off—placed in God's hand, you see," said Hugo Wahl, "and the responsibility would be His."

Markus Wahl reflected that the shock had actually lent his son imagination. He saw the interiors of those emigrant ships, the sick, the women, their children and their bundles; tossed by the wind and waves, colliding and drifting helplessly on to mine-fields. English cruisers would fire at the remnant of the squadron, unaware of the identity of these ships that sailed under the German flag. Such want of thought and imagination almost aroused his pity. Why could not these people put themselves in the position of others? Were they too young, too immature? Surely men with such crude consciences ought not to be masters?

"Nothing, of course, came of this precious plan," went on Herr Hugo Wahl. "Obstfelder dealt with the matter from the point of view of international law, quite dispassionately, as though he were treating of any other political measure. Not a word, not an intonation that would not have been perfectly appropriate in a speech on company law. Under international law Germany was pledged to provide for the needs of the population of an occupied area, as in Belgium. No measures that the German authorities might take could conceal the grievances of the Jewish masses; the organization of the world today made it possible for every man, in the last resort, to send news wherever he wished. Such a clearance of the occupied areas would expose us to a charge of violating international law; it would rouse all the neutrals, and provide inexhaustible material for enemy propaganda. The proposed scheme of evacuation, as likely to cause unnecessary hardship, and as a measure aimed against the Jews, would call forth a storm of indignation, especially in America, in the face of which the advocates of the German cause would be powerless. The so-called interventionists would then find it easy to bring in America on the side of the Entente, and the country most rich in raw material would thus be provoked into entering the ring of our foes; for in America no nice distinctions are made between Jews and other people. Jonas associated himself with Obstfelder, speaking with rather more warmth and intensity. For a generation he had been fighting to win respect for Germany among the Jews. In our just struggle for self-preservation, we needed all the sympathy that we could get, no section of humanity was beneath our notice; even the mouse in the fable helped the lion. He very well understood the anxieties of the Eastern Command, but he proposed to meet them in another fashion. It would be possible to collect funds in America, rather on the model of the American relief work in Belgium, to provide the population of the former Western provinces of Russia, without distinction of creed, with the necessaries of life, clothing, and fuel; and he pledged himself to obtain considerable contributions in Germany as well. With the assistance of the American Government, foodstuffs could be imported from the neutral States, and perhaps also from America, and the difficulties would thus be solved in a manner creditable to Germany.

"It was a sound and humane speech, you see, and Schieffenzahn realized this; I could not help feeling delighted when he summed up. He, too, was not able to ignore the objections that had been brought forward, and the scheme must be allowed to drop. Moreover, Herr Dr. Jonas's suggestions were worth consideration, and he favoured the idea of buying up foodstuffs in neutral countries —in any case, other methods must be found. And he brought the meeting to a close.

"Then with much clattering of boots and chairs, they all got up, stretched themselves, and suddenly began to talk at the tops of their voices; and we—we were non-existent. All we could see were backs, if you understand me. That was the staggering thing. These people had expected us to provide cover for their lunatic schemes; instead of which we brought forward reasonable objections, and suggested a better way out; in recognition, we were treated as though we were no longer in the room. The orderlies cleared away the chairs, collected the papers, the officers looked out of the windows, or gathered round Major-General Schieffenzahn, and lit each other's cigarettes. They presented a cheerful group at the far end of the room; while we must have had the air of tailors' dummies left behind. You should have seen Jonas. He was furious, and showed it without showing it—if you know what I mean. He took two steps towards the window, and signed to us to come forward. The noise lessened, though the cheerful gentlemen in uniform did not otherwise pay us much attention; still, the clear, cutting tones of the dialogue that followed made it clear that something was up. 'We must now take our leave, Herr General,' said Jonas, directly ignoring all the others. Schieffenzahn expressed his regret, and the hope that we had been suitably entertained as guests of the Commander-in-Chief. 'We are leaving this evening,' Jonas went on, 'and would ask you to convey our respects to the Field-Marshal.' 'We are glad,' Obstfelder said, in that husky voice of his, 'to have been of service to the Reich, and are grateful to you for giving us the opportunity.' 'Then nothing remains but to wish you a pleasant journey home.' We bowed, walked down the long room, bowed once more at the door, which I, as the last, shut. I caught the General's eye, and he looked to me slightly embarrassed. We took the night train; during the journey, we talked little, we were too conscious of our insignificance; indeed we spent most of the time asleep, each in his own corner. On our pass was stamped: 'Not to be deloused,' otherwise we should have been mercilessly bundled out at the frontier, to the great damage of our clothes. We were just civilians; men of no account. I simply would not have believed it possible. A friendly word, an invitation to spend a sociable evening, a little sensible talk over a glass of wine—was that too much to ask? Apparently it was."

Markus Wahl bent lower over his son. And then he did what he had not done for many years; he passed his hand gently over the smooth and carefully brushed hair.

At the touch, Hugo Wahl let his forehead sink on to his sleeve. Then he sat up. "For nearly fifty years I have admired our Prussians, and thought a soldier's tunic the finest wear in the world; and I would not listen to people who talked about militarism—including yourself, Father. Well, it's never too late to learn. Reason is the highest patriotism, and militarism is evil in its very essence. It will ruin Germany, if it is not kept within some sort of bounds."

Markus Wahl, with his hands behind his back, answered gravely: "But who will do so? There is no one."

"We can't," admitted the son. "We men of fifty are too old. The men of thirty must see to it; we can stand by and back them up. It is odd that you men of seventy judge the world more justly, while we let ourselves be deluded."

"Success deludes a man," observed Markus Wahl. "Anyhow, you can do something for your daughter. She wants to marry soon."

Hugo Wahl looked up—father and son surveyed each other quizzically. "I admit I didn't take this engagement very seriously; it seemed to be useful to have a connexion of the family at the front. But you are right—she shall marry the man. How old is our prospective son-in-law?"

"Getting on for thirty, I should think," smiled Markus Wahl.

Into Hugo Wahl's embittered, deeply wounded soul, came the memory of a verse, that he had learnt in his school days, a line of Virgil, with which Frederick William, the Great Elector, was said to have signed a disagreeable peace: *Exoriare aliquis nostris ex ossibus ultor.*—May an avenger arise from our bones in time to come.

Chapter 6

FRAU WAHL GOES INTO THE CELLAR

Since a certain day of this year Frau Wahl had been keeping a diary. It began with the words: "Today David was put back for six months. I kept my vow, and made many people happy; but nothing could express my own feeling of deliverance." And in her large pointed script she spread herself over the pages of the old-fashioned leather volume which she had extracted from one of her drawers, full of animation and excitement at the prospect of a wedding in a few months. "When she told me, it gave me a shock; I had to collect myself, and ask for time to think it over. I said: 'It is such a surprise, child, and these are hard times.' " And she enlarged on the difficulties in the way of setting up a new establishment at such a juncture. She sat in a corner of her boudoir, in a velvet-covered arm-chair, at an elegant little writing-table, where it was cool in the stifling days of summer, and warm when the streets were freezing outside.

Times were indeed hard. Every German, great or small, had then to live on a weekly ration of four hundred grammes of bread, half a pound of meat, nine pounds of potatoes, ninety grammes of butter (watered), some cheese, and from time to time an egg. In the cities, milk was kept for children and sick persons; but owing to the lack of transport, the farmer was able to feed his young pigs on milk. In addition, everyone received half a pound of oatmeal, groats, barley, beans, or—in summer—vegetables: white or savoy cabbage, spinach, swedes, carrots, seakale. But the dreadful thing was the uncertainty as to what would be available the following week; this was the burden that weighed upon housewives and children. When, after hours of waiting in a queue, customers at last reached the counter, it too often happened that their allotted shares had already gone. Potatoes, especially, were short, though the railways had orders to give them preference; however, the new harvest promised to be good. But before that, the months of May and June and July had to be got through; and no one can fill his belly with flowers. All this Frau Wahl pondered as she wrote. She made it clear to herself that one more person in the household would mean one more mouth to be fed. If Lenore ate less bread, David had the benefit of it. She noted that it was only for much-valued customers that shops were willing to set aside, and deliver—mostly at night—the best and dearest kinds of meat. She came to the conclusion that a separate household would involve her daughter in a great deal of trouble without any benefit to anyone. Then she laid down her pen, took a stick of chocolate out of a sidedrawer and nibbled it; which soothed her mind. She could not be charged with merely observing the many changes in every kind of trade since the end of 1915, without profiting by the experience she had gained in all her varied activities. She had bought a supply of soft warm cloth for the men of her household, for herself, and for Lenore, and as Christmas presents for the servants. And when, in the first months of the war, thousands of unemployed women were thronging the labour exchanges, and it became a patriotic duty to do all one could to help trade in this difficult time, she had bought fine linen, batiste, and lace, and had a trousseau made for her daughter, such as was given to young girls in those days; a chest full of night-gowns and shifts, dressing-jackets, damask tablecloths, and others for everyday, the finest bed-linen, underclothes lavishly trimmed with embroidery and lace, face towels, bath towels, towels for the kitchen and for every other household purpose. In all human calculation, the supply would last for ten years, if good soap were used to wash it. But for a long time there had been no good soap. For daily purposes a sort of fine pumice-stone had been introduced. It was called K.-A.-soap, and left a kind of brownish deposit that had to be carefully rinsed off, so that it should not soil the towels. In the country, it seemed, soap was boiled according to old recipes, and candles were made of tallow; but in the town, fat and oils were strictly controlled, and it was becoming more and more difficult to get these products by any form of subterfuge. Yes, her daughter should marry if she so wished. The object for which the engagement had been allowed would be secured much better by marriage; she should marry and live at home.

Frau Wahl put away the diary in a drawer, and took out of another an oddly old-fashioned key. Then she left her place and the room. In the hall, she put on an old frieze cloak; and she went down into her cellars. A glance into the coal cellar, the door of which she opened first, set one anxiety at rest; yes, the mild winter had been fortunate for all Germans, and for her as well. There was still a little mound of coke for heating the house, and briquettes and wood for the kitchen. In the laundry-room nearby, the bed and body linen of the past month lay soaking in a tub; the powdered cleanser had to be mixed with the greatest care, if it was not to corrode the fabric. Cautiously she stirred the mass with the huge wooden spoon; the linen swelled and gurgled with the inrushing air, and then again subsided. In the potato chest there was a layer of grey-brown tubers about a hand's breadth deep; Tornow must be sent to his country home to get further supplies as soon as possible. The wooden racks looked very empty; only a few heads of cabbage and half a dozen lemons. In the egg-chest, some bedded in chopped straw, and some lying in earthen vessels full of water-glass, gleamed the products of their industrious and faithful fowls, which had survived December and January under the veranda. And there were still apples from the garden, and winter fruit, sweet-smelling on their layers of straw. All this was carefully dealt out to guests, children, husband, and grandfather. There, too, were rows of tall glass jars full of dark cherries, raspberries from the further corner of the garden, and even blackberries from bushes that David had once planted to provide shelter for his hedgehog. The greengages had been eaten, so had the gooseberries, and so also had the fine pears and the sweet cherries. In their place stood two glasses, one full, and the other a third full, of honey which had run to the colour of wax. The winter was over. But at all this she would not look; she knew it by heart, and there was an inventory to show what had been used.

From the last chamber in the basement came a waft of chill air: it was the wine cellar, in which the bottles, ranged according to their vintages, displayed an array of red, yellow, and blue capsules. Part of the wall was hidden by a large piece of furniture once in use in the house, a hatstand, consisting of an expanse of planking covered in rep and set with a row of hooks for hats and coats, and large rings for sticks and umbrellas. From the hooks hung keys and old clothes. It led a purposeless existence here, because no one had the heart to throw it away, nor knew of any better place for it. Frau Wahl pushed it carefully aside. A door of bare boards freshly inset in the wall, was then revealed. This opened upon a deep embrasure in which Markus Wahl used to keep little casks of his favourite Southern wine which he imported from Hungary and Italy. Here Frau Wahl stored the food supplies that she had collected in the terror of the first few weeks, like many another comfortable German housewife, who, though much ridiculed and criticized, made provision as though the Mark of Brandenburg were going to be starved out by the enemy within the following few weeks. Although panic quickly vanished before the cheerful confidence that Germany was quite well provided enough to survive a war that could not last for long, from age-long housewifely instinct she preserved her hoard, especially as the grocers, corn dealers, and butchers, offered such a choice and abundance of goods as they had never done before. This state of affairs gradually changed, but the tradesman with whom she chiefly dealt, a large grocer in the main avenue, urged her to follow the example of the stewards who bought for their Majesties and the Princesses. He supplied the palaces; and without hesitating or troubling about high prices, with a half sheet of paper in her hand, she whispered her orders. The goods were delivered at night; little sacks and cases with the wares of warmer lands, carried home by ships which had long been rotting at the bottom of the sea. About ten pounds of wheaten meal from Hungary lay beside double the amount of rice, five pounds of cocoa from the Dutch East Indies, a square canister of English oatmeal, two thirds of a German sugar-loaf, a cluster of green lemons from Italy, a sealed chest of China tea, and another of Brazilian coffee. A large stone vessel full of so-called butter-fat—melted butter, which could only thus be preserved from growing rancid; and glass jars of precious goose and chicken fat, completed her treasure.

It was with a deeply divided mind that Frau Wahl lingered by this modest store, which would hardly have supplied a great hotel or a sanatorium for three days. Pride and satisfaction were written on her face; but her drooping shoulders were eloquent of the burden of an evil conscience. The press at that time was full of reproaches against those who hoarded for themselves and their families. The State had undertaken what was impossible—to carry on a war for several years, without imports, and with an untested and inadequate system of distribution; it was trying to feed the army and the nation on what Germany could produce, whereas only on paper could the land be made to yield enough to make this possible. The ruling castes could very well hold out—the landlords, the landed aristocracy in important State positions, the richer middle class, and the countless officers' families, who received foodstuffs from the Lines of Communications, consigned under various disguises by freight trains, or carried home by men going on leave. Frau Wahl knew very well what went on. She came into contact with all classes in her town, and also with many people in Berlin. The people, the broad masses of labouring citizens, professional men and artists, grew daily more exasperated by the insufficient and monotonous food that was to give them strength for their labours. No one yet regarded the final victory as a matter of indifference; everyone believed and hoped, and prayed, collected their scanty supplies and strictly dealt them out, and ate substitutes and tinned goods of very dubious origin. But beneath that tense mask of confidence, the soul of men began to stir with evil passions; envy, betrayal, and hatred were not far below the surface and only waited an occasion to leap forth. . . .

Frau Mathilde Wahl closed the cupboard, put the key in her apron pocket, pushed the hatstand back into its place, made up her mind to hang a few bright-coloured aprons on the hooks, and an emergency lantern, in case the electric light gave out. Then, still pondering, she climbed the winding cellar steps. Her daughter might marry with her mind at ease. Within the modest resources of her domain, she was not more ill provided than Her Majesty the Empress, the pattern of every German woman.

Chapter 7

A YOUNG LADY EFFECTS A MARRIAGE LEAVE

There was a musty smell in the room. "Take your clothes off, please," said Dr. Schimmel. Bewildered and almost frightened, Lenore stared at the grey-bearded figure, on whose table stood a pile of cigarette-boxes full of dried starfish and mussel-shells. "Well? Don't you understand?" he said roughly. "You are to strip the upper part of your body."

Lenore Wahl was very angry. In her house not even a dog was spoken to in that tone. "Humour polishes all metals," she said to herself, quoting an advertisement then very popular. Had she not better turn her back on this gaunt tobacco-stained personage, the Medical Officer of Health for the district, though he did not open his windows, probably to save the cost of heating? She had only come here to get an official stamp affixed to her old friend Dr. Matthias's certificate; and was she now to let herself be sniffed at and fingered by a stranger? The process of getting leave for Werner Bertin was certainly leading her into very odd places; but she would not shrink. Softly, and smiling to herself, she took off her jacket, her blouse, and let the ribbons of her shift slip from her shoulders. With her arms resting on the table she felt the old man's hairy ear tickling her ribs. As he tapped, and listened, heedless of the lovely curves of her shoulders, the room in which that woman's body was unveiled seemed to be transfigured.

But the red plush curtains, the chairs and the cloth on the desk soon wore their accustomed air of dusty desolation in the cheerful morning sunlight, while an elderly medical officer carried out his duties. His two sons, also doctors, were serving in reserve regiments with the Third Corps; he himself expected to be called up shortly; such an appalling number of his colleagues had fallen in the last two years, or were no longer fit for service. Dr. Schimmel had no intention of helping a private soldier to get leave merely because this young woman came of a rich family. A soldier's place was at the front, where he was none so badly off. If this woman, as her type would have led him to expect, had shown the slightest indication of a weak lung, he would have been delighted to refuse his "placet." But she was sound, and there must be children. Mortality in the home was fortunately decreasing; but out there—they had been far too wasteful with their human material. "You can dress now," he growled, shuffled across to his desk, wrote a few words with a scratchy pen, spat on to a pad, and stamped the sheet. Meanwhile Lenore, with deft quick movements, dressed herself. The glass over a portrait of the old Emperor Wilhelm, served her as a mirror; and she patted the bow in front of her blouse into its proper place.

The old man turned, and said: "Well, aren't you ready yet? Here you are." Lenore asked what she owed him. He glared at her through his spectacles, and snorted that this was his official duty, and there was nothing to pay. Good-bye.

"Poor old owl," thought Lenore; and she ran down the stairs with the feeling that she had escaped from some ghostly schoolroom. It was sweet to undergo humiliations for a man she loved—or rather, as she hurriedly corrected herself, in a good cause. For whether she could be said to love this man, was still very much a matter of debate. Now, all would go well.

Lenore had never yet engaged herself in such a complicated undertaking. She was accustomed to intercourse with authors, living and dead; for those who stayed at home, reading had to replace every form of life. She had journeyed with Herder from Riga to Bordeaux, wandered with Anton Reiser from Hanover to Erfurt, fled with Schiller from Stuttgart to Mannheim, strolled through Venice with Heinse, dashed furtively to the South with

Goethe, through Munich, past the Walchensee, and down over the Brenner to Rome; but she had returned with Hölderlin, bewildered, from the banks of the Garonne to the domain of Diotima. The salamandrine glow of Hans von Bülow flashed forth in letters that he wrote to his wife; and that loneliest of wanderers, Nietzsche's restless search for the true climate of his soul had carried her to Sils Maria and Turin. It was good to have done all these things; it cleansed her soul, renewed her youth, strengthened her perceptions, and purified her judgments. But for her present purpose it was, indeed—in David's elegant phrase—just so much tripe, and merely hindered her in her dealings with "this world." And she was astonished that the matter made no progress. She wrote an application to the Home Command of the Third Corps, to which, as she laboriously ascertained, Bertin's unit belonged. Perhaps she had been wrongly advised. The application came back after a while, with "Wrong Department" scrawled in red ink across the foolscap page. What on earth was she to do now?

Marriage was a woman's affair—*the* woman's affair in a very real sense. Advisory agencies of all kinds gave women information and help in all their complications as dependants or survivors of soldiers at the front. Before the war they had been denied all interest and understanding of the affairs of life, and even the most commonplace question was met with: "That's no business of yours. Go back to your saucepans." Men, themselves intimidated by the State machine, had made too much use of feminine dependence to exalt their self-esteem; and now the age had taken its revenge.

The women who worked in public had no easy time. They were worn down by miseries in all shapes and forms, due to the absence of men . . . but this stirred no misgivings in their minds, it only awakened their idealism. They stretched forth their arms, and their eyes shone proudly as they realized that they were servants that the State could not do without.

Lenore found that a good deal of arrogance coloured women's dealings with and for each other. In one room she was taken for a student who wanted to get work on the land, in another, because *stud. phil.* was printed on her visiting card, for a chemist looking for employment in an explosives factory. (Women could not carry on with this for many months; their eyes and skin grew yellow, and the brown gases given off by the nitroglycerine gave them an incessant cough.) She often felt herself longing to get out on to the landing, and sit down and cry. The world was suddenly full of female teachers, there was no sympathy, no fellow-feeling, work had swept away all the gentler feminine qualities.

In their company, Lenore felt useless and unwanted, she had no degree and no practical aim in life; for social work, too, she had no talent, at any rate none officially recognizable. She looked pretty, sensitive, much too well-dressed, and she took up busy women's time with so unfeminine and unpatriotic a matter as her request for marriage-leave for her fiancé. That could surely be managed without all this fuss, when Private Bertin came home on leave in the ordinary course. Every soldier in the field had the right to leave; sometimes after fourteen months, sometimes not until after sixteen, but every man came home on leave at last. Why all this trouble?

At last, at the Inquiry Office for professional women, to which she had been wrongly referred, she got some helpful information, when one of the officiating ladies, after pointedly observing to her colleague that she could not imagine why the young person had come to them, said: "Go to the Guards' Inquiry Bureau, Fräulein, and don't waste our time, please."

The barrack rooms bore unmistakable evidence of bad eating, bad sleeping, and bad tobacco. She had to explain herself first to a deaf clerk, then to a sergeant, and lastly to a sergeant-major. Here she was greeted with facetious benevolence. They eyed the outline of her body to see whether she was in an advanced state of pregnancy, for no one could conceive any other reason for a hurried marriage with special leave from the front. The Prussian soldier was not constructed to take account of the more delicate emotions. He could turn a Pomeranian peasant lad into a man;

but the essential soul of a great people, with a thousand years of spiritual history behind it, in which so much that was outworn had been sloughed away, and such rich qualities laid bare, was beyond the horizon of any military authorities in the world. And now, after two years of war, it was beyond the vision of this sergeant. Why did the Fräuleinchen want to take one of the Kaiser's soldiers away from him? There were so many at home, only slightly wounded, or fit only for garrison service, with whom one could play at marriage, with much less difficulty, and without having to wait for stamp and paper.

Lenore was not to be offended. She retorted with gay coquettish glances, and after listening to much waggish counsel of this sort as she stood in that stuffy barrack room, she got the information that she wanted, made little notes in a small leather notebook, thanked the sergeant politely, and passed on. At last she had it all complete.

The marriage of a private soldier in the mobile army was treated much like that of a serf in earlier times. If his own unit had consented, the reserve unit, like the House that he served, took cognizance of the fact; the change was entered on the register, paybook, and company list, it altered his claims to dependants' relief, and caused a good deal of trouble. All this did not apply to Army Service Corps battalions. They were dealt with by an administrative section in the Home Command established at a period when such battalions consisted only of civilian labourers engaged for the purpose. And in the Prussia of those days such men were treated much like labourers from the Eastern Elbe, or migrants from Poland for the harvest. Lastly, somewhere, and of secondary importance, hovered the dim vision of a Registrar, her parents' house, and a church.

After all these journeyings and hours of waiting, it was Lenore's habit to take a hot bath. As she lay in the soothing water and soaped her skin with a cake of carnation-scented soap that Bertin had sent her, she felt like a child that has escaped some irksome task. Since her schoolgirl days she had never been so directly conscious of the hostility of human beings. Had she, in sensibility and character, so greatly outgrown the average? "Good God," she thought, contemplating her slim legs, "where am I then? In Germany? In Potsdam—where I have always been so spoilt, and people used to stare after the car when I was sitting in it, where there was always someone to catch my hoop when it ran away from me in the park? Where the girls all imitated my way of doing my hair, and the ribbons in my plait? Didn't they let me help them with their exercises, and explain a passage in Lessing's *Nathan,* a difficult sentence in Taine, or a verse of Shakespeare? Have I grown of less importance because my fiancé has been sweating for twelve months as a private in the A.S.C., for the Kaiser and the Empire, though he's as good a man as any officer? Have I lost my caste? In my own heart, my little friends, I know I have not lost it." She laughed and splashed in contempt and exultation; she would not be defeated.

As she dried and then lay down to rest, she pondered on what would really happen when peace came again upon the earth. One could then take spiritual stock of oneself, and see how much of one's moral character had been eroded by the war. One would try to hide the horror that was past; to discipline the feelings, esteem the intellect, and love things of good report. She must wait her time. "We must go through much tribulation," she hummed softly to herself from an aria that she loved, "we must go through much tribulation before we can enter into the Kingdom of God." And she hoped that it might prove to be the kingdom of love and of the spirit, and of a better time. In the meantime let us preserve our sense of truth, that we may take up the fabric of civilized life at the point where we laid it down almost two years ago.

Thus, simply and without foreboding, did Lenore Wahl conceive the issue of the war. She may well be pardoned. It was generally so conceived, except by a very few.

Chapter 8

NEW ACQUAINTANCE, OLD ACQUAINTANCE

Without the presence of the minister of a recognized creed, a middle-class marriage could not be even imagined. Dr. Jacob Sommergast, rabbi of one of the synagogues in Berlin, shy by nature and by habit, still stood under the shadow of a paralysing experience when a certain Fräulein Wahl came to see him about her marriage. He had lately returned from Hungary where he had rendered the last service of love to his wife's brother, which was to convey him to the Jewish cemetery in Budapest. Of three members of his wife's family who were fighting at the front, two were still alive; the third, who had been called up for active service in the very first days of mobilization, and had been promoted lieutenant, had fallen near the frontier in a fight with Serbian infantry, by the side of his captain and a major. The regiment had made a grave for the three of them, in a farmyard near the scene of the fight. Frau Dr. Sommergast, who came of a house that deeply respected the Law, suffered great distress of mind while her favourite brother Sandor lay so far away from the other men of her family. Dr. Sommergast managed to secure a permit to enter Hungary, though not indeed until the spring of 1916. At Oderburg, where he crossed the frontier, he manfully endured a painful examination of his person. Newspapers, even scraps of printed paper, were removed from his luggage; he saw many mothers with children miss their connexion, the Austrian police were so insistent to discover whether any secret news was written on the skins of the little ones. This caused great surprise to his simple mind. Then he began to get much satisfaction from the rich and abundant food in that flourishing and fortunate land. At last he found out where the farmyard was situated; and without much difficulty a large grave was discovered containing the bodies of the major and the captain. According to the report of the sergeant on duty, the body of Lieutenant Barday Sandor had also slept there awaiting resurrection, laid in friendly fashion by his comrades' side, and covered by a plank in accordance with the Jewish custom. Dr. Sommergast then displayed an energy that surprised even himself. He had the whole yard dug up; and finally, under a dung-heap used by the swineherds, the body of the Jewish officer was found huddled into the ground—though it was not otherwise in bad state of preservation. Sommergast was not able to find out who had been responsible for this; but it was natural enough that he should feel it deeply, and he only told his wife about the conveyance of the body from the grave to the war cemetery. In sleepless nights knotty problems of the Law kept turning in his head; did the presence of unclean bodies deprive the burial place of its sanctity, or, on the contrary, did this outrage confer on his brother-in-law the halo of martyrdom even after death? He decided that if he could find no parallel case in the Sacred Writings, he would ask one of the great Eastern Rabbis for a verdict. He had a communicative disposition, melancholy eyes, and a little straggling beard. He believed in the cause of the Central Powers, but so far as his own experience had gone, he thought it badly handled; and he was much distressed not to be able to open his heart to anyone.

Fräulein Wahl's visit took his mind off all this; he received her first in a very businesslike manner. She wanted to be married! Excellent. When? Ah, that was the trouble. The fiancé's application for leave had been put in—God alone knew when it would get through, nor how suddenly. The bridegroom's name? Werner Bertin. Not Werner Bertin, the author! Dr. Sommergast flushed with satisfaction. Of course he knew his work. More than that: he had taught the Faith to two little cousins of his in a Berlin school. That was splendid news, a promise of good hope. He beamed sympathetically at the Fräulein, and became quite ecstatic. Like many Jews, he could not—owing probably to some disability of very ancient origin—pronounce his I's properly, and Lenore found it hard to keep a straight face at his odd dialect. She thought him a simple fellow; still, here she found a willingness to help, and respect for her man and herself. She could be married at any time, if she would telephone immediately Herr Bertin got home.

Lenore told David of this visit, and of another—to be later described—to Frau Laubschrey. They both laughed at the Minister and the Prophetess, while David, at the piano, let his fingers ripple up and down the keyboard in soft chords and cadences.

"Why are you being married in Berlin, and not here?"

"It's a silent understanding between the parents and myself. Because of the people here. A private in the A.S.C., you see!"

David nodded. Since he had been put back for military service, he went about in a dream. When she teased him he always replied in music—a theme of four parts, like an uprush of deliverance. "A prayer of gratitude to the Divinity by one who has been restored to health," he called the passage; it came from a Beethoven quartet. Then, after listening for a moment: "Why people call this 'difficult,' God alone knows. Difficult? It just runs off one's fingers. Grand stuff, these quartets."

Since the burden of uncertainty had been taken from him, he was bubbling over with inspiration. He was always scrawling five parallel lines and filling in the heads of notes. With the utmost self-composure he now saw his existence centring upon music. "That's all right, Lenore, you marry. I shall leave the house very soon—soon, though slightly ritardando."

He would anyhow have to do one year's military service; and this he would prefer to do in war-time rather than in peace. He would be promoted, to please his father, and as a reward, he would go straight out of uniform to the High School for Music. "Not another day in the Sixth, no leaving exam, no more of all that rot." Already every morning that tore him from his dreams of music, and his ideas for themes and phrases, seemed like a leap into cold water; one more day as a schoolboy and a slave. If he could get right out of the rut for nine months, or even six, he could rid himself of school for ever. By that time he would be nineteen or twenty, and the precious years of training, that he so longed for, would be at hand. He was resolved to be a pianist, a composer, a conductor, and to give concerts; to stand before an orchestra, and conduct the *Eroica,* or a Brahms symphony. That was a man's career and worth going hungry for, in case his father insisted on his passing the leaving examination. Art was long and our life was short. Everyone who had done anything in the world felt on his death-bed that he was just then ready to begin.

Lenore listened, amazed at the lad's calm determination, and the clarity with which he saw his aim, the destined development of his talent. "But you are talking," she said, "as if you were certain of coming back from the War."

"I must; I've got too much work to do," answered David confidently. "My head is just crammed with music waiting to be fired off, German music, mark you! Most modern stuff is pedantic rubbish. You wait until people like me get on to the job. I shan't be killed." And his voice quivered with impatient energy.

Lenore was horrified at this provocation of disaster, and put her hand over his lips. "Boy! Touch wood at once! Haven't we found out the sort of things that happens?"

David laughed, but he touched the piano. Fortunately it stood on glass feet, which insulated it, as he reminded himself with a secret smile. He twitted his sister with growing superstitions. "Well, and why not?" asked Lenore, and she insisted that the cards had told the truth. Step by step, everything had been fulfilled; peril, conflict, separation, and victory achieved by her alone. Even the date seemed to have come true; Bertin wrote that he might be back in July.

Yes, Lenore had remembered Laubschrey, the prophetess. She reckoned up the dates; from the seventh of May 1913 until the first of December 1915, nineteen months; add an equal period, and the result was—the first week in July of the present year. Prophecies were not to be pressed too closely, if they more or less came out. In the midst of all the fuss and excitement of that day of May, when Bertin's trunk arrived from Kreuzburg, she found time for a journey to Berlin.

By the window in Frau Laubschrey's sitting-room sat a stout old woman completely filling her chair, with one leg, swollen to the knee, resting on a footstool; greyhaired, and deeply lined from the nose to the sagging chin, and round the eyes. Only by those brown eyes, slightly slanting and still with a faint twinkle in them, did Lenore recognize her. One year! Last May she had been a middle-aged Berlin landlady, well able to look after herself; there unmistakable, lay the rug, orange and red with a Persian border on a black ground, which had disappeared from Bertin's room. What spell had transformed her into this old crone? Lenore stopped at the door and stood motionless, like a slender sapling. But Frau Laubschrey recognized her at once. In a faint croaking voice she asked her to come in.

"Why, it's the young lady as used to go about with No. 6 Brixenerstrasse. I remember how we laughed over that old trunk. Well, well, I've been in trouble since I saw you last, and there isn't much left of poor old Laubschrey now. No, you needn't sympathize. My head"—and here she clapped her hand against her forehead—"still works all right; even though I've got water in my legs, and my heart's nearly given out."

Lenore shuddered, but she came in.

"And now," croaked Frau Laubschrey, looking contentedly down into the street, "I can enjoy the sunshine again, and perhaps Laubschrey will come back on leave sometime soon. Just after I got into trouble, they called him up, as a punishment."

Then she unburdened herself, at first in a tone of indifference; but soon she became excited, and hammered on the floor with the stick with which she hobbled between her chair and the bed.

Next door to one of her apartment houses had lived a bank clerk, who was due to be called up at the end of April 1915, as a corporal. When he came to say good-bye, Frau Laubschrey met him and his wife on the common staircase, and they fell into talk about what lay before him. Her warm Berlin heart soon broke through the conventional words, and she said how truly sorry she was that Herr Zeitschel had to go to this filthy war. Before it was too late, couldn't he wangle some claim that he was indispensable, so that he could stop behind with his wife and child? He wasn't a great hulking fellow in Class A and it was a shame he should have to go now, when the Government were just out for conquest and wouldn't hear of peace. Frau Laubschrey had known the Zeitschels for more than three years, but, alas, she did not really know them. Herr Zeitschel puffed out his chest, rolled his little eyes, and called his wife to witness that this woman, a landlady, who housed German soldiers, had tried to persuade him to shirk his duty; she had said what was not true and was dangerous to the State, and lent assistance to enemy propaganda. He knew what was due to the Kaiser's uniform, to himself, and to his honour as a servant of the State.

"And he actually gave me away to the police. I couldn't deny what I had said. And the Zeitschels, whom I had so often helped with a taler or two, swore evidence against me—both of them—and I got five months. No appeal was any use—in fact the Court insisted they had let me off very lightly; they wanted to prove that I had been doing this sort of thing for some time, so as not to lose my lodgers' rents. I was sent to the women's prison in the Barnimstrasse. And Laubschrey was immediately called up for the infantry; they said they wanted to give him an opportunity of escaping from my bad influence. Now he has got a gun-shot wound in the hand, and is in hospital at Küstrin, waiting to be let out again—to go back to the front, of course. Yes, Fräulein, that's what happened to me. I wonder I've been able to last out till now, seeing that I've always liked to have things nice and tidy. And if I have, that's owing to Frau Luxemburg. 'Frau Laubschrey,' she said, one day, 'what you did, we have all done, or we ought to have done, do you see? all women that really are women. And the war won't ever come to an end until we have shaken these men into their senses. There is nothing heroic in being packed off to the front.' And as I was told afterwards, this kind lady with the soft eyes, was *the* Rosa Luxemburg, the member of the Reichstag, whom they laugh at but are all so frightened of, and call 'Red Rosa'—well, it was she who made me pull myself together. And when I was taken away in the Black Maria, like any woman of the streets, and had to undress to my chemise, and let myself be pawed about by officials, I said to myself: Laubschrey, courage. And I didn't give way. The doctor said my heart was sound enough and that I should do all right, but who knows? Zeitschel has been a sergeant for a long while and sends parcels home to his wife, a couple of rabbits or a joint of pork. And here I sit with the water in my legs. But I wish I could live and see whether they come home victorious—these folk who put a lady in prison because she talks a bit of nonsense. And now you must tell me why you've troubled to come here, and what you've got to say to poor old Laubschrey." And her eyes, the only part of her that showed any signs of life, glanced at the rug beside the bed.

Lenore, in her deep compassion, found it very hard to speak. She reminded Frau Laubschrey of the time she had laid the cards, and told her that everything had come true, even the date. Her friend was soon coming back on leave to marry her, their names were already sent in to the Registrar's office. "I thought, Frau Laubschrey, you would be glad to know what a marvellous gift you have."

Frau Laubschrey was genuinely delighted. She had housed many couples and was familiar with the ways of many young people, but she had seldom heard any more of them. Here had come someone to recall herself to mind, and someone who brought into these evil times a reflection of the fine times that were past. That did her good, so much good, indeed, that she wanted to get up and look for a bit of chocolate for her visitor. But Lenore thanked her and refused; people were kind enough to give her sweets now and again. This woman had brought good fortune to Werner and herself; they had been happy under her roof. She must not be allowed to die like a cat in a corner. She, Lenore, had committed a crime; she had, indeed, made herself liable to a term of penal servitude, by the views of the State in which they lived. She asked Frau Laubschrey what sort of doctor was treating her, and whether everything was being done to put her right again. Would she try to be at home tomorrow, or the day after, when a certain Dr. Obstfelder would call and examine her to see whether this nasty dropsy could not be treated? He had been invalided from the army after malaria, and was just the man to look after the old lady. She shook Frau Laubschrey by the hand, drew a deep breath when she got out into the street, and hurried across the embankment towards the station; a little lady with much purpose in her head.

Speechless, with her hands folded on the handle of her stick, Frau Laubschrey stared after that slim determined figure. Had she not said that something good would come of that young lady? And what, indeed, had come of her? She was going to send a doctor who knew more about heart and dropsy than the prison doctor. It all made her feel quite pious, and inclined even to believe in her fellow-creatures. She must tell all this to Frau Miele in the evening while the news was still warm. Cards: why not? She might earn some money that way, and some money that she needed badly. She must get Miele to go about a bit, and tell people about the student, and the lady, and the marriage at the exact time that she had predicted; then the women would soon be coming round. Yes, life was beginning to look up again—thanks to the little lady. . . . The rug? No, she would not give that back now. She had grown too accustomed to it, and it looked so well beside her bed.

BOOK SEVEN

FOUR DAYS

Chapter 1

CONVERSATION IN THE NIGHT

The night, pulsating with the roar of aeroplane engines, brooded in unearthly clarity between the hills. The moon, in her last quarter, poured a mild radiance over the roofs of the hutments. It was on such nights as these that the airmen went out after their prey. Not a shimmer of light appeared in the close-curtained windows. In the ground mist, the munitions park at Moirey was as little to be distinguished from any other part of the scarred earth's crust, as a line of hills from its valley.

Between eleven and twelve, clad in his great-coat, Private Bertin of the A.S.C. came out of the hutments to visit the latrine, and make water into the gutter lined with tarred pasteboard for that purpose. That came of flinging oneself on to one's mattress, dead tired, soon after nine o'clock. Within lay rows of snoring, coughing, reeking soldiery, a hundred and twenty men. In the faint glow of his pocket torch he could see them, rolled in their blankets, contorted like men in bonds, to whom even sleep brings no relief. Outside, wafts of odorous coolness floated down from the stars. And if rest had not been so essential for the toil of the coming day, it would have been pleasanter, instead of mounting the timbered footway to the men's latrines, to walk through the grass up to the wire entanglements that enclosed the upper end of the camp. Thence could be seen the white rockets with which the French controlled the fireworks of the front. With his hands in his great-coat pockets, and his trousers tucked into his boots, Bertin went about his business; his footsteps stumped along the timbered path, scaring away the rats that live under the huts, and fight squeaking for the offal. A little later he came back the same way.

In the meantime the scene had slightly changed; a sinister high-pitched humming could be heard far above them in the air. The soldier hollowed his fingers round his ear, cocked it skywards and listened intently.

"Now then, take care you get home safe, my lad," said a deep voice from the shadow of a corner.

"Evening, Hildebrand," replied Bertin, turning calmly towards the voice. He had to look sideways and upwards, as Hildebrand the blacksmith was the tallest man in the company; but for a weak heart he would have been in the Guards. "Hullo? No. 1 file of No. 1 squad on duty tonight? Almost like the New Year." And they shook hands.

They had now known each other for thirteen months. Both had been in the battalion from the beginning, and were delighted when they met. Very often the distribution of work kept them apart for weeks together, and when it was done they each found themselves with their immediate comrades in another hut or billet.

"Take cover, my boy," said Hildebrand, and drew Bertin from the half-lit timbered path into the shadow of the pent-house roof.

The rhythmic whirr of the home-faring airman was just then right above the ammunition park: German machines did not go out at night in order to avoid any risk of confusion. The two soldiers, one tall and the other middle-sized, peered upwards with misgiving.

"They don't see us," said Bertin with a careless laugh.

"But they might spot our shadows," persisted Hildebrand.

For all his hundred-fold experience, Bertin was lost in wonder at the radiance of that moon-lit night. They might well be in peril if these spectres of the air had been ordered to drop their bombs here. They could easily locate themselves by maps, as the district had long since been surveyed from all angles, and the ammunition park had not been established yesterday. It was masked as far as possible, but Moirey railway station, and the field railway lines, offered profitable targets.

Ah! a searchlight darted the milk-white tongue of a spectral beast of prey across the sky. A second followed, and a third; they swung in half-circles through the black firmament, tongues broadening at the end with which they caught their prey. Suddenly, with a sharp hoarse scream something shot up out of the night; far above them a red splash burst against the darkness, and three or four seconds later they heard the detonation.

"Do you see him?" asked Hildebrand.

Noiselessly the half-circles met and crossed, and with their point of intersection sought for a something that Hildebrand seemed to see, though Bertin could not, in spite of his thick glasses. All the more clearly he could hear that humming grow fainter; the many-voiced yet monotonously high-pitched roar of the French engines. The anti-aircraft batteries tracked the noxious creatures on their journey home. Those behind Flabas were no longer firing; they must be others, now, further to the West or to the South, near Romagne or Chaumont. The A.S.C. men had only the vaguest conception of the country in which they had been labouring for seven weeks. Not one of them possessed a map, and no one troubled to investigate their whereabouts. Bertin thought the sight marvellous; the bands of light reminded him of gigantic astronomical instruments, great arcs sliding across the hemisphere of heaven. He was glad he had had to go out.

"It's too damned tricky to hit them up yonder in the dark," observed Hildebrand.

"Well," replied Bertin, "it's fortunate they can't really spot where they're laying their eggs."

The night seemed to be falling silent; very far away Bertin could hear the familiar thud and crackle of the aeroplane motors. Towards Douaumont, where there had been heavy fighting yesterday and the day before, there was a constant flicker of rifle fire and the rattle of machine-guns. No peace in that direction.

"I wonder how many poor devils are lying dead out yonder, eh? Several thousand, I shouldn't be surprised," said Hildebrand grimly.

He would not have spoken thus to everyone; he was, as may be imagined, a Social-Democrat, a Swabian, who had roved about the world, and knew many places where Bertin had been; he had worked in Copenhagen and in Milan, and he happened to have been called up in Berlin instead of in Carnstatt. But he often talked to his writer friend, because he knew whom he could trust. He stroked his long moustache back from his mouth and decided he might now detach his shadow from the hut.

"Go to sleep, my lad," he urged his friend. "Ours is hard work for the likes of you who have spent your lives sitting down."

The other raised his face to the moon; his spectacles flashed and hid his eyes.

"There will be peace by the autumn," he said abruptly; "the whole damned show will come to an end here before Verdun."

That was his conviction; he had often proved it to his comrades while at work, with the best arguments in the world.

Hildebrand the blacksmith shrugged his shoulders significantly. He would have gladly believed in peace. It was now May; much might happen before October. But he was not so convinced of it as his friend the writer, who took too innocent a view of things, and was too fond of appealing to "reason." He was a novice in politics and did not see the threads that connect the interests of the ruling class with the opinions of the masses. He must be much more sceptical and learn to hold his tongue.

"Peace or not," said Hildebrand at last, with a yawn; "you had better go and sleep, my lad, until tomorrow morning." And they both started off.

"I wish I could believe in things like you do," he went on.

"Believe?" retorted Bertin angrily. "Do you believe that those fellows are going to stand more than another six months of it?"

Hildebrand did not answer. With slow gigantic strides, to one of which the smaller man had to take two, he tramped along to the writing-room; his head nearly touched the roof.

"I dare say, if it was only our business," he growled finally. "But the folk that should be making peace—at home or behind the lines—just draw their blankets comfortably up to their noses —see? Good night."

Bertin opened the door of the hut. He wished he could turn back again; the reek of that sleeping throng struck hot and thick against his face. Many groaned without awakening—and scratched away their lice; here and there, from fear of rats, a man had drawn his blanket right over his face. Tip-toeing along the room Bertin found his place, hung up his great-coat on its nail, stepped on a cross-plank, and swung himself on to a flock-stuffed sack suspended about four feet above the floor. Beneath him peacefully slumbered Private Heine Foth, the lousiest man in the whole company. The day before yesterday they had forcibly scrubbed his entire person, and under the inspection of two experienced comrades, eighty-four "bees" had been found in his shirt. He was then made to have all his garments deloused in Crépion. He had infected all his neighbours, even those who slept above him, such as Bertin. Perhaps it would now be somewhat better, but perhaps not. The company had been clean when they came to this camp, and, although they had carried wagonloads of dirt out of the hutments, and spent a whole afternoon on a thorough spring-cleaning, the lice of the previous occupation were not to be expelled. The torment of lice, the torment of toil, and the torment of continual obedience, aggravated for that company the burden of the war. Bertin stretched himself out on his lumpy mattress, wrapped himself in his blankets, blew a little more air into his pillow, and resigned himself again to the stale and poisonous atmosphere of the place. It was no longer so foul as it had been a fortnight before; at his insistence, some ventilators had been cut in the roof. Still, for a man used to decent conditions the stench was terrible, and a certain spiritual strength was needed if his resistance was not to be broken down. Bertin reminded himself that he had been in it for a year and a month without a break, and before that he slept with an open window, summer and winter. Soon he would be going away on leave, play at being a man for a couple of weeks, and be with Lenore. They could not well give him less than a fortnight—he had been in the field since the beginning of August. Behind his closed eyes he looked once more upon the starry heavens—and then he slid away into dream; and the scene of that dream was his old schoolroom. Before his inner vision towered the gigantic red-brick pile of his school at Kreuzburg; a little boy in little boots was trudging along to school, with his sealskin satchel and his lunch bag slung on to his back. At the top of the stone stairway gaped the black portal that guarded the domain of the Rector, Melkmann, whom Bertin remembered with the stump of a half-chewed cigarette eternally between his brown and broken teeth. But within, above the benches cut and carved by many generations, sat enthroned, with his great moustache, their terrible old master, Kosch, and beat, beat without mercy, little children with his savage cane.

In the company orderly-room electric bulbs were burning, and a silver watch ticked on a nail. Sergeant Diehl, the best man in the office, was telephoning to one Metzler, whose good temper and alertness had earned him a transfer to the orderly-room of the battalion staff. Metzler, a fat young man with a merry twinkle in his eyes, an astute Silesian, had an excellent memory, and this had in the course of a few weeks made him indispensable. The battalion staff lay at Damvilliers, an almost undamaged village of fine stone buildings, in which some of the civil population were still living—a few French peasants and old women. If a man could stand the unmistakable garrison odour that hung about the streets, if he was alert and prompt, if he polished his buttons and understood his job, he could live like a prince in France. Such was Metzler's opinion. He was twenty-two, and had been a clerk in an office in Breslau; he had been called up on the outbreak of the war, got what was coming to him on the Loretto heights (gunshot wound in the chest), and was glad to make himself very useful to his friends. No. 1 Company was more especially in the good books of the battalion; partly, of course, because it was No. 1, and secondly because it had more than once brought the major congratulations from the Ammunition Park Command, and (he hoped) the prospect of the Iron Cross, First Class. Sergeant Diehl asked the Park telephone exchange to put him through to Metzler of the orderly-room.

"Private or official?" asked the operator, Sperlich, of his friend.

"Both," snapped Diehl decisively, and Sperlich plugged the connexion.

These are the really important conversations. They set the temperature in the company, and in ninety—or even ninety-seven per cent of cases, things fall out as the little gods of the orderly-room may see fit to dispose; except for special events that may send the temperature suddenly down, or, more fortunately and more seldom, up. And with leave, the most important matter in a soldier's life, they are most particularly concerned.

To begin with, Diehl got Metzler to read him that day's communiqué from Headquarters. The Austrians had at last given the Italians another nasty knock; they had captured the Plateau of Lafraun, stormed several mountain peaks, smashed up some armoured positions—all between the eternal snows and the walls of the Dolomites. This, by the way. Over here, on the west bank of the Meuse, Height 279, at the southern point of Camard wood, had been taken, and that accursed graveyard called Height 304, in spite of a terrific resistance by the French, had been in German hands since yesterday. It appeared, however, that the summit had actually been lost again that day, but Cumières had certainly been stormed and the Mort Homme strewn with many dead. The road from Haucourt to Esnes was again within the German positions, so much of it as ran parallel with the front between Malancourt and Height 304. On the Esnes slopes the French had come under a very heavy fire and must have suffered tremendous losses.

Diehl held the receiver in one hand, and with the other he stuck pins into the map fixed on the wall near his chair.

"Wait a moment," he said to Metzler, "I don't follow. Of course," he muttered to himself, as he stuck his little flag into the grey hatched markings between Esnes and Height 304, "of course, the objective is Marre. So long as they can drop heavy stuff on us from there, we can't get forward on our bank."

"Quite a little Moltke, aren't you?" said Metzler approvingly. "The Bavarians have retaken the village of Douaumont."

"I'm glad to hear it," answered Diehl. "The men that will never come back from there . . ."

"I shouldn't like to have to make a list of them," agreed Metzler, and added a few further details. A quarry, near Haudromont, where there had been fighting since the beginning of April, and certain other little hills and gullies, appeared now to be regarded as very important. The Russian front was quiet at the moment, which was a good thing.

The report would be presented to the lieutenant next morning (the lieutenant being our old friend Grassnick); and then they came to the intimacies of the service.

"That dirty dog, Bertin, has got some marriage-leave coming to him, I fancy?" said Diehl. "The girl's family in Potsdam put in for it. Has it come through yet?"

"It came yesterday," broke in Metzler, "and will be sent on to you tomorrow for endorsement."

Private Bertin had been in the company as long as anyone. His conduct had been irreproachable; in the heaviest marches in Serbia, and over the foulest work that he had to do there, in Hungary, or here, he had never given the slightest cause for complaint; it was inconceivable that anyone should want to get in his way.

"Is there anyone of your people likely to turn him down?" asked Metzler cautiously.

The allusion could only refer to one person, and his name was Glinsky. Grassnick was merely lazy. But Herr Glinsky rejoiced in a quality of natural malignity, for the indulgence of which the service provided a wide scope. He was now letting his favourites go on leave, but alas for those who stood in the shadow of his disfavour. He had expected, when he was promoted to sergeant-major, that the more educated men would treat him with deference, just as he had had to behave in peace-time during his one year's service. In those days a company sergeant-major expected much obsequiousness and even presents from men in the ranks who needed his good offices. But in this company the one-year service men seemed to think they could get away with what they wanted without taking any trouble, and that galled him. This fellow Bertin withheld the incense that was due, the proper propitiatory offering to power and condescension. Should this be so?

It should not be so. The leave of Private Bertin, who was so popular with his fellows, was a precarious proposition if Herr Glinsky got to hear of it. Metzler and Bertin came from the same part of Germany—Silesia. Moreover, they had marched and toiled and slept side by side in Hungary and Serbia. Was he to be done out of a few days leave for getting married?

"I believe there is, my lad," said Diehl, "and that's why I rang you up. How can we fix it?"

Metzler pondered. Diehl could hear him take a deep pull at his pipe or cigar, and added: "Got a spot of good tobacco, eh?"

Metzler thought. He saw with his inner eye the town of Vranje, the mountain road that led up to it, and more especially a certain iron bridge. One of its girders would certainly have struck him on the forehead and flung him from the truck where he sat on a towering pile of railway lines, had not Bertin yelled at the top of his voice: "Look out—heads!" Privation and distress, drudgery and the wiles of Glinsky—a wholesome hatred of the men, had been a strong bond of union between the tenth and eleventh squads —the mountain marches between Jagodina and Nish, the filthy quarters at Jabukovac, Pojate, Paracin.

"He'll get his leave, but you must help."

Diehl was about six years older than Metzler: a teacher in an elementary school and a decent man, who was doing his utmost to get out of this company and away from Herr Glinsky, in the first instance to the battalion. At the moment his anxiety was that he might be combed out and passed as "Fit for Active Service." But when this menace, that was imminent in the shape of an early examination by the so-called "Murder Commission," was overpast, his ambition was to get into the battalion orderly-room at Damvilliers, where there were private billets, a Soldiers' Home, books, and newspapers. He hated his life in this place, with Glinsky everywhere—his filthy remarks and his contemptuous looks took away a peaceful man's appetite. Unfortunately there was only a very limited number of men in the company who could take his place as a clerk. Major Jansch had always and on principle refused to have Jews in the orderly-room. Moreover, there were ominous rumours of a question to be addressed by the Minister of War to all units, requiring them to report the number of Israelites thus employed. "Application refused" was the order of the day. Another bit of dirty work against the Jews, thought Diehl, who came from Hamburg; so like the Prussians.

"I'll do what I can to help, but I can't afford to make myself disliked with a wife and child at home."

Metzler reassured him: "I should think not. Never get across a Prussian! But as to Bertin. Give him a quiet tip to lie very low for a week and not say a word about leave. Then a certain person will be sent to Belgium to buy pigs for the battalion and the company, and there'll be a spot of leave for him to run down to Berlin, on duty, of course, to see his old mother."

It was so arranged. The orderly-room of the first company waited for the departure of the former quartermaster, Glinsky, like schoolboys for a holiday. It was held up by a dispute as to who should pay for the trip. Grassnick considered that it should fall to the charges of the battalion, since of the five pigs to be procured, only one was destined for No. 1 company. But the battalion insisted that the company should pay their own man. At last, however—by agreement between the two clerks—it was settled that Herr Glinsky should travel at the men's expense on the pence deducted from their pay for the canteen funds; such is the nicety of military justice.

Whereupon Metzler said: "If anything comes through here in the meantime—I mean from Potsdam and the girl's parents—I'll put it away in my drawer. Then I'll bring it out at the right moment; the adjutant will sign anything that's put before him. There mustn't be any inquiries from you, of course, so that he shan't know what's up. He's so down on Jews. After Glinsky has gone, just quietly put the leave-warrant, which will be stamped 'Approved by the Battalion,' in front of your lieutenant—and the trick's done; Bertin *allé, parti.*"

"First rate," said Diehl admiringly. "How long's the leave for?"

"Only four days, I'm sorry to say, with one day for the journey each way. No one can scrape any more. There's an Army Order about it—issued before the war."

Diehl shook his head briefly. Four days' marriage-leave seemed little enough after so long in the field. Still, it was better than nothing. "All right, we'll leave it at that. What about the Murder Commission?"

"Look here, my lad," returned Metzler with a laugh, "where do you live—at the back of the moon? It was announced long ago that we aren't to be combed out at all. Troops at the front are all 'On Active Service,' the General has decided."

Diehl sat rigid on his stool. His eyes, deep set in his long skull, seemed to be staring homewards through the wall. Then he drew a deep breath. The stark fear of death fell from him—all the suppressed misery of the man, whose right to existence depends on accident, on the caprice of other men. Air attacks would not disturb his sleep that night. All of which he expressed in the words: "That's a bit of luck again."

Chapter 2

WEDDING WITH ROSES

Unheralded, after chilly weeks of rain, in the middle of June, spring broke upon the world. In the hot sunshine the last drops sparkled on the buds, which in a few days grew round and many-hued, and then burst, filling the garden with fragrance and colour; roses, Jasmine, and lilac. Then came July. On the morning of the fifth, as a thunderstorm was rumbling immediately above the city and rain was pouring down, a voice, hoarse with excitement, rang up on the telephone; he was there, he, Werner Bertin; he had arrived at the Anhalt station, and he was just taking an underground train.

For a few days past the Wahls had been living in a hotel in the central district of the city, of which the kitchen seemed to give promise of producing a decent wedding breakfast. It was not very far from the synagogue, under the twin domes of which was to take place the spiritual sanctification of a union, for which the bridegroom had for week after week failed to appear. Neither had he been present for the betrothal—both absence and delay being, indeed, not his fault.

The asphalt pavements were awash with rain, and the broad streets were almost empty. Under her green umbrella, with green shadows flickering across her radiant face, arrayed in a green mackintosh, stood the girl Lenore; she felt so light that she was sure she could have flown. Only the glorious rain, the warm patter of the slanting threads of water, held her feet still firm to earth. From the side entrance of the underground railway came forth a soldier in full marching kit, splashing through the tiny runnels that poured down the steps; he stood before her, gripped her by the shoulders, raised her face to his, and covered it with kisses. His breath smelt, his beard unshaven from a night of travel, pricked her, the buckles and straps of his pack hurt her, and the badge on his cap tickled her forehead; and she stood, in ecstasy, in that palace of rain. She leaned forward, slender and half-hidden in those encircling arms. The good times were at hand. Her existence swung round sharply like the needle on a compass; how lovely it would be, now that she could be at peace with all about her. . . . They forgot where they were. Rain splashed from the tilted umbrella, passersby hurried into a house or into the entrance to the underground. But these two stood and looked at each other. Two faces, one rosy, grey-eyed, and wet with tears, the other tanned and brown-eyed behind damp spectacles.

"Forgive my kissing you," he said with a merry laugh. "I stink like a hoopoe. I've been eating, smoking, and I've hardly slept at all. You must take me like a bit of army bread—just as I am."

She laughed tenderly and told a lie: "Nonsense, I didn't notice anything. It's not the first time you haven't shaved. And the rain from my umbrella is dripping into your boots."

"So it is," he nodded, "I ought to have laced them up. You haven't changed a bit. You are lovelier than ought to be allowed by law. And am I to marry you? Out of the question!"

Her eyes shone. "Come," she said coaxingly, pressing his arm to her side. "Come and get dry."

They trudged along over the slippery asphalt, holding each other close, at about half-past eight in the morning; instead of shadows they flung reflections on the pavement; one green and the other grey with red stripes here and there, and hump-backed from the pack it carried. Often she would turn her face to his.

"I believe you have grown," she said wonderingly.

He had. His shoulders had broadened, his chest had filled out, and his back straightened, there was muscles in the arms that moved in the thick sleeves of his tunic, and his face, richly tanned, now sparkled with exultant health. A year under the open sky, in all weathers, on three or four different fronts, was calculated to vitalize any man's physique; the sea wind on the plains of Northern France, the Serbian snows three thousand feet above the sea, and then the impact of the Macedonian sun. The life of the intellect, as it was lived in peace-time, was certainly more wearing than the summer holiday from which he had just come. So, indeed, he thought he ought to describe it, from the outset.

"A rather long summer holiday," said she. "I think a change of air might have been managed for you cheaper. But you must be terribly hungry," she added, as they passed the dining-room of the Three Markgraves Hotel and went upstairs.

Hungry? Yes, but he could wait for a while. He had brought food with him. He would indeed be thankful for some good coffee. But what he needed most was a bath, although he was deloused. "You needn't be afraid."

Then he lay alone in a tiled bath, luxuriating in the warm water, and surveying the nickelled taps, and the calm space and height of the little room. It did not seem little to him. He looked at it with a professional eye; at a pinch it could house four men. Especially towards the ceiling, the space seemed to him completely wasted. He stretched himself out, soaped all the interstices of his body, scrubbed himself, and then plunged once more into the warm flood, twiddled his toes, turned over on his belly, ducked his head and raised it dripping: and wondered whether it was not all a dream. He shut a door behind him, and no one could hammer on it with his fists and cry "Open!" It was breakfast time. No one could bellow out: "Tumble up now and fetch the coffee!" He had not to stagger along the rain-sodden timber track to the kitchen, and the familiar clatter of the saucepans could not reach him. The noise of the great guns behind Caures wood, the eternal metallic rumbling and thudding of that cauldron of death, could not penetrate as far as this. A woman was there; a woman who was to be his, a magical creature, who for a whole year had existed only at the wrong end of a telescope, flinging letters from a Beyond, to which he replied into that same Beyond. Now her radiant face beckoned to him, and her eyes looked into his. When he got out of the bath and left the bathroom, the new world continued unbroken into a carpeted corridor. He hoped no officer was living in the hotel. He wanted to spend these four days untroubled by the world.

Four days. They had given him four days in which to marry. He had now been eleven months in the field, and fourteen months a soldier; not a day's leave had he asked for until now, and they had given him four days.

Four times four and twenty hours, counted from the morning of that day. One day it would be known who had measured out that time, Major Jansch or Acting Officer Grassnick. Glinsky had gone away—gone for ten days on duty; so this time it could not be he. Little Sergeant-Major Pohl, a schoolmaster in civil life, and Diehl, the orderly-room clerk, had stamped his pass "By D-train," and let him depart that same afternoon ("for delousement"), otherwise he would have had only three times twenty-four hours here in which to dream and live and breathe, and feel a woman's arms about him. One must take what one could get, and hold fast to memories; forget nothing, and above all, come back safe.

He got out of the bath, watched the water drip off him, and rejoiced at the sight. He rejoiced in the rough bath-towel that he flung round him like a toga. He rejoiced in his body, on which the shorn brown head sat like the black knob on a white skittle. He rejoiced in the fragrant mouth-wash that had been set ready for him, of course by Lenore. He scrubbed his teeth until they positively frothed, lathered his chin, and rejoiced in the smooth movement of the razor blade, and the soothing cream that he rubbed on afterwards. Then he put on a soft sleeping-suit that had been laid out for him, with yellow and white stripes and frogged like a hussar's tunic, surveyed himself in the mirror, laughed aloud, and listened to the echo of that laughter. It was lovely, it was grand to live in a solid house with silent doors, and to walk into a room where his parents were waiting.

He put his arms round his mother's thin shoulders, and held her lined and tear-stained face to his. Then he clasped a broad and powerful back, kissed his father on the beard and was told that his brother Fritz was getting leave for the wedding (he was at the moment on light duty with his regiment, the Fifty-Seventh at Brieg; he had been shot right through the left hand, in trench fighting with the Tommies near Lens. His mother had naturally been much upset. But the hand was healing perfectly, and he would be able to use it just as he had always done). Well, she was thankful he had got his leave, and the woman he had chosen—bless his heart. Yes, she had cried a great deal at the betrothal ceremony; but things were much worse now. Of his schoolmates, Rashke, Banjura, and the elder Pawlik had been killed; Hans Bensch was still missing, and his friend Kinsel had just been promoted sergeant and was stationed somewhere in Russia. Bertin laughed: Kinsel. The lad who had been afraid of coming too late for the World War, and missing the "generation of magnificent murderers" of which he had written so enthusiastically in a letter to him, in those days of August '14. And he asked after his mother's heart, which had long troubled her.

She stroked his hand with her thin ringed fingers. He did not need to worry about that; her heart was getting on all right. If only he would write often and tell her he was well; that would be the best medicine for her. There was no shortage of anything in Kreuzburg, as there were farms all round the town; the peasant women, who used to bring them butter, game, and fruit or early vegetables in peace-time, still came. Father was up to his eyes with orders. The guns and artillery simply ate up his crates and wickerwork containers. New machines had already been installed, and they would soon be thinking about buying the house in which they lived, and spreading themselves a little. Here Father's grave and kindly voice cut her short. This had been all Fritz's doing. He himself had the tradition of hand labour in his blood, and was too old to start a modern business like this. He could carry on, but he could not enlarge it. Well, the War could not go on very much longer, the enemy must at last see reason and realize that they could not get the better of us. Then Werner and his young wife must come and stay with them at Kreuzburg for a couple of months, and tell them all that he had been doing until his marriage with this fine young lady.

"Father has fallen in love with her," said his mother, happily. "Do you know, she is rather like me. . . . I mean, of course, when I was young," she added hastily. "I can see a likeness in the way she carries herself, and in her eyes. Except that," she went on proudly, "I was very fair, though you won't remember that. Wasn't I, Father? But brunettes are just as pretty. Now you must go and say how-do-you-do to your parents-in-law."

Embarrassed? Not a bit of it! A soldier is never embarrassed. Greetings, hand-shakings—victory. They all sat down to breakfast, and to Bertin the coffee was a delight. The fact that he was sitting here with Lenore, openly, and among her family—was a fairy-tale. A foolish fairy-tale; as incredible as the story about the man who wanted to learn to be afraid. They discussed the arrangements for the following days.

"I assume, to begin with, that you have ten days' leave," asked Herr Wahl, "or is it fourteen?"

"Four," replied Bertin, chewing contentedly. "Four. I'm only a private in the A.S.C., remember. Ninety-six hours, of which the first two and a half have been glorious."

A short silence. Lenore half-raised both hands helplessly. Had he got into any sort of trouble? asked Herr Wahl, who had paled a little. In that case, of course, he could not use such influence as he might have. But otherwise—*his* daughter—*his* son-in-law—and he was silent; the impotence of his anger struck at his heart.

And Bertin, unconcernedly intent upon his egg, assured him that if he had committed the slightest contravention of the most trifling military regulation, he would certainly not be sitting there that day. Perhaps Herr Wahl might come across the Prussian War Minister at some meeting or other; if so, he might take the opportunity of telling him that his cancellation of the order for a return of Jews employed in orderly-rooms, had been of great service to the Jewish soldiers in the whole army; it had, for instance, procured him this generous marriage-leave. Everyone, of course, believed that this had been intended solely to disprove the slanders that had been put about, as witness to which he sat there. "And now, that being so, what is the programme to be?"

At twelve that day they expected the Registrar, Herr Wahl said, still rather pale. Tomorrow morning there would be the ceremony in the synagogue and the wedding breakfast.

"Thirty clear hours, then," broke in Bertin, looking at Lenore. "We certainly can't allow you any more, the rest we need for ourselves."

Frau Bertin wept silently into her handkerchief. She saw only too clearly that her son was right; they, the parents, must renounce their claims. Renunciation was a very important word in the lives of such folk as they; it was gladness enough that their son had grown from a mutinous young schoolboy into a clever man who knew his mind.

Frau Wahl, an imposing figure in a light brown silk dress, with her hair beautifully waved, agreed with her son-in-law; and she told herself that he had an expressive head. The wedding breakfast would have to be over in time for them to catch their train to Oberstdorf in the Bavarian Allgäu. The Potsdam house was at the young people's disposal; Tornow would drive them there and back in the car. Grandfather Markus, had, in any case, promised to spend a few days with his friend Obstfelder on the Scharmützelsee; so the couple would be quite comfortable, with books, piano, garden, and a whole house in which to roam about. David laid a brown boyish hand on his sister's shoulder, and whispered: "Well, we've got through worse than four days like this, eh?" He was going with his parents to Bavaria, he had grown a great deal in the past year, his dark pelt of hair topped all the company at table.

No one wanted to linger over the delights of that breakfast table, the potted salmon, the real honey. A tall grandfather clock in brown wood, hitherto unremarked against the wall, suddenly dominated the room with a whirring of wheels. Coffin-like it towered up near the door, impaling the fleeting hours of life with dagger-like fingers.

Bertin yawned. "About twelve?" he asked. "Then I shall have an hour's nap."

Lenore, too, looked tired, and she also wanted to rest.

"I'll take you to your room," she said, and got up from the table.

Frau Wahl looked disapproving. For a young girl to announce that she proposed to accompany to his room a young man to whom she was not yet married—was that quite proper? But she did not want to scold her daughter in front of the new relations.

"I'll be all ready in the hall at a quarter to twelve," cried Bertin, greeted the company with a comprehensive gesture of embrace, kissed his mother, and left the room, with his arm round Lenore's shoulder. This in the presence of her parents: and they did not throw their knives and forks at his back. "Can you imagine it? It's the most tremendous fairy-tale I ever heard of. Robber abducts princess to the applause of much-affected parents."

She nodded faintly, and pressed her cheek against his. A voice within her kept on murmuring—four days. Would there be opportunity for saying all that must be said in those four days, which were, indeed, only two and half—from tomorrow afternoon? To reach an understanding with him she had scaled a formidable peak. The ascent had begun in Frau Nocks's room. Yes, and with a child in her vitals that had had to be removed. Soon she would be able to go to bed with him in all honour, under a permit stamped with the Prussian royal arms. But between then and now lay many things. . . . Life had a hard grip and showed little mercy to the laggard. Well, she had got him back, and she herself had done it; she had become engaged to him; and now she was marrying him. *She* was marrying *him*—and no one suspected anything whatever. It was well that it was so, and so it should remain. Her strength sufficed. But he was her friend, her man; in four days she would be seeing him into a train.

At a quarter past twelve, in the presence of a dignified and benevolent-looking gentleman in a frock-coat, sat Werner Bertin in the uniform of a private in the A.S.C.—round service cap, high boots, bayonet buckled to his belt—and Lenore Wahl in a light grey costume, very demure and maidenly. They stated their desire to marry, confirmed it by their signatures, and brought with them as witnesses Herr Hugo Wahl of Potsdam, the father of the bride, and Herr Berthold Bertin of Kreuzburg, father of the bridegroom.

The Registrar, as he filled in the necessary details, liked the look of the young couple. They seemed to radiate a sense of solid companionship. They appeared neither crude nor cynical, neither stiff nor shy. This marriage would endure, thought this expert of humanity, before whose table so many, many couples had come and gone. He hoped the young man would get back safe. And he sighed. He had lost his eldest son nine months ago, a cheery young sub-lieutenant in the navy. In the Dogger Bank battle a shell explosion had flung him overboard. Life went on.

The newly married pair kissed each other with laughing eyes. There was much joy but faint hope for the future in their first encounter; it had been just youth and love, without misgiving and without set purpose. And now they were here, in a place that seemed so inaccessible and so remote in those days of 1914, at the village of Polling near Munich.

In the hall below, on a carved oak bench, Markus and David Wahl, and Fritz Bertin of the infantry, waited for them as they came down.

"Done it, old boy?" cried Fritz to his brother, and embraced him, though both men felt a little awkward in the process. Then he insisted on kissing his new sister-in-law on the lips, kindly explaining to Private Bertin of the A.S.C. that it was not his place to object.

Tornow, in the great red car, shook the bride by the hand, and then the bridegroom. He thoroughly approved. The man was a private soldier like his own nephew. Quite right. Great folk had to come down a bit when a stout lad won't give up his girl. And a fine young lady like the Fräulein must be allowed to have the one she had set her mind on.

"Now let us go at once to the registration office and get my bread and meat cards, potato cards, fat cards, soap cards, sugar cards, and report myself generally—and do the whole business at one visit. Otherwise we shall waste more minutes, and," he said to Herr Wahl, "you will not be angry with us, sir, if we are rather mean about minutes just at present."

No, Herr Wahl was not angry with them. All his life he had

worshipped the Prussian tradition—every aspect of it, and in all sincerity; his relations with his father had often been strained because the latter viewed it with scepticism. The Eastern Command had given him a shock; what had now happened was the last straw. His own daughter—and only three and a half days more. Of course, it was wartime; no one needed to tell him that: soldiers must get back to their job. But did life therefore stand still? Were not the young women, here in Germany, growing more and more dependent on men's companionship? Food was getting worse, clothes more difficult to buy, and all the pleasant amenities of youth—travel, scents, and silk, were slipping more surely from their grasp. How was a young woman to be true to her husband, if he was to be torn from her side again after three days? Of what use to him, Herr Wahl, was a pocketbook stuffed with green and red notes? Middle-class morals, all those usages that from the days of their fathers and forefathers had so wisely regulated human relations, would collapse if they were treated with such contempt. For the peace, whatever it might be and whenever it came, the strictest discipline must be preserved, or social order would break down; marriage, morals, security, and property. The war had fertilized business; they had all got used to that; was it at the same time undermining the foundations of society?

"Children," he said, turning round abruptly, for that morning he had contented himself with the front seat. "In all this turmoil we have forgotten your wedding present. We'll put all that right later on, when you come to set up house. But I also owe you a betrothal present, my dear fellow. I hope you won't be too proud"—and with this he took Lenore's bag from her lap, slipped a crumpled object into it, and closed it again. "At any rate you won't mind taking it from your wife. Buy anything you fancy, when you are your own master again."

Bertin laughed; yes, he said, he had grown very sensitive! Such a drive in a car was quite an adequate betrothal gift for a common soldier; and he saluted an officer by sitting up stiffly in his seat.

Lenore looked surreptitiously into her bag; three thousand-mark notes! Everything came right if only one had courage. The fictitious bankbook with the supposititious five thousand marks could now become a real one, which genuinely belonged to them. She took her father by the ear from behind, turned his head round, and kissed him.

She was in the wildest spirits all that day until the evening; she ran about the hotel, bright-eyed and tingling with excitement. She danced with Herr Berthold Bertin, with her father, with her brother-in-law, Fritz, and even with her husband, who regarded himself as a bad dancer and proved very reluctant; she drank wine at dinner—champagne—and flirted with her husband, while Frau Wahl's eyes grew rounder and rounder; was this woman her little daughter, her blue-stocking, usually so haughty and fastidious? Where had she learnt all this, or rather, where had she concealed it all? They must take care she did not follow him to his room that night, as was mostly the custom after the ceremony at the Registrar's. What must the parents of the young man be thinking? They were indeed merely thinking what a dear creature she was; and they all sat up rather late together. A brief understanding between the young people was responsible for this. They had settled that this evening was to belong to their parents, and that they would then have their sleep out by themselves. On the morrow they would look into each other's eyes, alone.

Yes, strange anxieties beset Frau Wahl. She was taken aback by the thought that she now had a married daughter, would soon be a grandmother, and on the shelf. Her hopes lay in shipwreck all about her. No ascent into exalted circles—relegation, rather, to a synagogue. Her son-in-law's parents were excellent people, honest people, but—dear, dear—very small people indeed. Her daughter's husband was an author, he had written banned plays, and a novel, certainly, and had won some reputation in good society, rather more than he deserved. . . . Did such an income as his bring fame or honour? Would it be a distinction to be called Frau Werner Bertin? And yet she had done right. It was no such easy matter to get a husband for a girl in these times—bad times as they were. . . . Now she had a member of the family at the front, so much so that he could only get four days' leave, and no one could look askance at her David, even if he got stronger, and was again put back in April, next April, April of 1917. She now had something she could pray for in every church and every synagogue—that this boy might be rejected for the army, definitely and for ever, so long as this awful war went on. . . . She lay awake, she did not sleep well in a strange bed. Round about her lay Berlin, and starved. A glance at the children was enough—their thin little arms and legs, their wizened faces, as they played silently in the sunshine, or squabbled on the pavements. Anyone who wanted to buy meat cards could get them cheap in the North or East of the city, in spite of the maximum prices; field-kitchens for mass feeding drove through the streets, twenty pfennigs a portion. The bread was full of potatoes and very dubious flour. Sausage skins were made of paper and filled with intestines. Eggs—there were none. Herrings—seldom. Fruit had disappeared. (Those marmalade shares of Hugo's clients were going up encouragingly.) Sugar was scarce, artificial honey paid better. People had begun to smell, having only clay soap with which to wash themselves; it was more and more of a task to keep linen in order and get shoes repaired—indeed the clatter of wooden soles was becoming more and more frequent in the streets. Thin faces, helpless eyes, clothes wearing out. Two shirts a year had to suffice, two pairs of shoes, and one overcoat. No, it did not look like peace. . . . Thank God that there were still warm, enveloping feather beds, and that demons had not revealed the future.

In the morning she sent Bertha, the maid, out of the room to fetch the bride's bouquet of white roses, and said to her daughter: "I hope you will stand before the altar a pure girl."

Lenore, in white underclothes, with her shoulders bare, nearly laughed aloud. Her little girl, or little boy, which she had borne for a time within her, would still have been too small to have carried her train, as she had once seen a child do in Potsdam. . . . Coolly she asked in answer what her mother meant. She had never had anything *explained* to her, if that was the proper word. And Frau Wahl believed her. She was too accustomed to combine the ideas of a wedding with those of a wedding night, of painful and even tragic surprises, distress, and outraged womanhood. But here was her daughter walking about, excited indeed, and perhaps rather short of sleep, but fresh, girlish, maidenly, and innocent of any painful experience.

Lenore went up to the mirror to wish herself luck. Two years ago she had conceived it possible, but very difficult, to marry the penniless Bertin with the consent of her parents. Now, like any other girl of her station, she was putting on a white silk wedding dress and a long trailing lace veil; Bertha's verdict was that she looked rather pale, but very lovely. To begin with, Werner had been inclined to object to all this ceremony; it meant time lost. But out of regard for his parents it would have been impossible to dispense with it—that he realized. Nothing would have induced her to forgo this triumph; but that she did not tell him. Men are sly enough; there are some things it is not good for them to know. Her victory would not have been complete without the boom of the organ, an address by a minister of religion, and a public exchange of rings. This was to be the pinnacle of her life. It was with an eye on marriage some day that the little girl was induced to let her hair be plaited, and with an eye on marriage that she had been taught to shake hands prettily and curtsy. With this intent, throngs of girls like her went eagerly to school; their lot as wife and mother was the very purport of lessons in grammar and in languages, and indeed it lay at the base of their whole system of education; it even inspired their visits to the dentist and the dressmaker. "Ladies, you hope one day to become careful housewives," thus had the sewing mistress initiated them into the mysteries of cross-stitch. . . . It was therefore in prospect of this moment and not to fulfil her destiny, according to the views of people such as these, that she had developed her mind, exercised her body, formed her character, refined her emotions by contact with great works of art—to be delivered up, as an unsuspecting creature of the female sex, into the hands of a male. "No, my dears," she thought, as she smiled at Bertin, who had stopped in the doorway, pale and excited at the vision of this tense and vivid apparition. "We have upset all your calculations, and made as many holes in your ideas as there are in a Gruyère cheese; and it could not have been otherwise. Your sentimental world, your rancid ideals, are out of date. They had to go sometime, even though it was only this loathsome war that got rid of them at last. Now let us begin afresh. We'll find some cleaner way of managing human destinies. And if you find out about us"—she clapped her hands above her head—"so much the better. How I should just love to tell you all outright. But there's no sense in hurting your poor feelings."

They stood trembling, and deeply moved, before the altar. Their vision was a haze of red and gold lights, an organ, curtains, steps to the left and right. He had only to speak one formula; by it the woman was sanctified to him, in the ancient Hebrew phrase, which means that she was both consecrate and set apart, And following the age-long usage, he put on her finger the ring which binds and exalts the woman, and which she, together with its twin, had had made from an old-fashioned wedding ring. The organ and the choir of men's voices stirred the depths of their souls, dimmed their eyes to all about them, called up the spirit of their childhood days; spellbound they stood. Then a man in a robe addressed them, a man clad in dignity by the mouths and hands of men long since dead, and his simple words burned into their minds. . . . The birth of a new hope in these years of war, a union, begun in happy days, and brought to fulfilment in these dark and ominous times, when the nations looked up fearfully to Providence; so this pair, trusting in their stars, was ready to separate for the Fatherland's sake, to come together once again in the intention of marriage; to triumph over death, if God had so ordained.

Werner Bertin frowned and set his lips, but he could not find it in his heart to be angry with Dr. Sommergast. His eyes were only for the girl at his side, now his wife, entrusted to him, sanctified and pledged to him, to be his charge. It would be his to preserve her from the great disasters of existence, and from the small mishaps that can be so very painful. Could he do that—if he might now be allowed to wipe out what was past? Two and a half days more, he thought, looking down at himself as he stood there;

heavy boots, grey trousers, red stripes, his thumbs in his belt. He had even flatly refused to buy a cap with a peak. He had been thus arrayed by the people who had given an educated man two and a half days more for his wedding—a man who had always done his duty under great hardship, and had a clean record; he had no intention of adorning himself to cover up the deplorable treatment of the intellectual classes in Germany. So he stood before the company as he was, and indeed the synagogue was packed. What a difference in the shadows cast by himself and Lenore. His appearance in that clumsy uniform was in fact regarded as something of a provocation; a feeling which was emphasized by the fact that Lenore Wahl, in her silk dress, white roses, tea roses, and roses that were almost green, her diaphanous train, and the coronal of myrtle looked like the Princess of a Royal House in exile. "She's lovely, but what a sight he looks!" cried a deaf old woman in a shocked tone; one Frau Saltz, who dealt in goose-dripping and giblets. . . . Such then was the Wahl-Bertin wedding, and it gave rise to much talk and excitement among the congregation. They even forgot to listen to the closing toccata on the organ, by J. S. Bach and David Wahl. By the aid of a manuscript in the Royal Library, he had worked up the Chorale, "I will feed all nations," into a fugue with Schumann's *Grenadiers,* in which, as is well known, there is an echo of the *Marseillaise.* Never had more surprising strains accompanied bride and bridegroom and the wedding guests into the anteroom, where acquaintances wished good luck to the newly married pair.

Then they drove to the hotel, and ate many excellent dishes, a feast that did not exceed what was allowed by law, but amplified by the aid of a certain Kliem, who had appeared at the Three Markgraves Hotel. He brought a huge sturgeon from the Havel, bigger than many a great ocean fish. David had invited him to the wedding, and Kliem had decisively refused—he had no inkling of how closely he was involved in the issue of this affair. . . .

At the head of the table sat a bride who did not know how pathetically lovely she looked, and a bridegroom who was quick to notice it; a dry sob rose into his throat as David, at the hotel piano, accompanied Paula Weber-Bunge in the first movement of Mendelssohn's E-flat concerto. Bertin's heart throbbed in slow pulsations. He would never learn to play the fiddle like that. His hands were spoiled for the delicate sweeping movements of the bow, his brain had coarsened, and his accumulated strength was claimed elsewhere. If he survived the war uninjured he would have to work very hard to get back to the point where he had been before. He would then have to labour to subdue much intractable material into speech, drama, and narrative. No more time for fiddling, Bertin. No more would he bend over his violin and draw forth those rhythms that soar so lightly upwards, hover, pirouette, and fall, caught in a falling ripple of notes from the old piano.

"Old pianos are David's strong point," whispered Lenore, as he laid his hand on her arm.

"I shan't play any more," said Paula, putting down her violin amid applause. "It gets sad now, for a day like today especially, and our couple haven't the time for three movements."

Frau Mathilde Wahl was a marvellous impersonation of a bride's mother, youthfully radiant, with her delicate pink skin, and arrayed in an imposing dress of grey silk; but Frau Lina Bertin wept bitterly as she bade her last farewell to the young people. Once more the two stood in a circle of those who loved them. They kissed the grandfather, whom Bertin looked forward to seeing much of in the years to come, Herr and Frau Wahl, wishing them a good holiday at Oberstdorf, then David, "our best friend," and last of all the two simple folk from Kreuzburg, Father and Mother in their old-fashioned clothes, but very ceremonious and correct. The little white-haired lady fell to sobbing helplessly, but the grey-bearded gentleman in the frock-coat with a gold chain across his waistcoat, reasoned with her kindly; she must not agitate herself, all would be well, she must not make it so hard for the children, it would soon be over now. Then he pressed into the hand of his young daughter-in-law a small and rather weighty little package wrapped in tissue paper, not much bigger than a heavy ring; five twenty-mark pieces—half the treasure he had managed to lay by when gold was being requisitioned. They not merely weighed heavier than Herr Wahl's three thousand-mark notes; one day they were to be much more valuable. But that was something that no one could then know.

Bertin had often to clear his throat and take off his glasses, as he said a quick and almost cold good-bye to his parents, caught and torn between Lenore and them, between the new love and the sweet familiarity of childhood. But it had to be, and therefore it was better that it should be sharp and quick. Privates Fritz and Werner Bertin wished each other a safe and speedy return; then bride and bridegroom got into the car, and sat behind Tornow's hooting horn and his new yellow leather gloves.

The car glided out to Schöneberg and the places that Lenore and Bertin knew so well. It crossed the main street of Schöneberg, lined with blossoming trees, left the Steglitz town hall on the right, slid up the hill to Zehlendorf, and sped on under the oaks of Lichterfelde. Berlin lay in the melodious light of early summer, pale grey, arched above with blue, embowered in green, fragrant with many roses, and all the gardens gay with sunflowers (now grown for the oil extracted from their seeds). In the streets the children ran shouting after the great car; their parents stopped and watched it and wondered how the man came to be sitting in it.

Lenore's hat-veil fluttered out behind her from the deep-cushioned seat. "We'll live somewhere about here later on," she said, as they left Zehlendorf behind them.

He pressed her hand. "If only I could get some decent leave. They told me definitely that these four days wouldn't be counted against me nor taken off my next leave. But what are promises?"

Then the grey forests of the Mark opened out to welcome them; the broad and gently undulating avenues, edged with green foliage, led along Wann lake, dotted with white yachts, as far as Potsdam. Tornow drove them carefully but fast. He felt a sympathy with this bridegroom who had to go to the war again so soon. Yes, he reflected, as they crossed the Glienick bridge, his car was soon due to be requisitioned; indeed, his master had been left the use of it longer than most people. Horse and carriage would regain their honourable estate. Well, that would suit him just as well. He, Tornow, could manage them just as well as a car. And there was much to do in the garden in the way of cutting the grass, looking after the fruit trees and the rabbits, and so on. After all, he was not too old, he might well marry and have a child. The notion warmed him, and settled in his mind. He would certainly be on the look-out for someone who would suit him. A nice war-widow might do very well, possibly one with a child. And with a cheerful hoot of his horn he braked the car in front of the Wahl mansion. The wheels grated on the gravel, the car stopped, Tornow got down from his seat and stood gravely at attention while Lenore and Bertin got out.

Behind the great double doors they stopped and stood; the great staircase, that circled upwards round the vestibule to the second story, was hung with roses, and with no other flower but roses.

"Bertha!" cried Lenore, "Tornow, Frau Mahnke! What are you thinking of? Am I a Princess from the New Palace?"

"In God's name, Fräulein Lene," sobbed Frau Mahnke, her apron to her eye. "We had to do what we could, now that everything is rationed, and you can't buy anything decent, no trousseau, and no silver, and nothing—just promises, till things get better. So we thought you should not go short of roses anyway, gracious lady; and we want to wish you health and happiness, and we hope this awful war will soon be over so that you can live in peace and quiet with your husband. We have looked forward to this moment for such a long time," and with a burst of tears she fled into the kitchen to make the coffee.

Entwined about the banisters, and almost hiding them, fragrant with the rich scents of summer, the great bank of roses swept upwards. Dark red blossoms, dark with the deep colour of untransparent wine, honey-coloured blossoms, golden, and rosy white—roses of all kinds and sizes breathed here. Some slim and meerschaum-brown, like tapering pigeon's eggs; some with an array of yellow stamens in spreading petals of pale yellow. Great greenish white ones with open calyxes, and others, flesh-coloured, with curled outer petals like pallid mouths. Even the stairs were strewn with short-stemmed roses and dog-roses, and scattered petals. The pair stood silent, and breathed as they looked and marvelled. "You see how they all love you?" said the man softly.

"How often have I made them walk up and down those stairs," she answered. "Really, I don't deserve it. . . ." Then she added briskly: "Now we'll have some coffee and play at man and wife for fifty-six hours."

"Wrong, Fräulein, you have started by making a mistake. Exactly sixty-three hours."

What a symbol of victory it was to change her dress in her own room and with his help! She chose the white low-cut summer frock that she had worn a year before at Wilkersdorf, with a grey silk belt, and trimmed with pink braid.

He recognized it at once, but said no word. It was on the tip of his tongue to remind her that it was fifty weeks ago to the very day. But she was silent, she had learnt to wait. She merely looked abstractedly in front of her, thinking of the crooked course her life had taken since that day, over the mountain of supreme ordeal, down into the valley of desolation, and then through misery to this moment when he, with his tunic off, was hooking her dress between her shoulders and kissing her the while. The vision passed before her mind. . . . It was hard to conceive of all that lay behind her. . . .

"How was it that it all came right so quickly in the end. Do you understand?" she asked, over her brown shoulders.

In the middle of the night Bertin awoke with a start from a deep sleep. The Forty-Second had fired over yonder at the edge of Thil wood. The shock of the detonation had gone through his whole body. The rats scurried squeaking from under the huts, as scared as if there had been an earthquake. Indeed, the earth was really quaking, he felt a blast of wind against his face, the saucepans rattled on their hooks, the sleepers snored and groaned in sunk oblivion. But he—where was he? He had left his post, the post he had taken over from the man beside him, who had gone home on leave, to marry. Wild-eyed he stared about him; there lay a face, averted, beside him in the moonlight. With a deep breath he lay back on the white pillows; he realized where he was. Somebody must have shut the glass door down below. From far away came flooding in the full chorus of the Havel frogs, and the passionate song of a nightingale in the tall trees of Sanssouci. He had not left his post. He would take up duty once again, his place in the community to which he now belonged; deeply he loved its spirit, that spirit he served and championed with the utmost of his strength. He was a little rivet on the ship that was Germany, now labouring in heavy seas, with dubious pilots, an unduly magniloquent captain, and very supercilious persons at the wheel. At such a time, not even a rivet should give way in a ship's hull that held so precious a charge as the woman who lay at his side.

Lenore slept—the sleep of an ancient mother of the world. The disordered balance had at last been readjusted. Sleep after such a night of love meant a plunge into the deepest deposits of the soul, the abandonment of the little ego, and the discovery of kinship with the spreading tree of life, on which she was a tiny blossoming twig. Her breathing was faint. The coverlet on her breast rose and fell, her arms lay loosely by her sides, one hand hung down from the bed, and a ring on her finger glittered in the radiance of the moon, now nearly at the full. The windows stood open, and between them the windowsill shone white.

Bertin got softly out of bed. From Lenore's writing-table—two beds like two yoked and faithful horses now stood in her room—he took pencil and paper. Since the days of spring in Serbia he had hardly written any poetry. Now he sat in striped pyjamas, and shining spectacles, while line after line of verse covered the sheet of paper. Beyond that rose-decked staircase he called up the forests of Verdun, where men were dying and still dying in their tens of thousands.

What will become of this and when shall be the end?
But what are roses? Tomorrow they are dust.
And dead men? Tomorrow mouldered into mire.
These circling moons? Hate, convulsed and shrill.

But thou—we dully agonize that such as thou,
O home, may live and breathe in sweet placidity.
And with thy silent hands may make us whole.

He wrote as he had always written verse. He could indeed sit for long hours and labour steadily at his work; he had proved it. But poems must be written at the first flush, except for trifling alterations. Verse gave scope for the improvising instinct in his nature, and as such he valued it. He did not care about publishing such poems, indeed, he did not really know whether they were good or bad. They were his, like his handwriting, the colour of his hair, the lines on the palm of his hands. He was always amused and rather pleased to think that people regarded him as devoid of lyrical feeling. He hid the sheet in Lenore's blotter, which she would certainly not open before he went away. He looked at the clock, it was nearly two. Of his leave five-and-fifty hours were still his. And as he walked to the window to look out into the strange garden, a surge of memory swept over his mind—a memory of those days at Polling, when, at night, before he went to her or after he had left her, he had laboured at his task, moulding the figure of the great Bishop to whom his conscience gave no rest, and compelled him to turn his ego inside out like a glove. In those nights the beloved meadows lay outspread in the moonlight; from the dark edge of the wood came the call of the screech-owl, and now and then a deer would wander forth, lower its head and browse. Where were those days? Where were the leaves of last autumn? Where was the Bertin of those days, untroubled, unsuspecting, free as a wild animal and answerable only to himself? Was there a task that still confronted him? Here was one that would last him all his life. Unperturbed, she followed the precepts by which she had always walked, she unfolded her being in utter loyalty to what she was—soft, with the softness that, as the Chinese teach, overcomes what is hardest in the world. It overcame war, absence, estrangement even, hatred, and indignation. He brought that grey letter back with him in his pack, and was quite ready to discuss everything with her—her childish reproaches that his letters were didactic, descriptive, and cold. Why were they so? Because he wanted to spare her the humiliating servitude which he had himself kept steadily at a distance, that he might, untroubled by the events of every day, preserve the true sense of his service as a soldier. The defence of the idea that was "Germany" against Sergeant-Major Glinsky, of the principles of human decency against Acting-Officer Grassnick, and to contend for what was just in the presence of Major Jansch's predatory profile—all this called for no mean effort. And this was reflected in his loveless letters. . . . But she herself did not speak of these trivialities; she ought to have done so at once, it was certainly too late now; and for him—and he laughed shortly—to waste one hour of the five-and-fifty left to him—what pitiable folly! Cautiously he lay down beside her. Later on, he could sleep again elsewhere, where men snored and stank. Here he wanted to feel a heart beating against his own, her heart, her skin, and the inside of her arms against his ribs. He awakened her with gentle kisses. She, still deep in her sleep, murmured like a peevish child.

She eyed him sideways as he wandered through the room, picked up books, stroked their backs, and opened them. He had come upon Schiller's letters on æsthetic education; together they read the passage in which he writes: "I hope to convince you that this subject is far less foreign to the needs than to the taste of the age; and even that it is through æsthetics that the way lies to the solution of every political problem, since it is through beauty that mankind moves on to freedom." He put the book back, looked at her and nodded. It was so, and it remained so—merely postponed for a while until the bugles blew for peace. Lenore was faintly sceptical, but said nothing. She sat and watched him as he eagerly put on the civilian suit, which he had no right to wear, so that they could not leave the house and garden. Tubular trousers reaching to the ground, that caught the dust when the wearer was walking; beneath them the inevitable underpants, which effectively kept all air from the skin. Stockings, called socks, which for some inexplicable reason stopped at the middle of the calf, and had to be secured beneath the knee by an ingenious arrangement of india-rubber and metal hooks. An up-and-down collar of four-fold linen, chafed the sensitive eye-nerves all round the neck. Between its two thicknesses lay squeezed man's sole adornment, a gaily coloured strip of silk, wound into a knot that enabled it, with some physical effort, to be drawn through the collar and set into its place; its purpose was to cover the bare stud that untied shirt and collar. . . . It was only at the braces that he struck. He held out the strips of webbing at arms' length, burst into a shout of laughter, whirled them round his head, and threw them into a corner. "What a pity I haven't got a tennis shirt in my trunk. Look here, let's go and buy one! We're quite rich enough!" He stood there, narrow-hipped and slim, straight-legged from waist to ankle—only to be destroyed one day by a bullet or a shell? She shook herself. . . . She sat by him at table, he loved the look of everything, the spoons, the milk-white plates, the damask tablecloth, and the flowers in the vases. His senses thrilled to the least contact, his finger-tips delighted in the rough grain of stuffs and wood paper. From time to time she glanced at him sideways, or pondered, with her hands over her eyes, when he presented, in some sort, a picture, such as when he filed his nails, or took his ring off his finger and put it back again.

They were always together. He went with her into the kitchen; she lay beside him under the great beech tree; they stood side by side under the shower in the bathroom, splashed each other, and shouted. When he shaved she held the mirror, and brought him hot water. While she combed her hair, he read reviews. Then, behind the curtain of her hair, she cried out to herself: "Take the paper from him, and speak to him about . . . it! Didn't you bring him here to come to an explanation with him on certain matters, so as to live in truth of intercourse again? Didn't he fling you to the ground, frighten you, get you with child, compel you to an abortion, and let himself be carted off to France like a sheep. Think of his letters, advice, and his fine speeches—so condescending, so cheerful, and so unconstrained." Engagement, marriage, leave—all this he took as a matter of course, the incredible creature! Such, no doubt, had been his scheme of life since Polling. Circumstances had favoured him in surprising fashion; the unbelievable became possible thanks to the War, all went smoothly, and here he was. And now she could not tell him what she had so often dreamed at nights of telling him, what she had cried out against him in her heart? The obsession of a year collapsed at the touch of reality. Was she doing right or wrong? Calmly she pushed her hair aside, and revealed her forehead and her eyes, childlike and womanly. Once more she surveyed the cheerful youth who now shared her life. No, she did not want to humiliate or reproach him, she wanted but to love him and to be his; she did not want to send him from her, but to burn his image into her heart. There he sat, tanned of cheek and pipe in mouth; how kind his eyes were! Man lived for his career, she reflected, as she plaited her hair—but when the hour came, he could live, as a man then should, for love. That heart of his was very likely obstinate, unknowing, and even foolish; but it throbbed and yearned for her only, belonged to her only, and it loved her. And she loved him. Well, she would gently guide him on the way that he should go; understanding was what he needed—a man like him must not live in such ignorance of his fellow-creatures. That she saw as clearly as she saw the shadow of the elder branches on the floor at her feet. Perhaps he was fated to suffer, and that might make him wiser. Well, if he were not to be too deeply stricken, let him suffer. But he must come back safe to his Lenore. Then they would go forward hand in hand, and make something of themselves. "Shall I do them up or let them be?" And she held out her plaits to him. He smelled their soft fragrance, swung them to and fro, and said: "Let them be, my darling."

The birds were singing their morning songs in the black and

green massed foliage of the beech tree, and darting through the latticed palings of the garden. The warm scent of summer steamed upwards from the earth to the light clouds that drifted across the sky as the harvest sun mounted higher.

In those days, in that summer, the German battleships left Wilhelmshaven to try and break through the British stranglehold on Germany. Wireless messages flashed back and forward, and those from Germany were deciphered by the British. With streaming funnels the ships dashed out to sea; they would drown these upstart squadrons like dangerous young cats, who thought they could one day get the better of their elders. They met, and many ships were sunk. Vast elaborate steel structures, produced at the cost of better schools, hospitals, and pensions for the poor, turned over in the lashing North Sea waves, and plunged keel upwards to the bottom, with their crews, and more of them were German than English. The English long-range guns reached farther, and did more damage than the latest German guns. When the fleets parted, both believed that the battle had been drawn, but later on each side announced by wireless that they alone had won the victory. The world believed the British; and the blockade still held, in spite of all the bloodshed and brave deeds, and the drowning of more than eight thousand red-cheeked German lads and English boys. In the deep currents of the treacherous sea, dead men swung dumbly to and fro; they could not praise the German nor the English admiral, for they were being slowly eaten by the fishes, or lay perhaps imprisoned in corroding steel. One of these was called Klaus Fischer; he kept afloat on the black waters longer than most because he swam so well. He had learnt swimming from a man by the name of Kliem, who was his father—though this was a secret. For Anna Fischer, who had borne this son to him, he could not marry; but his heart was in the boy, and it was him he really sought in his friendship with young Wahl, at first, at least, until he learned to value David for himself. He hoped Klaus would rise higher in the world than it had been granted him to do, and Klaus grew up into a fine lad in the little town of Ribnitz in Mecklenburg, on a broad lagoon near the Baltic. But Klaus had had to sink down very deep, and for the first time ever, Kliem, the cheerful Kliem, for a whole day long held his pipe cold between his teeth, grim lines appeared about his mouth, and his hold on life, or most of it, was taken from him. He went to Ribnitz and came back sorrowful; but when he found a card from Upper Bavaria on his kitchen table, he was glad; here was something. Someone was still alive. It was a long while until the spring of 1917. . . .

At that time, too, it came about that the war was once again to be finished; and the brave Russian warrior, Russki Voynik, was to finish it. For the Tsars, for the true faith, for little mother Russia, and for peace, he once again came forth from his trenches. The long hordes of his riflemen were to sweep like great brown sea-rollers through the entrails of the Austrian, and so make an end. For the French had dealt the Germans a heavy blow at a place called Verdun, and at that very moment the English were attacking on the Somme in France, advancing pipe in mouth and with an air of nonchalance, but skilful and determined soldiers. And now came the valiant Russians! Well, something must be very wrong if he did not manage it this time. The Japanese had sent artillery, guns, gunners, the Americans had sent vast masses of ammunition through Vladivostok, and General Brussilov, a soldier every inch of him, crouched over maps and telephone, peered through long-distance periscopes, and sent his men forward to the attack; the men of the North, from Vyatka and Vologda, the men of the South, from Perm and Saratov, the men of Great Russia, from Moscow and Smolensk, and the men of Georgia, Caucasia, Siberia, the Cossacks, and the Letts. Up above, by the Baltic, the unarmed Corps of the Bulgarian General, Radko Dimitrieff, hurled themselves against the German positions, regiments without rifles, which had to get them from the men they killed; but it was in the South that the storm burst. There they fell upon each other after a hurricane of gun-fire that lasted many days; the earth quaked and roared, the air was shaken and rent by thundering, screaming, whining steel, on the Styr, and on the

Stochod, on the Ikwa, the Strypa, and the Pruth. The very earth seemed to come to life in the effort; it seemed to shake off the thin lines of Germans, who held on savagely, while their Generals crouched over telephones and maps, and peered through long-distance periscopes. But the main blow fell upon the light-blue Austrians—Czechs, Bosnians, Hungarians, Croats, men from Carinthia, Salzburg, Egerland, from Linz, Vienna, and the Corps from Prague. General Brussilov's offensive swept onwards, for many lessons had been learned of late. The Russians drove in the front, leapt over the trenches, and killed; they killed their enemy by thrusting a bayonet into his vitals, smashing his skull with a rifle-butt, or blowing him to pieces with a hand-grenade. They killed, took hordes of prisoners, and tore a great archway in the enemy front, through which victory must pass. But it did not pass. Through it nine hundred thousand men were sent back, and engulfed in Russia, eleven thousand officers, and a rabble of German and Austrian guns and plunder. But behind, where General Brussilov's proud offensive had not yet reached, new fronts were formed. Men began to grasp the fact that it was now too late to believe in a break-through. Fresh fronts were built with trenches and men's bodies, with nerves of barbed wire and ligaments of railways. Summer nights, summer days—nights and days of screaming agony and thirst, when men died in tens of thousands. As they lay strewn upon the earth they truly looked no more different from each other than men from Berlin East and Berlin North-West. The offensive came to a standstill, but the war—no: it had already outgrown such offensives. This, General Brussilov's offensive, was to have finished it off; and so were the former ones of General Knobelsdorff, General Mackensen, Herr von Falkenhayn, and Herr von Kluck, one after another. But the War laughed silently, and grew and grew; the limbs of it spread among the nations like lowering mountain chains, and the war played with them, exulting in the offensives that were to have destroyed it. On the Sereth, the Stochod, the Narocz lake, the Dwina, the Isonzo, the Somme, the Meuse, the

Yser, and the sea, the war ravened, and slew and wallowed in the wreckage of men.

Those were the days in which Werner Bertin and Lenore Wahl made their marriage. In those same hours and days and weeks, the cities behind the fronts were swarming with smart uniforms; orderlies appeared on leave bringing boxes of eggs for the Frau Major; lace, trinkets, and rugs, or smoked fish, butter, and tea from the cities of Russia, macaroni, peas, lentils, and beans. In the officers' messes well-cooked food was plentiful; from Headquarters war-correspondents in breeches drove to the former battlefields, where, after an address by their guide, they stumbled about, duly impressed with all they saw. At the moment, A.S.C. men were possibly burying the dead, Germans, Russians, and Austrians of all races. This process they did not describe; they announced that they were confident that Germany would be victorious, just as a cow gives forth milk, when its udders are properly squeezed. At the same moment, the allies of two very Christian Emperors, the Turks, were exterminating one million three hundred thousand Christian Armenians, including three hundred and thirty thousand children; on the barrack-yards, sergeants were drilling the youngest class of recruits, the eighteen-year-olds; good-humoured sergeant-majors were receiving a small income from persons against whose names a cross had inadvertently been marked in the register, signifying "killed"; and the man newly called up was trying to get a safe job. A great mass of the German people, the educated classes more especially, the readers of the newspapers, the professors and their satellites, the female intellectuals, doctors, judges, teachers, authors, bankers, industrials, and great land-owners, both men or women, all these had long ceased to live in the war as it really was. Those who lived in the real war were the survivors of the killed, the womenfolk of men on service, and the workmen and workwomen in businesses and factories who were expected to work very hard on very short rations. But the others all lived for the realization of the ideals of Germany, by which they meant the control of mineral deposits, Channel ports, Russian provinces, Turkish concessions, and oil as far as Persia. The purpose of the war as they conceived it was to be read in many places; much had been written about the exalted and historic mission of Germany, the new Rome, the Gothic race, the modern Imperium. For them the Field Greys died, uncomplaining, dignified, and grave; they fought, and they were killed, with their young heroic leaders at their head. For these men, all that counted now was the imperishable memory of the slain, and the pose that they adopted for their grandchildren's benefit. Cheap actors, they bore their own troubles without a murmur, they gave up their living sons, and gloated on the burden of their sacrifice, that would shed a solemn glory over this age; mighty destiny of a mighty people. If an officer went forth into this offensive and fell, what then? Lieutenant Lederer (one of the many thousands), Dr. Theodor Lederer, a man of trained intelligence and an expert on the arts. The mountain fighting had failed to kill him, but he fell very promptly in the new offensive. Returned from leave, assigned to a fresh unit, sent to the front and into action, shot dead and buried—finished. Who would take up this man's life work, half-achieved? No one. Was this man, so deeply versed in religious art and the Christian myths, no longer needed in the West? Surely. . . . But Lieutenant Lederer was mouldering to dust with a horde of his comrades in a common grave; centuries later, perhaps, someone would dig up that finely moulded skull and marvel at its contours. What, in the meantime, had become of that high-hearted woman, Mela Hartig-Lederer, the pianist? She did not recant her views, she wept in secret, she held that Tirol peasant's head of hers as high as ever—but she grew gradually silent. She was less and less able to play in public. Her memory began to fail her strangely; the notes she was actually playing, the next bar, the onward rush of a Beethoven theme, slipped suddenly from her mind. Her existence was corroded by grief, her great impulsive heart was turned to stone, she shut up her house, crept away into the mountains with her young son, and her aspect vanished from the memory of her contemporaries. Only Lenore asked after her from time to time, as a woman who had impressed her in her girlhood more than any other, a woman both honoured and feared—and, later on, Bertin. Hermann Lorcher alone went to see her occasionally, until he, too, passed over into the multitude of victims. But that is quite another story.

When Werner Bertin reminded his wife that they only had four-and-twenty hours left, she put her hand over his mouth; which was wise, as his lips were faintly trembling. They lived through the day, from the rising of the sun until its setting, close at each other's sides. They smoked, they talked, sometimes they ate, and sometimes they slept. They looked at pictures, photographs of old times, that alone seemed real; they grew intent on plans, schemes for work and for their coming life together. Must this day pass? Must it rise to the peak of noontide, pass into a warm and murmurous afternoon, then sink into twilight and evening? But night came at last. "We shall have to start very early—" and she put her hand over his mouth. Furtively he collected his soldier's belongings, and the heart within his breast felt like lead. Lenore came up to him, laid her hands upon his shoulders, and wept; then she helped him pack. Clean underlinen, shirts, socks, the wrappings for his feet, which he always said were better than stockings. Then the last night enfolded them. Wine stood upon the table, dark, precious wine, candles, roses, the freshest roses from the staircase. They spoke in a whisper, and their eyes gazed beyond their words. All would be well. The war could not possibly last over the winter; everyone knew how the nations longed for peace. The nations of Europe were a match for each other, and the fight would end in a draw. The two lovers would write to each other, and think of each other, thankful that they had been born and lived and breathed in the same epoch of time. On one matter they fell out; Lenore was not to come with him to the station.

She assured him that she would not cry, but she must positively go with him.

But the leave-taking would only be an added agony.

She insisted: she would get up at four o'clock and go with him to the station.

He asked her not to think too much of the hardships that faced him when he left her: "You are to be left behind alone, but I am going back to my company, to the place where I belong. When I have that tunic on, when I hook this belt, only my heart is still yours. I myself, you may be very sure, am changed, and have become partly a soldier, a private—tenth squad, third section, first company of the X/20, mobile A.S.C. battalion. From the window of the railway carriage a private in the A.S.C. will look at an exquisite woman, as remote, for me, as the goddess of the moon. I may still hold your hand in the car; but my company still holds me in the grip of comradeship—those lousy, swaggering, toiling men, who for ten hours on end will drag shells from the trucks to the dump, from the dump to the field railway, and walk beside the little trucks to the breech-blocks of the guns. I couldn't deceive you, that's the truth."

And she answered: "This is your hand, and these your eyes, and these your cheeks, and this your mouth. We have twelve hours more."

"Fourteen."

At breakfast in the morning she said: "Three hours."

Then he took a last bath, put on his grey-collared red-tabbed tunic, buckled an untanned cowhide belt about his middle; on his arm was a band marked: Mob. Arm. Bat. X/20. I. Comp. He stepped cautiously across the parquet floor in his great nailed boots. With lingering eyes, but smiling now, he bade farewell to the breakfast china, silver, crystal, vases of roses, eggs, ham coffee, and honey. When he drew Lenore into his arms once again, and slung his pack over his back, both of them looked sickly pale, and thin, and, for the moment, beaten. His throat was thick with sobs. He could not breathe—he could not sit and wait—they must go, and go at once.

In a dress and shawl of which he was especially fond, and a hat that they had bought together, she got into the car. When it slid away, and the house, the corner of the road, and all the roads nearby were gone, he found himself gasping for air. He must tell the man to stop! Surely he had left something behind? No, a man leaves nothing behind when he has spent fifteen months with the Prussians, eleven of them in the field, not indeed in the trenches, but in places where life was hard and rough and very dirty, and where men trod barefooted in stale filth and offal. They longed to say something that would have fixed this moment; but nothing came. Gently he stroked the rounded forearm, dark brown under its sheen of pale down, grasped the girlish waist, and kissed the back of her hand.

"Four such days as these," he said; "that will not pass. That will last out the summer, and the autumn, and by the winter we shall be together again."

"If only you come back safe. Don't worry about me—I shall be all right."

At that same time and in just such a tone, thousands of women over the whole earth were saying the same thing in all the chief languages of white humanity.

Chapter 3

L'ENVOI

The travel warrant had been examined and stamped in the Railway Transport Office; on the Charlottenburg station the D-train waited with steam up. The platform and the train seemed to stretch away into the distance; like tresses of the giantess Berlin, the railway lines coiled out into the Mark of Brandenburg. From the long, rocking D-train carriages, peered the faces of men returning from leave. There are but few to watch this departure, the women have to work on the morning of a weekday, and a leave-man must set forth unaccompanied back into the West, whither that huge machine will soon be thundering on its way.

From the windows of the second-class officers' carriages, curious eyes looked down the platform to the men's compartments. Beside one of them stood a very noticeable figure. A young lady in a jade-green silk dress, high-waisted, and reaching down to her small feet. Over her arms and neck was a silver-grey silk wrap. Her brown hands hung at her sides, ringless, except for a wedding ring; but round her neck glittered a necklace of bluish-green South Sea shells. Her face was shaded by a soft broad-brimmed hat of Florentine straw. She looked up at a third-class compartment, whence, beside two others, peered the tanned, clean-shaven, bespectacled face of a private in the A.S.C. And her eyes burned into his.

There he stood, the beloved, foolish lad. She had spared him her reproaches; anger and resentment lay in ashes at the bottom of her soul like last year's foliage. She would watch him go, she would smile, she let the yearning of her heart be seen only in her eyes, and in her fluttering shawl; weep she would not.

Werner Bertin had little to say that could be said in public. Was that his wife? a gigantic artilleryman had asked him, and induced an infantryman to give Bertin his place at the window, so that he could see better. It was a bad job, he observed, to have to go back to the front, leaving something like that behind. With parted lips Bertin gazed at the woman who had given herself to him, who, after a secret union, was now publicly pledged as his.

The stationmaster whistled, late comers jostled into the last compartment, the train backed slowly, and then slid forward. In that moment, Lenore's whole soul flashed into her face, the eager, pure, sweet soul of a young woman, tried and yet immaculate. It looked so sad and yet so lovely, that an old woman came up to her hesitatingly, and with many excuses, asked if she were Greek.

Lenore started. Stupid question. It must be the way she had done her hair she thought, in coiled masses, and because she was dark and wearing a long dress. With a shy faint smile she shook her head: "No, I come from hereabouts."

The train, with arms still waving from the windows, swung round the inexorable curve. Lenore Bertin walked up the stairway: her sorrow had passed. Something inevitable had been brought to pass; that parting had to come. The hem of her dress brushed the stone steps which had just been sprinkled and swept for the day.

At home, in her sunlit room, she gave way. Her eyes fell on Werner's trunk. Frau Mahnke had had it put where it now belonged. There was the hollow stone in which Bertin's whole existence lay folded and put away, clothes and books, pictures and music, notes and diaries. Everything that was to carry him from his earlier world into the world that would succeed it, lay there, a brown and battered object, on the floor of her own room. Here was now his home, and this made his absence the more terrible. She slipped down on her knees beside the trunk—only to see if there was a key attached to it. It was fifteen months since she had sat on it, utterly light-hearted and unforeboding of the fuure. All, alas, was not yet well; there might be much evil yet to come.

She bent down, clasped it in her arms, passed her hands over the cracked leather, and then clutched it with convulsive fingers. She sobbed on to her arms, biting into her skin, so that the maid should not hear. "Dear lad, come back—Oh come back!" It was none other than love that had come upon her—love that suffers, schemes, creates; just love.

THE END

Afterword

This book was begun in the summer of 1928, and was intended to be the first part of the novel, *Education before Verdun.* In the course of the work it became apparent that *Education before Verdun* would have to be preceded by a self-contained and complete story, to be called *Young Woman of 1914.* Owing to various accidents the author was prevented from finishing both books as soon as he had hoped. In this long interval, he felt impelled to construct a separate and smaller work out of the first two books of *Young Woman of 1914,* in the shape of a prelude, to be called *Advance of Youth.* The whole work, the central section of which is represented by *The Case of Sergeant Grischa,* will, in addition to those already mentioned, be rounded off by a final volume, *The Crowning of a King,* and will, it is hoped, be brought to a conclusion by the end of 1933. Until then, the author would deprecate any misinterpretation of his intention.

A. Z.

Berlin, November 11th, 1931.